the
skeleton
clock

hickory crowl

WISHINGSHELF
PRESS

The Wishing Shelf Press, 32 Rectors Gate, Retford, DN22 7TX, UK

Edited by Therese Rasback, Alison Turner

www.hickorycrowl.co.uk @HickoryCrowl

ISBN 979-8-6360119-6-5

FOR DAD
who always took me to feed the ducks

A bullet knows no mercy
It will simply go where it is sent

The Skeleton Clock

Part I
Amaryllis Storm

I

The comet hurtled boldly through the galaxy. It clipped the icy rings of Saturn and shot by Jupiter's ever-circling moons, hunting for a world to destroy. Skimming the red orb of Mars, it homed in on a tiny pinprick of light. As the rock thundered closer, the light grew bigger, turning into a shining, blue planet.

The third planet from the sun.

The Skeleton Clock
2 months, 3 days, 0 hrs, 27 mins, 41 secs

I'm human. Or I think I'm human. I sleep when I'm tired. I drink when I'm thirsty. I only kill when I must. So I must be human. I must be.

Over and over, I tumble in my bed, my sheets twisted and knotted, my only blanket, now old and shabby, thrown to the floor. As I try to sleep, I see them on the backs of my eyelids. All the howlers I have killed. Murdered. Shadowy ghosts, twisted and bloody. In my poor, tortured mind, they hunt me. But not with swords and not with crossbows. No. They hunt me with a word. "Why?" they mercilessly cry. Over and over and over...

The implant in my wrist sends a bolt of electricity surging through my body and, in a whirl of terror, I shoot up in my bed. My skin is drenched and my jaw hurts from being clenched too tightly. Frantically, I check my body for slugs. Armpits. Nostrils. Bellybutton. The cracks in my blistered feet. But there's nothing there. I'm still me. I'm still Amaryllis Storm. With a sob, I curl up in a ball, my knees pressed up to my chin. But my whimpers disturb nobody, for there is nobody here to disturb. There is nobody here but me.

This is my burrow. It's not much, just a big hole of sorts, dug into a hill in a tiny thicket of dying trees. The roof is low, sickeningly low, the timbers holding it up dry and cracked. There's not much in here and what there is, is smothered in a thick layer of dust. A bed, a rickety stool, a low bench spilling over with scraps of paper. Over in a corner there is a bathtub, a cracked sink and a bucket, and, just by them, there's a fat-encrusted log burner with a wonky tin chimney sprouting up from the top.

My puffed-up eyes drift to the untidy bench. Over the bench, pinned to the wall, there is a poster. On it, in big, black letters, it says,

SSPs (Strict Survival Protocols)
1. Stay Alert
2. Keep Moving
3. Never Sleep for Too Long

There is a fourth protocol, but it's so depressing, so horrific, I ripped it off long ago and tossed it in the log burner.

The Skeleton Clock

Below the torn poster, on the bench, this is a tatty photograph of a family. A mum, a dad, a boy and a girl. But I don't know any of them. The little girl with her gappy teeth is not me and the boy's not my brother. Other photographs sit there too, of mothers in flowery skirts and sun-freckled boys with rosy cheeks. All of them sit under tall, green trees. Back when trees were tall. Back when trees were green. But I don't know any of them; just strangers to me

My burrow is closed off by a wall. There is a door in the wall. It's two feet thick. Triple-locked. Always triple-locked. It helps to keep out the monsters. To the left of the door there is a tiny, egg-shaped window. Through the bars, I see it is still dark out, the sky inky-black with just a splash of clouds and dots of stars. It is not yet dawn, but I know it will soon be time.

Reluctantly, I swing my legs off the bed and patter over to the corner of the room. There, on the floor, is the rusty bucket. I bob down and pee in it, splashing my feet. Then I step over to the sink. It is full of dirty water, the hole stoppered with a cork. Cupping my hands, I scoop up the water and throw it over my face, allowing it to trickle down my neck and chest. It is horribly hot in here, and it helps to cool me down.

Over the sink, hooked to the wall, there is a cracked mirror. I look in it and, almost instantly, I wish I hadn't. For I do not see my soft, freckled cheeks or the strong set of my jaw. I do not even see my bloom of red, wavy curls; impossible to miss. No. All I see is a chipped tooth, a scar on my left temple – ugly, crooked – and hollow, bloodshot eyes. My face is, I think, not so much the face of a sixteen-year-old girl, but of a devil; a horrifying monster with a thorny hallow of brutality.

The clock on my bench rings, making me jump like a startled deer. Almost tripping over the stool, I hurry over to it and slam my hand down on the vibrating bell. Cursing my stupidity, I shut my eyes and listen. No footsteps and, thankfully, no howling or snapping of jaws. I sigh as the thump in my chest slows.

Just then, the spying moon strays through the window, whitening the bench and the scrawled-on Top Secret papers lying there. On the bench there is a box, the front of it a jumble of levers, bulbs and tarnished, grey buttons. To the left of the box there is a 12-volt car battery; this is what powers it. A thick cable is attached to the back of the box. From there, it winds up the wall to the roof of the burrow where it is connected to a tall, steel pole. This is Comms. This is how they contact me.

Ballooning my cheeks, I pick up the stool. Then I carry it over to the bench and drop down on it, crossing my feet at the heels like a bow. I sit there, watching the clock's hands tick off the seconds.

Soon the bulbs will light up. For today is the day I get my orders.

Three.

Today is the day...

Two.

...when they tell me...

One.

...who I must kill.

12

II

According to the few surviving records, the comet impacted 101 kms north of Mexico City at 21.45hrs on 25th September 2032. Burying deep into the planet's crust, it sent burning rocks spiraling up into the sky, showering the forests and towns, and filling the rivers. Then a blast of scorching hot gas, travelling at over 1500 kph, rolled over the continent. In the blink of an eye, North and South America were destroyed, from the northern tip of Alaska all the way down to the foot of Chile. The mighty Mississippi river evaporated, the streets of New York and Washington melted, and the Amazon forest burnt to ash. In less than two hours, over 1,000,000,000 men, women and children were wiped off the planet.

It was only the beginning.

The Skeleton Clock
2 months, 3 days, 0 hrs, 13 mins, 22 secs

Suddenly, three of the bulbs on the box start to blink rapidly. "Sniper Two Seven, Sniper Two Seven, this is the Nest. Respond, over."

A smile tugs on my unwilling lips. It's him. My controller. It's always him. I suspect he's from Bravo or possibly Whiskey Sector, sectors now overrun by the howlers. I can tell by his melodic accent and the way he drops his vowels.

I jerk the stool closer to the bench, walloping my knee on the wood. "This is Sniper Two Seven," I respond instantly.

There is a hiss of static, mocking me. I feel my cheeks burn. I'm like a child ripping off the wrappings of a present. Then, "Identify."

I sit there for a second, thinking. "My lucky number's seven," I say at last.

There is a rustling of papers as he checks my file. Computers don't work very well. There's too much dust and it clogs up the microchips. "Confirm scramble," he says at last.

I flip a switch on the box. This is old tech. No microchips. Just resistors and copper wiring. But it works. "Confirmed," I reply. We don't want the howlers to listen in.

I often wonder what he looks like. With any luck, he's sixteen like me, but taller with perfectly trimmed, hawk-like eyebrows. His lips will be full, and his green, misty eyes will be all hooded and sorrowful. I sigh wistfully. I know I will never meet him – Rebel HQ, or the Nest as most of the rebels call it, is strictly off limits to snipers – but, if I ever do, I will tell him how I...

"Verify SSPs."

Confident he can't see me, I roll my eyes. "But why?" I protest. "If I'd stopped following them, I'd be infested. Then I'd not be sitting here. I'd be off, y' know, killing rebels."

I chuckle. That was sort of funny.

Silence.

Or possibly not.

"Verify SSPs," he says, his words much sterner now, a command, strongly hinting if I don't do it, he'll cut comms.

"Okay, okay." My eyes drift to the poster pinned to the wall. "Keep alert," I drawl, sounding anything but, "keep moving and never sleep for too long." I stop there.

"Go on."

Pursing up my lips, I stay stubbornly silent. I ripped the fourth protocol off the poster the day I got here. But I can still remember it. No, that's not the problem. The problem is, I don't want to say it.

"You know the drill, Two Seven. It's just," he sighs, "it's just protocol. If you don't say it, I don't tick the box. And if I don't tick the box, there'll be hell to pay."

I jerk up on my stool. What's he implying? That if I don't do it, they'll send me back to the Netty, the refugee camp I grew up in. I may be lonely, but I'm not going back there. No way. So, grudgingly, I do as he orders. "If I'm infested," I mutter, "I must -," I grit my teeth, "- I must kill myself." I spit it out as if it's worm-infested food.

"Better," he says. "Much better." I can almost see the box being ticked. "Now, to work. There's a forest, or what's left of it, thirty-three clicks to the southwest of you. On the old maps it's called Sherwood. Tall conifers mostly. Chestnuts, a few silver birch. Do you know it?"

"Oh, em, yes. Yes!" Focus, Storm, I scold myself. Urgently, I snatch up a map from off the bench and unfold it. I hardly need to. I know Zulu Sector better than anybody. It's my patch. It's where I work. With my index finger, I track a path southwest into howler territory. The rest of Zulu, the top half of it anyway, is controlled by the rebels. My burrow sits on the enemy front between the two. But there's not just me. Most of the front is manned by snipers. When I say manned, I'm being ironic. Every sniper's a girl. We shoot much better than boys. Every 10 kms or so there's a burrow, and in every burrow there's a sniper. The front's just over 600 kms long, so there must be 60 snipers in all.

I frown at the map. There's not much there now, just desert and a lot of rubbish left over from the old days. Skeletons too. Hundreds of them. Finally, my finger hovers over the forest. "Thirty-three clicks southwest. Got it."

"New intel just in. There's been a report of howlers there destroying it. We, er, think there's a troop of them."

I blink rapidly, a scowl creeping over my dripping brow. The enemy's plan is devilishly clever but remarkably simple. To destroy all the trees and plants left on the planet. They absorb CO_2 so, if the howlers do it, CO_2 levels will spiral higher and higher. It's now at 5%. When it hits 6%, it will be too toxic for humans. But not howlers. They don't seem bothered by it at all. The comet, the tidal wave and the duststorms did a lot of the work for them, destroying 90% of the planet's trees. But there's still 10% left. They all need to be destroyed if the howlers' cowardly plan is to work.

My job is to stop them.

"How big a troop?" I ask.

"Unknown. As of today, there's been no fly overs. Too risky. It's too deep in enemy territory. So, the intel is presently a little, er – sketchy."

I glower at the microphone. Too risky! Who for? The helicopter pilots flying recon? Not for me anyway. "Oh, wonderful," I mutter. Bad intel is the best way I know of to get a sniper killed. To get me killed.

"But Major Crow suspects there must be over twenty," he adds.

My teeth clench. "Hubert Crow?" I bark. "From this Sector? From Zulu?"

"Correct. He's the new Zulu commander."

Slowly, my hands curl up into fists. I begin to rock on my stool, my eyelids fluttering. I can feel the anger welling up in me, flooding my belly like hot bubbling acid. Hubert Crow. A hero in the Battle of London, a city now lost to the howlers. A man I have never met. A man I very much want to put a bullet in. And now, at last, I know where he is. He's in the Nest.

"Is there a problem?" he asks.

"No, no, I, er..." My mind is swirling, and I don't know what to say.

"Sniper Two Seven, is there a problem?"

Yes, I'm tempted to yell. Yes, there is. Hubert Crow murdered my mum. But I say nothing. It's difficult but I know I must not let on how I feel. Crow might be listening in. "What happened to Major Striker?" I muster, referring to the old Zulu commander. "Was she demoted?"

"No. Infested. She shot herself."

I'm lost for words. In truth, I never met her. Just another rebel giving orders, telling me where to go and who to shoot. Still, she'd been a good boss. She'd never got me killed.

"Do you know Major Crow?" he asks.

"No, I don't," I reply, my teeth still clenched. I'm in shock. All I want to do is sit in a corner and concoct a way of finding the Nest and getting my hands on my mum's killer. But I can't. If I cut comms now, Crow will be informed. And I don't want him to suspect anything. So, as discreetly as I can, I switch subjects. "Will there be any serfs in the forest?" I ask him, referring to anybody captured by the howlers and forced to work for them.

"Yes. If there's a troop of howlers, they'll be fifty or so serfs."

I thumb the cleft of my chin, tracing a scar. He's right. Howlers never do the dirty work. Not when serfs will do it for them. "Do we even know if the forest is still there?"

"We suspect it is. Most of it anyway."

"Suspect," I hiss. I'm now gripping the mic so tightly, there's a strong possibility it'll snap. "If you think for a second I'm going to plod over thirty..."

"But it won't be for long," he interrupts me. "They work fast. They must be stopped, Storm. They must be stopped now."

I scowl at the wall of grey buttons. My controller never calls me Storm. Always Sniper Two Seven or, simply, Two Seven. So why now? Unless... "The Skeleton Clock. Is it accelerating? Is it..."

"Yes, it is," he hastily cuts me off. "Two months, three days and, er, sixteen seconds."

The Skeleton Clock sits in the Nest. Connected to hundreds of sensors all over the Sector, the clock predicts how long is left until CO_2 levels hit 6%, ending all human life on the planet.

I crunch my teeth over my lips. Just over two months. So short. So very, very short. "I see," I say soberly. "My orders?"

"I'm pulling you off the front. Proceed A.S.A.P. southwest to the forest. Destroy the enemy there. Understood?"

I almost topple off my stool. "What? All of them?"

"Yes," he says simply. It's as if he's asking me to shoot rubber ducks. "That's the major's orders. No prisoners."

"And the serfs?"

"Expendable." But he answers a little too abruptly. I suspect he's under orders too, and I suddenly wonder if Major Crow is in the room with him.

I sit there, not knowing what to say. Water drips from the cracked sink ticking off the seconds. This is insanity. There must be a different way or soon they'll be nobody left in the world. Even the enemy will go extinct. "I can't terminate twenty howlers," I stubbornly tell him. "Nobody can. Not even Sniper Six Six."

"Sniper Six Six took out thirty howlers yesterday," my controller retorts.

I swallow a torrent of dirty words and mutter, "Good for her."

Sniper Six Six is a girl in Victor Sector. I have never met her but my instructor in boot camp told me she's the best sniper in the rebel army. Another hero, but of Victor Sector, not Zulu. I often wonder if she's still better than me. Still sharper. And, if she is, by how much?

"If I miss any of the howlers – any of them! – they'll attack the serfs," I tell him. "They'll kill them. All of them." Soberly, I add, "They always do."

"Understood."

My eyes narrow. His cold, velvety drawl suddenly annoys me. How can he know, hidden away in a steel bunker in the Nest? It will be me, not him, who kills the howlers. And it will be me who will be forced to witness the bloodbath if I miss any of them and they turn on the serfs. I swallow and rub my swollen eyes. It will be me who will remember it for the rest of my days.

"What do I do?" I growl.

"Don't miss," he growls back. I can tell by his blunt reply he's angry too. "Remember, Two Seven," his words soften - slightly, "for the good of the many."

My controller can't see me, but I nod anyway. "For the good of the many," I say flatly. It is the rebels' moto; what they live by. It is supposed to help them to sleep better at night. But it never helps me. Just hollow words. But then, I'm not a rebel. I'm a mercenary who works for them. I often wonder if what I do is for the good of anybody, or if I'm just a lump of driftwood trapped in a raging river.

Absentmindedly, I rub the back of my hand. If I was a rebel, there would be a tattoo inked there, a six-pronged star representing the six sectors in Cinis still left in the fight. All islands. Salt water frightens the bejeebers out of howlers, so islands have a natural defense. There's Foxtrot, formerly called Cyprus, Golf (Iceland), Kilo (Malta), Victor (Sicily), Yankee (Crete) and my Sector, Sector Zulu. On the old maps, it's called the United Kingdom. Recently, I met with Rufus Splinter, a crook and a seller of, well, whatever I want. If I can pay for it. He let slip Golf Sector is all but overrun. The man's a fool but, still, I can't help but wonder how difficult it'll be for the rebels to rub off part of a tattoo.

"I don't even know your name," I suddenly say. "What is it?"

"Controller," he says.

I roll my eyes at the microphone. "No, no, not your job. Your name!"

Silence.

I drum my fingers on the top of the bench. Wow, this is difficult. "Everybody's got a name," I lecture him. "Unless it's top secret." I frown. "Is it top secret?"

"No," he snaps back.

"Excellent! Then what is it?"

For a long, long second, all there is, is static. I sit there, struggling to inhale, to exhale, to do anything, my eyes tightly shut, praying he'll reply. Then, in a very husky whisper, he says, "This is not protocol."

"Yes," I swallow, "yes, I know. It's just..." I gnaw on a dirty thumb, my cheek twitching rapidly. I want to tell him how lonely I am. How I just want to talk to him. Tell him how I feel. But I don't know how to say it. I'm a sniper. My job is to kill howlers. My job is not to feel anything at all. So I open my eyes and say what I always say. "Orders understood. Inform Major Crow the mission is a go. I will be off the enemy front for six, possibly seven days. Sniper Two Seven out."

I jump up. I'm such a tool. I'm such a, a – coward! With a growl, I kick over the stool and slam my fist down on the bench. I stand there, just – stand there, my eyes to my feet.

Then, in a whirl of static, two words. "Nicolo Lupo."

My spirits lift and, with them, my gaze. "Hello Nicolo," I say.

He's silent for, well, it seems like forever. Then, "Two Seven, listen to me. This is important."

"If you want to, you can call me Amaryllis. Honestly, I don't mind."

"Two Seven!"

"Okay! Okay!" I wonder what he's going to say. How he's madly in love with me? How all he thinks of is crushing me to his chest? I suddenly feel the need to put on a pretty dress – if I had a dress – and to brush my teeth – but to do that, I'd need a toothbrush...

"Two Seven."

"Yes." My cheeks flush as, expectantly, I shuffle closer to the mic. "What is it?"

"Don't trust anybody."

"Sorry?"

"Don't trust anybody. Anybody. Understood?"

Is that it? It's not very, well, romantic, is it. And to be honest, I'm a bit miffed. "Not a problem," I reply waspishly. "Who's there to trust? There's just me here."

"Not for much longer," he says flippantly.

I scowl. "Not for much..." I stop short, my mind puzzling over my controller's words. Then, suddenly, I get it. "I don't need a spotter," I thunder. "Understood?" I snatch up the mic and press it to my lips. "UNDERSTOOD!?"

He responds with a chuckle. Then the bulbs blink off.

III

Seconds after the comet hit, two walls of water over 1,000 feet high travelling at 800kph raced over the Pacific and Atlantic Oceans. Crossing the Pacific, the wave swept away Fiji, the Solomon Islands and Japan, crashing into China, only stopping when it was lapping at the hills of Tibet. Things were no better in the Atlantic. Most of West Africa including Morocco, Mali, the Republic of Congo and even as far inland as Chad were lost to the tempest. Further north, Portugal, France, the fjords of Norway and much of the UK, including London, vanished under the rushing water. Trees were uprooted, cars were swept away, even Big Ben was destroyed.

Weeks later, when the water finally receded, another 2,000,000,000 had been killed.

It was still not over.

The Skeleton Clock
2 months, 2 days, 22 hrs, 40 mins, 55 secs

My name is Amaryllis. Amaryllis Storm. My mother was a sniper, but she was killed in the Battle of London. A battle we lost. She was the best shot in the rebel army; or so they say. As for my father, I don't know what he did. It seems it's Top Secret and nobody will tell me. I often try to remember what he looked like, but he's always out of focus, blurry, as if I'm seeing the memory of him through a dirty window.

The Skeleton Clock

I love to draw. Flowers mostly. And trees. But I draw them the way they were. The way my mother described them to me. Not the way they look now, all knotted and twisted and burnt by the sun. Oh, and I'm a sniper too; a mercenary, temporarily in the employ of the rebels. My job...

...to shoot howlers. To stop them from destroying what's left of Cinis.

I look to my old, wind-up clock. It is almost 0600hrs but it's July, and in July the sun is almost always up. Or it seems to be now the planet's spin has slowed and a day is much longer. Even now, it climbs up over the distant hills and, with the help of my window, basks my burrow in a soft glow. To be honest, I'm tempted to set off now. But I know it's too risky. They'll be howlers everywhere. No. Best to travel after dark. It'll be cooler then too. If only slightly.

I feel woozy, so I pull a bottle from off the shelf over my sink. Tipping it up, I drop two OxyPills into my palm. The oval-shaped tablets, dotted with tiny, oxygen-enriched crystals remind me of speckled eggshells. Reluctantly, I swallow them. They taste bitter, like betrayal, but with CO_2 levels rising so rapidly, they help a lot and, within a few seconds, my mind sharpens. Then I throw on belted shorts and a ripped t-shirt followed by my cowboy boots; calf skin, they stop just below the knees. Armed with my rifle, a rucksack and a net fixed to a wire hoop, I slip from my burrow. I creep out of the dying woods and down a hill to a river. Only now it's not a river. Now it's just a tiny brook clogged with sand and old, ripped plastic bags. I want to catch fish for my supper. To be honest, it's not difficult. There's so little water in it, the gasping salmon seem almost happy to see me, and jump wildly into my net. I drop them into my rucksack. Later, I plan to descale them, pepper them and then fry them on my log burner.

Two hundred feet to the north of the brook there is a well. This is where the rebels drop everything I need. I never see them, but they always do. Mostly food and ammo for my gun; payment for the work I do. Snipers, it seems, don't cost very much.

As I plod over to the well, I feel eyes on me and, suddenly, a growl erupts from a nest of rocks just to my left. Alarmed, I jump back. If it's a wild dog, I'm okay. Even if it is infested by a slug. But if it's a howler... Swiftly, I unsling my rifle and step over to the rocks. But, oddly, there's nothing there to shoot.

Unnerved, I shuffle on until, finally, I stop by the well. Partly covered in a low, stone roof, the shallow water is murky and choked with moss, old crisp bags and the wrappers of sweets I have never tasted and never will. There is a rope knotted to a metal hook in the roof, the end dangling into the water. I drop to a knee and, slowly, hand over hand, I pull it up. After a few seconds, a bucket clatters over the top of the wall. I peer in. The bucket is filled to the brim with clay pots. I pull off the cork lids and, in them, I discover sweet chestnuts – they'll go perfectly with the fish – salted beef, lentils and many kinds of herbs. I often wonder where the rebels grow the food they send me. When I'm on patrol, all I ever see is desert. I'm not much of a gardener, but sand can't be the best of composts. They left OxyPills too, a battery for my torch and a box of hollow-tipped shells for my rifle. Gently, I pick up the pots and rest them in the bottom of my rucksack with the fish. When the bucket is empty, I lower it back down into the water.

Then I do what I always do when I'm here. I hunt in the dirt for a pebble. Finding a jagged shard of flint, I drop it into the well. It lands in the still water with a satisfying kerplunk. I then shut my eyes tightly hoping that my wish will be granted. Sadly, it never is, and today's no different. For, when I peek out from under my eyelids, there's still nobody here but me.

As I rest there in the dirt feeling sorry for myself, I spy a hornets' nest nestled under the roof of the well. It's big, the size of a football. I know the yellow-striped insects can kill - when the power plants exploded, the toxins changed them; and not in a good way – so, warily, I clamber to my feet and creep by it. Then, thankful to be away from there, I set off back to my burrow, snatching up a few sticks for my log burner on the way.

When I return, I empty my horribly smelly bucket. Then I check on the howler traps encircling my home. Only I know where to find them. And my controller. He insisted I send him a map – a sort of X marks the spot map – showing where I'd hidden them. Steel-jawed, sharp-toothed and almost impossible to spot, the traps rest just under the sand. Step on any of them and SNAP! The jaws shut and the unlucky victim will be trapped there until it rots. Or until I put a bullet in it. Nasty, I know. But war's war. They don't take prisoners, so we don't take prisoners.

The Skeleton Clock

As I work, I try not to think too much. It's important not to, for I know if I do, I will be overwhelmed with self-pity. So I keep to my list: sort supper, sort smelly bucket, sort traps. And so on and so on. Just don't think, I sternly tell myself. But it's difficult. My only contact with the rest of the world is my weekly comms with the Nest. But for the crook, Rufus Splinter, I never meet anybody. It's as if – I swallow – as if there's nobody left in the world but me.

Whilst checking my traps, I inadvertently get a whiff of my left armpit and I almost throw up. I stink terribly. Time, I think, for my monthly bath.

My tub is my only luxury. Steel with splayed, brass legs, it sits in the corner of my burrow. I discovered it in a tumbled-down barn when I was on patrol. It took me a day to lug it back here and two weeks to scrub off all the grime. But it was worth it. It's the only way I know to wash off the horrors of what I do – and the dust. In this world, there's dust everywhere. Dirty grey, it sits in every nook and in every cranny, so thick it looks like fur. Eyes weep from it, cuts sting from it and lungs fill up.

The tub's not plumbed in so the taps don't work, but I remedy this with water from another well in the cellar. Worryingly, I must unwind almost all the rope before the bucket hits the water with a muffled splash. Soon, I suspect, baths will be just a memory; a topic for history lessons like the internet, MediPods and pepperoni pizza. Then I'll be forced to scrub off the dirt with a wire brush. It's a lot of work carrying the slopping bucket – a different bucket to the bucket I pee in – up the ladder, but it's worth it, and I enjoy a long, cold dip.

As I lay there, my mind drifts to my controller, Nicolo Lupo. It is, I think, a very odd name, Lupo. But when I say it – which embarrassingly is rather often – it still fits comfortably on my lips. Anyway, with a name like Amaryllis Storm, who am I to talk?

I wonder if he ever thinks about me. Not just the assassin, Sniper Two Seven, but me, the sixteen-year-old girl. It's silly, I know. I have never even met him. I never will. No mercenary has ever been allowed into the Nest. I'm not even allowed to know where it is. A mercenary, it seems, is not to be trusted. But when I'm here, day after day, my mind tends to wander. To hope for the impossible. I rub my tired eyes. Anyway, he's probably not sixteen at all. Or tall. Or with perfectly trimmed, hawk-like eyebrows. He's probably sixty, bent over, with smelly feet and warts on his chin.

I frown as I remember Nicolo's words to me. I'd told him, "There's just me here." His reply, "Not for much longer." Did the rebels intend to send me a spotter then? Many snipers work with a spotter, to help them to find the enemy and to assess humidity and wind speed. Hubert Crow had been my mother's, until Crow killed her. I thump the bottom of the bath with my foot. I may be lonely, but I still don't want a spotter. And I never will. They can't be trusted.

There is a dull throb over my left temple and, tenderly, I rub it with my thumb. There is a scar there. I can't remember how I got it. A howler's claw possibly. To be honest, I can't remember a lot of stuff. I don't even know when my birthday is. I do know I'm sixteen. I begged my controller to tell me. But, as to when I'm seventeen, it seems that's top secret; on a need to know only. And I don't need to know.

After my bath, I towel myself dry and dress. A rumble of thunder tells me a storm's rolling in. Perfect! I'm hungry. Now, when I cook, the howlers won't see the telltale smoke from my log burner. With the wind pummeling my door, I light the burner and fry the fish, enjoying it with the chestnuts from the well.

Full of food, I reluctantly pack my rucksack for the mission. I bring only what I need. A compass, a torch, flint, a hunting knife, a hollow stick and a little food. I fill my canteen from the well and set it in the bag too. There's still a lot of salt in the wells from when the Atlantic swept over England almost a century ago. But there's a filter in the canteen that cleverly gets rid of most of it. I pack twenty shells and, very gently, seven blocks of C4 explosive and a box of detonators. That's all. I find it's always best to carry what I need in my mind, not slung on my back. Much lighter that way.

I yawn, stretching my fingers up to the timbers crisscrossing the roof. I feel horribly sleepy, dizzy almost, but then, that's how I always feel. It's hardly surprising when there's so much CO_2 in my blood and the enemy will try to infest me if I sleep for too long. That's not going to happen to me. No way!

My old doll, Miss Moffit, is sitting on my pillow and, just by it, there is my rifle. Slumping down on the bed, I pick it up. Then I recklessly thumb off the safety, cock it and pull the trigger. There is a hollow click. Empty. Carved from maple, the barrel of hammered steel, it is over three feet from the tip of the barrel to the butt of the stock. Battered, dented, it is still a powerful tool. In the right hands. With the help of the scope, I can hit a howler from two hundred feet away; I can shoot off a howler's thumb from a hundred. I run my fingers over the barrel. It is icy cold. There are not many of them left now so I know I must look after it. It, in turn, looks after me. With it, I'm a predator. Without it, I'm a predator's food.

Hunting in my bag, I pull out a shell. I sit there studying it, the shiny, steel casing, the bullet's stubby nose. I still remember my first kill in sniper camp. A kitten. A test to see if I'd do it. To see if I'd follow orders. The thinking being if I'd shoot a fluffy kitten, I'd have no problem shooting a howler. Well, I passed the test. To this day, I still remember my instructor's words to me as I stood weeping over the kitten's tiny body. "A bullet knows no mercy, Two Seven. It will simply go where it is sent."

"But I sent it!" I'd stormed back at him. "Me! It's my finger on the trigger. I'm the assassin."

"No." He smiled then; the only time he ever smiled at me. "The assassin is the bullet."

I'd not admitted it back then in sniper camp; not to him and not to myself. But I know now he'd been right. The assassin's job is to simply go where he or she is sent. I am the bullet. Regret, morality, whatever they call it, is forbidden. It's a luxury the rebels don't allow. Still, it's there. It's part of me. I can't just cut it off and throw it away. I so want to be the cold, hard killer they want me to be, but I'm not. And I don't think I ever will be.

The Skeleton Clock

With a sharp crack, I pull back the bolt. Then I slip the shell into the firing chamber. To cock it, I push the bolt forward and down. Why, I wonder, don't I just end my misery? Just to see if it will fit, I upend the gun, pressing the tip of the barrel to my chin.

It fits perfectly.

Very gently, I rest my finger on the trigger. Why not do it? There's nobody here to see. Nobody to stop me, to tell me how everything's going to be okay. Nobody will even know. Or care.

I sit there, unmoving, only the ticking of the clock keeping me company.

Why not, I think.

Why not?

Then I will be with my mum, where I belong.

But I don't. I can't. I'm a survivor. Even if the howlers kill off every human on the planet, I'm still determined to be the last to go. Lowering the gun, I click on the safety and, almost reverently, I return it to my pillow.

It is now almost 1700hrs. Still too soon to go. I know the night will be full of terrors too but, still, it's safer than travelling by day. So I pull my stool over to the tiny window and slump down onto it.

The storm's now over and, from my perch, I can see most of the wood. Many of the trees look horribly sick, the spindly trunks twisted, the bark charred and brittle, peeling off like the skin of a serpent. When the comet hit, flaming rocks showered the planet, burning the forests. Then, as the planet's spin slowed, the winds whipped up the dust, blocking the sun and slowly killing off many of the trees that were left. But not every tree. Even in my tiny wood, there is a sprinkling of green. A sprinkling of hope.

To my surprise, I spot a snapdragon bravely sprouting out of the dirt. Sadly, it too looks dry and withered, the petals smothered under a film of dust. Soon the desert will engulf this dying woods. That, or the howlers will burn it down. So, if I wish to draw flowers, even a flower as poorly as this, I must do it now. For tomorrow it will not be there.

I peer down at the floor. There, by my feet is a pad and a wooden box. The lid is up, showing off a mix of pencils, a brush and six ink pots. The pots sit in two rows of three, a present from my mum on my seventh birthday. She even had Amaryllis etched on the lid, a flower climbing the leg of the first "L".

Suddenly, there is a tremor. It is the third this week. I grab for my ink pots to stop them from spilling over. Why do they keep happening, I wonder, battling to stay on my stool. Is it another effect of the comet strike? Is the planet splitting apart? I do know, if they get much bigger, my burrow will collapse on top of me.

When it finally stops, I set the paper on my knee, snatch up a grey pencil and start to sketch.

With a sweep of my hand, the jutting stem of a snapdragon is drawn. I find this is the best way to do it; it is important the stem flows and is not jerky or bumpy. The top of the stem bows over to the bell-shaped flowers. Charily, I sketch the borders of the petals and pepper them with dots.

The Skeleton Clock

Drawing is how I relax. But, today, it is difficult. My mind is too swamped with problems, the biggest being the howlers I must soon find a way of stopping. It's the intel from the Nest. It's just too – sketchy. Crow thinks – thinks! – there's a troop of howlers in the forest. But think is no good to me. The word 'think' is just a shorter way of saying 'I don't know'. Yes, there might be twenty. Or there might be thirty or forty – or even fifty! It's as if – as if I'm blindfolded. I don't know how many there will be. I don't even know where in the forest they will be.

But it's not just the howlers that bother me. It's my mum's old spotter, Crow, who's now my boss. I know where he is now. He's in the Nest. The problem is, I don't know where the Nest is. I never go there. Rebels don't trust snipers, so I'm not allowed. I think they think we'll suddenly turn on them; uncover the Nest's secrets then run off and sell them to the enemy. All I do know is what Rufus Splinter told me. It's a steel bunker dug deep into a hill. Six levels in all, protected by guns, tanks and a fleet of attack helicopters. It's encircled by a fifty-foot steel wall too. The rumor is it's electric; touch it, you'll fry. So, as much as I want to, I know I can't get to him. Suddenly, I'm overwhelmed with misery. I can't get to the man who killed my mum and destroyed my life.

I know I must not dwell on it. If I do, I'll go crazy. So I try to swallow my feelings and focus on my drawing.

I see it is now in need of a little colour. But the flower I see from my window is all dusty and grey. That will not do at all. So I unstopper the ink pots and dip the brush in the yellow. Thankfully, my mind is soon blanketed in much sweeter thoughts of snowy-tipped, yellow petals and green-speckled stems.

I feel happy.

Content...

Sadly, in the end, a second storm rolls in. A swirling brown blur of dust. Almost the instant it hits, the sun is hidden, and the flower is lost to the sandy blizzard. As lightning shreds the sky, I reluctantly stopper the ink pots, wash off the brush in the sink and rest the paper on my bed to dry. Then, as I towel my hands on a dirty cloth, there is a thud, the three trusty locks on my door fly off, and a howler storms in.

IV

After the comet hit and the Pacific Ocean swept over China, the Wuhu Atomic Power Plant was submerged for sixteen days. When the water finally receded, all seven hundred and thirteen employees had drowned. With no engineers left to keep the atomic rods cool, the power plant finally exploded at 16.22 on 17th December 2032, throwing up over 76,000,000 tons of toxic gas. Strong winds soon pushed the gas west, over China, Iran and Iraq, killing as it went.

On the day of the impact, there were six hundred and seventy-three atomic power plants in the world. The hundred and seven in North America were instantly vaporised when the comet hit. The rest of them, all five hundred and sixty-six, like Wuhu, soon exploded too.

The Skeleton Clock
2 months, 2 days, 11 hrs, 10 mins, 8 secs

I can tell the howler's a man. But, sadly, there's not much left of him now. Now his jowly cheeks swarm with slugs, his yellow eyes crackle and spark – it's almost as if he's swallowed a lightning bolt – and his crocodile teeth erupt from car-crusher sized jaws. They SNAP! SNAP! SNAP! the way howlers' jaws always do.

Suddenly, he howls, the sheer power of his fury forcing me to cower in terror. When a howler howls, it is from deep within. Fists clenched, eyes bulging, it's horrifying.

With my knees almost buckling with fright, I stagger over to my rifle. But the howler lumbers after me and, with a brutal kick, he flips over the bed. The rifle – and my sketch – are instantly lost in a messy jumble of pillows and my old, crusty blanket.

I spy a poker by the log burner. Urgently, I dash over to it and snatch it up. "Get out!" I yell, puffing up my chest and waving the poker at the monster. But my bravado is lost on him and he simply growls.

He creeps slowly over to me. Cornered, I press my back up to the wall. I can smell him now. A sickly-sweet, rotten sort of stink, like eggy vomit. It wafts up my nostrils and I feel my stomach lurch. It's the way all howlers smell. They all rot in the end. But, still, this howler is different. He looks bigger. Stronger. And the way he's dressed is different too. He's got on a bowler hat. A bowler hat! And a stripy, buttoned-up jacket. There's even a hanky peeking up from the top of his pocket. He looks as if he's off to a party. But why? He's just a shell; a host to the parasite hidden in his skull. Who's he trying to impress?

"They say y' the hero of Zulu Sector," he sneers, his bulging eyes wild, craving for blood.

My eyes widen in shock. A howler who can talk! How odd. They tend to just drool a lot. And howl.

He steps even closer to me. "It must be a joke. Look at y'. Sniper Two Seven's no hero, she's just a skinny runt."

He knows my number, I think wildly. But how can he? It's, it's – impossible. Unless there's a spy in the Nest. Or comms is compromised. I feel his eyes travel over me, as if he's sizing me up for a coffin. I suddenly feel horribly dirty and in need of another bath.

Very, very slowly I lift the poker. But he sees me and kicks me so hard in the belly, I'm almost knocked to my knees. I swing my poker at his chest, but the howler's too fast, so fast I can no longer see his fists or his feet. But I feel them, in my eye, my jaw, my poor ribs.

With a screech, he jumps up, his foot hunting for my chin. But I block him and punch him in the belly. He staggers back, his bushy eyebrows arched. I think the howler did not expect me to fight back. With fists flying, he clumps back over to me, but I drop low and sweep my foot. Nimbly, he jumps over it. And now it's his turn.

He thumps me, an uppercut to the jaw. Then he twists and flips me over his shoulder, cartwheeling me to the floor. I clamber drunkenly to my feet, but a hammering fist wallops me on the cleft of my chin, cracking a tooth. I lurch back, hitting the wall and dropping the poker. Blurry-eyed, I watch him march up to me, murder glinting in his pot lid-shaped eyes.

"Stop!" I cry. "This is crazy." But faster than a lightning bolt, he's on me.

Gripping me by the neck, the howler slams me up to the wall. I feel his sharp claws digging into my skin. I grab for his fingers, trying to wrench them off, but he's too strong. In fact, I'd say he's the strongest howler I've ever battled. By far! I suddenly wonder if I should pray, but I can't remember any of the words.

From nowhere, a rage fills me from my cowboy boots all the way to the tops of my curls. I thrust up my chin, the man's stubbly chin scratching the tip of my nose. "Get off me," I hiss.

The howler snorts, his laugh harsh and rasping like the sharpening of a blade. But, in that split second, I see my opening. Gripping hold of his skull, I jam my thumbs into his eye sockets. He howls and, instantly, he unclasps my neck and drops me to the floor.

Splayed like a puppet, I lay there. Just – lay there. Then, slowly, not wanting to, I look up. The now blind howler is darting to and fro, bulldozing into the walls like a badly-wired robot. I know I must kill this man. This – monster! If I don't, when he recovers – and he will recover; howlers always do – he'll kill me.

But, first, there are a few things I need to know.

I snatch up the poker and storm over to him. "How did you get by my traps?" I demand to know. I thump him mercilessly in the stomach with the poker. "And how do you know I'm Sniper Two Seven? Is there a spy in the Nest? Is comms compromised? ANSWER ME!" I cry.

But the howler just snorts, drops to the floor and curls up in a ball, rubbing at his bloody eyes.

The fury in my chest drops to a simmer. I can't help but feel sorry for him. I can tell he's not much older than me. Nineteen. Possibly twenty. He didn't ask to be infested. He's simply the host. He's innocent just like the rest of them. But I know I must finish him off. If I don't, if I ever stop doing what I do, the rebels will never win this war. It's my duty. It's in my blood. And, most importantly, it's what they pay me to do. So, with all the venom I can muster, I lift the poker...

"Sister," the howler mutters.

I stop, the poker's sharp tip hovering over his chest. Did he just say...

The monster claws at my boots and I pull away. "I'm not y' bloody sister," I hiss. And, with a growl, I send him to hell.

The man yelps, a wretched, lost sort of cry that seems to dribble off his lips. For a second, he is still there. Then his eyes roll over and he's not. Everything the man was, everything he ever wanted to be, is simply – lost.

My knees crumble and with a pathetic, almost babyish whimper, I fold to the floor. Pulling my knees up to my chin, I rock to and fro. There I stay, the bloody poker still clenched in my fist. I can't keep doing this. I just can't. It's killing me. I try not to cry. Only when I'm tucked up in my bed do I weep for them, often crying myself to sleep.

The howler's body suddenly judders and jerks. It's as if he's having a fit. In horror, I scamper over to my sink and cower under it. I watch as his left nostril grows slowly bigger and bigger until, finally, the flesh splits and it bursts open, spraying the room with blood. I almost throw up as a slug drops from it. It is well over a foot long with yellow, pulsating skin, bulging eyes and snapping pincers.

I look on in disgust as it slithers over to me hunting for a new host. It is this, not the man, who is my enemy. It is this that wants to destroy my world; the flowers and the trees I love so much. It is this that killed my little brother, Benji. With fury rumbling in my belly, I jump up. Then, I lift my boot and stamp down on it. Hard! And, this time, I don't feel sorry at all.

V

In the months following the comet strike, grey, swirling dust filled the sky, blocking out the sun and burying the world under a blanket of gloom. The dust polluted the rivers, killing the fish. Crops, deprived of light, slowly withered away. Even the birds, lungs filled with it, dropped silently from the sky.

There were by now only a handful of working governments left. They did what little they could, dispensing emergency food to the hungry and deploying the remnants of NATO's army to keep law and order in the city streets. But, by the second month, everybody was hungry and most of the army had deserted. So the governments did what governments do best. They looked after the rich and the powerful, escorting top ministers, bishops and prancing pop stars to well-stocked and well-hidden bomb shelters.

From Sweden's old capital, Stockholm, to the tiny town of Piza, from USSR's Moscow to the walled city of Jerusalem, wild mobs now ruled the streets. They looted shops and killed anybody who stood up to them. But, by the third month, there was nothing left to loot. Every can of spam, every Pepsi, every peppermint Tic Tac had been consumed.

Slowly, the world began to starve.

The Skeleton Clock
2 months, 2 days, 8 hrs, 27 mins, 55 secs

The Skeleton Clock

It is a difficult trek to the forest. Admittedly, thirty-three clicks is not very far – not for me anyway – but, although it's night, there seems to be howlers everywhere. In packs, they hunt the wilderness for survivors of the Uprising. They need serfs to work the land; to destroy what's left of Cinis. But to see so many howlers. It's odd is all. Disturbing. It's almost as if they know I'm on the way.

It's shockingly hot too. Even now, when the sun's dropped away, there's no let up from it. It's stifling, as if I'm cocooned in a woolly blanket. My shirt is soon sodden, my eyes stinging from the salt dripping off my brow. Even my lungs burn. It's not helping that my ribs hurt so much from being pummeled by the howler. But relentlessly, I struggle on until, at 0200hrs, a dust storm rolls in.

The night is suddenly charged with electricity, bolts of lightning ripping at the sky as if it's just flimsy paper. They say the storms began just a few months after the comet hit, as if God was angry at seeing his planet destroyed. Now, almost a century later, they still fill the sky, the rumbling thunder promising a watery tempest. But it hardly ever happens. A drop of water hardly ever falls.

The wind picks up; a sudden, unrelenting blast rocking me back on my heels. It's so strong, I worry I will blow away. Pulling up my dust mask, I battle on, my eyes, narrowed to tiny slits, hunting for shelter. Luckily, I soon spot a rusty, blackened tank, a relic from the Uprising – or World War Three. It's always difficult to tell. A French T-27 Terminator by the look of the 120mm gun. I crawl up onto the turret, yank up the hatch and drop down.

The Skeleton Clock

I sit there spitting dust and blinking grit from my eyes, trying not to listen to the howling wind, or look at the two charred skeletons sitting there with me. The storm is now so strong, it is rattling the tank like a toy. Still, this is a good hotel to hold up in until it lets up. It's steel and the turret's bunged up with rust and old crow nests. The slugs will find it difficult to get to me in here. The only problem is, it's terribly hot. It's as if I'm being slowly cooked. But I can't risk opening the hatch. If I do, the tank will fill with sand. So I drink from my warm canteen – the filter permitting the water to drip out frustratingly slow; much slower than my thirst demands - and try to keep my skin away from the tank's burning hot metal.

I do try to get a little shut eye, sitting up, my chin resting on my chest. There's a Sleep and Toxicity Alarm (S-TOX, the rebels call it) grafted to my left wrist. It was surgically implanted there the day I turned seven. The day I went to sniper camp. But for my rifle, this is my most important tool. It can do two things. It lets me know if toxicity levels climb dangerously high and I must turn back. And it stops me from sleeping too long. I see it is now 03.20hrs. I set it to go off at 03.35hrs. I can't risk sleeping for longer. If a slug finds a way in here and it infests me, it's end of days for Amaryllis Storm. I will just be another host. A shell. So I power nap. I'm the master of power naps.

When I'm woken up by the blast of electricity from my implant, instinct sets in and I check my body for slugs. Nothing. Then, feeling thoroughly fed up, I just sit there listening to the muffled growl of the storm.

The Skeleton Clock

It is moments like this when I feel most lonely. Most vulnerable. In many ways, loneliness is my biggest enemy. It is like a black hole. It fills me, growing larger and larger every day. I'm frightened it will soon swallow every part of me, good and bad, until all that's left is a human-shaped shell.

To pass the time – and to keep my sanity – I try to think of other things. Other things being the oddly-dressed howler I killed in my burrow. It knew my number. Not only that, it slipped by my traps. All of them! But how? Is comms compromised? Can they listen in to everything I say? Or is there a spy in the Nest; an informer, who's selling secrets to the howlers? Then there's the possibility it had been hiding in the rocks when I visited the well and followed me back to my burrow. Then it had simply watched where I'd put my feet. And where I'd not put them. Were howlers truly that clever? Were they evolving?

But what's bothering me the most is what the howler called me just before I killed it. It called me sister. But why? A host can't remember anything. And slugs don't have sisters. A slug's just a, well, just a slug. And, anyway, I'm nobody's sister. Not now they killed Benji.

Luckily, on the second night, the storm drifts off to the north. With a nod to the skeletons – by then, I'd named them Slim and Skelly McRibbs - I clamber up onto the turret. From there, with the help of the moon, I see the storm did a thorough job. Everywhere I look all I see is sand. It's as if the world's been covered in a silvery-brown duvet.

There's always a lot of CO_2 after a storm. I don't know why, but there always is. So I swallow two OxyPills. Then I jump down off the tank, my boots sinking instantly into the soft, powdery sand. I check my body for slugs. My feet. The crooks of my knees. Armpits. They love to curl up in there. Then, cocking my rifle, I click the safety to off and go on my way.

Valley after valley, I trudge on and soon I feel my eyeballs will overflow with tall, fork-shaped cacti and sandblasted rocks. It is no longer the lush, green England of long ago. Skeletons too. Lots and lots of skeletons. They rest like dolls in the golden powder, limbs set in such a way they cannot be asleep. Once so full of life, now left to rot in the open, or to be consumed by the ever-circling crows.

I only ever stop to pee – and to check my map and compass. I know Zulu Sector well but, even when there's a full moon, everything looks different at night. Particularly after a big storm when many of the landmarks I know get hidden under a fresh layer of sand. Here, anybody can get lost. Even me.

Thankfully, the sun soon shows up, popping up on the horizon in a mess of reds and runny yellows. The land is soon shimmering under it, the barren, parched dirt cracked like a wizened face. The sun's rays lick at my burnt cheeks, seeming to wrap around me like a hotblooded serpent. I'm tempted to stop now; hold up in another rusty tank till nightfall. I can spot three of them from here. But I know every second lost is another tree felled. So, I push on, my bravery – or stupidity – rewarded when I plod over the top of a hill and spot a town nestled in the valley. I know the town well. It's called Hope; ironic I always think, as there's very little in the way of hope there now.

As I plod along Hope's deserted streets, I see what I see in every town in Zulu: bent lampposts, doors peppered with dry rot, and lots of rusty, mangled cars partly submerged in sand. There's always a church tower too, and the clock on it is always silent. The only thing I see different here is a set of working traffic lights. Powered by the sun's rays, they switch from red to amber to green. And, every time they switch, there is a tiny click.

Click! Click! Click!

It's disturbing. Unsettling. There's been no cars to stop for almost a century. The town, the streets, all of it, just a carcass, stripped of any flesh by scavengers. Now, there is only the wind for company, and the persistent click of the traffic lights.

Suddenly, a crow sweeps over me, landing clumsily on the roof of a shed. Ruffling ink-black wings, it caws at me, the rasping cry scornful, as if mocking me for returning. I smile grimly. The town of Hope is just a dot on a map. And when all the maps fade – and they soon will – it will not even be that.

Another crow drops to the shed's roof. Stroking the trigger of my rifle, I warily eye the two birds. Infested, I wonder, or not. I decide - not. The thump in my chest slows. If they were, they'd be trying to peck out my eyes by now.

I look down and see a yellow slug slithering up my left boot. I stopped for too long. I forgot Strict Survival

Protocols 1 and 2: Keep Alert, Keep Moving. I pry the slug off with my thumb and then step on it. The resulting pop is wonderfully satisfying; a bit like popping a zit.

As I peer down at the grisly mess, I spot a paw print in the sand. I kneel down and study it. A dog's by the look of it. Deep too. It must be big. Or fat! With so many dust storms, footprints never sit for long. With a frown, I look up and down the street. So this must be recent.

A tremor rocks the town, rattling the doors and sending a slate tumbling off the church steeple. When the shaking stops, I warily stroll on, only stopping when I get to the door of a tiny cottage. It looks a sorry mess, the thatched roof patchy and frayed, crows nesting in the broken gutter. The crumbling, stone walls seem only to be kept up by a tangled web of withered ivy and lichen, the tiny windows framed in rotten and blistered wood. Cupping my hands, I press my nose to a window, but the glass is thick with dirt, reducing everything to a yellow smudge.

The door, I see, is grey. It is like tarnished silver, dull and spotted with endless summers of sun and driving winds. The handle is a shaft of dark, cold-looking metal. I close my fingers around it, but they simply slip off, coming away blackened with dust.

With a screech, the door suddenly opens as if yanked by a mighty hand. Startled, I jump back. But when I peer in, there is nobody there. I stand perfectly still not knowing what to do. There is much evil here. I smell it; a stench of decay, and feel it oozing from the darkened windows glaring down at me. I know I'm in a hurry, but I feel I must go in there. For I suspect in there I'll find what I'm looking for. What I'm always looking for. So, with a hardening jaw, I lift a trembling leg and step into the blackness.

A wind blows down the corridor, grasping me in a chilly embrace. Its icy fingers seem to encircle my body, fondling me, making me shiver and pull my shoulders tightly together for warmth. I see the furthest door from me has been left ajar, allowing a glow of amber to fill the hallway. My mind tells me not to go there, but my body drags me to the light. Every step is met by a dissenting rasp from the rotten floor, but still I keep on walking. My legs tremble, my feet twitch as I battle the impulse to whirl around and sprint back down the shadowy corridor.

At last, I get to the door. It is set into the wall at an odd angle like a tooth grown wild in a witch's mouth. I lift my hand to knock but, as my fingers curl up into a fist, I stop. The time for knocking passed a long time ago. Mustering all of my strength, I kick open the door. It springs open with a crash. With my rifle clutched in my hands, I lurch into the room.

But the dank kitchen I find myself in is not full of braying, bloodthirsty howlers. Or monsters of any kind. In fact, scanning the room, there seems to be nothing frightening in here at all. Apart from the stink! Wrong-footed, I slowly lower my gun. Still, I'm wary. My gut, my – instinct tells me there's danger here. And my gut's never wrong.

It's a big kitchen, oblong in a crooked sort of way, and very, very messy. As I step further in, empty tin cans crunch under my boots and cobwebs brush my cheeks.

The Skeleton Clock

There's a filthy cooker in the corner and, just by it, a sink filled to the brim with rusty pots and pans.

Just to the left of the sink, there is a door. I creep warily over to it and, very gently, I twist the knob and pull it open. There, I discover a set of wooden steps. Smooth and slightly bow-shaped, they spiral up into the darkness. I do not want to go up there, but I know, if I do, I might find what I'm looking for. I fumble in my rucksack for my torch. Then, with my rifle clutched in my left hand, and the torch in my right, I start to climb.

Up and up I go.

The steps are narrow, the low, spider-infested roof only a foot over my skull. I feel smothered. Suffocated. My burrow's bad, but this – it's almost as if I'm entombed.

At the top of the steps. I find a corridor with just two doors off it. I see that the door on the left is slightly ajar, wedged open by a chipped brick. Boldly, I elbow it open, and step over the threshold.

I'm now in what looks like a children's nursery. Old, yellow wallpaper hangs limply off the walls and battered toys litter the carpet. Standing there, a feeling of horror creeps over me. This is no nursery. This is a cemetery. Children slept here. Played here. And were killed here. I can feel it. I don't know how I can, but I can. Whether they were infested by slugs or simply starved, I don't know. And, anyway, it's not important. My stomach spasms, vomit filling my mouth. To me, it's as if every toy is splattered with blood.

All I want to do is get out of there. But then I spot a dresser and there, perched on top of it, I find what I'm looking for.

Warily, I creep over to it. Three silver-framed photographs sit there. I pick up the biggest of them and blow off the dust. There's a woman in the picture. She's sitting on the grass by a tree, a girl in a red, frilly dress perched on her lap. The woman is looking down at the girl, a soft glow to her eyes. There is the inkling of wistfulness there, of wishing she'd sit on her knee forever. For a second, I see my mum's eyes there. Grey. Grey like swirling smoke. I wonder if my mum ever looked at me that way.

My mind drifts to a fuzzy memory. I was only six or possibly seven, and we were living in the Netty. I remember there were rows and rows of shabby, green tents, and everywhere old women stirred pots of bubbling stew. My mum was holding my feet and spinning me. I remember the tents turning to a greenish blur. I remember thinking, "I'm flying. Flying!" It is my most important memory. Not for the smells wafting up from the cooking pots, but for being with her. For being with my mum. Sadly, it is just the wisp of a thing. But it's all that's left. And when I'm frightened, I cling to it with all my might.

As I stand there wondering what it'd be like to have a family, what it'd be like to be loved, a deep hollowness fills me. It is like a cramp in my gut. My only thought is of my mum. I miss her so badly it hurts. If only she was here. If only... I clench my fists. But she's not. And, thanks to Crow, she never will be. Finally, I rub my tired eyes. This will not do at all. Sentimentality is no ally in a war. So, mentally, I shift the memory of my mum to a cobwebby corner in the back of my mind. I pull off my rucksack and slip the photograph in it, nestling it between the box of ammo and the flint. It will go on my bench with the rest of my pretend family. Then, turning to go...

...I see the dog.

VI

The survivors, now numbering fewer than 500,000, cowered in the bunkers, praying for the sun's return. The days turned to weeks, the weeks to months, but still the choking dust filled the sky. Thankfully, on 1st April 2033, when all seemed lost, the dust settled, the sun peeking back down at the grey, withered planet.

But the lucky few creeping out of the bunkers were now met by a new horror. Within days of venturing up into the sunlight, a sickness swept over them. It was the toxins from the powerplants. They drifted on the winds, bringing fever, sending the survivors staggering back to the bunkers. Soon, cramps set in, clawing at stomachs, making them vomit blood and cry like colic children. Then the victims' necks swelled up, big seeping lumps the size of plums erupting up from the skin.

With no hospitals to go to and no doctors or working MediPods, the sick just lay on sodden sheets, drifting in and out of sleep, minds so dulled, they hardly knew where they were.

Within weeks, the toxins killed over 200,000. With food in the bunkers running low, the rest were destined to follow.

The Skeleton Clock
2 months, 0 days, 22 hrs, 46 mins, 41 secs

It's over by the bedroom door. The door I stupidly left open. It's a big fellow; a pit bull by the look of it, with jet-black, bridled fur and drooling jaws. I can tell it's infested. The yellow tint to the eyes, the snap, snap, snap of needle-sharp teeth. All of this topped off with a hefty dollop of hostility. This dog, this – pet! – is now a killer.

To my left, over a baby's cot, there's a window. Keeping a wary eye on the pit bull, I very slowly creep over to it. But I stop when I see the window catch is rusted up. I'm trapped.

The dog snorts, spraying the floor with blobs of yellow snot. I can tell it's hungry; the way the ribs stick out, the way it's eyeing me as if I'm a chicken fillet. It thinks I'm his dinner.

On silent feet, the pit bull pads closer.

"Now, now, boy." Slowly, I cock my rifle. "Don't do anything stupid."

But the dog just growls.

Then...

...it happens. What always happens when a howler is going to attack.

The eyes spark.

"Oh no," I mutter.

With a blood-curdling snarl, it sprints over to me. It's only ten feet away, but there's still time. Calmly, I drop to a knee, level my gun, and rest my finger on the trigger. Then, when the dog's only a foot away from the tip of the barrel, I blow off the top if its skull.

I stay kneeling there, the dog's body twitching on the floor. I feel no joy in the kill. No joy in this tiny, pathetic victory. Yes, I'm a sniper. A mercenary. I know many in the Nest call me an assassin. But what I do is not what I am. And this...

I eye the bloody mess.

...this is just butchery.

~

Just to the west of the town, there is a deep, narrow gully. There's a bridge going over it. I often cross it when I'm on patrol, so I know it drops a hundred feet to a dry, rock-strewn riverbed. As I drag myself to the top of a sand dune, the bridge looms over me. It's old and rusty, the metal girders bumpy with tired-looking rivets and bolts. I don't want to cross it. I don't even want to step foot on it. But it's the only way I know of to get to the forest.

Wary where I put my feet, I creep over it. When I peer down between the cracks in the steel, I see the bottom of the gully is littered with broken and twisted girders. I eye the mess thoughtfully. If the bridge is going to collapse anyway, it might as well help the war effort and bring a few howlers with it. So I stop and plant a little surprise for them.

At midday, I see the forest – or what's left of it. Even from here, it is pitiful to look at. The trees droop dankly, old, crumpled, with knots of twisted limbs. As I creep closer, I must clamber over hundreds of felled conifers, most of them now just skinny, blackened sticks, the bark charred and peeling away. The howlers did this. They cut them down and then burnt them. It is crazily hot, but it still chills me to see the forest this way. My trigger finger curls up. The enemy will pay for this.

I jump as the toxicity alarm on my S-TOX suddenly beeps. With a sinking feeling, I check it. Although the power plants exploded a long time ago, there are still a few pockets of toxic gas left. At the mercy of the winds, they wander the planet, so nobody knows when and where they'll turn up next. I see from the digital display, levels just hit 200 REMS. Thankfully, that's not lethal and, so long as it stays below 300 REMS, I'll be okay. But if it keeps on climbing, I'll be forced to turn back. Vomiting blood is, I think, the most horrific way of dying.

There is a path going through the forest but, concerned I might be ambushed, I decide not to risk it, So, reluctantly, I venture in amongst the trees. Although the sun is high in the sky, it is dark in here. I can feel it closing in on me, pressing down, suffocating me slowly as I step gingerly through the thick maze of dying woodland. The tightly-packed trees loom over me but, oddly, they stay perfectly still, seemingly unaffected by the hot breeze pulling on my curls. The light is slowed to a trickle and my eyes must work hard, only to see a path of gloom in front of me. Even the forest floor is dying, the moss dry, withered and kelp-like. If this isn't hell, it's where the devil enjoys his holidays.

All afternoon, I hunt for Crow's troop of twenty – or so – howlers, only discovering them when I almost step on the outstretched feet of a sleeping sentry. He's sitting, his back resting on a tree trunk, snoring gently. When a slug infests a host, it alters the host's DNA. This is the result, a mess of a man, repellent; all humps, bumps and dripping skin. Even his lips look old, dry and brittle-looking like twigs. He looks harmless lying there, but I know he's not. He's a killer, his gigantic jaw full of needle-sharp teeth giving him away. With narrow eyes, I watch his chest. I can tell he's only snoozing. I must find a way to help him to sleep a little deeper.

I drop silently to my knees. Then, digging in my rucksack, I pull out a hollow stick. I put the tip of it to my lips, level it at the howler and blow sharply. A tiny dart shoots out of the end, hitting his cheek. The sentry's eyes blink open, and he flaps a lazy hand at his face, knocking the dart onto his lap. I scowl and pull my knife. But I need not worry as, a second later, his chin drops to his chest. The dirt's tip had been dipped in a powerful toxin; he'll now sleep deeply for two days.

I drop to my belly and, like a snake, I slither over the dry, prickly moss. Stopping by a small rock, I peer over the top of it. I'm now on top of a low cliff, and there, below me, is the howlers' camp. Scruffy tents held up with frayed rope, barrels filled to the brim with brownish-looking water, a horse hooked up to a wagon filled with muddy turnips. Oddly, I see only six – no, no, seven howlers. The seventh is over by a tree peeing up the trunk. I scowl. According to Crow, there'd be twenty. Where can the rest of them be?

My recon is disturbed by a slug crawling up my leg. I flick it away, pulping it with a satisfying splat under my fist. Then I check the toxicity level on my S-TOX. 250 REMS. I scowl. Still not lethal but still going up. Knowing I need to get a shift on, I return to watching my enemy and to formulating my plan.

From here, the enemy look only to be carrying rusty swords and crossbows. It's the 22nd century but, in many ways, it's closer to the 16th. Most technology's been lost; the skills to fix it lost too. Yes, there's the odd helicopter still flying – just – and, yes, comms still works – sort of – but when it's broken, it stays broken. There's nobody to fix it. Now we only know how to kill. During the Uprising in 2108, we killed with hypersonic bombs and laser canons. When the silos were empty, we turned to bullets and old World War Three tanks. Now, in 2132, it's mostly swords and crossbows. Soon, I suspect, it will be just feet and fists.

I turn my eyes to the serfs. There must be fifty of them down there. Possibly sixty. Men, women and children, all of them dusty, bedraggled and skeleton-thin. And all of them judged by the slugs to be unworthy of being hosts. So, every day, the howlers set them to work. The men hack at the trees with hatchets, the women and children spray sulphuric acid on any greenery they find. They work sluggishly, shoulders bowed, blood-encrusted feet dragging through the dirt. At night, the howlers keep them in camps. They feed them too but not much. Mostly turnips laced with Devil's Dust, a drug to keep them docile. Like cattle.

A few feet from the horse and cart, there's a pit. I'm too far away to see how deep it is, but I do know what it's for. If the serfs stop working – even for a second – they'll be tossed in there. Serfs work until they drop. Then, when they drop, nobody's allowed to help them up. It's the howler way. Sickening.

I spy a boy helping an elderly woman to spray acid on a bush. He's tiny, possibly just six or seven, with a crooked crew cut and sunburnt cheeks. Like me, he's dressed in a ripped t-shirt and shorts. My belly twists when I see how spindly his legs look. He's as withered as the trees. The serf working with him suddenly trips over, accidentally spraying her sandaled feet with the corrosive acid. Instantly, the boy runs over to a barrel and cups up a handful of water. He sprints back over to her, throwing the water over her blistering feet.

I'm impressed. It's not often I see a serf helping another serf. He's a plucky kid. If he's seen by a howler, he'll be punished.

Sadly, he is seen. With a wolf-like howl, a big, trollish-looking fellow storms over to the boy, a whip clutched menacingly in his fist.

I don't know why I do it. Or, possibly, I do. It's the dog I killed. It's poor Slim and Skelly McRibbs left to rot in a steel box. It's seeing so many trees being destroyed. It's, it's – I frown – it's the boy. He reminds me of my brother, Benji. A brother I was too cowardly to protect.

With a sneer shadowing my lips, I thumb off the safety on my rifle and rest my finger ever so lightly on the trigger. It must be a hundred and sixty feet from here to there. A difficult shot for many. But not for me. I look up to the few trees still standing. The wind is blowing from the west, left to right, ten, possibly eleven knots. I sight my rifle an inch or so to the left of the howler. "Bully," I mutter. And, as he lifts the whip to hit the boy, my nostrils twitch and I pull the trigger.

The shot I know is good.

To the accompanying 'Boom!' the howler falls to his knees. He sways a little. Just – a little. Then, with a howl, he drops the whip and slowly keels over.

I rest there on my elbows, smugly congratulating myself on my shooting skills. But I'm forced to stop when the rest of the howlers turn and look at me. I gulp. So much for formulating a plan.

VII

Just thirteen months after the cataclysmic event, the lands of the world were black. The sky, in the beginning filled with choking dust, was now a horrifying brew of electric storms and toxic gas. Every city, from London to New York, from Moscow to Tokyo, stood like a skeleton, the flesh ripped from them, deserted but for the scavenging rats.

The last of the survivors hiding in the bunkers clung determinedly to life. But even the strongest of them knew the clock was ticking. Time was running out. For all of humanity's technology and for all of humanity's prayers, it had been bested. Wiped out by a rock.

But it was not to be. For, in the end, when everything seemed lost, when humanity was on the very brink of going extinct, a man stepped from the shadows. A man who knew a way of surviving on a toxic planet. A man who called himself...

...JANUS.

The Skeleton Clock
2 months, 0 days, 10 hrs, 14 mins, 33 secs

With a wild cry, I storm down the hill and over to the boy. The six howlers – and most of the serfs – look on in astonishment. Bulging eyes, trembling, all of them frozen to the spot. They must be in shock. But I suspect, they won't be in shock for long.

I skid to a stop in front of the boy. "Hello," I say brightly. "I'm Amaryllis Storm."

"Er, hello." His mouth is hanging open and his lips look all blubbery. I hope he's not going to cry. "I'm, er, Twig."

"Twig! As in tree. How sweet." I grin so wildly, I feel my jaw click. "So, Twig, we seem to be in a bit of a pickle."

Rocking and dribbling, he says nothing. He's in shock too.

I drop to a knee, gripping hold of his hands. I need to get through to this boy and the only way I can think of doing it is to be blunt. Thankfully, I'm excellent at being blunt. "The thing is, Twig, if we stay here, we'll be horribly murdered. Horribly! But, if we run for it, we possibly won't. The clock's ticking. What do you want to do?"

"Go with her," mutters the serf the boy just helped. She's lying on her back, her feet terribly burnt from the acid.

"But Granny..."

"Run," she begs him. "There's nothing for you here. This girl is a rebel. She'll help you."

He nods, a sharp jerk of his neck. "O – okay. We'll fetch help."

"Good," she says. "I'll be here."

I jump up. "Excellent!" Blunt, it seems, did the job. "Let's be off then."

I look fleetingly to the boy's grandmother. When the howlers see her feet, they'll kill her. Throw her in the pit. But I can't help her. She's too old and too injured to run, and there's no way I can carry her and still fight off howlers. "I'm sorry. I can't..."

60

"Don't worry," she says, stopping me. She knows I can't do anything for her; and she knows nobody's coming to help. "Protect the boy," she says.

"I'll do my best."

"No." Although it must hurt terribly, she crawls over to me and grips hold of my hand. "Do better."

I nod. I can see in her eyes she's broken. "I will," I tell her. I can hardly deny the wish of a dying woman.

I let the boy hug her. Then I urgently usher him over to the turnip cart. But, as we get there, a gang of sword-brandishing howlers thunder over to us. I eye them stonily. Three men. Two of them tall and thin. The third I see is beginning to rot. He's misshapen, lumpy, as if he'd been molded by a child out of clay. Jaws snapping. Eyes sparking. Howling the way howlers do. All of them killers. All of them stronger than any human. But still just flesh and blood. They can be killed too.

The boy creeps closer to me, his tiny hand tugging on my t-shirt. "What do we do now?" he mutters.

I smile coldly. "Now, Twig, we fight."

I wonder if he's going to panic and try to run. I'd not blame him. But no. He steps over to the cart and picks up a shovel and bucket lying by the left wheel. He then scampers back over to me and stands by my elbow.

He is a plucky kid.

In a flurry of wolfish howls, they charge. It's too late to go for my rifle, so I duck under a sweeping sword, twist and elbow my attacker ruthlessly in the stomach. I hit flesh. Wheezing, he bends over, and I wallop the back of his skull with my fist.

The boy, I see, is still on his feet fending off a howler with the shovel and bucket. I hurry over to help him but then a second howler jumps me. This fellow is colossal with the stumpy legs of a rhino. His sword sweeps up, grazing the cleft of my chin. I scurry back but he doggedly follows me, jabbing relentlessly for my chest. He's a hunter and he can smell my blood. Using my rifle, I block his thrusts. Then, with a howl of fury, I suddenly step up to him and push him up and over the pit's low wall. He plummets to the bottom.

The swish of steel and I instinctively duck, a shimmering sword skewering the cart by my shoulder. My third attacker yanks on the hilt trying to wrench it free but it is jammed in the timber.

In the past, I'd do the howler the civility of stepping off; he'd been unlucky and that is no way to win a fight. But not now. Not today. Today, I cuff him brutally on his snapping jaw.

A volcano spits and growls in my chest, pummeling my rib cage. I see my blurred eyes in the back of the blade; they burn yellow, and fervently I look for the next howler to brawl.

My eyes flit to the boy. He is slumped by the feet of his enemy. I don't think the boy's hurt; there's no blood anyway. But, by the look of the howler's snapping jaws, there soon will be.

"Throw the sword." A whisper, sweet yet terribly toxic, invading my mind. Whatever it is, wherever it's from, it knows my instincts, my primal instincts. "Be all you can be," it suddenly bellows. "Throw it now!"

So, I do. Dropping the rifle, I pull the sword from the cart, the outstretched blade quivering in rage and, with all the venom I can muster, I let fly. It tomahawks over the pit, hitting the boy's attacker with such ferocity, he is thrown twenty feet, striking a tree and landing with a bone-crunching thud in the dirt.

With fury simmering under my skin, I storm over to the body. I must...

"Yes, yes, you must."

...claw open his chest. Gnaw on his ribs.

"Don't forget the liver. Lots of iron in liver. It will keep you strong."

I must...

"Feed on him!"

I drop to my knees and rip open the howler's shirt. But, then, new words spiral in my mind. Softer. Dampening the fury. They block the whisperer's playful temptings and, with a whimper, I slump to the dirt.

The boy scampers over to me. "Amaryllis, get up," he begs, pulling wildly on my left foot. "When she sees what you did, she'll kill you. She'll kill me too."

"I don't want to get up," I mutter. I feel wretched, as if my energy has been sucked from me. Still, a tiny part of me is wondering who 'she' is.

"But, but – WHY!?" he stutters.

I press my cheek firmly to the dirt. "It's safer down here."

But I know the boy's right. We need to go. What I don't know is why I just did what I did. Why I just felt the way I felt. The hunger to kill. To feed. I detest killing howlers. I detest killing anything. I frown. Don't I? Slowly, my eyes flutter shut. I can see it now. The whisperer. It is hidden in the very corner of my mind. It torments me, plays with me and fills me with a terrible anger. I'm just a puppet and it, whatever it is, is my puppeteer.

Clumsily, I get to my feet. The world is spinning, black spots inking my sight. I'm suddenly surprised by how tall I am; how far from the forest floor I seem to be. I step away as the howler I just killed jerks and judders, his nostril growing bigger and bigger until the skin splits and a slug drops out. It crawls over to me, but I simply stamp on it, crushing it under my heel. Still wobbly on my feet, I snatch up my rifle and herd Twig over to the horse and cart. There, I pick him up and, with the last of my waning strength, I toss him onto the hill of turnips.

"Try to get comfy," I tell him, grinning lopsidedly. "It's going to be a long trip." I'm trying to be all cool, as if everything that's happened is just what I expected to happen. As if it's all part of my well-thought-out plan. But, by the look of the terror in the boy's eyes – and the fact he's wet himself – I don't think he's falling for it.

The horse is snorting and thumping the dirt with his hoof. He's spooked by all the fighting. But, when I rest my hand on his trembling cheek, he stops. I grunt. If only it worked so well on dogs.

I feel the boy's eyes on me, and I turn and wink at him. "Just a little trick I know," I say flippantly.

At the front of the cart there is a low, wooden bench. I scramble up onto it and snatch up a discarded whip. Lightly, I flick the horse's rump. "Let's go, boy."

The Skeleton Clock

As the cart clatters up the bumpy track, I can't help but look back. The serfs just stand there, eyes glazed over, rooted to the dirt like the trees they fell. When the howlers see what happened here, they'll kill them. All of them. It'll be a warning to the rebels. Kill six howlers, we'll kill sixty humans. "Run!" I holler to them. A few of them do. Most of them don't. But I can't help them. Nobody can. They were bred for this work. I look to Twig now up to his elbows in jiggling turnips. But the boy seems different. Alert. If the Devil's Dust hasn't destroyed his mind, possibly I can help him.

My eyes drift to the pit where, only moments ago, I tossed the stumpy-legged howler. There, just by it, I spot another howler. The host's a woman. She reminds me instantly of a shard of glass with her thin, sharp-looking body and her jutting-out chin. I can tell she's a howler, the way her eyes spark. But, still, she looks almost human compared to many of them. I can't even see any slugs in her cheeks! Two silver muskets sit on her hips, the belt holding them so thick it seems to almost cut her in two. She's toying with a lock of her ginger curls, her jaw working slowly up and down.

So that's where the sixth howler went. Oddly, I see she's smiling. Smiling! Is she mocking me? Then she begins to slow clap, and I know she is.

"Bravo," she calls to me. "Bravo!" I frown. Or did she? Her lips stayed perfectly still.

I'm tempted to shoot her. Admittedly, it's a difficult shot from a jiggling cart and, to be honest, I don't need to. She's not in my way. But, still, the way she's acting bothers me.

It's, it's – disrespectful. And, anyway, Major Crow's orders were explicit. Kill ALL the howlers I find here.

I lift my rifle and put my eye to the scope. I see she's still smirking. Then she winks at me. Winks! It's as if she's daring me to shoot her. A deep burn sparks in my gut, a tingle crawls over my scalp. The whisperer's back. "Do it, girl. Do it!" With a growl, I rest my finger on the trigger. I can't fight it. But, luckily for her, the cart turns a corner and she's hidden by the trees.

Slowly, I lower my rifle. Who was she? And why did she not try to stop me? The way she acted; it was so odd – for a howler. Howlers do two things. They sleep and they kill. That's it. The end. They never smile and they never, ever wink! But I do know this. Whoever she was, she frightens the bejeepers out of me.

VIII

In the city of Bern in the west of Switzerland, a crowd stood silently. Men, women, even children, they'd left the safety of the bunkers, travelling from all over the world to see Janus and to listen to his sermons. By ship from Finland, in tiny fishing trawlers from Greenland. From North Africa, they walked most of the 6,000 kms, many dying on the way. Within weeks, the city's inhabitants had swelled from 1,000 to over 10,000. Within a month, there were 20,000 survivors there calling on Janus to help them.

As the sun settled over the crumbling city, they looked up in wonder at the man sitting crossed-legged on the top of a red, overturned bus. To be honest, he did not look very inspiring. Dressed in filthy rags, he had the hollows eyes of a man who enjoyed very little sleep and the thick bushy eyebrows of a man who no longer had any interest in trimming them. But the crowd was not interested in how he looked. They were only interested in his words.

"It was not the comet that destroyed this planet," he told them, his sunken, left eye twitching rapidly. "It was humanity. Forests destroyed. Elephants shot for ivory. Rivers polluted and clogged with rubbish. A third world war. All for profit. All for greed!"

"Greed," the crowd chanted angrily. "GREED!"

"Now, we must do things differently. This planet is the mother to all of us. She must be respected. Cared for. If not, everything is lost."

Lifting his hands, the crowd cheered and called his name. "JANUS! JANUS!" Over and over and over. As they cheered, the man on the bus smiled and, for just a second, his eyes flashed yellow.

The Skeleton Clock
2 months, 0 days, 8 hrs, 44 mins, 21 secs

The wheels of the cart bump wildly over a rock, but I don't slow down. Too risky. This is the enemy's territory. Hooking my feet under the juddering bench, I slap the horse with the whip. "Get going!" I cry. "GO!" I twist my neck to check on Twig. I see he's trying to hold on too, up to his knees in jiggling turnips.

"There's a deep gully," I holler to him. "There's a bridge going over it. If we can get to it, we'll be okay."

His blond eyebrows drop to a frown. "But, but – she's smart," he stutters back. "If we can cross it, she can cross it too. She'll find a way."

She? Is he referring to the skinny woman I saw in the forest? I wink impishly at him. "We'll see."

Just then, the wheels hit a second, even bigger rock and I almost tumble off the cart.

"Is there not a smoother way to get there?" the boy asks with a whimper.

"Yes, there is," I admit to him, "but the howlers will know it too, so we can't risk it in daylight. Sorry," I add with a shrug.

He nods. Well, I think he nods. That, or the cart's simply jerking him up and down. "This way is a lot safer," I tell him, "even if it is a bit, er, bumpy."

I feel sorry for the boy. It can't be a lot of fun swimming in rotten turnips. But things will not be better if the howlers catch us. Not by a long way. "Just hold on," I bellow.

"To what?" he snivels. "A turnip?"

It's now afternoon and, thankfully, there's been no sign of any howlers. Including the skinny woman. But, now, there is a new enemy. The wind. Howling and whistling, it throws up dust making it difficult to see. The cart is slowing too, the horse battling to tow us up a steep hill. His chin is almost scuffing the dirt and, every so often, he almost trips. I know what the problem is. He's suffering from the effects of too much CO_2. But, having given all of my OxyPills to the boy, there's nothing I can do to help him. As the horse staggers over the top of the hill, I'm frightened any second now he'll keel over.

As the juddering cart travels further and further away from the forest, the anger I felt there drops away from me. So much so, I can hardly even remember how it felt. I try to but it's sort of like trying to remember how it feels to be cold on a swelteringly hot day. I don't know what happened to me in the forest. Why I felt the way I felt. Why I did what I did. But it seemed to be triggered by a whisper! A whisper that's now been silenced. I do remember how alluring the whisper was. How tempting. To be free of morality in that way, to feel no regrets at all was, in many ways, liberating. Now, as my internal conflict returns, knowing I must destroy the enemy but, to do so, I must destroy the host too, I find I miss it. I miss the whisperer's gift. The freedom to not feel anything at all.

I'm so consumed by my thoughts, I don't see the enemy. Only when there's a sudden howl do I look up, instantly spotting the horse and cart nestled by a rock only a short way from the path. To my horror, it is crowded with howlers. So that's where the rest of them went, I think grimly.

"Look!" I cry. I stretch over and jab the boy in the ribs. But I didn't need to. I can tell by the terror in his eyes he's spotted them too. I whip the horse. "Go, boy! GO!"

The enemy is moving too, trundling down the hill, trying to cut us off. If we don't hurry, they'll succeed.

"Stop!" yells Twig. "Go back!"

"Never!" I trumpet. I clench my teeth and feel my cheeks redden. "We can win this."

"It's not a race!" the boy howls.

"Yes, it bloody well is," I mutter back.

The enemy's cart careens wildly onto the path just as we thunder by. Then, two things happen. An arrow from a howler's crossbow ricochets off the bench and sinks deeply into my leg. I yelp and clutch for my thigh, blood seeping from between my fingers. Then, with a crunch, the two carts collide. Thankfully, we seem to be going the faster of the two and bulldoze the howlers' cart out of the way.

Clattering off, I shoot a look back. The driver, a pasty, hollow-cheeked man in a tatty shirt, is trying to turn the cart, whipping the horse brutally on the rump.

"They, er, don't seem to be giving up," says Twig.

Soberly, I nod. "They never do."

I peer down at my bloody leg and the arrow sticking up from it. Gripping hold of the shaft, I try to yank it out, but I only succeed in snapping it in two. "Oh, crap," I hiss. With the tip still deeply embedded in my flesh, there's no way I'm going to get it out now.

We get to the crest of a hill and, as we rumble down the other side, the wind drops a little. Instantly, the dust thins and I spot a nest of rocks not twenty feet from the path. Anger stirs within me. I'm getting sick of running away. "I'm going to jump off," I call to the boy.

"But, but – why!?"

"Ambush," I say simply. "They'll never know what hit them."

"Should I jump off too?"

"No," I snap. "Stay on the cart. It'll be safer. Just remember to keep going north."

"North?" He frowns deeply. "But how will I know? I'm not very good at..."

"Keep the sun where it is." I nod to it. "Over the hill there. Then you can't go wrong."

"But..."

"Don't worry, kid. It'll be okay." It won't be, I'm lying. Storybook endings don't exist now. But I grin lopsidedly in a pathetic attempt to look confident. "I'll meet you by the bridge."

"You will?"

"Yes."

He nods reluctantly. "Thanks, Amaryllis."

"For what?"

"For stopping the howler from hitting me. Nobody but Granny has ever helped me before."

Surprised – and not a little embarrassed – I ruffle his curls. It's not often I'm thanked. "No problem, Twig. It's my job." Which is a rather odd thing to say, as saving serfs is not my job at all.

I help the boy up onto the bench. Then, after throwing him the whip, I jump. My boots hit rock, my injured leg buckling under me. With a cry of agony, I cartwheel over, landing in a spaghetti-tangle of arms and legs. Gritting my teeth, I drag myself up. I know my leg needs attending to but, right now, I must find cover. I'll see to my injury later. If there is a later.

"Good luck," hollers Twig, as the cart clatters away.

"Thanks," I holler back, giving him a thumbs up. I wonder if I will get to meet him by the gully. And what will happen to him if I don't. He's suddenly, oddly, very important to me.

Clutching my gun, I limp over to the rocks I'd seen from the cart. There, I drop to my knees. Not a second too soon for, suddenly, there is a 'Thump! Thump! Thump!' of hoofed feet. Emptying my mind of Twig and the dull throb coming from my leg, I peer warily over the tops of the rocks.

Instantly, I see the howlers. Six of them in all. But it's the driver who interests me the most. If I can kill him, they'll be forced to stop. I'd shoot the horse, but I don't know if it's infested or not. And I'm not killing anything that's not infested.

The Skeleton Clock

They must be a 100, possibly a 110 feet away, travelling say, 30 kph. I twist the lens on my scope three clicks clockwise, focusing in on the man's chest. My instructor told me to shoot them between the eyes. But I can't. I just can't. Very gently, I rest my index finger on the trigger. The important thing is not to rush the shot. Not to pull sharply. Not to jerk it. If I do, the split second the bullet's still in the barrel, it will be knocked off target.

The problem is, I can't stop my hands from trembling. I honestly don't want to kill this man. But, if I don't, the slug in his skull will force him to kill me. I know I must focus on the fact he's no longer human. He's nobody's dad, I grimly tell myself. He's nobody's son. He's just a host. A shell. Shooting him is like shooting a doll. It looks human but it's not. Thankfully, the trembling stops, and I do what I must do. I pull the trigger.

A swarm of crows fly up as the driver slithers off the bench, dropping to the path with a bone-crunching thump. Bellowing and hollering, the rest of the howlers jump off the cart and run for cover, ducking in amongst the rocks.

The number one skill in the sniper's handbook is to keep moving. If they can't find me, they can't kill me. But it's difficult when my leg is hurting so much, I possess the agility a baby with a box of bricks. But I do my best. With arrows from the howlers' crossbows whizzing over me, I drop to my belly and slither over to a nest of cacti. There, I nestle down, ignoring the jabs of the thorns.

I stay perfectly still. Staying still and listening is a sniper's second most important skill. After a few seconds, I'm rewarded by the snap of a twig over to my left.

Pressing my eye up to the scope, I slowly swing my rifle, focusing in on a trembling thorn bush. There's a howler peering over the top of it, a crossbow clutched in his hands. He looks old. Sixty. Seventy. Possibly even older. I grit my teeth and pull the trigger. With a startled cry, he grabs for his bloody chest, tumbling to the dirt.

I drop low and, on my hands and knees, I scurry away. A split second later, the cacti nest I'd been hiding in is smattered with arrows.

This is madness; there's no way I can shoot all of them and not get hit too. There is a frightened whinny. Peering over a rock, I spot the howlers' cart. The horse hooked up to it is not looking happy, baring his teeth and kicking wildly. All this fighting is making him jumpy. He wants to run away. Perfect! So do I.

Scrambling to my feet, I hop up on a handy rock, jump and land crookedly on the bench. "Let's go!" A brutal whip and, to the urgent yells of the howlers, we gallop up the path. Only three of them left, I think coldly. Much better odds. I shoot a look over my shoulder. Howlers can run like the wind and my enemy is only thirty feet back, looking grim and determined in my wake.

Reluctantly, I whip the horse even harder. Twig must be a long way off by now. But, speeding recklessly over the top of a hill, I'm surprised to see his cart. "Go, boy!" I howl, urging the horse on.

Cantering up next to him, I jump, landing by the startled boy's elbow. But the jump is too much for my injured leg and I topple over, flopping down with a grunt onto the bench.

"Did you miss me?" I ask Twig with a wink.

IX

Every month, it grew hotter, CO_2 thrown up by the comet's impact trapping the sun's rays and turning the world into a slow-burning cooker. But, as the deserts grew, Janus and his followers prospered. Slowly, over half a century, industry developed and farming improved. And, as the toxicity levels dropped and the water receded, the land they lived on grew in size. Soon it stretched from the north of Sweden to the very foot of Italy, from as far west as England to the Polish city of Warsaw.

Janus, in his wisdom, renamed it the Cinis Kingdom, Cinis being the Latin word for 'embers'. For, if anything had risen up from the embers, it was this. On the border, a steel wall was constructed separating Cinis from the rest of the world, a now lawless land called the Wilds.

By now, it was impossible for Janus to directly rule such a vast territory. So he divided it up into sectors, from Alpha Sector (Switzerland) all the way through to Zulu (the United Kingdom). Every sector was assigned a sheriff who worked directly under Janus. The Cinis Assembly was formed, a monthly meeting of Janus and his sheriffs. The Assembly decided everything. Controlled everything.

They were the law.

The Skeleton Clock
2 months, 0 days, 5 hrs, 29 mins, 44 secs

The Skeleton Clock

Halfway over the bridge, I pull up sharply and the old cart clatters to a stop. "Jump off," I holler to my passenger.

The ashen-faced boy looks to me in horror. "But, but – why!?" he stutters back. He's clinging to the top of the bench so hard, I wonder if his fingertips will mark the wood. "If we stop here, they'll catch us," he tells me. "She'll catch us. Then we can't help my granny."

His granny! I'd forgotten all about her. For a second, my jaw hangs open; I don't know what to say. How can I tell a little boy his granny's lost to him? So I don't, I put it off. Tomorrow. Yes, I'll tell him tomorrow. "Don't worry, kid," I say, smiling comfortingly. "I won't let anybody hurt you. Trust me, okay?"

He's shaking with terror and there's nothing in the way of trust in his wild-eyed gaze. But he nods anyway and jumps down.

The arrow in my leg is hurting a lot, but there's no time to try to dig it out now. The howlers will soon be here, and we must hurry. So, recklessly, I jump off the cart too. Swallowing a whimper – and a few very dirty words – I limp over to the horse and hastily unfasten him from his harness. "Good job," I tell the trembling animal. I rub his clammy cheek. "Now, off you go." Gently, I slap his rump and send him trotting away. He'll not last long in the desert, but it's better than being whipped all day by howlers.

Pulling on the cart, I try to shift it, but it's surprisingly difficult. It's all the bloody turnips. "Help me then," I order the boy.

The Skeleton Clock

Huffing and puffing, we turn the cart until it is blocking most of the bridge. I feel the rusty steel under my feet shift a little. Fingers crossed it'll hold. Pulling the shard of flint from my rucksack, I set light to the bed of straw. It is dry and brittle, and it is almost instantly ablaze. I step swiftly back. Fire frightens me. But I'm still happy to see the drug-laced turnips burn.

Snatching up my rifle, I drag a wobbly-legged Twig over the bridge to the far bank. There, I turn and, with my finger resting on the trigger, I look back over the gully. My leg is torturing me. And, to add to my misery, it is swelteringly hot. But I stay perfectly still. They'll be coming soon. I know it. I can feel them.

To begin with, I see nothing, only the sun as it dips below the rolling hills. The very top of the glowing orb hovers there, as if frightened of the coming night and the horrors it brings. Then, in a rush of vibrant pinks and sizzling reds, it slips from sight as if it was sucked into a vast melting pot. It is then, in the dusk that follows, beyond the swirling smoke, that I spot a howler. But, surprisingly, it's not any of the howlers who were chasing us. It's the skinny woman from the forest. She is standing on the other bank, her gaze fixed on me like a cat eyeing a bird with a broken wing.

I watch as she puts a walkie talkie to her lips. Now what's she up to, I wonder. I don't need to wonder for long.

There is a low rumble. Louder. LOUDER! From the dust thunders the enemy. A dozen, two, three – no! I swallow. Hundreds! Hundreds of teeth-baring, eye-bulging howlers. With swords in fists and teeth bared, they look like devils from the pits of hell.

With my enemy only two hundred feet away, I look up to the darkening sky. The crows hover over us, keen to enjoy a supper of soft flesh. All I want to do is shoot them. All of them. But I can't. I'm going to need every bullet.

A hundred and fifty feet.

An unstoppable tidal wave of sharpened steel and guts.

A hundred feet.

Snarls and wild eyes, they jump the burning cart.

Fifty feet.

"Amaryllis! AMARYLLIS!" Twig yanks urgently on my shirt, ripping yet another hole in it. He's stronger than he looks. "We must run," he begs.

I pull a tiny box from my shorts' pocket and show it to him. "No," I reply, ruffling his curls. "No, we don't." As gently as I can – which is not very gently at all – I push him over, my body falling on top of his. Then...

...I do it.

I push the button on the detonator in my hand. I don't want to. It's horrifying. Raw. Wretched. But I must. If I don't, they'll kill me. They'll kill me and the boy. THIS IS WAR!

Instantly, the clods of dirt under us shiver, and the screech of twisting steel rings in my skull. I feel the skin on my cheeks almost melt and my eyebrows burn. Then, a hot wind blows over me and all is silent.

As the dust slowly thins, I stagger to my feet. I see the bridge is no longer there. This morning, when I crossed it, I planted seven blocks of C4 in amongst the girders. They did the job perfectly. All of the slugs were blown to smithereens. The hosts too, the poor sods. The thought of so many humans dying at my hands sickens me. So much so, I retch, throwing up over my boots.

Then, with sick dribbling down my chin, I see her. The woman. She's still there, glaring at me over the yawning chasm.

I watch as tiny bolts of lightning erupt from her eyeballs. Nobody seems to know why howlers' eyes spark the way they do. But I suspect it's the storms. The slugs must be channeling the electricity from them. But how do they do it? How can they be connected to the planet in this way? A planet they don't even know. A planet they crashed on.

"I'm the new sheriff of Zulu Sector," she suddenly calls to me. Or did she? Her lips stay oddly still as her words echo in my mind, low and gravelly. "But do call me Lily."

I eye her warily. I don't often do 'chit chat' with howlers. I find most of them – no, all of them – just want to kill me. Still, why be rude? "Hello, Lily," I reply coolly. Then, not knowing what to say, I add, "What a very hot day it's been."

She responds with a joyful hoot. It seems she finds my attempt at civility amusing. As if she's happy I'm playing her game. "Yes, it has. Too hot for me anyway. It's not good for my chest."

"Oh, I'm sorry. Possibly tomorrow it will be cooler."

"Yes," she nods, "possibly."

This is crazy, I think. Nuts! I can tell by her eyes that she just wants to shoot me. And, here I am, showing concern for her wellbeing.

"Did you kill him?" she suddenly asks me.

"Who?"

"My brother. He dressed a little, er, differently."

I frown as I recall the howler who attacked me in my burrow. His bowler hat, his pinstriped jacket with the hanky peeking out of the pocket. And how he'd called for his sister just before I'd killed him. I thought he was talking to me. That, in his madness, he thought I was his sister. But, no. his sister's Lily. I lick my lips; they suddenly feel puffed up and dry. I killed the Zulu sheriff's brother.

"I see you do remember him. How gratifying. Tell me, Sniper Two Seven – or may I call you Amaryllis Storm, yes?" Her eyes narrow to tiny slits. "Tell me, where did you dump his body?"

I clench my fists, trying to keep hold of my rising temper. Why is it every howler I now meet seems to know who I am? It's beginning to upset me.

"She's crazy," the trembling boy by my elbow whispers. "We must run."

"Never," I hiss. I'm not showing this howler my back. If I do, I suspect she'll put a bullet in it.

I feel Lily's yellow eyes flicker over me, as if she suspects the truth is hidden in the folds of my skin. "TELL ME!" she barks, jutting out her chest like a cockerel.

I put on my best poker face and keep my lips stubbornly still. I burnt it. I always do. It's the only way to get rid of the stink. But if I tell her, I suspect she'll get even madder. "Walk away," I lift my gun, "or I will kill you too."

Lily snorts at me. Oddly, her contempt feels like a slap in the face. Why, I don't know. When did I ever need the approval of a howler? "I do enjoy the hunt," she says in a scarily detached sort of way. "You see, I never stop. Ever. Not until I catch my prey. And today's prey is so - now, how to put it?" She frowns, then snaps her fingers. "Worthy! Yes, worthy." She's over fifty feet away but, oddly, I still catch her every word. "This trap I set today is just the beginning."

Trap! Is she saying what I think she's saying? That the howlers in the forest were just a trap. A trap to catch me! But how did she do it? I was sent there by the Nest. I frown. No, I correct myself. I was sent there by Hubert Crow, my mum's killer. Is he in on it then? Is he the spy who's working with the howlers? Is he trying to kill me too?

Suddenly, she pulls the muskets from off her hips and twirls them in her hands. "This is the end," she says, "for Amaryllis Storm."

There's pity in the crook of her smile; in the twist of her lips. And, suddenly, I see red. "No," I tell her icily, blowing a red curl out of my eyes. "This is the end," I level my rifle and shoot her in the chest, "for you."

A pool of blood blossoms on her shirt. Her jaw drops open. She looks, if anything, confused, as if she expected me to hug her, not to shoot her. "Why?" she says. Then, letting go of the muskets, she drops to the dirt with a thump.

The Skeleton Clock

I stay there, totally still, gazing at her upturned feet and wondering why she seemed so surprised I shot her. She is my enemy. For a second, all seems well. Then, her left foot jerks and slowly, little by little, she sits up. "My, my," she says, spitting blood, "that wasn't very gentlemanly, was it."

Horror creeps over my skin. Throbs in my chest. But I just shot her. I JUST SHOT HER! I never miss. EVER! Not from fifty feet away. But I didn't miss. Her shirt, I see, is drenched in blood. Then how...

With jelly for knees, I stagger back.

"Don't try to run," Lily says, picking up her muskets and standing up. She grunts, a sort of bullish snort, and her thin, coppery lips curl up. "Why bother? Remember, I always catch my prey. It's just the way it is."

A tidal wave of hurt slams into me. I clutch for my scalp, my teeth clamped over a paltry whimper. It's torture, as if a bomb just exploded in my skull.

"Welcome to my family, Amaryllis Storm," she says.

Oddly, for a second, possibly even two, I feel, well...
...comforted.

Then, three terrible words. "I own you."

Then, I do run. Pulling Twig with me, I run and I run...
...AND I RUN!

X

Over time, hundreds of Cinis's children developed a yellow tint to the pupil of the eye. There were other symptoms too, vomiting and sudden mood swings. The kingdom's doctors blamed it on toxins from the power plants. Concerned parents were told not to worry, the doctors insisting the children's eyes would return to normal when they grew up.

Inexplicably, only the strongest and the cleverest suffered from it. So much so, it was soon seen not as a sign of sickness, but of strength and powerful intellect. And there was another benefit too. The children could see in the dark.

As to it fading...

It never did.

The Skeleton Clock
1 months, 28 days, 16 hrs, 50 mins, 11 secs

I'm in a stinking temper. Shivering, I'm slumped by a rusty stepladder under a trapdoor, my fingers hidden in the folds of my armpits. It's horribly hot in the tunnel, but to me it feels icy cold. It's the wound on my leg; it's given me a fever. Gingerly, I roll up my shorts, drawing in breath at the sight of it. The gash is red and rawer than uncooked beef. I put my finger to it and, instantly, the throbbing deepens, almost putting me to my knees. I grip hold of the ladder as fuzzy dots stab at my eyes. The arrow's tip is still in there. I can feel it. Luckily, there's no puss yet and I can't smell anything bad. But that'll soon change if I don't pull it out.

As soon as we got back to my burrow, I called up Rufus Splinter using comms and told him to bring penicillin. I'm hoping it will help to stop my leg from getting infected. The smuggler had agreed to, but at a hefty price.

With a snarl, I punch a barrel, the torch perched on top of it almost toppling off. "Where the hell is he?" I growl.

Seemingly on command, the trapdoor shudders, a thundering "Boom! Boom! Boom!" echoing through the tunnel.

I clamber awkwardly up the ladder, unbolt the door and elbow it open. A second later, a man in a dirty, patched-up tunic follows me back down, pulling the door firmly shut after him.

"Evening, Gov'nor," he rasps. He looks at me and scowls. "Blimey! You look terrible. What's up with you? It's not leprosy is it. If it's leprosy, I'm off. I don't want my bits falling off."

Annoyingly, he's right - although not about the leprosy. I do look terrible. My front tooth is missing, there's a gash on my chin, and most of my eyebrows have melted off. And I mustn't forget my blood-drenched shorts. But I'm in no mood for the smuggler's silly banter and I eye him coldly. "Where you been, Splinter?" I scold him.

The torch on the barrel casts a silvery glow over my late-night visitor, showing off his ferrety eyes, rotten teeth and wind-scuffed cheeks. The index finger on his left hand is missing, sawn off at the knuckle like a missing key on a piano, and there is a moon-shaped scar connecting his top lip to the corner of his left eyelid. He reminds me uncomfortably of a troll out of a terrifying children's story.

Splinter sniffs and limps over to me. The smuggler tells anybody who will listen that he got shrapnel in his knee. "Shot in battle," he would say, but he would never say which battle. Anyway, I know better. Six months ago, the fool had fallen drunk in a ditch and broken his leg.

"Ay, well, nobody's in much of a rush to visit you just now." Gnawing rattishly on his rotten gums, the crook eyes me warily. "They say you killed the new sheriff's brother." He steps back. "They say she's after you?"

"Is the sheriff called Lily?" I ask him.

He nods. "Yep."

"And is Lily skinny, madder than a wet hen and keeps two silver muskets," I slap my hips, "right here?"

"That'll be her."

"Then, yes," I tell him evenly, "I killed her brother. And, yes, she's after me."

The smuggler gnaws on a dirty thumb, his left cheek twitching rapidly. Then, he yanks a filthy rag from his tunic pocket and puts it over his gappy, yellow teeth.

"I'm not infested," I growl.

The crook shrugs. "This'll, er – by my last visit for a month or so," he mutters, passing me a clinking sack before snatching his hand away. "Here's the meds you wanted. All good stuff. Most of it. That'll be twenty OxyPills, Gov'nor."

"Twenty!" I look at the old smuggler in astonishment. With CO_2 levels so high, the OxyPill is the new currency.

Thankfully, the rebels supply me with plenty of them. Payment, in a way, for my work. And my loyalty. Still, twenty's a lot. "You must be kidding," I growl. "It's meds y' selling, not the Nest's map reference."

The smuggler titters hollowly, as if I just told a joke that turned out not to be funny at all. "I can sell you that too if you want," he says.

I eye him skeptically. I suspect he's full of it, still... "How much?" I ask.

"Too much. You can't afford it."

"Now, listen here, Splinter..."

"No, you listen. Sniper. OxyPills, they don't work so good now. Too much CO_2. And now the sheriff's after y', I'm risking my neck coming 'ere. So, it's ten pills for the meds and the rest is hazard's pay. Got it?"

"Bleeding robbery is what it is," I mutter. Digging in my shorts' pocket, I hold out my hand. Splinter looks at the tiny bottle, his brow wrinkled up like a hill of elderly laundry. I sigh irritably. "If you don't want it."

"Now, now, Gov'nor, keep y' pinny on," the smuggler rasps, whipping the bottle from my palm and pocketing it. He rubs his fingers briskly on the tatty hem of his tunic. "I'll be seeing you then," he says, turning back to the ladder. With a chuckle, he adds, "Or not if Lily gets her claws on you."

"Who is she?" I suddenly blurt out. Rufus Splinter knows everybody in Zulu. So, if anybody knows her – and what she's up to - it'll be him.

Slowly, he turns back to me, a smirk playing on his misshapen lips. "It'll cost you," he says.

"No kidding," I mutter, rolling my eyes. Nothing's free from this man. I hunt in my pockets, pull out a second bottle of OxyPills and toss it to him.

"How many's in there?" he asks, rattling it.

"Two."

"Two!?"

"It's all I got," I fib.

He nods, slipping it into his pocket with the first. "She's a hunter," he says. "A predator. She was in command of Golf. She killed every sniper there."

I scowl. "So, Golf, it's..."

"Fallen, yep. Thirteen days ago. There's not a tree left standing. Or a rebel," he adds with a snigger.

I look at him with contempt. The man's a dirtbag in every way. Golf's been overrun and he says it as if it's the punchline to a joke. Just a bit of gossip to sell on. He's lower than a howler. If I didn't need him so much, I'd end him here and now.

"Do it." The whisperer's back. "Go on. He's scum."

I focus on Splinter and try to block out the tempting words. Difficult to do when they're ricocheting off the walls of my skull. "Why's she here?" I bark.

"Janus sent her. She's a psychopathic monster. Relentless. The best there is."

"At what?"

"Killing rebels," he says with relish. I can tell he's enjoying this. I feel my fingers curl up. But I bet he'll soon stop smiling if I rip off his...

"She killed all of them in Golf. That's why it fell. And that's why she's here in Zulu Sector. To kill every sniper on the enemy front and then march on the Nest. And now you killed her brother, well, they'll be no stopping her now."

"But she's a howler," I retort. "There's a slug in her skull. So how can she even remember she had a brother?"

Splinter shrugs. He's now scowling so hard his face practically folds in two. "I don't know," he says. "But there's been talk."

"Talk?"

"They say she's – different from the rest of 'em."

I step up to him. This is getting interesting. "Different? How?"

"The slug allows the host to think. To – remember stuff. They work together."

"Rubbish!" I hiss, my temper rising. "Hosts never knowingly help slugs."

"But what if the hosts don't know?"

I don't know what to say to that. So I just screw up my lips and eye him stonily. I want to deny it. I want to tell him he's wrong. But Lily acted so oddly. She winked at me. Winked! Howlers never wink. Ever. Up until now, I always hoped hosts were forever fighting the slugs; trying to find a way of getting back control. But now it seems they work in harmony.

It's a creepy thought.

"Who is the host?" I ask him.

"A rebel sniper, or so I'm told. She's clever too," Splinter adds. "Cunning as a fox. The slug picked well."

"The slug didn't pick her," I growl. "It just," I shrug, "got lucky."

"If you say so," Splinter says with a smirk. "All I can tell you is she's got a lot of howlers with her. And when she's killed every sniper on the enemy front, she'll destroy the Nest. The rebels can't stop her. Not now. There's too much CO_2; they can't fight in it."

"I can."

"You!" he scoffs with a snigger. "I don't think so."

Still chuckling, he turns to go.

"That's it?"

"For two OxyPills, it's all you get."

Stony-faced, I watch him clamber back up to the trapdoor and push it open. He lets it slam shut after him. "Bloody crook," I mutter. Thankfully, the whisperer is silent now; possibly upset with me for not killing Splinter. I know I must report this new intel to the Nest but, right now, I need to sort my leg. With that in mind, I peer greedily into the sack.

I pull out a bottle. It's very old-looking. And very, very sticky. On the faded label, it says, Expiry 07/2030. Christ! It's over a century old. I peer closer. Thankfully, I see it is penicillin. I blink. It can't be. It's for pigs! I gnaw angrily on my lower lip. I'm going to kill Rufus Splinter.

"I did tell you to," the whisperer grumpily reminds me.

I stand there in the gloomy tunnel, rats scampering over my feet, glaring at the label. Finally, with a, "What the hell!" I untwist the cap, put the bottle to my lips and swig it back. It'll fix me up or it'll kill me. There's also the tiny possibility I'll grow trotters.

After bolting the trapdoor, I hurry as best I can back down the tunnel. If my burrow's ever attacked and I'm trapped there, this is my only way of escaping. Thankfully, my torch is doing a good job at keeping the shadows at bay, but I still feel pins of terror prickling my scalp. The sickeningly low roof feels like a tomb to me.

At the end of the short tunnel, there's a ladder. It's wonky and brittle with age, but it'll hold. Gripping the neck of the sack in my teeth, I clamber up it, emerging from the top of a wooden barrel. I'm now back in my cellar. I jump down. Finding the lid I'd discarded on the floor, I set it firmly on top of the barrel. My 'Emergency Exit' is now well hidden.

Returning up to my burrow, I creep over to the bed, my feet expelling little puffs of dust as I go. I stand watching Twig's chest slowly rising and falling. He looks terribly ill. His skeletal body is trembling, and his skin is so papery-thin, it's almost transparent. When we returned to the burrow, the boy was hit by a sudden fever. Sweeping over his body, it robbed him of his strength and sent him staggering to my bed. And, from the look of the drenched mattress, he's not getting any better

Luckily, I know why he's sick. It's withdrawal symptoms. His body's craving for Devil's Dust, the drug the howlers lace the turnips with. He's going to be this way for weeks. It might even kill him. Wetting a rag, I rest it on his hot brow. All I can do is keep him cool and try to get food and water into him.

Ever so lightly, I brush my fingertips over his hot, puffy cheeks. He looks so sweet lying there, so very innocent, his lips a dusty pink, his freckled cheeks, a gift from the sun, flushed from the fever. Even his golden curls look perfect, falling over his eyes in lazy ringlets. He reminds me so much of my baby brother; a brother I was too frightened to protect. I remember cradling Benji in my arms, kissing his face and begging him to open his eyes. I remember how his fingers twitched, how his eyelids fluttered; it was as if he so wanted to live but just didn't know how to. To this day, I still wonder if he saw me, just for a moment, before his chest stilled and he slipped away.

"I will never let them hurt you," I whisper to the boy. "Never." Twig's my responsibility now. I promised his granny, and I'm not going to let her down.

Allowing the boy to sleep, I limp over to my cracked sink. Over it, on a shelf, there sits a box. I pry off the reluctant lid and peer in. It is jammed to the top with broken thermometers, crumpled half-empty packets of pills and dirty eye dressings. I bravely fish in amongst the clutter and pull out an incredibly old and very sticky bottle of antiseptic. Digging deeper, I discover a bag of cotton wool, sleeping pills and a rusty set of tweezers. Laying my finds on the sink, I eye them with distrust. But they'll have to do. It's not as if there's a hospital I can go to.

For a second, I stand there staring at myself in the mirror. I remember when I first got here there'd been no mirror at all. So I went hunting. It took forever. It was as if they'd all been spirited away. I only discovered this mirror by luck. I'd been sheltering in a garden shed from a sandstorm and discovered it under a hill of smelly blankets. Yes, it's got a long crack in it, but it's better than nothing. A girl, even this girl, needs a mirror.

The Skeleton Clock

I see the yellow tint to my eyes is still there. But why? Is it the toxins from the power plants? Or is it... I stop myself. It's too awful to even think it. But it can't be that. It can't be. If it was, I'd not be me.

Deciding I can't put if off any longer, I pull over the stool and drop down on it, hooking my foot up on the lip of the sink. I roll up my shorts and study the cut on my thigh. The tip of the arrow is still in there. I can't see it – it's way too deep – but when I press on the skin, I can feel it. I balloon my cheeks. If I don't pull it out, my leg will turn septic. Even with the penicillin.

There was talk in sniper camp of there being a working MediPod in Rebel HQ. Developed in 2030, the long, torpedo-shaped cannisters were a wonder of the 21st century. Just sit in them and POW! Cancers sorted, broken legs mended; they even cured the common cold. But there's no MediPod here so I must resort to surgery and popping pills.

Gritting my teeth, I go to work with the tweezers, sucking in sharply as spasms spiral up my body. But I don't stop. I can't, determinedly digging further and further into my raw flesh.

At last, when I'm only seconds from blacking out, I find the arrow. Clamping the tweezers onto it, I steel myself. Then, very slowly and very gently, I begin to pull it out. Red spots blur my eyes and I have to bite my lip from the agony of it. Finally, with a sickening sort of 'Plop', it pulls free. I drop it into the sink and study the blood-drenched tip with morbid interest. It's barbed! No wonder it hurt so much.

Luckily, although the cut's deep, it's not very long, and there's nothing much to sew up. So I drench it with antiseptic and wrap it tightly in a bandage. I sit there for a second admiring my handiwork. Not a bad job considering how blunt the tweezers were and how badly my hand was shaking.

I swallow a fistful of sleeping pills. Too many, I know, but I'm past caring. If a slug finds me and infests me, so be it. I need to sleep. Tossing the tweezers and the bloody ball of cotton wool into the sink, I drag myself to my feet. Instantly, the room begins to spin. I feel my stomach lurch and I throw up all over the floor. As I sway there, my feet sticky with evil-smelling vomit, I wonder if this is possibly the worst day of my life. Then I remember how horrible my life is and I decide it's probably not.

Feeling terribly sorry for myself, I limp over to the bed. Twig is still asleep, sprawled over the lumpy mattress like a starfish. As gently as I can, I shift him over a little. I see he's cuddling Miss Moffit. Not so gently, I snatch it off him; she's my doll, not his. Then, as my knees finally buckle, I drop down onto the warm spot he's left for me. I rest there, curled up in a ball, drifting in and out of sleep. My leg throbs, but soon my mind is so dulled from the pills, I hardly feel it.

Soon, I hardly feel anything at all.

XI

After thirty years of rule, Janus declared Burn the capital of Cinis. He renamed the city Potens, the Latin word for powerful, and a new flag was designed. Fluttering over the city, it depicted a phoenix, claws extended, rising up from a pit of burning, red cinders.

But Alpha Sector was a long way from the other, outlying sectors and, to keep law and order, they needed policing. So the sheriffs picked the strongest and the cleverest citizens to be knights. Working under the sheriffs, they policed the towns of Cinis, ensuring everybody followed the Assembly's laws.

If any citizen did dare to defy a knight's order, they were branded a criminal. Every Sunday, in every sector, the Whippings were held. There, crowds of onlookers were forced to witness the criminals being punished.

As time went by, there were whispers of discontent. Why, many wanted to know, did the sheriffs enjoy such luxury? And why were only citizens with yellow eyes ever picked to be knights? Many called Janus a tyrant. A dictator. There was even talk of an uprising.

But, still, Cinis grew. Still it prospered. But it was not to last, shattered...

...by a sniper's bullet.

The Skeleton Clock
1 months, 28 days, 12 hrs, 39 mins, 52 secs

Clawing at my pillow, I twist and turn in my bed, my feet tangled up in my sheets. I suddenly see him. The howler I killed in my burrow. Lily's brother. With cheeks riddled with tiny slugs, bulging yellow eyes and colossal teeth erupting from alligator-sized jaws, he's a monster from the pits of hell.

"No," I sob. "NO!" I press my fists to my eyeballs. "Stay away from me."

A burst of red-hot fury erupts in my chest and, with a strangled cry, I tumble from my bed. With my chin to my chest, I curl up like a baby in a womb, praying for the suffering to stop. I will do anything – anything if it will just stop.

"Now, that is interesting," the whisperer in my mind rasps slyly.

Then, just as abruptly, it's over, as if a bucket of icy water has been thrown over my scorched and blistered bowls.

All night long, as the boy sleeps, I rest there on the floor, the whisperer's sly murmurings caressing my mind. They are oddly melodic; sweet yet terribly toxic, like a cake filled with a layer of venom. Alluring, swaying, showing me the way. Until, finally, a slug, fooled by my stillness, creeps over my outstretched legs. Like a striking python, my hand shoots out and I snatch it up. I sit there studying it. It is mildly interesting watching it wriggle. Watching how hard it clings to life. But, in the end, I grow bored of it and drop it to the floor. I go to crush it with my heel, but I stop. I stop and let it crawl away.

Only then do I smile.

XII

London, a city of rubble, where scorching, soulless winds whistled between the broken-backed skyscrapers, whipping up the dust and making the buckled streetlamps judder. Mangled, upturned cars and yellow skeletons rested in the streets, a reminder of the day the comet hit and the tidal wave crashed over the city. When the Atlantic receded, the few things not snatched by the tumbling water were later snatched by looters. Plundered. Even the shops' floors were bare, the worn, soggy vinyl ripped up by greedy hands.

There, only a stone's throw from the city's river, in the shadow of the derelict London Eye, a crowd stood silently. Surrounded by hundreds of knights, they'd traveled from all over Zulu Sector to witness the Sunday Whippings. Most of them did not want to be there but they knew, if they refused, they risked offending Sheriff Frost.

Stood on a wooden platform only feet from the riverbank, Frost looked out at the crowd. It was gratifying for him to see so many there. He'd put on his best tunic for the event, plush, red velvet with silver buttons and a row of shiny medals pinned to the lapel. Glancing down at the medals, he saw they were glittering in the sun. He smiled. It was important to look the part.

"Citizens of Cinis," he boomed. "Welcome to the Whippings."

He turned to a boy who was cowering by his feet and brutally kicked him. "This crook took cow's milk. Three pints of it. Three! And, under the powers given to me by the Cinis Assembly, I must punish him for his sin."

"But I was thirsty," whimpered the hazel-eyed boy. He was lollipop skinny, his ragged shirt draped over his body like a bell over a toothpick.

"Theft is theft," thundered Frost, swelling up his chest, "and you will pay for it with the skin off your back."

Brutally, he ripped the boy's shirt off and flung it away. He knew he was being a little over dramatic, but he wanted to put on a good show.

With the crowd looking on, the Sheriff picked up a long, knotted rope. But, as he went to strike the boy, a shot rang out and, with a cry, he keeled over, blood pumping from his chest.

The crowd, even the knights, stood there in shock. Then, as Frost's body twitched and jerked in front of them, his nose suddenly exploded...

...and a slug dropped out.

As the crowd pulled back in horror, Frost's deputy, an ugly, bullish-looking man, cocked his revolver and started shooting.

The knights killed everybody, even the children. No mercy was shown, and nobody was spared. Or so they thought. But they forgot the boy who lay half-crushed under Sheriff Frost's cold body. That night, under the cover of darkness, he escaped, dropping into the fast-flowing river and swimming away. He escaped to tell the rest of Cinis what he'd witnessed.

And, so, the Uprising began.

The Skeleton Clock

The Skeleton Clock
1 months, 28 days, 6 hrs, 22 mins, 40 secs

Silently, I sit by my cluttered desk. The boy is still asleep, snoring gently, curled up like a cat on a blanket. My blanket. But I don't mind; he needs it. For three days, the boy's been terribly sick. Shaking, vomiting, whimpering in agony. Coming off Devil's Dust is no picnic.

As I watch his tiny chest slowly rising and falling, I feel oddly perturbed. Up until now, it's just been me. There's been nobody to fret over. But now there is. In a way, it feels good. It's what I wanted anyway. It's what I always wished for when I dropped the pebble in the well. But, if I'm honest, it's scary too. I don't even know if I'm up to the job of being this kid's big sister. I lost Benji to the howlers. What if they kill Twig too? What if I let this boy down the way I let my little brother down?

I thump my skull, trying to dislodge the memory of Benji's murder. But it never works and, when I uncurl my fist, the memory's still there. It's almost as if it's scorched into the back of my eyelids. The image of me, cowering in a cellar, Benji's yells for help only partly drowned out by the cowardly chatter of my teeth.

With a snarl, I rip off the cap on the bottle of penicillin, put the bottle to my lips and swig it back. Unlike the boy, I'm feeling much better. My fever's dropped and my leg is hardly throbbing at all. It's always the way with me. I always seem to mend in no time at all. I don't know how I do it, but I do. Although, this time, I possibly had help from Splinter's pig medicine.

I watch the clock tick off the seconds. Three, two, one... "Sniper Two Seven, Sniper Two Seven, this is the Nest. Respond, over."

I scowl at the flashing row of bulbs. Who is this? It's a man, yes. But it's not my controller, Nicolo. Whoever he is, I can tell he's older. Much older. "This is Sniper Two Seven," I respond tentatively.

"Identify," he barks.

I'm tempted to say, "No, you identify." But I don't. Better to first know who it is I'll be upsetting. I think for a second, then, "My left foot's bigger than my right." I know it's stupid, but it's all I can think of.

He grunts. "Confirm scramble."

"Confirmed," I reply, flicking the grey switch up.

"Success?"

I scowl at the mic. What's the big rush? Normally, I'm asked to verify SSPs. Is he – whoever he is – in a hurry? I suddenly wonder, rather childishly, if he needs the loo. "Yes," I reply just as sharply.

"Is the forest still there?"

"Most of it."

"Good. Confirmed kills?"

"Seven." Then, remembering the bloodbath at the bridge, I correct myself. "Possibly a hundred and seven."

"A hundred and..." He stops and, for a second, all there is, is static. It seems I rendered him speechless. "Perfect!" he suddenly erupts. "Bloody perfect!" It seems I didn't. "That's just what we need. I will add a hundred and seven to your tally."

Perfect! Why is it perfect? Why is it just what WE need? THEY KEEP A TALLY!? But I let it go. There's too much intel to report. "Be advised, a howler attack is imminent all along the front."

"Enemy numbers?"

"Unknown, Sir. But, according to my intel, it's going to be big. There's a new sheriff and she's planning to march on the Nest."

"This intel. Is it good?"

I think of Splinter. He's hardly good. Still, I think he was telling the truth. Why wouldn't he? There'd be no profit in it.

"Yes," I say. "It's good."

"Understood. I'll put the rest of the snipers on alert. And I'll send troops to the front to support them. Anything to add, Two Seven?"

I think for a second. Then, "I had a visitor," I tell him. "A howler. It knew me."

"I don't follow."

"It knew who I was. It called me Sniper Two Seven."

"Impossible."

"No, it's not," I hiss back. I'm trying to keep my cool, difficult when it's so hot in here and I'm so upset. "I was there. And not only that, it knew where I'd hidden my traps."

"How do you know?"

"How do I know!" I jump to my feet. The man's a moron. "I'll tell you how," I yell into the mic. "IT GOT INTO MY BURROW AND DIDN'T STEP ON ANY OF THEM!"

Keeping my cool is not going well.

"Did you, er, kill it?" he asks flatly. He seems annoyingly unruffled by my angry outburst.

"If I hadn't, I'd not be here," I shoot back.

"Pity. Level Six, that's, er, R and D, they need howlers. Experiments," he adds. "How did it know where the traps were hidden? It's top secret."

"Yes, I know it is." I feel my pulse slow, and I sit back down. "Only I know, and the Nest knows. That's it."

"I see," he says slowly.

I scowl. What's he trying to say? Is he thinking what I'm thinking? That there's a spy in Rebel HQ who's working for the howlers. Is it possible he suspects Crow too?

"Have you moved them now?" he asks.

Doubt crawls under my skin and begins to itch. For a second, I don't reply. Why's he so interested? I try to think but it's as if my mind's a can of tuna and I need a tin opener to get into it. If there is a spy in the Nest, whether it's Crow or not, and I tell this man, the intel might be passed on to the howlers. I can't risk it. I don't want another uninvited visitor. "No," I say at last. I'm lying; I moved them yesterday. "I'll do it in the morning."

"No," he says. "Don't bother."

Startled, my eyes widen. "I'm sorry, did you just tell me not to bother?"

"Correct. Orders from the top. We need you here in the Nest for a new mission."

Speechless, I sit there. Is he messing with me? I don't know of any sniper who even knows where the Nest is, never mind a sniper who's been there. But here, at last, is my opportunity. Finally, I can get my hands on my mum's killer. I can get my hands on Major Hubert Crow.

"Whose orders?" I ask him.

"My orders. Major Hubert Crow, rebel commander of Zulu."

Instantly, my hands curl up into tight fists, so tight, my fingernails cut into my fleshy palms. "I see," I say through clenched teeth. It's difficult but I must not let on how I feel. I don't want him to know I'm coming for him; that the avenging angel is on her way. "What's the mission?" I ask.

"Sorry, Two Seven, it's top secret." There's a wariness to him now, as if he's unpacking a box full of sharp objects. "On a need to know only," he adds.

I feel my blood pump. "And I don't need to know?"

"Correct. Not yet anyway. Too risky. If the howlers catch you, well, you know what'll happen."

"Understood," I reluctantly mutter. He's right. They'd pump me so full of Devil's Dust, I'd end up telling them everything. I suddenly wonder if Crow knows who I am and if he suspects I know what he did. Possibly there's no mission at all. Now I survived Lily's trap - a trap I suspect Crow helped to set - he possibly just wants me in the Nest so he can find a way of getting rid of me. Now he's the new rebel commander, he'll not want me telling the world he's a murderer.

But there's nothing I can do. I must follow orders. Or pretend to. "I'll set off after dark," I tell him. "But I'll need to know the Nest's grid ref. Then I can..."

"No," he interrupts me. "This is too urgent. You will be picked up by helicopter. It's on route to you now, ETA 0700hrs."

I check the clock. That's in just over one hour. "Understood," I say. "I'll keep my eye on the sky."

"Good. And don't forget to set the self-destruct."

"I won't be returning?"

"No."

"Never?"

"Never. Blow it up. All of it."

My eyes travel over the burrow where I have lived for so long, the dry, brittle timbers holding up the roof, the cracked mirror, the dusty photos of my pretend family, and, oddly, I find I'm not bothered at all. My old ragdoll, a present from my mum, is sitting on my pillow, her left eye jammed shut as if she's winking at me. I wink back. Miss Moffit will be coming with me. "Understood," I say, my gaze settling on the bed. "By the way, they'll be a boy with me."

"A boy! Who?"

Emboldened, my lips curl up impishly. "That's on a need to know." I tell him. Then, feeling wonderfully spiteful, I add, "And you don't need to. Over and out." With a flamboyant flick of my wrist, I pull the power.

Dragging my feet, I wander over to the bed and drop limply down on the stool there. There's so much stuff I didn't tell Crow, most of it – if not all of it – to do with Lily. How she's the new sheriff of Zulu. How, according to Rufus Splinter, she and her slug work together. And, most worrying of all, how, when I shot her, she simply got back up. I'd intended to tell Rebel HQ everything. Good intel is how you win a war. But I'd expected Nicolo to contact me, not Crow. And I don't trust Crow. How can I? He murdered my mum.

It is still only 0600hrs, but the summer sun seems keep to begin the day, creeping up over the hills and basking my bunker in a soft glow. As I peer out of the window, I'm surprised to see a sparrow sitting in a tree. It's amazing it's survived so long in a sky full of toxic gas and killer crows. The sparrow chirrups, reminding me of a lullaby my mum sang to me when I was a kid. Smiling at the memory, I brush a stray ringlet from the boy's eye and begin to sing.

A little cock sparrow sat in a tree,
Looking as happy as happy can be,
Till a girl ran by with a bow and arrow,
Says she, "I'll shoot the little cock sparrow."

In a flurry of speckled, brown wings, the sparrow darts away. I watch it go, wondering what frightened it. Possibly the storm looming on the horizon. Or possibly my singing. But it turns out not to be any of them. It's the three howlers I suddenly spot creeping through the trees.

Urgently, I shake the sleeping boy. "We gotta go," I whisper.

He answers with a yawn, sitting up and rubbing feverishly at his reddened nostrils. "What's going on?"

But there's no need for me to answer him for, suddenly, there is the thump of steel jaws and the howl of the trap's victim. "Howlers," the boy mutters, his eyes widening, his fingers curling up into tight, white-knuckled fists. "Do – do you think she's with them?" he stutters.

We lock eyes. We both know she is.

Untangling himself from his blanket, he jumps up from the bed. Then, abruptly, he sits back down. "I feel giddy," he mutters feebly.

I nod. I'm not surprised. He's been ill for days and he's still got a fever. "Stay here," I sternly tell him.

Sprinting over to a rusty box screwed to the wall over my desk, I flip up the lid. Under it, there's a red button. I slam my hand down on it. "This is Sniper Two Seven. Destruct. Destruct. Destruct."

Silence! For a split second, I worry the mechanism is a victim of the dust and has stopped working. Then there's a click and a whirling of hidden cogs. "Confirm destruct," a computer responds in a cold, metallic tone.

"Seven three six..." Scowling, I stop. "What is it?"

"Incorrect."

"No, no, hold on! Em, two – or is it three? No, two! Seven three six two."

"Seven three six two is confirmed. Sniper Two Seven, six zero zero seconds to destruct."

Hooking my rucksack over my shoulder, I snatch up my rifle, run back over to the boy and begin to steer him over to the trapdoor. "Blast! Hold on." Dashing back over to the window, I pick up my pencil box and stuff it into my bag. Then I snatch up Miss Moffit from off my bed. "Did you think I'd forgotten you?" I mutter, stuffing her in too. Sprinting back over to Twig, I wrench up the trapdoor.

"What's down there?" he asks, peering wild-eyed at the hole.

"The way out," I reply with a cold smile.

I follow Twig down the ladder, softly shutting the door after me. Then I herd him over to the barrel. But the thud of boots on the cellar roof stops me. Dust in the rafters showers my skull, and a spider in a trembling web rolls up in a ball. Abruptly, the thuds stop, replaced by a terrifying hush.

I nod at the barrel. "Under there is a tunnel," I whisper, pulling off the lid and gently placing it on the cellar floor. "Let's go."

The boy rubs the end of his nose. "Okay," he says with a sniff, fishing a snotty-looking rag from his pocket.

"No," I hiss.

But there's no stopping him and he trumpets wildly into it. The resulting 'BOOM!' ricochets off the cellar walls and, instantly, I feel a shiver of terror run up my spine.

"Sorry," the boy mutters, sheepishly. "I can't help it."

Gritting my teeth, I nod. "I know," I say gently. Which is remarkably sweet of me as, to be honest, I just want to slap him.

The trapdoor is suddenly flung back, and I look up to see the heels of a howler's boots clomping down the ladder. A howler with a thin, sharp-looking body and ginger curls. A howler with two silver muskets hooked to her hip. She stops at the bottom and grins at me.

"Hello Amaryllis," she says.

I thumb off the safety on my rifle and cock it. "Hello Lily," I reply.

XIII

In the beginning, the war did not go well for the rebels. The howlers, as they were now called, were stronger than any human and, within month, the Uprising had almost been crashed. Captured rebels were forcibly infested with slugs, further swelling the enemy's numbers, and any prisoners deemed not worthy of being howlers were fed a mind-controlling drug called Devil's Dust and forced to work as serfs.

But slowly the rebels got organised. Refugee camps were set up for the children, and the old bomb shelters were converted into Rebel HQs called Nests. From them, the newly-promoted commanders directed the troops, forcing the enemy to fight for every foot of Cinis land.

On the third month of fighting, the rebel successfully captured a howler. They transported it to the Zulu Nest to be experimented on. There, using blunt scalpels, the doctors discovered the slug hidden in the host's skull, its tiny suckers fused to the host's cerebrum. When they removed it and tested the DNA, they discovered the shocking truth. The slugs were not not from this planet. They were invaders, having travelled here deep within the bowels of the comet.

As the war rumbled on, the enemy proved relentless, and kept on advancing. Sector by Sector, they took over Cinis until only six of the sixty Sectors were left under rebel control. Then, in the summer of 2124, they invaded Zulu. The Battle of London lasted three long, bloody weeks. But, in the end, the enemy proved too strong and the city surrendered.

The Skeleton Clock

The Rebel Commander took the last of her troops north, to the Nest. There, she ordered them to dig in. But deep down she knew, when the enemy got to them, there was no way of stopping them.

The end was coming. It was just a matter of time.

The Skeleton Clock
1 months, 28 days, 4 hrs, 53 mins, 55 secs

With a cocky, cowboy sort of swagger, Lily walks over to me, her muskets and a short, ivory-hilted sword swinging menacingly on her hips. A second howler clomps after her. Paler than chalk, I suspect he's not the cleverest of fellows, having the melancholy look of a paddocked donkey. He's rotten and stinks terribly. I see there's a sword on his belt too but his is rusty with a blunted tip.

They stop just in front of me, Lily plonking her feet so firmly in the dirt, I doubt even a herd of elephants would uproot her. "The boy there," she snaps, stabbing at Twig with a bony finger. "He's a serf, yes? A subject of Janus."

Reluctantly, I nod.

"Then return him to me. He's my property."

"He's nobody's property," I snap back. "He's a boy."

"NOW!" she thunders.

I feel Twig huddling into the crook of my left knee. He's trembling and I wonder if it's from the fever or from being so frightened. "No," I reply coldly. "He's with me." I know, according to Rufus Splinter, that she's a psychopathic monster but I'm still determined not to let her bully me.

Lily's cheeks burn a nasty, ugly red. This sheriff's not accustomed to being disobeyed. Nonchalantly, she drops her hands to the hilts of her muskets. I step back, a chill flooding my body. Is she going to try to kill me right here? Right now? Looking into her cold, yellow eyes, I shudder. There is such insanity in her. I can see it in her stare. I suspect the slug has stolen her mind, seeding a new personality and muddling up the rest.

Splinter's right. Lily's a butcher.

With a click, she thumbs back the hammers on the two muskets. But she's still not drawn them; they still sit snugly in her belt. "Drop the gun, Amaryllis."

I level the barrel of my rifle at her belly. "I don't think I will, Lily," I reply. It feels odd calling my enemy Lily. It's such a pretty flower, so soft, so – fragile, and not at all like this murdering howler.

"Don't be a fool," she scolds me. "Three days ago, you shot me right here." She slaps her stomach. "Remember?"

"I remember." She's so condescending, it's maddening. I'm not a child. She can't send me to bed with no supper.

She pulls up her shirt showing me her midriff. Much to my dismay, I see there's not even a scratch. "Well, it didn't work, did it?"

"No, I reply, "it seems not."

"So trust me, girl, it'll not work now. DROP THE GUN!"

"Three days ago, I was sixty feet away," I retort. Boldly, I step up to her. "Now I'm under six." I drop my eyes momentarily to the gun in my hands. "This here is a Winchester rifle. It is the most powerful rifle in Cinis. In it, there's a 9mm hollow-tipped bullet…"

"Don't tell me," Lily interrupts. "It's the most powerful bullet in Cinis."

"No, it's not. But at six feet..."

"Under six feet," she corrects me with a smirk.

I frown at her. I don't get this howler. It's as if she thinks being shot is a joke. As if she knows I can't hurt her. Well, we'll see. "Yes, yes, I'm sorry. At under six feet – better?"

"Much."

"I'll carry on then."

"Yes, do." She nods fervently. "It's all so very interesting."

A deep burn sparks in my gut. I know she's trying to needle me. Get under my skin. The problem is, it's working. "At under six feet," I say, keeping my words as even as I can, "it'll go through rock." I eye her up and down. "And, by the look of it, I'd say your skin is considerably softer than a rock."

She is now shifting from foot to foot, and she can't seem to keep her fingers still. I can tell she wants to draw her muskets. But this sheriff's no fool. She's crazy, yes. But she's not reckless. She wants to win.

Suddenly, she grins wildly. It's not pretty, her jaw full of needle-sharp teeth. "Honestly, Amaryllis, don't be so melodramatic. I only wish to chat."

I eye her skeptically. "Chat?"

"Yes." Then she plays her winning card. "Anyway, if we all start shooting, who knows who'll be hit. Possibly the boy there. And we don't want that, do we."

The male howler stomps up to me, pulling his rusty sword. With his other fist, he thumps his chest like a baboon. I sigh, crushing my teeth over my lips. It seems I must do as she says. If I don't, they'll kill Twig. So, almost numb with misery, I rest the rifle down by my feet.

"Kick it away," she barks.

Reluctantly, I do as she orders.

"That's much better. Now, tell me Amaryllis, do you know who Darwin is?"

"Darwin!" Totally bewildered, I stare at her. "Er, no," I say.

She nods. "I didn't think so. I suspect history is not part of the sniper syllabus."

"It wasn't," I admit. "But they did instruct me on how to kill howlers -," I smile, "in lots of different ways." I know I'm being cocky, but I can't help it. I'm sick of cowering to this woman.

"I bet they did," Lily says. She frowns, eyeballing me with the sort of puzzled interest doctors show when they see a particularly nasty rash.

"I'm very talented," I add. "Top of the class. If you wish, I can show you."

"I'd be most interested to see. But first, let's discuss Darwin. 1809 to 1882. A very clever fellow. Shall I tell you why?"

"If you must."

"Yes, I must. It would be remiss of me not to."

I frown. Remiss is not a word I know. But I don't want her to think I'm dumb, so I nod for her to carry on.

"You see, Amaryllis, Darwin understood why humans ruled this world. Simply put, they were the smartest. The rest, well, they bowed to the whims of the dominant animal. Or they perished. The elephant. The rhino. The dodo bird. All of them killed off by humanity, which, let's face it, is not incredibly good at sharing."

I try to look bored, as if nothing she says is worth listening to. But I am listening; and she knows it.

"When we – slugs you call us, yes?" She snorts. "How silly. Anyway, when we – slugs find a host, the result is, well, perfect. Flawless. A howler is stronger and cleverer than any human."

"And this monster here?" I nod to her knight. There is a sort of cold, blank look to his eyes, empty, as if he's been hypnotised. "He looks as if he's got the IQ of a turnip."

"Grr," growls the howler.

But Lily just shrugs. "Admittedly, not every howler is – how can I put it? – up to the job. But he's strong and respectful."

"He smells strong," I mutter, childishly wrinkling up my nose.

Lily shoots me such a wintry smile, I almost shiver. "Howlers represent the next step on the evolutionary ladder," she tells me. "It is time for humans to pick. Perish or bow to the howlers' will."

"Rubbish!" I snarl. "We…"

"Now, now, Amaryllis," she says, shushing me, "don't upset yourself. The old must be replenished with the new. It's the way of the things. It is nature."

Unwaveringly, I stare at her. There is an intolerable stiffness to this howler; she's like a rusty bolt that will not budge. "So, you plan to kill every person in the world so you can be – what? The master race?"

"Yes and no. Yes, we do intend to be the rulers of this world. But to kill every person! No, no, no. Think of it in this way. A human is much cleverer than, say – oh, I don't know – a dog! But humans don't kill dogs, do they. No, they keep them."

"As pets," I hiss.

"Yes. As pets. The trick is not to let them breed."

A cold chill floods my body and I suck in my cheeks. I must act, and I must act NOW! But I need a plan. I know. WING IT!

Shoving Twig away, I lurch at Lily's knight. My boot ricochets off his shin. My elbow thumps his jaw. Teeth splinter. A howl and, with a whimper, he drops to his knees.

Snatching his sword, I lung at Lily. I know I must be crazy. All the sheriff has to do is pull her pistols and shoot me. But surprisingly, she pulls her sword too. As I hack and lung and cut, I discover why. She's much, MUCH better than me, faster too, with a hint of 'look at me' flamboyance. Effortlessly parrying my attack, she swings her blade, sending my blade clattering to the floor.

Still determined to kill her, I plummet to my knees, my hands hunting for the hilt.

"Don't be a fool, Amaryllis," she warns me. "Let it be. I do not wish to kill you. Not yet. But, if I'm forced to, I will. Understood?"

Slowly, I get to my feet, eyeing the sheriff with bristling contempt. I must find a way of stopping her. But how? I can't get to my gun and she's expert with a blade.

She flicks her wrist, slicing a gash in my chin. "UNDERSTOOD!?" she thunders.

"Yes, yes," I growl, stumbling back. Gently, I press a finger to my bloody chin. Another scar, I think glumly.

I see the boy's crept closer to the barrel and is now only a foot away from it. He looks helpless cowering there, his hands stuffed in his armpits. I feel so sorry for him. But not only that. I feel frustrated too. Frustrated that I can't help him. That I can't protect him from this psychopath. If only there was a way of distracting her and her knight. Then, possibly, he could escape down the tunnel.

"The Zulu Sector's a difficult nut to crack," Lily says, lowering her sword. "There's the Nest to destroy. Not only is it deep in rebel territory, it's cleverly defended too. Your Major Crow's seen to that. There's a wall topped with razor-sharp wire. Hidden traps. Tanks. Even helicopters. It's a fortress. I don't know how I'm going to..." She peters off, apparently lost in thought. "And let's not forget the sixty snipers camped out on the front," she suddenly says, her eyes refocusing. "We must kill them too."

My jaw hardens, my hands curling up into white-knuckled fists. All I want to do is lash out.

"Oh, yes." She smirks. "We know how many. And we know where to find them. Intel is important in war."

But where's this howler getting the intel from? That's what I want to know. There must be a spy in the Nest. There must be! But who is it?

"And a rebel army of -," her eyebrows arch, "- what? Sixteen hundred? Seventeen?"

I press my lips together. I'm not telling her anything. To be honest, I don't know anyway. The rebels keep me in the dark on most things.

She shrugs. "They must all be killed too. Or infested and turned into knights. Yes, an exceedingly difficult job. Even for me."

Although I'm spitting-mad, I can't help but wonder why she's telling me all of this. I'm her enemy, not her ally. Then, I find out.

"We need you, Amaryllis. Your skills."

My eyes widen in astonishment. "You want me – ME! – to work for – YOU!?"

"Just so. The rebels, they pay you, yes?"

I nod slowly. "They pay me well."

"Do they now!" She snorts scornfully. "I don't think so. Tell me, what do they stuff down that old well ever month? Food? OxyPills? Ammo? Not incredibly good is it. Well, we pay better. Much better. And, if I'm not mistaken, a mercenary works for the highest bidder, correct?"

"What can howlers possibly pay me?" I hiss.

"Well, let's think, shall we?" She rubs her chin in a cliched attempt at playacting. "I know," she says with a snap of her fingers. "This war will soon be over. There's just the odd sector still putting up a fight. But it'll not be long now. Sadly, we lost a few sheriffs along the way. When the war's won, they'll need replacing."

I look at her in utter astonishment. "You want me to be a sheriff?"

"Yes, why not?" she says.

"Why not! Well, to begin with, I'm not a howler."

"That's not a problem."

I scowl. What's she saying? That it's not a problem to jam a slug up my nose or...

"Think of the power," she says.

"Power!" I scoff. "I'm not interested in power. I don't get it. I killed your brother. Didn't you tell me how much you enjoy the hunt? That you will never stop until you catch your prey?"

"Yes, I did, didn't I." She shrugs. "There's no denying it. But to be honest, my brother was beginning to rot. And, anyway, Janus overruled me – annoyingly," she adds with a low growl.

Lily, I can tell, is not a howler who enjoys being told what to do.

"It seems he wants you to do a job for him."

"A job!" I'm shocked Janus even knows I exist. "Well, you can tell him I'm not interested. I'm no deserter and I work for humanity."

She tuts and rolls her eyes. She seems to enjoy the opportunity, tossing her head back and letting his mouth gape open. "Loyalty! How, er – well, how inspiring! But loyalty to the rebels! Tell me, do the rebels ever show loyalty to you?"

I keep my lips firmly shut, eyeing her with as much contempt as I can muster. But, if I was a target, she just hit the bullseye. She knows it too.

"Every month, a sector falls. And Zulu Sector will be next. By the end of today, every sniper burrow on the front will be overrun. Then we will march on Rebel HQ. Oh yes,

I know where the Nest is. In three weeks, we will crush it. And, trust me, every rebel in there will be killed."

"The Nest will never fall," I snarl.

"Will it not? You know, in Golf Sector a rebel I tortured there told me that too. "It'll never fall," he yelled at me. "Never!" To be honest, I was impressed by his fortitude. It's so exceedingly difficult to yell with so many teeth broken. But Golf's Nest fell anyway. As did Omega's. As did Beta's. Etc. Etc. Must I go on?"

A swell of fury floods my body. "I will never work for Janus!" I hiss, baring my teeth. "Never! His howlers murdered my brother. I will only truly be happy when I put a bullet in his skull."

Even I'm surprised by the brutality of my words. It seems Lily is too. She's now paler than chalk and looks for all the world as if she's swallowed a chili. With a snap of her jaw, she jams the sword up to my neck. I expect it to be cold and raw on my skin, but my numb body feels nothing. Nothing at all. Paralysed, all I can do is look into the howler's eyes and the terrifying madness living there.

Trembling, I lift my chin, tempting her to end it here and now. Half hoping she will. A drop of blood drips down my neck, but I don't try to pull away, stubbornly returning Lily's cold stare. I feel her grip on the sword shift a little, the blade cutting deeper into my flesh, dying my t-shirt a crimson-red.

"I was surprised to see a mirror up there," she suddenly says. "Tell me, be honest now, where did you find it?"

I can't help but gasp. How is it she knows so much? It's as if she's been following me for months, watching everything I do. I swallow, trying to gather my wits. "I didn't," I say slowly. "It was here when I..."

"Stop lying!" she howls, her eyes sparking. "There's never a mirror in a sniper's burrow. The truth now or I will kill you right here, right now."

I can tell she's not bluffing. There's too much pent-up fury in her for that. I swallow. Why not, I think. It's not as if it's top secret or anything. It's just a mirror. "I took it from a shed," I say at last.

"It was hidden?"

I nod.

"Where?"

"Is it important?"

"Where!?" she growls.

"Under a blanket."

"Under a blanket! I see. Then it was not hidden well. Is there a possibility a..." She tapers off, eyeing me with such intensity, I'd not be surprised if my flesh melted. "It's interesting," she says with a sudden curl of her lips, "the speed you can run."

I look blankly at her. Now what's she up to? It's difficult to keep up with this woman. She's like a ship in a storm, always twisting and turning.

She snorts. "Now, now, Amaryllis, don't be coy. Even I can't run that fast. But that's not your only skill, is it. You shot my knight in the forest. Tell me, how far was that? A hundred feet? A hundred and fifty?"

"A hundred a sixty," I tell her stonily. I don't know why I'm telling her this. Why I'm trying to impress her. But I can't stop myself.

Her eyebrows arch. "A hundred and sixty!" She nods slowly. "Yes, possibly it was." Is it envy I see in her eyes? Or hatred? It's difficult to tell. "Then, if I remember correctly, you got into a punch up with the rest of my knights. My best. But, still, you won. I must say, Amaryllis, I'm mightily impressed with your work."

"I do a lot of press ups," I tell her.

She rewards my flippancy with the ghost of a smile. "So do I," she says. Abruptly, she lowers the sword and steps up to me. Eye to eye, her smell fills my nostrils. But oddly, I'm not repelled by it. Not at all. She smells of flowers.

Her fingertips find the scar on my temple. "You don't know how you got this, do you?" she says silkily.

I don't know how to answer this, so I say nothing.

"I do," she says.

Stunned, my eyes widen. She can't possibly know. Can she!? I feel cornered. This howler knows way too much. It's my job to be in control but, with her, I'm anything but. So I do the only thing I can do. I call her bluff. "Why don't you enlighten me?" I hiss.

She nods. "Okay," she says, with a smirk. "I will."

I steel myself. It's as if all the clocks in the world stop ticking. As if I will be replaying this moment for the rest of my life. Her lips part. For a second, I don't know if she's going to tell me or try to kiss me. But then, the most annoying thing happens...

My burrow blows up.

XIV

With London lost, the howlers thought it was the beginning of the end for the rebels. Most of Cinis's sectors were now under howler rule. The Uprising had been crushed.

But the rebels on six of the outlying islands – Foxtrot, Golf, Kilo, Victor, Yankee and the now partly overrun Zulu Sector – were determined to hold on. Armed to the teeth, they refused to surrender. Then Janus did the unexpected. He switched tactics, ordering his troops to cut down the trees. With CO_2 levels skyrocketing, it was not difficult for the rebel commanders to work out Janus's plan. If he couldn't kill them with bombs and bullets, he'd suffocate them.

But still the rebels battled on. A chemist in Victor Sector HQ developed a pill to help combat the effects of CO_2 on the body. Sniper camps were set up too. Orphans, of which there were now many, were sent to them. Then, when they were deemed Fully Skilled, they were deployed to the fronts. From there, the Nests directed them into enemy territory with orders to stop the howlers from destroying the forests.

But the howlers numbered so many and the snipers so few. It was an impossible task. No matter how many enemy troops the snipers killed, the trees kept falling and CO_2 levels kept spiraling up and up.

On 13th April 2127, Major Striker, Rebel Commander of Zulu Sector, ordered a clock to be constructed. The clock's job was simple. To calculate how long was left until CO_2

levels hit 6%, ending all human life on the planet. Cpt. Felicity Brady, an engineer in the Nest, was given the task. It took her and her troops three months to construct the clock. They then connected it to CO_2 sensors all over the Sector.

Cpt. Brady christened the clock Casper 3636, Casper being the name of her son who was killed in a howler attack, 3636 being the number of days he'd lived for. But the rebel troops called it by a very different name.

They called it...

...the Skeleton Clock.

The Skeleton Clock
1 months, 28 days, 4 hrs, 40 mins, 42 secs

There's a numbness past terror. That's how I feel – or don't feel – as I stumble my way through the tunnel, dragging the dazed-looking Twig with me. It's almost as if my mind's given up. That or I'm simply putting up walls to stop the truth from getting in. The only thought I do allow myself is whether Lily was killed when the cellar roof caved in. But I know it's just wistful thinking. She's too strong and way too wily to be stopped by a few falling timbers. No, she's coming. She's coming for me. She's in my skull. Her lust to kill, to kill me, is almost overwhelming.

So I'm doing what I promised myself I'd never do. The only thing I can do. I'm running away. I'm running away as fast as I can.

The Skeleton Clock

Down the rat-swamped tunnel we sprint till, finally, we get to the trapdoor. Scrambling up the ladder, I wrench back the bolt and fling the door open. Then, still dragging the boy with me, we stagger out into the storm.

Thunder booms over the woods, the wind howling, blowing up dust and sandpapering my cheeks and chin. The storm is not so much over us, but everywhere! Even with my mask on, I can hardly see a thing. But I don't slow down. Not even for a second. I can't. I know Lily won't stop. She's relentless. Now that I turned down Janus's offer, she'll keep hunting me until she kills me. A snarl curls up my lips. Or I kill her.

The boy is slowing me down. Badly. But I can't just abandon him. I won't. I couldn't live with myself. So I trap the terror and grip his hand even tighter.

"Amaryllis!"

Her icy tenor bursts into my mind and, reluctantly, I slither to a stop. I stand perfectly still, my darting eyes hunting the storm for my enemy. My gut tells me – no, yells at me – to run and to keep on running. But I'm frightened she's herding me into a trap. I always trust my gut. Always. But not now. Now...

...I just don't know.

"Where is she?" the boy howls over the wind.

I shush him with a frantic flap of my hand. I know Lily's out there, her and her gormless monster, hunting for her prey. But to shoot her, I need to see her. And, right now, I can hardly see a thing. Then it dawns on me. "Oh no," I mutter, my shoulders slumping. My rifle! I left it back in the cellar.

"Why bother to run?" A holler from the wall of spiraling sand. "There's nowhere to run to."

She's right. I know she's right. But, pulling the boy with me, I step back anyway.

"Remember, Amaryllis, I always catch my prey."

With a gulp, I backpedal faster...

And faster...

And FASTER...

"Got you!"

I twirl so swiftly, I crick my neck. But I'm still too slow. With a terrifying growl, Lily's knight is on me and I'm shoved brutally to my knees.

Urgently, I push Twig away. "Run," I hiss.

"But I can't just..."

"Run, you fool!"

He nods jerkily. "I'm so sorry," he says. Then he twists on his heels and scampers away.

Still on my knees, I watch him go. I watch him right up until the second he's swallowed up by the swirling dust. He'll not last long. Not in this storm. But when he falls and the sand covers his body, he'll be free. Free from slavery. It's all I can offer him.

With sorrow festering in my chest, I peer up at the howler. Oddly, he seems not to be interested in the boy, letting him run off. This is incredibly good news. I feel horribly woozy and not at all up for a fist fight.

"Sheriff!" he booms. "I got her. She's over here."

Thankfully, the wind drops a little, and I can now see a lot better. I pull off my mask. I'm surprised to see I'm down by the river. Twenty feet to my left there is the well with the hornets' nest in the roof. And, just by it, is Lily. As my tormentor strolls over to me, her muskets swinging menacingly on her hips, she seems to glow with danger.

"Such a short hunt," she says, stopping in front of me. "I expected a sniper with so many skills to do better. To put up a bit of a fight. I'm almost," she shrugs, "upset."

But I can tell by the smirk sitting on her lips that she's not. Not at all. It's Janus who wants me for his ally, not her. And now I turned him down, she can do what she wanted to do all along. She can avenge her brother and put a bullet in me.

But I do not cower – no way! – meeting her smirk with a perfectly good smirk of my own. Surprisingly, most of the anger I felt back in my cellar has now seeped away. The whisperer is silent too which is good. I'm not giving up, but such an all-consuming wrath did no sit comfortably in me. I'm focused now. Lethal.

"Good work," Lily croons, turning to the other howler. She slaps him on the back and a puff of dust blooms up, instantly whipped away by the wind. "Okay, let's do this." She brutally kicks my injured leg. "Get up!"

Battling to my feet, I stonily eyeball the sheriff. But I see two, no, three of her. My eyes will not focus. Possibly it's from all the sleeping pills I took or from being walloped by so many clods of dirt when my burrow blew up. Or possibly it's the CO_2. Whatever it is, I can't fight her if I can't see her properly. I must keep her talking until I recover.

"Why?" I ask her.

Her eyes narrow. "Why – what?" she snaps. "I'm going to need a noun."

"The planet. Why destroy it?"

"Destroy it!" She laughs mockingly. "Don't be stupid, child. Janus is saving it. Or trying to."

"From who?"

Thoughtfully, she plays with a gold ring on her finger. "Truthfully?" She says the word slowly, almost timidly, as if it is a word seldom on her lips.

I nod.

"From humans." She bends down and pulls a rusty tin can from the dirt. "Thankfully, when CO_2 levels hit 6%, the planet will be free of them and the harm they do. Then, all this rubbish," she throws the tin at my feet, "will rot. It will not happen overnight. A century. Two. It's not important. What's important is the planet will recover and there'll be no humans – no vermin left to destroy it."

I'm speechless. She thinks she's the hero. She thinks by killing off humanity, she's saving the planet. She's crazy. "But the trees!" I cry.

"They will be replanted."

"How?"

"Seeds," she says simply. "But only when the Uprising is crushed. Until then, we will cut down every tree we find."

I rub dust from my eyes, trying to gather my thoughts. I always assumed Janus was simply a power-hungry tyrant who wants to rule the world. But, according to Lily, he's saving it. From humanity! To him, humanity is a virus. A virus which must be cured. Wiped out.

I shoot Lily a long, withering look. My lips curl up into a snarl and I feel my eyesight sharpen. "Go to hell!" I hiss.

"No, Amaryllis," she says. "But I think I'll send you there." Abruptly, she pulls a musket off her belt. "Here!"

She throws it to me and, nimbly, I catch it. Now what's she up to? I'm tempted to shoot her here and now but, if I do, her chum will attack me. You only get one shot with a musket – and he's got a sword! Yes, it's a rusty sword, but it's still a sword.

"Tuck it in your shorts," Lily says.

"Why?"

"Just do it!" she snaps, her words bullish and sharp.

Confused, I do as she orders.

"Excellent." She abruptly turns and walks off. When she's over by the well, she stops, turning to face me. "That's perfect," she says. Very slowly, she rests her hand on the butt of the musket in her belt. "We'll draw on three."

"Sorry – WHAT!?"

"The way the old cowboys did it, yes? My host's a Western buff. Silly, I know but," she shrugs, "I try to keep her happy."

I nod slowly. This howler's as crazy as a box of frogs. "On three it is."

"One," Lily growls, her eyes hardening.

So, this is it. I know, even if I kill Lily, her knight will be on me in a second. I can try to fight him but he's got a sword. Steel vs. flesh; never good odds.

"Two."

I don't let her get to three.

"For Benji," I cry. With red fury exploding in my chest, I pull my musket and shoot...

...the hornets' nest.

Two things then happen. First, the nest blows up, hundreds of angry, buzzing hornets flying up, swarming all over Lily and her knight. Second, and this is most unexpected, a rope ladder – A ROPE LADDER! – thumps me in the chest!

Unthinking, I drop the musket and grip hold of a rung. Then I'm whisked off my feet.

Up and up I go.

With a cry of fury, the musket in Lily's fist jerks. There's a billow of smoke followed by a sharp crack. But there's no way the bullet will hit me. Not when I'm on a swinging ladder and she's being attacked by a swarm of hornets. "Do you think this is over?" she bellows, slapping wildly at the buzzing insects. "It'll never be over. NEVER!"

But there's nothing she can do. And she knows it. But as is often the way with this sheriff, her fury is suddenly replaced with a smile. I see it for just a second before she's hidden by the storm.

Why, I wonder. Why the smile? She lost, didn't she? And I won. What is it she knows that I don't?

There's a long, low growl. I look down in horror. Now I know why. Directly under me, clinging to the ladder, is Lily's gormless knight.

With a hiss, he claws at my boots.

Scrambling up two of the rungs, I pull my knife from my rucksack – a difficult thing to do on a swaying ladder – and begin to saw at the rope just below my feet.

"Stop!" he yells. "STOP!" But I don't stop. I can't.

I don't want to kill him. He's just Lily's tool. But he's a monster now. And he'd happily kill me. "War's war," I mutter as the twisted stands suddenly pull apart with a twang. The howler plummets silently to his doom.

Swallowing bile, I look up. But there's so much swirling dust, I can't see what the ladder's hooked on to. But, when I listen, I do catch the whirl of a motor. It must be the helicopter Crow sent to fetch me. But who's flying it? Ally or enemy?

Gritting my teeth, I begin to climb. It's difficult with the wind buffeting me. And there's so much dust, I'm almost blind. The ladder's not helping, swaying and wriggling like an angry snake. But I keep on going. Hand over hand. The sooner I reach the helicopter, the sooner I can look for Twig.

Higher and higher I climb. The ladder is old and bristly, the rungs cutting deep welts into my palms. To add to my discomfort, it's beginning to get colder. Much colder. The helicopter must be going up, dragging me up with it. Suddenly, I burst from the storm into bright sunlight. I look up. It's a US Army Chinook; I can tell by the twirling twin motors and the sheer size of it. It's huge. A bus in the sky. I see the ladder is hooked to the bottom of a door in the helicopter's port side. The door's been slid back but there's nobody peering down at me. If I'm lucky, the pilots don't even know I'm hanging here.

Whoever's up there was sent by Crow to collect me. But I don't trust Crow. Now he's the new rebel commander, he'll do anything in his power to keep his dirty little secret hidden. He'll not want anybody discovering that he's the sort of man who deserted his post and left another rebel fighter, my mum, to be killed by howlers. If Crows knows I know, he'll want to shut me up. So, is this just a trap? Whoever's up there, were they sent to bring me to the Nest? Or simply to kill me?

Determined to find answers, I keep in climbing. Then, when I'm just below the door, two hands yank me off the ladder and I'm tossed into the helicopter. I lay there, winded, nursing my bloody palms. Then, knowing I'm unarmed and at the mercy of whoever's in here, I look up.

There's a rebel fighter over by the open door. I can tell by the markings on his combats that he's a gunner. I can also tell – by his cocky grin no less – that it was him who yanked me so unceremoniously off the ladder.

"I didn't hurt you, did I?" he asks with a chuckle, confirming it. Then he frowns and adds, "What the hell happened to your eyebrows?"

I don't bother to reply.

Looking past him, I see there's a small boy lying on the helicopter's juddering floor. I blink in astonishment. It's Twig! A second boy is kneeling over him, but he's much older. Sixteen? Seventeen? I don't meet many boys so it's sort of difficult to tell. I watch as he puts a blanket over Twig, tucking it under his chin. Then he jumps nimbly to his feet and strolls over to me.

The helicopter is swaying and pitching, but the boy keeps his footing so perfectly and, seemingly, with so little effort, I'm reluctantly impressed. As he stops in front of me, I look him over, noting his beefy body and bulldog jaw.

I see his left cheek is all wrinkly and badly scarred. I know this injury. This boy's seen battle. He's been burnt.

For a long, long second, he just looks at me...

...looking at him. I suspect I see sympathy in his soft, green eyes. Even pity. Which annoys me. I don't like pity. Then, with a wild grin, he offers his hand. "Hello, Two Seven," he says. Instantly, I recognise his drawl. "I'm Nicolo Lupo, your controller."

"Oh," I say. "Hi." I muster up a smile, allowing him to pull me to my feet. I'm just thankful he's not sixty, bent over, with warts on his chin.

XV

By 2132, CO_2 levels had skyrocketed so high, the OxyPills were no longer of much help. Undeterred, the rebels battled on but, with lungs full of the suffocating gas, they were no match for the howlers. They were losing. Badly. Then, in April, Golf Sector fell. Janus's plan was working and Cinis was almost back in his grasp.

Luckily, Major Hubert Crow, the recently promoted commander of Zulu Sector, had a plan of his own. A plan so daring, yet so clever, if it succeeded it would win the war. But for it to work, he needed the best sniper in the rebel army; a sniper capable of hitting a target 5,327 feet away. An impossible shot.

He needed Amaryllis Storm.

The Skeleton Clock
1 months, 28 days, 4 hrs, 9 mins, 16 secs

Cross-legged, I sit on the floor of the shuddering Chinook, warily eyeing the rusty bolts and willing them to hold together. There's a row of circular windows in the grey, wire-strewn wall. The window closest to me is grimy and badly pitted, but I can still see the sun through it. It's on the port side so we must be flying north. Towards the Nest. Towards the man I'm going to kill. I'm just keeping my fingers crossed this bucket of junk will get me there.

There is good news. Nicolo, my controller, is not at all interested in murdering me. Not yet. And the second rebel fighter, the gunner, well, he's not even bothering to look my way. Dressed in desert combats and a badly dented Kevlar helmet, he's over by the door draped lazily over a rusting M16 that's been welded to the helicopter's floor. Nicolo, who's dressed in combats too, is busy playing doctor. He's strapped Twig into a canvas cot and hooked him up to a complicated-looking monitor. But my controller seems to know how to work it, pressing buttons and nodding knowingly when it beeps.

All I want to do is sleep, but I feel bad just sitting there watching Nicolo do all the work. Anyway, the boy's my responsibility, not his. So, reluctantly, I drag myself up. Every part of my body is hurting, from the popped blisters on my hands and feet to a very nasty swelling on the top of my skull. So much so, as I limp over to them, I can't help but wonder – I little selfishly, I admit – why it is Twig's hooked up to the monitor and not me.

"How's he doing?" I ask, stopping by Nicolo's elbow.

The helicopter suddenly rolls, tipping alarmingly to port. I almost grab for Nicolo to stop myself from toppling over. Almost. But I don't, gripping hold of Twig's cot. I don't need his help. I don't need anybody's help.

Nicolo shrugs. He's still upright and, annoyingly, he didn't seem to feel the need to grab hold of anything at all. "He's doing okay, I think," he says. "I'm a medic, not a doctor, so there's only so much I can do."

"A medic!" Now I'm confused. "I thought you were my controller."

"I am. But I'm a medic too. When there's fighting, my job's to help the injured troops. Mostly I just try to stop the bleeding. Then I stretcher them off. Did you think I just sit in Comms all day on the off-chance Sniper Two Seven will call in?"

"No, no," I say, "that'd just be silly." I feel my cheeks redden. That's exactly what I thought.

Upending a canteen, Nicolo drips water onto a towel. He then rests it on the boy's glistening brow. "His skin's clammy and cold," he says. "He must be in shock."

I balloon my cheeks. "I know how he feels," I mutter.

"Sorry?" He turns to look at me.

"Oh, er, nothing," I stutter back, suddenly very glad the helicopter's rotors drowned out my words. I must stop being so selfish.

"He's coming off Devil's Dust, yes?"

I nod, trying to keep my eyes from lingering too long on Nicolo's burnt cheek. "I think so," I say. "It's been just under a week."

"That'll be why his pulse is so erratic. Don't worry, Two Seven, there's a medical unit in the Nest. It's not very big but there's a doctor there. A Doctor Atchoo..."

"Atchoo! No way. As in..."

"Sneezing, yes." He grins disarmingly. "When you meet him, try not to giggle."

"I never giggle," I tell him. Still, I grin too. It feels odd. I think it's been so long, my mouth's almost forgotten how to do it.

"Doctor Atchoo, he's, er, well, he's okay. He's a doctor anyway."

"Of medicine, yes?"

"Possibly." He shrugs, then prods his disfigured cheek. "He fixed me up. He'll know how to help the boy."

Eyeing Nicolo's cheek, I can't help hoping Doctor Atchoo's better with drug addicts than he is at doing skin grafts.

"So, if the boy -." He frowns.

"Twig."

"Sorry, yes, Twig. If Twig's hooked on Devil's Dust, he must be a howler slave, correct?"

"Correct. He's a serf."

"I see. Where did you pick him up from?"

"On the mission," I tell him without thinking. "I discovered him in the..." His scowl cuts me off. "What?"

"The mission!" He stiffens, eyeing me shrewdly. "If I remember correctly, I instructed you to..."

"Intel," I interrupt him, mentally kicking myself. It's all I can think of. I don't want my controller to think I'm going soft; that I don't follow orders. "Who knows what he knows," I add.

He nods slowly. I can tell he's not convinced but, thankfully, he drops it and turns back to the screen. Peeking over his shoulder, I see Twig's body temp is flashing alarmingly. It's only 35°C. Suddenly, I get why the boy's hooked up to the monitor and not me. He's dying.

Feeling properly ashamed of myself, I kneel down by the cot and, very gently, I rest my blistered hand on his. I hardly know him but he's still important to me. To me, he's the brother I didn't protect. He's Benji. As I kneel there, I remember his grandmother's dying words.

"Protect my boy," she'd begged me. But how can I protect him from this?

"Try not to worry," says Nicolo. He puts his hand on my shoulder and, without thinking, I pull sharply away.

"Oh, sorry," he splutters, his left cheek reddening, his burnt cheek staying oddly pale. "Is the shoulder hurting?"

"No, no it's just -," I sigh. I feel angry with myself. He's just trying to be kind. "The thing is, for so long it's just been me. I, er – well, nobody's ever…"

"It's okay. I understand."

I don't think he can – I don't think anybody can – but I nod anyway, thanking him. I don't know why I'm being so difficult. After so long in the desert, I should be happy to see another human being. I should be hugging everybody I meet. But no; I'm as prickly as a cactus.

"Twig will be okay," Nicolo says. "Trust me."

Sadly, he is not the most accomplished of actors, his words hollow, his smile a little too forced.

I say nothing. I don't trust anybody.

"It's just lucky we got to you when we did."

"How did you find us in the dust storm?" I ask, happy to change the subject. "There was almost zero visibility."

"Sensors."

"Sensors!" I eye him skeptically. "You gotta be kidding me. On this – thing! It's a relic. With so much dust, it's amazing it can even fly."

He laughs. It's deep, rumbling, fitting him perfectly. "Well, this – relic spotted you from twenty clicks out. There's all sort of tech in the Nest. Major Crow's seen to that. You'll see when you get there."

"In sniper camp we were told the Nest is off limits to us." I know it sounds as if I'm accusing him. But that's okay. That's how I want to sound.

Nicolo frowns. "I think it still is."

"So why am I being taken there?"

"I'm not permitted to tell you," he says slowly. "I'm just following orders. Sorry."

"Why? Is it top secret?"

His lips tilt up. "In the Nest, everything's top secret. But there's going to be a meeting tomorrow morning at 0600hrs. Then you'll find out what's going on."

"I'm invited?"

"Oh yes. Amaryllis Storm is the only item on the agenda."

I scowl as I mull this over. I'm the only item! What's the major up to? "Will, er, Crow be there?" I ask. I chew on my thumb, trying to look indifferent, as if I'm just making small talk.

But I don't need to worry; the boy only seems interested in my evident lack of respect for his boss. My boss. "Major Crow," he corrects me. "And, yes, he will. Well, he'd better be. He called the meeting."

Slumping down on the end of Twig's cot, I look out of the window. So tomorrow I get to meet Crow, the man responsible for my mum's death. I don't know how it happened. All I know is what I saw in my file in sniper camp. A file I wasn't even supposed to see.

AMARYLLIS STORM

STATUS: Fully Skilled
DOB: Top Secret (Project Liberty)
POB: The Netty, Zulu Sector
FATHER: Top Secret (Project Liberty)
MOTHER: Cpt. Holly Storm (Medal of Valor), rebel sniper, killed 27th July 2124 in the Battle of London.
NOTE: Sgt. Hubert Crow, her spotter, survived. Suspected of deserting his post but unproven. CASE CLOSED.

Case closed! CASE CLOSED! Not for me, it's not. And it never will be until I discover the truth. I suspect the mission went terribly wrong and that's why Crow deserted. But what happened? Were they fed bad intel? Were they outsmarted by the howlers? Or were they simply overwhelmed by enemy numbers and Crow bottled it? Did a runner. And why was it never proven? Was there no witness? I need to find a way of getting Crow on his own. Just him and me. I clench my fists. By the time I'm finished interrogating him, I will know everything there is to know.

Gazing moodily out of the window, I see it is very much a desert here too. I do spot the odd town dotted here and there, but there's not much to look at, just a bunch of roofs and red-bricked chimneys sticking up from the sand. Only when the pilot's forced by a duststorm to do a detour do I see anything of interest. A rebel camp! A nest of wooden huts encircled by a rusty-looking, barbed-wire fence. I see lots of troops hurrying here, there and everywhere, and three Challenger tanks puffing smoke.

"What's going on?" I quiz Nicolo. "Is the rebel army mobilising?"

Frowning, he steps closer to me, bending over and peering out of the window too. I can smell him now. He smells sort of musky. Sort of, oh, I don't know – honest. Which is stupid. How can anybody smell honest? But that's how he smells to me. "Yes," he says simply. "There's been reports of a new howler sheriff who's..."

"There is," I interrupt him. "Crow got the intel from me. I met her. She calls herself Lily. According to a smuggler I know, she was a rebel sniper."

"And she's not rotted?"

"No. She smells of flowers."

"Flowers!?" His mouth drops open. "And you met this, er – Lily?"

"Yes." I chew on my top lip. Possibly telling my controller I'm on first name terms with the new sheriff is not such a smart move. "On the mission," I go on. "She was in the forest."

"But you escaped."

"Yes, I escaped." I keep my eyes locked on his. "Is that a problem?"

"No, not at all." He keeps on looking at me, no doubt trying to unlock my secrets. Then, with a shrug, he lets it go. "She's ordering howlers to attack all along the front. Major Crow's ordering the troops to fortify it, but..." He rubs his eyes and stands back up.

"Too many howlers?" I volunteer.

"Way too many. And that's not the only problem." Picking up a fresh towel, he gently mops Twig's burning cheeks. "The level of CO_2 is now almost off the chart. It's difficult for the rebels to fight in it."

"But the OxyPills. Don't they help?"

"They did. Not so much now. The lab's trying to develop stronger pills but," he shrugs, "the clock's ticking."

I nod. He's right. When I first got to my burrow, I was taking two OxyPills a week. Now I'm taking two a day. "And the rest of the snipers on the front?" I ask.

"Mostly overrun. Sorry," he adds with a sympathetic smile.

I feel my guts twist up. So many snipers, I think numbly. Sixty of them. All killed. I didn't know any of them. The rebels forbid snipers from meeting up. Even in sniper camp, we were stopped from mixing. But, still, SIXTY! It is a terribly bitter pill to swallow, and I tightly shut my eyes. I'm rocking now, all hunched up, my hands stuffed in my armpits. And if it wasn't for Crow and this mission he wants me for, I'd be amongst them. I sit there, struggling to inhale, to exhale, to do anything. Then I remember Nicolo's watching me. Keen for him to keep thinking I'm a cold, hard killer, I drag my eyes open. "They knew the risk," I say offhandedly. Typical of me. Trying to show I'm independent. Strong. Nothing can dent me. Is it bravery? No. It's survival. It's the only way I can get through a day. Not wanting him to see how badly I'm trembling, I turn back to the window. I'm just in time to see three Chinooks fly by, all of them going the other way. All of them going to war.

"Do you know what Project Liberty is?" I suddenly ask him. I know I should be looking at him, watching for signs he's lying. Itching, fidgeting, shuffling his feet. But I don't; I keep looking out of the window.

"No," he says.

It's only then that I spot the big, black cloud. I scowl deeply. It's getting bigger too – much bigger! – so it must be coming this way. Then, as it fills my window, I see it's not a cloud at all. Terror fills me. It's a flock of birds.

CROWS!

"NICOLO!" I yell, trying to warn him. But it's far too late.

The Chinook rocks to and fro as the birds slam recklessly into the hull. The gunner, to his credit, is firing madly into them but, like a raging flood, they gush in the open door. There's nothing I can do to help him – or the pilot – so I duck down, wedging myself between Twig's cot and the wall. I try to look for Nicolo, but with all the birds I can hardly see a thing. I'm just hoping Twig is properly strapped in.

Suddenly, the helicopter tips to port and, with a yell, the gunner is flung out of the door. Without thinking, I jump up and sprint over to the smoking M16. I cock it and shoot wildly into the swarming birds. Within seconds, I kill hundreds. I know it's hopeless – the sky's filled with them – but I do this or I do nothing. And I never do nothing.

Keeping my finger curled tightly around the trigger, I risk turning to check on the boys. Through the swirling crows, I see Nicolo. He's standing over Twig who's curled up in a ball by the older boy's feet. Nicolo's swinging his fists wildly at the birds, trying to keep them away. Even now, when I'm fighting for my life, I find it interesting how different I am to everybody I meet. My controller's instinct is to protect the younger boy. But it never even crossed my mind. It seems I'm just not wired that way. My instinct is never to protect. Always to fight. Always to go for the gun.

Suddenly, Nicolo drops to his knees, flinging himself over Twig and covering the boy's body with his own. Why? Is he hurt? Then it hits me; the doom-filled silence. A cold shiver runs up my body. The thrum of the rotors has stopped. The helicopter's going down.

There is the howl of a siren. 'We-oow! We-oow! We-oow!' It rings in my skull. I do the only thing I can think of. I drop to the floor too, rolling up in a tight ball. Then, with a bone-crunching thump, the helicopter hits, the steel walls buckling in with a screech. But it's not stopping there, rolling over and over, jagged splinters of glass spilling over me, cutting and slicing, ripping my skin to shreds. When the helicopter finally stops, I'm lying on the floor, hot sticky blood dribbling down my chin.

Rocking gently, the Chinook rests there. As do I. I want to pretend this is not happening, but I know I can't. I must find Twig and help him. I must find Nicolo and help him too. Then there's the pilot to think of. So, ever so slowly, I sit up. The cabin's a mess of injured, dying birds, twisted steel and torn wiring. Everything is sparking. Or smoking. Fingers crossed it's not going to blow up. The only silver lining I can think of is that the siren's stopped blaring.

Numbly, I look down my cut and bleeding body. Everything is hurting. EVERYTHING! But is anything working? Gingerly, I clench and unclench my fingers.

They work. I try wriggling my feet. They work too. The only problem is the M16 is lying on top of my legs. I'm pinned to the floor. Bending my knees, I twist my legs, wriggling my feet to and fro. But I can't get them free. I'm going to need help.

My eyes hunt the wreckage for any signs of life. "Twig!" I holler. "Nicolo!" But there's no reply. Possibly they were thrown from the helicopter. A sudden coldness fills me. Possibly they were killed.

I sit there for – I don't know how long: forever, it seems, drowning in a river of hurt.

I feel...

I feel...

Broken.

But I don't weep. My spirit will not let me. If I cry, I will be lost. I fill my lungs. I will never stop fighting. 'Giving up' is not in my DNA.

"Amaryllis!"

I look up expectantly. "NICOLO!" I cry. But it's not. And it's not Twig or the anonymous pilot. The thump in my chest runs wild, my skin turning icy-cold. No. NO! It can't be...

Over by the helicopter's mangled door is Lily.

My clawing fingers hunt the floor, looking for anything I can throw at her. Anything I can protect myself with. But there's nothing. I'm totally helpless.

She ducks low, picking her way over to me. I see she's smiling. The thought of killing me must be putting her in a very good mood. She stops in front of me. "I did tell you," she says, pulling her sword, "I always catch my prey."

She lifts it up.

"I'll do it," I cry, my instinct for survival kicking in.

"Do – WHAT!?" she sneers, pressing the sword's tip up to my neck.

"The job."

".Job?"

"Yes. Janus, he wants me to do a job, right? Well, I'll do it. Whatever it is, I'll do it."

Her eyes widen, a flush creeping over her sallow cheeks. I can tell she's torn. I can tell by the way she keeps pressing the sword up to my neck. She so wants to kill me. But, to do so, she'll be defying Janus's orders. And, from what I know of him, he's not the most forgiving of monsters.

"How do I know I can trust you?" she growls.

"You don't," I growl back.

Her eyebrows arch hawkishly. I see most of her skin is covered with oozing yellow spots. Hornet stings, I think with relish. "Honesty," she mutters. "How very unexpected." She licks her lips. Then, slowly, she pulls the sword away. "Okay, Amaryllis," she says, dropping to her knees, "the job's not difficult. Well, not for such a talented girl."

I say nothing, strongly suspecting the compliment was not a compliment at all.

"When you get to the Nest," she says, "Janus wants you to find Level Seven."

Confused, I scowl. This is not what I expected at all. "Sorry, did you say Level Seven?"

"I did. Why, is there a problem?"

"No. Well, yes. Sort of." Now, how to put this and not upset her so much she kills me? "The thing is, er, Lily, there is no Level Seven. A Nest only has six."

She laughs scornfully. "That's what they want you to think. Honestly, Amaryllis, try not to be such a puppet?"

"I'm nobody's puppet," I say with venom.

"Excellent! Then show it. Cut the strings and find Level Seven. Remember, they'll try to stop you. Just don't let them."

Deciding it best not to annoy her further, I play along. "Let's say I find this Level Seven. What do I do when I get there?"

"Find the truth," she says simply, hopping to her feet. Then, almost as if it's an afterthought, she adds, "Then put a bullet in Major Crow's skull."

I feel my eyes grow to the size of dustbin lids. So Crow's not the spy! If he was, they'd not want him murdered. He'd be too important to them. "Kill Crow!" I gasp. "But, but – he's my boss!"

"Yes, I know he is," she says nonchalantly, slipping her sword in her belt. "Don't fret, Amaryllis, when you see what's hidden there, you'll shoot him whether Janus wants you to or not." She turns to go but stops. "By the way, don't think for a second I can't get to you. So, if this is just a ploy to stop me from killing you here and now, well, let's just say there'll be hell to pay." Her cold, yellow eyes drill into me. "Understood?"

"Understood," I growl, stubbornly returning her gaze.

"Wonderful! We don't want any, er, misunderstandings, do we?"

I say nothing.

She kicks my foot. "Do we?"

"No, we don't."

She nods. "Then, I'll be off. So many snipers to kill, I hardly know where to begin."

My eyes follow her as she picks her way through the smoldering wreckage to the helicopter's mangled door. "Sheriff," I suddenly call out.

"What is it?" she snaps, turning and glaring at me. "I'm in a hurry."

"Yes, I know. Sorry," I then add. I don't want to upset her. I'm still trapped. I'm still at her mercy. "Back in my burrow, you were going to tell me how I got the scar. I need to know."

"You will," she says, turning away. She ducks down, exiting the helicopter. "Follow Janus's orders," she calls back to me, "and soon you will know everything there is to know."

And so I'm left there, two worrying thoughts swirling in my mind. Firstly, what can be so important that it's kept hidden on a level nobody knows exists? And, secondly, if I kill Crow now, I will be helping the howlers. I will be helping my enemy to win the war!

The Skeleton Clock

Part II
The Nest

XVI

The Skeleton Clock
1 months, 27 days, 6 hrs, 13 mins, 10 secs

My eyes flicker open and, with a cry, I bolt up in my – I look down – my bed. I'm in a bed! Where's the helicopter? Where's Nicolo and Twig? And why's there a dripfeed going into the back of my hand? Then it hits me. I FEEL WONDERFUL! For the first time in forever, oxygen fills my lungs and not CO_2. And nothing hurts. Nothing! Not even the gash on my leg.

As my eyes slowly focus, I see I'm in a tiny room. It's empty but for me, the bed and, sitting on the end of it by my feet, a sunken-cheeked man in a crisp-looking, white gown.

"Where am I?" I demand to know.

"In the Nest," he answers, hoping off his perch. He sniffs. "This is Medical and I'm Doctor Atchoo." Then, as if to prove it, he pulls a hanky from his pocket and trumpets into it.

With a scowl, I eye the doctor up and down. He's a dumpy-looking fellow with a sort of waxy, buffed-up sheen to his skin, and the most crazy, wiry curls ever. EVER! So crazy, I can't help but conclude he's been recently electrocuted.

The Skeleton Clock

As I sit there wondering if I trust this man or not - and, if not, whether I should hit him and leg it or simply leg it – it suddenly occurs to me that the bed I'm in is not a bed at all. I'm under a sheet, yes. There's even a fluffy pillow. But there the similarity ends. To begin with, it's constructed of glass. And it's egg-shaped but cut in two and I'm lying in the bottom of it. By my feet, where the doctor had been sitting, there's a row of glowing, red buttons and a huge LCD monitor with lots of numbers on it. Staring at it, I see my body temperature is 37°c, which is perfect, and my pulse is 60bpm, which is low. Oddly, under the word BLOOD, the letters U, N and K are blinking red.

"It's a MediPod," the doctor enlightens me. "The only working MediPod in Cinis."

I nod slowly. So they do still exist.

I peek under my sheet and I'm shocked to see I'm totally nude. And that's not the only thing that's shocking. My skin! It looks so shiny; glowing almost. "Where did all my scars go?" I ask in wonder.

"The MediPod grafted new skin over them." He rests his fingertips on the monitor and, almost lovingly, he pets it. "Remarkable, isn't it?"

"Yes," I say. "Yes, it is." I feel newborn. Everything is tingling. Everything! From the bottom of my feet to the top of my scalp.

Instinctively, I feel for my broken tooth with my tongue. It's grown back! But, when I put my fingers to my temple, I find my scar's still there.

The doctor shrugs. "Sorry. I don't know why the pod didn't fix it. I'll talk to engineering. There must be a glitch."

But I don't mind. If I'm honest, I'm glad. It's been there for as long as I can remember. If I looked in mirror and it wasn't there, I'd not be me.

"Feeling better?" he asks.

"Yes," I reply. "Much."

"Good. Good. Although, I'm not surprised. I had a corpse in yesterday in better shape than you."

I eye him coldly. I hardly know this man but already I'm beginning to find him annoying.

"Now, let's see," He unhooks a chart off the end of the pod. "You had skin cancer, liver cancer and lung cancer. Remarkably, they were all stage three."

"Is three, em, not good then?" I ask.

"Not good! NOT GOOD!" He laughs so wildly, I wonder if he's having an asthma attack. "Three's terrible."

I smile feebly, idly wondering how much trouble I'd be in if I punched him.

"There were two other cancers I didn't even know existed. But, don't worry, the pod cured the lot of them. Amazing!" He grins wildly, spittle forming at the corner of mouth. "Amazing!"

Doctor Atchoo, it seems, is very much in love with his electronic toy. "So, just the cancers, then?" Best to check.

"Oh, no," he says cheerily. "It's a very, very long list." He consults the chart. "Six broken ribs, a torn bicep, no, no – sorry, two torn biceps, blisters -," he frowns, "- everywhere, cuts everywhere, a broken pelvis and, er –" he flips the page (there's another page!) "- oh, yes, a broken tooth, melted eyebrows and a dislocated left pinky."

"Bloody hell," I mutter. I feel for my eyebrows. Yes! They grew back. "It's a miracle I'm still alive."

"I don't think so," says the doctor offhandedly.

"Sorry?"

"Well, it's not, is it. Not with you being so – different."

"Different! How?"

The doctor's eyes slowly widen. "They didn't tell you?"

"No, they didn't. And who's they?"

"Oh my, how, er, embarrassing." He's now chomping wildly on his lower lip and his eyes keep flickering to a spot on the wall over my left shoulder. "I'm sorry, Two Seven, it's not for me to say."

"Doctor..."

"It's not for me to say," his tone turning stiff and surly.

I glare at him. My instinct is to jump out of the pod and throttle him with my dripfeed. He'd soon tell me then. But he's my doctor and he just saved my life. So, reluctantly, I don't. "Where's Twig?" I ask with a sigh.

He cocks his eyebrow. "Twig? I'm not a tree doctor."

"The boy," I say coldly. "He was in the helicopter with me."

"Yes, yes. Sorry." He has the decency to blush. "He's presently in ICU; that's the Intensive Care Unit," he adds in response to my blank look. "To be perfectly honest, he's not doing too well."

My shoulders slump. "Was he badly hurt in the crash?"

"No, no. Just a bit shook up. No, that's not the problem."

"So what is?"

"He's addicted to Devil's Dust."

"Oh. I know that," I say. "He's a serf. It's how the howlers control them."

He nods. "The problem is, if I ween him off it too suddenly, it will kill him."

"Then do it slowly."

The doctor sighs. "To do that, I'd need a supply of Devil's Dust. Then, as you say, I'd dripfeed it to him, a little less every day. But, the problem is, I don't possess any."

I rub my eyes. How am I going to get my hands on Devil's Dust? The only person I know who could help me is Rufus Splinter. But he's a long way from here. "Can't we just put him in the pod?" I ask.

"He's a drug addict, Two Seven. No pod can fix that."

As I sit there mulling over the problem, there's a knock on the door. It springs open with a hiss and Nicolo walks in carrying a tray and a crumpled-up paper bag. Suddenly mindful of how naked I am, I pull the sheet up to my chin.

"Look who's up," he says, ambling over to us. I see he's limping badly and there's a nasty cut over his left eye.

Doctor Atchoo jumps to his feet, dropping my chart on the floor. "My, my, is that the time!?" he splutters, which is a very odd thing to say as there's no clock in the room. With trembling fingers, he yanks the dripfeed from my hand and slaps a plaster over the punctured skin. "Pop in tomorrow for a checkup," he says. "I'll be here all day."

"Okay, Doc," I reply, wondering why he's suddenly so jumpy. And, at the same time, thinking, 'Excellent! Tomorrow, he can expand on the word - different.' "When can I see the boy?" I ask.

"Soon. Very soon." He is now almost halfway to the door. "He's asleep just now."

"Tomorrow then? When I'm in for my checkup."

"Yes, possibly. If he's awake." He casts a final, wary look at Nicolo and scampers out of the room.

"What a very annoying man," I mutter as the door swings shut behind him. I turn to Nicolo. "Hi," I say.

"Hi."

There then follows a very long and very uncomfortable silence.

"What you got there?" I finally ask, nodding at the stuff in his hands.

"A uniform," he says, dropping the bag on the stool, "and a gift from the kitchen." He rests the tray on my knee. On it, there's a blunt-looking fork and a bowl of what can only be described as cat sick.

"Is that cat sick?" I ask.

"In a way, yes."

"So, the cook..."

"Can't cook, no. It's chicken," he adds with a grin.

"Is it!? I think it's pulsating."

I pick up the fork and prod a particularly grisly-looking bit, half expecting it to jump out of the bowl and run clucking from the room.

"It's very grey to be chicken," I say.

"Well, it is."

"Is that an eyeball?"

The boy nods slowly. "Possibly."

I'm so hungry, even this bowl of slop is making me drool. So, with a shrug, I tuck in and, although it's a bit slimy, I wolf it down.

Looking bemused, Nicolo stands there watching me. "Hungry?" he asks.

"Famished," I reply as a grisly lump rolls down my chin and lands back in the bowl with a splat.

"Good shot," he says.

"I'm a sniper," I reply. "I never miss."

Finally, when there's not a speck of food left, I put my fork down. "According to the doctor, I was dying," I tell him. My gaze shifts from the bowl to the cut over his eye. It's being badly sewn up and is red-looking and swollen. The doctor's work I suspect. No wonder he ran out of the room. Nicolo probably wants to murder him. "You look a bit battered too. Were you hurt in the crash?"

"Yep." He scowls. "I buggered up my knee too. Twisted it."

"I know! Why don't you hop in here?"

"With you!?"

"Yes, why not?" Then I remember I'm naked. "Oh, er, no." My cheeks burn crimson, "But I can hop out. Oh no, I can't." I balloon my cheeks. Get a grip, Amaryllis, I tell myself. "Okay, this is the plan. Shut your eyes, I'll get dressed, then the pod's all yours."

"Thanks for the offer," he says, looking bemused, "but I can't."

"Why not? The doctor told me I had five cancers. five! And this pod cured the lot of them. It'll sort out a twisted knee in a jiffy."

"I'm not allowed to. The pod needs a lot of power to work, so it's kept for VIPs only. The higher ranks: pilots, doctors, engineers."

I cock my eyebrows. "And I'm a..."

"A Very Important Person, yes."

"I see. And you?"

"I'm a lowly medic so I'm not very important at all." He shrugs. "So I must mend slowly."

"But who'll know?" I persist. "Who's going to tell? There's just you and me here."

"No, there's not," he says, his eyes shifting to the left. He's now looking over my shoulder just the way the doctor kept doing.

This time I turn to look too and I spot a camera bolted to the wall, a green light under the lens blinking rapidly.

"They know everything," he whispers.

"Bugger," I whisper back. Now I know why the doctor refused to tell me how I was 'different'. Next time I ask him, I must remember to pull him into the girls' loos first. Unless there's a camera in there too! "How did I get here?" I ask, switching to what I hope is a safer subject. "Everything's sort of fuzzy."

"We were lucky."

"Lucky! We were attacked by crows and almost killed in a helicopter crash. How's that lucky?"

"Before we went down, the pilot sent out a mayday. It was picked up by the Nest and Major Crow sent a second helicopter to pick us up."

"Oh, okay, that's sort of lucky," I admit.

"Twig and I were thrown from the helicopter and knocked out. But you were jammed under the gun. When the medics cut you free, you were in a bad way, so they injected you with morphine, putting you under. Then they transported the three us back here to the Nest."

"Three? What happened to the pilot?"

"Sgt Bolt was killed in the crash."

I slump back down onto my pillow. The corpse the doctor had in yesterday. "I'm, er, sorry." I say, which I know is not very original, but it's all I can think of saying. "And the gunner?" I ask, referring to the rebel who fell out of the helicopter.

"Cpl Brooks. We were two hundred feet up, so - ." He shrugs.

I nod silently. Nobody could survive such a long fall.

"War's war," Nicolo says grimly. "They knew the risks. We all do. For the good of the many, remember?"

I say nothing. I suddenly feel sort of pathetic. I've always been so proud of my 'mercenary' label. Of not caring. Of not being expected to care. 'For the good of me' is my moto. That and the thirst for revenge. But is that it? Is that all I am?

Suddenly, Nicolo sits down on the end of my bed, snapping me out of my trance. "The meeting with Major Crow will begin soon," he tells me.

"Where's it being held?" I ask.

"In the Map Room on the top level. It's a bit of a hike so you'd better get dressed." He nods to the bag on the stool. "I didn't know your size so I went big. Sorry."

"Why didn't you check my file? Everything's in there, probably even my bra size."

Did I just say that!? All this talk of honor is making me feel uncomfortable. And when I'm uncomfortable, I say stupid things. It's my way of trying to shock him; of saying I don't care.

But he just nods, totally unfazed. "Yes," he says, "it probably is."

As he sits there grinning at me, it is my cheeks that redden, not his.

"Get dressed," he says, standing up, "and I'll escort you up there. I'll be in the corridor."

He thumps a green button on the wall, the door instantly sliding open. "By the way," he says, "you look better with eyebrows." Then he steps out, the door springing shut behind him.

For a second, I just sit there. This boy is so – oh, I don't know – good! So honest. He's like a bloody nun. It's bugging. Still, I like him. I know it's just a silly crush, but I can't help it. "Okay, Amaryllis," I sternly tell myself, "focus." It's time to go to work.

I look over at the bag. Now, how to – got it! I pull the cover off my pillow and throw it over the camera lens. Clambering out of the pod, I stretch, my fingertips brushing the glowing panels in the ceiling. I feel wonderful. New! As if I was dismantled, all the broken bits replaced and then put back together. I don't know how the pod works, but I do know this...

It works!

The Skeleton Clock

I drop to the floor and do two hundred press ups. It's a doddle. So I do a hundred sits up too. Then I inspect the uniform Nicolo left for me. Green with two pockets and a zip up the front. It's hardly a Cinderella dress. I put it on only to discover it's way too big for me. But it's this or I meet Crow stark naked. So, with a sigh, I roll up the legs. I then put on the boots. Amazingly, they fit perfectly.

Before going from the room, I pick up the fork and slip it up my droopy sleeve. Who knows who'll I'll meet; what dangers I might face. A girl must protect herself.

Pressing the green button, I step out of the door. I find I'm in a long, dimly-lit corridor. Nicolo is there, slouching on the wall, his hands shoved into his pockets. With a grin, he looks me up and down. "I think, possibly, I picked the wrong size," he says with a chuckle.

I stare stonily back at him. "You think?" I mutter. I don't like being laughed at.

He taps his watch. "We gotta go. It's 0530 and Major Crow's expecting us at 0600."

"But I can't meet him in this," I protest, waggling a sleeve at him. "I look like I'm dressed in a bin bag."

"Oh, I don't know," the boys says. Annoyingly, he's still smirking. "I think bin bags look better."

"Not funny," I hiss.

"Chill, Two Seven. It's a meeting, not a dinner date. Anyway, there's nothing we can do to fix it now. Let's go."

And, without another word, he turns and limps off.

For a second, I consider stomping back into my room in a huff. It's not the badly-fitting uniform that bothers me. I'm not interested in how I look. I'm just not very good at

157

following orders. I remember in sniper camp, the doctor there scribbled 'belligerent' on the bottom of my psych report – in big, red letters! But I know if I ever want to discover what happened to my mother, this might be my only chance. So, with the fork's cold steel pressed reassuringly up to my skin, I set off after him.

I follow him down the corridor, my boots clanking on the wire-meshed floor. Everything looks spotless. The steel walls, the grey struts holding them up; even the nuts and bolts holding the struts up. There's not a speck of dust anywhere. Or rust. But I do see plenty of doors and I wonder, idly, what's behind them. By ever door, there's a tiny keypad and it occurs to me, if I'm going to try to look for this secret level, I'm going to need the code that unlocks them. I know I don't need to find it. Lily can't get to me here. Still, I'm intrigued. What did Lily say? "Everything you need to know is in there". It's just too tempting to pass up.

To begin with, the Nest seems deserted. Not a rebel in sight. Then there's the blast of a siren and, as if by magic, the corridor fills with troops. Hundreds of them. Men, women, even children. But they all look identical to me. Sternly so. Skulls shaved, boots brightly polished, uniforms zipped up to the very top. I don't know why, but many of them stop short when they see me, whispering excitedly as we trudge by. It feels odds to be the focus of so many sets of eyes. I'm unaccustomed to it and I find it horribly unsettling. So much so, I begin to feel like a bug under a magnifying glass, and I wonder if soon they'll ask if they can dissect me to see how I work.

With my shoulders hunched, I follow the backs of Nicolo's boots to the end of the corridor, to a set of spiral steps.

"The Nest is on six levels," he tells me as we start to climb, "but only the top level is not dug into the hill. The Control Room's up there – that's where I sit when I'm on comms with you – and the Map Room, which is where I'm taking you now. There's the Armory..."

Armory! My eyes narrow. That's just what I need.

"The Skeleton Clock is up there too. Oh, and the inverters."

"Inverters?" But for us, the Nest now seems deserted. I much prefer it this way but, still, I wonder where everybody went.

"The Nest is powered by solar energy, but the DC electricity from the sun must be converted to AC electricity for it to work."

"And that's what the inverters do?"

He nods. He's two steps in front of me so I can't see his face. But I suspect there's a big grin on it. He's enjoying showing off his knowledge. "After the electricity is converted, it's stored in a battery so we can run the Nest at night. The inverters run whenever the sun's up which is why everything is juddering."

"I see." Even now, I can feel the steps vibrating under my feet.

"Medical's on Level Two. That's where we just were. So, thankfully, it's only a short climb to the Map Room."

I peer past him, trying to see the top. But the steps seem to spiral endlessly up and up and up. "How short?" I ask him skeptically.

"A hundred and thirty-three steps."

"A hundred and – y' gotta be kidding me! And there's no lift!?"

"No, sorry. But it'll keep you fit."

"Not if it kills me," I mutter.

In truth, such a long climb is not a problem for me. The pod worked wonders and I feel a hundred percent. But I don't want Nicolo to know that. Not yet anyway. Better he underestimate me until I work out if I can trust him or not.

"What's on the rest of the floors?" I ask him.

"Oh, all sorts. There's the kitchens, a school..."

"A school! Here, in Rebel HQ?"

"Yep." He nods. "The Nest's full of children. Over a hundred I think."

"Can Twig go there when – " I correct myself, " – if he ever gets better?"

"I don't see why not. I'll check, okay?"

"Thanks," I say. The boy's being remarkably helpful. Why? What's in it for him? Is he, I wonder, just being kind? And, if he is, why's it making me feel so uncomfortable?

"Most everybody sleeps on Level Five. There's a library and a gym. The canteen's there too. Oh, by the way, I sorted a room for you. It's not very big, but I think it'll do the job. When Twig's well, he can stay there too. It's, er, just down the corridor from where I sleep."

"Oh, how handy."

"Yes, it is. There's a sink, a shower. The bed's a bit old; two of the springs were shot but I fixed them. Now, where did I get to? Oh yes, the lowest level..."

"Level Six, right?"

"Right. A lot of it's R & D."

"Who works in there?"

"Just a bunch of boffins. They try to develop better ways to kill howlers. It's all top secret. All very hush hush. To be honest, we don't mix with them much. The rest of the level is taken up by the farm."

"Farm?"

"It's where all the food is grown."

I frown. He must be joking. "But how? It's impossible. There's no sun down there."

"We don't need the sun," he answers cryptically. "Hydroponics."

"Hydro...?"

"...ponics, yes. It's very clever. I'll show it to you."

It sounds interesting. But, at this moment in time, I want to discuss other things. "So Level Six is the lowest level, correct?"

"Correct."

"There's no Level Seven?"

"No." He stops on the steps so suddenly, I almost bump into him. "Who told you there was?" he asks, turning to me.

"Oh, em, just a smuggler I know," I fib, moving up two steps until I'm eye to eye with the boy. "I know it's silly but he insisted there's a secret level in the Nest where they do – stuff."

"Stuff? What, er, sort of stuff?"

I shrug. "You tell me."

With a roll of his eyes, he turns to go. But I grip hold of his arm. "It's important, Nicolo."

"Why?"

"It just is."

"Well, there's not. Trust me, if there was, I'd know. This is where I grew up. When I was a kid, this is where I played. I know every nook and cranny of this Nest. If there was a Level Seven, I'd know. Your smuggler is full of it."

"So there's not?"

"No, Two Seven, there's not." He pulls free of my grip. "We need to keep moving."

I nod. "After you." I don't like having anybody behind me; not when there's a chance they'll stick a knife in my back.

I keep on following him up the spiral steps. They seem to go on forever, and, soon, I'm hot, grumpy and horrible thirsty. But, when we get to the top, I'm not met by a cold drink but the cold stare of a beefy-looking sentry. Over her, screwed to the wall, there is a sign. 'Level One' it says in big, bold letters. Then, under it, in red, 'Restricted. Intruders will be shot'. Charming! As the sentry eyes me up and down, she rests her hand on the butt of her pistol.

"She's not going to shot me, is she?" I ask Nicolo, shuffling to my left so I'm partly hidden by the boy.

He turns to me. "Possibly." He winks. "But don't worry, I'm here to protect you." There's a playful twinkle to his eyes but, still, I suspect he's only half-joking.

Turning away, he limps over to the sentry. "She's got a meeting with the boss at 0600hrs. I'm her escort."

"Name?" she barks, looking past Nicolo and directly at me.

"Sniper Two Seven," I reply.

She checks a list that's been taped to the wall. I see it's a very short list. There's only my name on it. But the sentry's in no hurry, enjoying exercising what little power she has.

In the end, she ticks a box and steps back, letting us past. She delivers a smart salute as I walk by. I return it, my flapping sleeve smacking me in the eye.

I follow the Corporal down a long, narrow corridor. The lighting here is much brighter than on Level Two and, for the first time, there's a thick carpet under my feet and not a steel mesh. Suddenly, there's the whirling hum of a motor, and I look up. I spot a lens protruding from the wall and I wonder who's watching me.

"This is it," the boy says, stopping in front of a red door.

As Nicolo enters a code into the keypad, I put on a show of fiddling with the zip on my uniform. But, from the corner of my eye, I see him tap in Two Seven Two Seven. Well, that's not going to be difficult for me to remember! I just hope it will open the rest of the Nest's doors.

The boy knocks sharply.

"Enter!" The command, although muffled, is still surprisingly shrill. It's still a command.

Then it hits me. I'm going to meet Hubert Crow, the man who I suspect is responsible for my mother's death. I know I'd be crazy to try to interrogate him now. He probably has a panic button. All he has to do is press it, and the beefy sentry down the corridor will sprint in, guns blazing. But what if this is it? What if this is the only chance I'll get? I just wish I had a pistol hidden up my sleeve, and not a blunt fork. But there's no going back now as Nicolo ushers me into the room.

The Map Room is surprisingly small, filled to the brim with desks and stools and lit by a single, green bulb. Not so surprisingly, most of the wall is covered by a map of Cinis and the outlying Wilds. It is colored red and yellow and sprinkled with tiny arrows. The red, I know, represents the enemy, the yellow the rebels. There is the odd splodge of yellow, but most of the map – 90% I'd say – is red. There's so much of it, it looks as if the map's been dipped in blood. My eyes drift to the top, to Golf Sector. I see it's red too. So Rufus Splinter was telling the truth. It has fallen.

A cow-eyed man with a shiny, mole-speckled skull is stood under the map. He's dressed in full military uniform, perfectly pressed, the buttons shiny, the collar adorned with three gold pips. I see the row of medals pinned to his chest look almost as polished as his skull.

With a toothy smile, he walks stiffly over to me. "Well, well, this must be the legendary Two Seven. Welcome to the Nest."

Legendary! Am I? Nobody bothered to tell me. Gripping my hand, he pumps it energetically up and down. I expect him to try to crush my fingers, but no, his grip is limp and wet, sort of like shaking hands with a fish.

"I'm so delighted to meet you," he says. "Over three hundred howler kills, yes? Outstanding. Truly outstanding!"

".Just doing my job," I mutter.

"And modest too! How very - ." his eyes narrow, "- unexpected."

I suppress a gasp. They were Lily's exact words to me only yesterday on the crashed helicopter.

He lets go of my hand and ushers me over to a desk. He pulls a stool out from under it and I sit down, covertly wiping my clammy hand on my uniform.

"I'm Major Hubert Crow," he tells me with a noticeable puffing up of his chest. "I'm commander of Zulu Sector. Or what's left of it." I note he stays on his feet, forcing me to look up at him. "I must say, Two Seven, we were very concerned."

"Concerned?" I say, giving him a puzzled look.

"Why, yes." With a tut, he plucks a speck of dust off his perfectly pressed tunic. I see there's a ring on his finger; it's gold but badly tarnished. "I was in Comms when the helicopter pilot sent the mayday. We thought we'd lost you."

"Oh, I see." My eyes lock with his. "Don't worry, Major, I'm very difficult to kill."

For a second, he says nothing. He even forgets to blink. Then he nods feverishly. "Yes, yes, which is why I sent for you."

What's he saying? I'm difficult to kill so he sent for me so he can kill me here, on his turf? Or the job he needs me for is so risky, he thinks only I can do it? The problem is, I don't know this man so I can't tell.

"The helicopter pilot was killed," I tell him. "Cpl. Bolt."

"That's a pity," he says. "We need pilots." Suddenly, he steps closer to me, perching his bony-looking bottom on my desk. "I have a secret," he tells me.

"Everybody has secrets," I reply, looking up at him.

"Yes, they do. But the thing is, Two Seven, my secret's bigger than most."

"Now y' just showing off."

Shuffling even closer, he whispers, "Can I tell it to you?"

He's almost on top of me now and I can smell his stink. He smells old, dusty, like a forgotten room. I want to pull my stool back but the leg's jammed up to the wall. Under the desk, out of Crow's sight, my hand slips free of the dangling sleeve. In it is the fork. "If you do," I say, "it'll no longer be a secret."

"Oh yes it will. I think I can trust you not to tell."

"Possibly," I say, playing along – although I have no idea what it is we're playing, "But I'm a mercenary, remember? Nobody trusts a mercenary."

"I do," he says. "I trust you." Then, with no warning whatsoever, he springs it on me. "I knew your mother, Holly. I worked with her."

I say nothing, just staring back at him. What's he up to? Is he trying to discover what I know? If he is, I'm not falling for it. I tighten the grip on my fork, preparing to strike. "Is that the secret?" I ask him.

"No." He lowers his gaze. "But I very much wish it was."

My eyes flicker to his neck. To his jugular. The fork's blunt but, if I stab hard, it'll do the job. He'll bleed out in sixty seconds. And that's all the time I'll need to discover the truth. Still, I hold off. I want to know what the secret it.

"Has it anything to do with Project Liberty?" I ask.

He looks up sharply. "How did you..."

"Sir!" It's Nicolo. I'm surprised to see he's still skulking over by the door. Good job I didn't kill his boss. "Sorry to interrupt, but did you wish me to stay?"

Startled, Crow jumps off the desk. "Corporal Lupo! I didn't, er..." The major rubs his eyes. Then, with an urgent flap of his hand, he beckons the boy over. "Sit down, sit down. There's much to discuss. And if this mission is going to succeed, I'm going to need both of you."

XVII

The Skeleton Clock
1 months, 27 days, 5 hrs, 07 mins, 49 secs

"Tremors," says Crow. He's standing under the map, his fingers pinching the folds of his trousers, his bony chin at a perfect 90° angle to his Adam's apple. He looks so rigid, so - brittle, I wonder, if he bent over, would he snap in two? "Tell me, Two Seven, how often do they happen?"

When I was seven and living in the Netty, I went to school. When I say 'school', it was just an old, tumbled-down shed filled with hungry kids who didn't know why they were there. Sitting here, being barked at by Crow, I'm reminded of it. So much so, I'm tempted to put up my hand. I resist and don't. "Every day," I say.

Nicolo, who's sitting next to me, nods briskly. "There were two in the night."

"Do you remember the day they started?" Crow asks.

"No, I don't," says the boy.

I think for a moment, drumming my fingers on the top of my steel desk. I think I'd just got my mirror so, "May," I say. "And they seem to be getting bigger and bigger."

"May 7th, 2132," Crow informs us, "Just a day short of three months ago. And yes, Two Seven, they get bigger every day."

Although I suspect whatever Crow's going to say next is going to be bad. I can't help feeling a little smug. I got it right. "I got it right," I whisper to Nicolo.

The boy sighs.

"Do you know what's triggering them?" I ask the major.

"Yes, I do. Janus. He's been dropping bombs."

"Bombs!" All joking forgotten, I sit up on my stool. "Where? Not in Zulu Sector. I'd know if he was."

"No, not here." Then, worryingly, he adds, "Not yet anyway. According to intel, he dropped a bomb into a volcano in Whiskey Sector. It erupted, spewing over 100,000,000 tons of CO_2 into the atmosphere."

"So that's why the Skeleton Clock's speeding up," I mutter.

Crow pretends to shoot me with his index finger – which, to be honest, I find a little disconcerting. "Correct, Two Seven." He picks up a stick and thumps the map, the tip hitting a small island in the north of Cinis. "Which is why, when the howlers took over Golf Sector, we grew concerned."

"Why?" I ask.

"Golf Sector is volcanic."

"Oh." My cheeks redden. "I see."

"The biggest volcano in Golf Sector is Esja. A Chinook did a fly by yesterday and took a ton of photographs. It's dormant. But there's a lot of howler activity by the crater."

"And Janus is planning to do what?" asks Nicolo. "Drop a bomb in it?"

"Yes. In just under two months. And when Esja erupts – and, trust me, it will erupt," he sighs, "well, let's just says the Skeleton Clock predicts CO_2 levels will hit 6% within days."

"Bugger," mutters Nicolo, which I feel sums everything up perfectly.

"What's stopping Janus from dropping the bomb in the volcano now?" I ask. "Today?"

"We got lucky," says Crow with a grin. "According to intel, it must be transported there by ship from the old USSR."

My eyes widen. "Isn't that in the Wilds!?"

Crow nods. "The howlers discovered a military bunker just north of Moscow. It was full of old SATAN rockets left over from World War Three."

"Atomic?"

Crow nods. "Six of them. Over 40,000 kilotons. They won't fly but the bombs still work."

"So, it's over," says Nicolo miserably. "We lost."

"I don't think so," I say, looking at Crow. "If it was, I'd not be here. The major has a plan."

Crow grins. "Possibly. And, if it's successful..." If I'm successful I'm tempted to say, but I don't, "...it will not just stop the howlers from blowing up Esja, it'll win the war too."

"Win!" gasps Nicolo.

Crow nods. "I think so."

I roll my eyes. There's that 'think' word. Why is it, whenever the rebels think a mission is going to win the war, it never happens? The war just keeps rumbling on. "Who is it you want me to shoot?" I ask resignedly.

"For now, that's top secret," says Crow.

"There's a shocker," I mutter. I try a different tack. "This intel on the bomb. Where's it from?"

"Sorry, it's..."

"Yes, yes, I know. It's top secret. The thing is Major, if you want me to risk my neck, I'm going to need to know everything. Or I'm off."

The boy shifts on his stool. "Two Seven..."

"It's okay, Corporal. She simply wants to know what she's getting into."

I nod vigorously, "I'm a mercenary, not a 'yes sir, no sir' rebel grunt."

Crow eyes me coldly and I wonder if I'm pushing it. Then his lips twitch up. "There's a spy in the howler camp. She reports Janus's plans directly to me."

"She?"

"Yes."

"And she's a howler?"

He nods.

"Then why's she helping the rebels? What's in it for her?"

"Why's not important."

"Not important! Don't be a fool," I hiss. "Why's always important. What if she's playing you. What if it's a trap."

"She's not playing me and it's not a trap." Unblinking, he meets my gaze. "I trust her."

"Then let her do it."

"She can't."

"Why not?"

"She'll be standing next to the target."

My scowl deepens. Finally, this is getting interesting. "How long is the shot?" I demand to know.

Crow licks his lips. "Sorry, it's, er..."

"How long?" I spit. Suddenly, I know why I'm here. Why he needs me for the mission. It's the length of the shot. "Tell me," I insist.

"5,327 feet," he says.

I feel my eyes growing wider and wider. I don't know whether to laugh or cry. He must be joking, so I laugh. I turn to the boy. "He's joking."

"No, I'm not," says Crow sternly. "And it's a night job."

I almost topple off my stool. "I'm sorry, did you just say,,."

"It's set for midnight on September 25th," he interrupts me, looking annoyed. I must be pushing it now. "That's in seven weeks and three days."

"Why then?" asks Nicolo.

"On that night, for just a few seconds, the target will be exposed."

I frown. "September 25th," I say slowly. "The 100th anniversary of the comet strike?"

"Yes."

"But if Two Seven is unsuccessful, they'll only be a few days left until they drop the bomb in the volcano," says Nicolo.

"Corporal Lupo, if Two Seven is unsuccessful, it's over. The war will be lost. There'll be no opportunity for a second shot."

"I don't get it," I say. "Cinis is overrun with howlers. Just look at the map. How can they be stopped by just a single bullet?"

"I know this will be difficult for a mercenary," says Crow, "but you must trust me that it will."

I hold in a laugh. I'd sooner trust a snake. But, whether I trust him or not is not important. What's important is, I can't do it. Nobody can. "A nine millimeter bullet travels 1,500 feet per second," I tell him. "For it to hit a target over 5,000 feet away, it's going to be travelling for 3½ seconds."

The major nods lazily. He was my mum's spotter, so he knows this stuff. But Nicolo's listening intently.

"Will the howler be in the open?" I ask Crow.

"Yes."

"Then everything will be in play. Everything. Temperature. Humidity. The wind too. At 5,000 feet, even a soft breeze will be a problem." I'm almost talking to myself now as I try to figure out how to do it. "The target. Do you want me to kill him or just injure him?"

"If my plan is to succeed, he must be killed."

So, the howler's a 'he'. Interesting. "Then I must hit him here," I prod my brow, "between the eyes. Will he be sleeping?"

"No."

I sigh. Pity.

"He'll be giving a speech."

"Will he be standing still or will he be moving?"

"I don't know."

"You don't know!" I balloon my cheeks. This is nuts! "So I must hit a target the size of a button from over 5,000 feet away, yes?"

"Yes."

"At night," Nicolo adds unhelpfully.

"Yes, at night. And, on top of that, I'll need to shoot him where he's going to be in 3½ seconds time, not where he is when I pull the trigger. It's impossible."

"Is it?" Crow unexpectantly says. "Corporal Lupo," he turns to the boy, "did you know, in sniper camp, when a sniper is deemed 'Fully Skilled', they must try to shoot a tin can off a rock from 5,000 feet away?"

"No, I didn't," says the boy. "Has anybody ever hit it?"

"Oh, yes. Two Seven did. The only sniper to ever do it."

I feel my cheeks redden. "I got lucky," I protest. "A sunny day, no wind…" the major eyes me sceptically and I feel my temper rising, "…and let's not forget, tin cans tend to keep still!"

"Rubbish," he snarls.

I shoot him a long, withering look. But, deep down, I know he's right. I still remember taking the shot; how it felt as I pulled the trigger, 3½ seconds later, the can jumping up, skipping off the rock. It was as if the target was only a foot away from me. As if it was impossible for me not to hit it.

"The only sniper who might possibly hit this target is you, Two Seven." Crow sighs. "Which brings me to the next problem. The other sectors want in on the mission."

"How?" asks Nicolo.

"The Foxtrot commander wants to send her best sniper, the Victor commander wants to send his. And so on."

"But why?" demands the boy. "If Two Seven is the only sniper who we know can do it."

"They think this mission will win the war," I volunteer. "So they want in on it. They want the glory too."

Crow nods. "Two Seven's correct. So, to keep everybody happy, there's going to be a contest. We plan to drop the best sniper from every rebel sector into a deserted town. There, with a little help from spotters, they'll fight it out. Whoever's left standing will go on the mission."

My chin hits my chest. It's not often I'm shocked, but I'm shocked now. "I'm sorry, I got a little lost there. Did you just tell me, no, no – order me, to kill the best snipers in the Rebel Army?"

"No, not at all. All of the snipers will be dressed in full Kevlar. Body shots only. Ammo will be low velocity with blunted tips. If – when a sniper gets hit, it'll sting like hell, but it'll not kill her."

This is crazy. Nuts! The howlers will soon be on Zulu Nest's doorstep and Crow's sending me off to play hide and seek with a bunch of rebel snipers.

"Here's who you'll be competing with." He pulls a sheet of paper from his tunic pocket, unfolds it and rests it on my desk. I see it is a list of sorts showing Confirmed Kills by the sectors' top snipers.

Sniper 66, Victor Sector, 727
Sniper 101, Kilo Sector, 699
Sniper 369, Foxtrot Sector, 522
Sniper 07, Yankee Sector, 409
Sniper 27, Zulu Sector, 361

I glower at it. Annoyingly, Sniper Six Six tops the list, whilst I languish at the bottom with less than half her tally.

"It looks as if you'd be better off sending the girl from Victor Sector," I mutter sourly.

"No, I don't think so," says Crow. He's talking in a whisper now, so low, the words seem to drop through the floor. "I know Sniper Six Six. She enjoys her work. She enjoys killing howlers. That's why she's at the top. She's not the best shot. She just keeps on firing until she hits the target. But you, Two Seven," he tuts, "that's a very different story. I suspect you don't enjoy killing anybody. Not even howlers. But, when you do shoot, you hit the target first time, every time. Am I correct?"

I don't reply. Considering I only just met the man, he seems to know me disturbingly well.

"So, let me get this right," I say. "You expect me to..."

"Us," butts in Nicolo. "I'm going with you."

Surprised, I turn to him. "Why?" I ask. "I don't need a medic."

"But you do need a spotter," he counters. "Yes, yes, I know I don't possess the right skills. But how difficult can it be? Spotters just – spot the enemy, right?"

I rub my eyes. Where to begin?

"Look, Two Seven, every spotter in Zulu was killed yesterday in the howler attack. There's me or – well, there's just me,"

I shrug. Why not? Although I can't help but wonder why he's volunteering. Is Crow forcing him to? Is his job to spy on me? To stop me from running off? "Now, where did

I get to?" I say, turning back to the major. "Oh, yes, you expect me, sorry, us..."

"Thank you," mutters Nicolo.

"...to fight it out with a bunch of highly-skilled snipers. Then, if we win, we get to go on this totally impossible mission."

"Not totally," says Crow with a half-smile. "But, yes."

"And on this mission, we must travel to who knows where and shoot who knows who from 5,327 feet away. If I'm successful, the rebels win the war. If I'm not..."

"The war's lost," says Crow. "The howlers win."

I turn to Nicolo. "And this ridiculous plan is okay with you?"

"With me!?" The boy grins. "Remember, I'm just a 'yes, sir, no, sir' rebel grunt. I do as I'm told."

I sigh. I possibly deserved that.

"The contest will begin in two weeks," Crow says. "Until then, you stay here, in the Nest. There's a lot to do."

"Such as?" I ask.

"Shooting. As you rightly say, it's going to be a very difficult shot. A little practice will help."

A little! A lot, I'm tempted to say. But I just nod. "Yes," I agree, "it will."

"Excellent. And I wish you to work on a few other skills too. Speed. Agility. They'll help you to win this thing. And I do expect you to win. Understood?"

"Understood."

"Tomorrow, you'll meet your tutor."

"Tutor!?"

"Yes, she's the best there is."

"At what?"

"Killing."

I nod slowly, my mind doing cartwheels. I'm not interested in Crow's stupid contest. And I'm not interested in going on this mission. Let Sniper Six Six risk her neck, not me. But, if I pretend to go along with it, I'll get to spend two weeks in the Nest. Two weeks! Plenty of time to find Level Seven – if it exists – and to get my hands on Crow and discover what happened to my mother. Under the desk, I push the fork back up my sleeve.

"If I'm going to do this," I say, "I want two things in return."

The major's thin, colorless lips curl up. "Why am I not surprised?" he says with a sigh. "Go on."

"I need access to comms. Not long. I just want to contact a, er, smuggler I know."

"A smuggler! Why?"

"I need Devil's Dust. It's not for me. It's for Twig."

"Twig? Oh yes, the boy in ICU. How's he doing?"

"He's dying," I say bluntly. "And he's my responsibility."

"He is!"

"Yes, I told his..." I stop. I can't tell Crow I promised the boy's grandmother I'd try to help him. Crow will know I didn't follow orders. He'll think I'm a sucker for a sob story.

I can feel the major's eyes boring into me. It's horribly unsettling, like being caught in the glare of a searchlight. "Okay," he says at last. "Corporal Lupo, see to it will you. And show her the Armory. Trigger's got a new rifle for her. If he's not too drunk to find it in all the mess."

"Yes, sir," says the boy.

"And the second thing, Two Seven?"

I nod at Nicolo. "He gets to go in the MediPod. A spotter with a limp's no good to me."

XVIII

The Skeleton Clock
1 months, 26 days, 8 hrs, 33 mins, 59 secs

The tips of the two swords meet and my tutor, Akiyo, is on me. She's brutal, her sword not so much a sword, but a bolt of lightning. Parrying her thrusts, I step hastily back, tumbling over a barrel. She steps off, allowing me to find my feet. Nicolo, sitting on an upturned bucket, rolls his eyes at my clumsy footwork. I feel a fool. A schoolgirl in a room full of scholars.

The boy had woken me at 0600hrs with a prod in the ribs from his shiny, steel-tipped boots. I did not sleep well, the clunk of hidden machinery preventing my eyes from closing. But it wasn't just the water pumps that kept me tossing and turning all night. I'm unsettled by so many things. In the helicopter, Lily knew I was going to the Nest. But how did she know? And, back in my burrow, why was she so interested in my mirror? What were her words now? "There's never a mirror in a sniper's burrow." What is it the rebels don't want me to see? Is it my eyes, the way they glow yellow when I'm angry? But I can't be a howler. I can't be! If I was, I'd not be Amaryllis Storm.

After throwing my boots at Nicolo and ordering him to get out of my room, I then discovered he'd left three perfectly folded uniforms by my bed. A little surprised he'd remembered, I picked up the top uniform and put it on. It fitted perfectly. But when I went to thank him, he just shrugged. "It's my job," he answered, limping off. Annoyed to discover he thinks helping me is just his job, I sullenly followed him down hundreds of steps to Level Six. To the Farm.

Level Six is very different to the rest of the Nest. Amazingly, this is where the rebels grow the food they need. IN A CAVE! Here, the floor's not steel, it's dirt. And, everywhere I look, I see the tops of carrots, turnips and parsnips poking up from it. And there's not just crops. I see pens full of sheep, cows, even chickens. Scruffy children tend to them, feeding the sheep, milking the cows and collecting eggs from under the roosting chickens, The children remind me a little uncomfortably of serfs. I always wondered where the rebels grew the food they sent me. Now I know.

I'd been about to ask Nicolo how all of this was even possible. I'm in a cave! THERE'S NO SUN! But, just then, my new tutor turned up, a Japanese woman who, in spite of having the wrinkly skin of a walnut, is strong, remarkably nimble, and much better with a sword than I am.

"If you wish to win this contest," she says, "you must master the skills of the ninja."

"Why?" I hiss. I'm still annoyed by how badly I'm performing. "The best sniper will win, not the best – swordsman." I almost spit the word.

"Two Seven," she says sternly, "the rest of the snipers know how to kill in many different ways. Not just with a bullet. And so must you."

"There's not going to be any killing," I retort. I know I'm being difficult, but I can't help it.

"Is there not?" she says.

I scowl crossly at her. My mind is a jumble, the thump in my chest vibrating through my body. I don't trust this woman. I know her job's to help me, but she works for Crow, the man I intend to kill. And, when I do, she'll turn on me.

All the rebels will.

With a roll of her eyes, Akiyo lowers her sword. "How many kills has Sniper Six Six?"

"Seven hundred and twenty-seven," I reply instantly. I remember the stats Crow showed me all too well. And how I was bottom of the list.

My tutor nods. "And she wants to win, yes?"

Sullenly, I nod. "Possibly."

She sighs, then rubs her face so vigorously, I half expect, when she pulls her hand away, for her nose to be missing. "Two Seven, I'm going to tell you a story."

She sits, crossing her legs in a bow. But I stay standing. I'm in no mood for a children's story. And, anyway, I'm itching to get my hands on my new rifle. "I was wondering if..." I peter off under her hard, uncompromising glare. "I'll do it later," I mutter, and, reluctantly, I sit too.

"A viper wants to cross a river," she begins, "but he can't swim..."

"I know this story," I interrupt her.

"Then tell it to me."

"Okay," I say, wishing I'd kept my mouth shut. I'm not good at storytelling. When we lived in the Netty and mum was away fighting, my job was to look after Benji. At night, he was always pestering me for a story. But it was difficult.

He wanted bold knights and dragons, but all I could think about was whether mum was coming home and, if she didn't, how long it'd be before we starved.

"The viper sees a crocodile sitting on the bank," I begin, "and asks him to carry him over the river. The crocodile knows the viper can't swim and, if the viper kills him, the viper will drown. So he agrees to do it. The viper slithers onto the croc's back and off they go. But, half way over, the viper kills the crocodile anyway."

"And the viper drowns, yes?"

"Yes."

"So, why did the viper do it when he knows he'll be killed too?"

"He's stupid?"

"Two Seven..."

"Okay, okay," I sigh, "I guess it's – instinct. It's what vipers do."

Akiyo jumps to her feet. Yes, JUMPS! It's mind blowing. She must be seventy! "A sniper's job is to kill the enemy. They do it every day of the week, every week of the month. It's the only thing they know how to do."

"And now I'm the enemy."

"In this contest, yes."

"You think the other snipers will try to kill me?"

"Not try to, no. But when the bullets begin flying, they'll go for the killing shot."

"Instinct," I say.

"Yes."

Reluctantly, I nod my understanding. Then I stand up too. I don't wish to dwell on the fact that I'm a sniper too.

That it is the only thing I know how to do. Determined to do better, I lift my sword.

But my tutor's not finished yet. "The other snipers know how to kill in many different ways," she says. "The girl from Victor Sector is lethal."

"Sniper Six Six," I mutter. "Do you know her?"

"She's my granddaughter."

"Oh," I frown deeply, "I, er – I see." To be honest, I don't see at all. Shouldn't she be helping her granddaughter to win, not me? But, when I open my mouth to ask her, she holds up a warning finger. "It is not a story I wish to share," she says.

I nod slowly. "No problem."

"You must excel in Kenjutsu, the sword, kyujutsu, the bow and bojutsu, the stick. All skills of the ninja."

Wow! So much to do in just two weeks. "I'll do my best."

"No," she snaps. "Do better. Now, to work. There's much to do."

"Let's go, Amaryllis," hollers Nicolo. "A little effort, yes?"

I eye him coldly. I'd throw my sword at him if I didn't need it. Seeing him sitting there, I wonder why he's still here. Then I remember. I'm his job! And I bet a big part of it is to report to Crow on how I'm doing. He's Crow's spy.

Akiyo attacks me but I shoulder her off, twirl my wrist and thrust. Our swords spark and, just for a second, I see a way in. But I stop. I don't want to hurt her. Then, to my horror, I feel cold steel under my own chin.

Slowly, I lower my sword.

"You remind me of a doddery old woman with a broom," Akiyo mocks me. She too lowers her sword. But I think she knows I had her. Just for a second. I can tell by the arch of her eyebrows, the stony set of her jaw. Oh yes, she knows. "But there is a hunger in you, Two Seven. I can see it." She shoots me the jackal's eye. "Skill too, I see."

Akiyo drops low, her left foot sweeping me off my feet. Swiftly, I throw up my sword but it is torn from my fist.

Dropping to her knees, she eyes me keenly. Stubbornly, I return her look. "Do you want to be the best?" she asks.

"Yes," I reply, "I want to be the best." I know it's what she wants me to say. But, the thing is, I honestly do.

"Good," she says. That's it. No smile. Just cold, glassy eyes. She's like a robot. She jumps up, pulling me up with her. "We will work here, on this patch of grass by this old shed. Every day, 7 o'clock sharp. Got it?"

My eyes widen. "What! Seven in the morning!"

She just looks at me.

I sigh deeply. "Got it," I say. So much for sleeping in.

"If you do everything I tell you to do, in two weeks you'll be the best killer in Zulu Sector."

"Then I might win the contest?"

"No." She throws me my sword. "Then you might live through it."

XVIV

The Skeleton Clock
1 months, 26 days, 3 hrs, 21 mins, 20 secs

I spend a long, blister-inducing morning with Akiyo working on my sword fighting skills. As we swing and cut and thrust, she endlessly reminds me - often with a scowl and always with a prod of her sword - to bend my knees and to tighten my grip. Nicolo sits silently on his upturned bucket, his green eyes watching my every move. His gaze is unrelenting; so much so, it's unsettling. But I know why he's still here. He's been ordered to stay. He's Crow's spy.

By midday, my uniform is drenched, I'm starving hungry, and my armpits smell disgusting. "Lunch," barks my tutor. "Return here tomorrow, 7 o'clock sharp. And don't be late."

I'm surprised. I thought I'd be stuck here playing ninja all day. But it seems Crow has other plans for me.

With my stomach rumbling merrily away, I accompany Nicolo to the canteen, stopping off en route for a shower and to put on a fresh uniform. Thankfully, the canteen's on Level Five so it's not far to go. That's good for me - I'm feeling stiff from my workout - and good for Nicolo who is still limping. "I thought Crow promised to let you go in the MediPod," I say as we trudge along a corridor.

"Major Crow," he corrects me. "And, yes, he did. I spoke to the doctor and he's booked me in for tomorrow. Oh, and, er, thanks by the way."

"Happy to help." If I'm honest, I didn't do it for the boy. If I didn't try to help him, Crow would wonder why. He knows there's no way I can win this contest if my spotter can't run. "Will it sort out the cut too?" I ask, referring to the nasty gash over his eye. "And your burnt cheek?"

"No," the boy says morosely. "It'll just fix my leg."

I stop and turn to him. "But why?"

"Do you remember I told you the MediPod needs lots of power to work?"

I nod.

"Well, it'll take ten seconds to fix my leg and another ten seconds to fix my face. Twice as long, twice as much power. And, anyway, the doctor says I don't need to look pretty to fight."

I roll my eyes. The doctor's a moron. When I see him tomorrow, I'm going to be having words.

When we get to the canteen, I'm astounded by how large it is. And how messy. Everything is steel, everything is grey, and everything is covered with food. Even the tops of the stools which is hardly inviting for the bottom. Bits of broccoli, chicken legs - and the floor! There's so much coffee and gravy all over it, if I want to cross it I might be forced to swim.

"What happened here?" I mutter, inspecting my boot and finding a string of spaghetti stuck to the heel. "A food fight?"

"Lunch," Nicolo says with a smile. "It's always a bit - chaotic."

It suddenly occurs to me that nobody's here. I look at him in horror. "We didn't miss it, did we? I'm famished!"

"Don't worry, Dorothy will feed us."

We slip and slide our way over to the kitchen where we find a woman with her hands in the sink scrubbing away at a dirty pot. She's old, shrunken and has a copper cross dangling from her neck. When she sees us, she grins, startling me with her bright, white teeth. "Ah, it's Sniper Two Seven," she says, waddling over to us. "I'm Dorothy."

"Hello," I reply trying not to show my surprise. How is it she knows me, I wonder. She's the cook!

"Now, pet, what can I get you? The hotpot's very tasty."

"No, it's not," says a ferrety-eyed men wandering over to us. He's holding a dishcloth so I suspect he's the dryer. "It's disgusting. I know, she cooked it and, trust me, it's not going in my belly. I'd be crapping for a week."

"Oh, just ignore him," says Dorothy, snatching the dishcloth off him and whipping him on the bottom. "He's just jealous of my culinary skills."

I don't mind if it's good or not. I'm hungry and, to me, food's food, in one end, out the other. "I'll try the hotpot," I say.

"Crickey!" gasps the man who's cleverly keeping out of dishcloth range. "She's a plucky lass. Maybe I'll put a bet on her after all."

Confused, I turn to Nicolo. "Why is he betting on me?"

"I'll tell you later," he says.

We follow Dorothy over to her rusty-looking cooker. Perched on top of it there's a big pot. "Here you go," she says, spooning a gigantic dollop of the bubbling stew into a bowl and handing it to me.

"Thanks," I say. I sort of want to ask her why it's so green, but she's still holding the dishcloth and I don't want my bottom whipped too.

"A bowl for you?" Dorothy asks Nicolo.

He shrugs "Why not? It's not gonna kill me."

"That's what you think," mutters the man.

As we turn to go, Dorothy whispers to me, "Good luck in the contest, pet. I'm rooting for you."

I nod and muster up a grin. "Thanks," I say. It seems the cook knows everything.

Balancing trays, we trudge out of the kitchen and over to a table. I wipe gravy off the stool with my sleeve and sit down. "So, if the cook knows why I'm here, I'm guessing everybody knows."

The boy nods, dropping down onto the stool next to me. "The contest is top secret so, yes, everybody knows. It's the way it is here." He pulls a napkin from out of his pocket and, with look of disgust, scrubs vigorously at a splodge of jam. "It's disgusting in here," he says. "If Major Crow sees it, he'll be hopping mad."

"He's a very tidy fellow," I remark, remembering yesterday and how smartly he was dressed.

"He's old school," the boy says. "Discipline, discipline, discipline, and everything should be spotless. But not everybody here agrees with him."

"Including Dorothy."

"Yes, but it's not only her. The biggest culprit is Trigger. He's up in the Armory. He keeps it in a right mess. They remember the old ways, how it was when Commander Striker was in charge."

"Did she let them get away with it?"

"Let's just say, she didn't run a very tight ship."

The Corporal skewers a gristly-looking lump of beef with his fork, puts it to his nostrils and sniffs it.

"Good?" I ask.

"No," he says.

Stiffening my jaw, I boldly sniff my own food. I feel my stomach lurch. It smells rotten. But, on the plus side, if I do throw up in my bowl, it won't look any different to what's already in there.

"Do the rebels know why the contest is being held?" I want to know.

"Sort of yes, sort of no," he says. With a long sigh, he drops his fork into the bowl. "They know the winner is going to be sent on a big mission, but they don't know what that mission is."

"Did Crow tell them it will win the war?"

"Major Crow," Nicolo corrects me with a tut. "Honestly, Two Seven, a little respect. And, yes, he did."

"And they trust him?"

"Yes, of course, he's the Nest Commander." He turns to look at me. "Don't you?"

For a long time, I don't reply. I'm not being rude and I'm not thinking about how to answer. The problem is, I just put a forkful of hotpot in my mouth and now my jaw's cemented shut. With a monumental gulp, I swallow it down. But it gets stuck in my esophagus and I begin to cough.

Nicolo helpfully thumps me on the back. "Better?"

"Better." Although, now it's in my stomach, who knows what damage it's doing. "You don't remember, do you," I gasp.

"Remember what?"

"Two weeks ago when we were talking on comms, you told me not to trust anybody."

"Oh yes." He nods slowly. "So I did."

"Well, I'm just following my Controller's orders."

So, everybody knows about the contest. As I strongly suspect there's a spy in the Nest, this could present a big problem. I did suspect Crow of being the spy, but now I don't think he is. According to Lily, Janus wants me to kill him. He'd hardly want me to do that if Crow was working for him. If the spy is not the major, then he, or she, must only know there's a contest and the winner is going to be sent on a 'big mission', but not what the big mission is. I suspect the spy's informed the enemy of this. So how will the enemy respond? Is that why Lily is marching on the Nest now? Has Janus ordered her to put a stop to Crow's plan - whatever it is?

I prod my food and try to decide what to risk next. No - I copy Nicolo and drop the fork into my bowl - best to let my stomach lining do battle with the lump of gristle first.

"Everybody here is rooting for you," Nicolo says. "We need to win."

I scowl at him. I don't get it. "I don't get it," I say.

"Everybody in the Nest knows the howlers will be here within weeks." He talks slowly as if to a child, and it's sort of bugging. "When they get here, the rebels must try to fight them off. They'll need to be motivated to do it. And what better way of motivating them is there than giving them a hero to root for."

"Who, me? You gotta be kidding." I'm here to kill Crow and to find out if Level Seven exists or not. If I must first win this contest to do it, then so be it. But I'm a mercenary. I'm nobody's hero and I never will be.

"For the good of the many," the boy loftily reminds me.

"That's your motto," I reply, with just as much scorn. "For the good of me is so much better."

The Corporal eyes me coldly. Then, shuffling his stool closer, he grips hold of my hand. He did this in the helicopter and I remember I pulled away. This time I don't. "The rebels here in this Nest will soon be fighting off hundreds off howlers," he says. "They need inspiring. Major Crow's hoping this contest will help to do that."

"But how?" I'm still not getting it. And the hand's not helping, turning my mind mushy, stopping me from thinking. "I thought it was going to be held in a deserted town."

"It is," he says, letting go of me.

I clench and unclench my fist; it's feeling abandoned. "Then nobody will see it."

"Yes, they will." Then he drops the bombshell. "The contest is going to be filmed and shown on big screens in every Nest."

I feel my bowels churn - and it's not just from the food . "But, but - that's nuts!" I cry.

"Why?"

"It just - it just is!"

"No, it's not. It's very clever. Look, Two Seven, everybody expects Sniper Six Six to win, right?"

"I know I do," I mutter.

"But when they see you fighting on, not giving up, the rebels here in Zulu will be inspired to fight on too."

So now it's my responsibility to inspire the rebels to fight! This is crazy. CRAZY! Suddenly, I don't feel hungry and I push my bowl away. "But what if I don't win?" I protest. "What if I'm shot in the first second of the contest? How's that going to inspire anybody?"

"You can do this, Two Seven. I know you can."

"How do you know?"

"I just do."

I scowl at him. I remember, before we ever met, I imagined him to be really tall with big lips and perfectly trimmed eyebrows. But he's no taller than me, thin-lipped, his eyebrows full and sort of bushy. But I did get his eyes right. I thought they'd be green, sorrowful and full of secrets. As I sit there looking into them, I see plenty of secrets hidden there.

"I don't get you," I say. "Why did you volunteer to go with me?"

He shrugs. "I'm just trying to help."

"That's rubbish! Tell me the truth."

"It's not rubbish. It is the truth. Is it so difficult for you to comprehend I'm not in this fight for me, that I'm in it for the rebels; for humanity?"

I don't know how to respond to this. How can I admit it to him - or to myself - that it is difficult for me to comprehend? Everything I do is for me. For me only. I don't know why I'm this way, but it's almost as if 'survival' has been programmed into my DNA.

"I was born in Whiskey Sector," he suddenly says. "Italy," he then adds in case I don't know.

I nod. I thought so; the rhythmical way he talks, extending his vowels. Then it occurs to me, Whiskey Sector was where the howlers just exploded the bomb in the volcano.

"In 2121, when it was overrun, I escaped with my family. We ended up here in Zulu."

"They let you into the Nest?"

"My mom was an engineer, so they needed her to help keep the helicopters flying."

"Was?"

"They were killed."

"Oh, I'm sorry. Did the howlers get them?"

"No, cancer did."

"But in Medical the other day, you told me 'engineer' is on the VIP list. So why didn't the rebels simply put them in the MediPod?"

"My dad was a cook." He shrugs. "Engineer's on the list, yes. But cook's not. They'd only help her."

"But that's barbaric!" I cry.

"I guess my mom thought that too, so she refused to go in it."

I sit there trying to think of what to say. "She must have loved him very much," I muster at last.

"I was only six so I don't remember them very well. But, yes, she must have loved him a lot." He grunts and bitterly adds, "More than she loved me anyway."

For a split second, I don't follow him. Then I do. She picked to end her life over being with her son. No wonder he's bitter.

"Thankfully, the rebels welcomed me in. I grew up here. Every rebel in the Nest is like a brother or a sister to me." He looks to me, his eyes filled with urgency, willing me to understand. "If we win this contest, I think it will help the rebels here in Zulu. They'll be inspired to fight on. And that can only be a good thing, right?"

I nod. "Right." My eyes flicker over him as I try to work him out. He's very different to me. If the rebels refused to do anything to prevent my mum and dad from dying, I'd not be looking to help them. I'd be looking for payback. But best to play along. "For the good of the many," I mutter.

The Corporal grins. "Now y' getting it." He sighs, pushing his bowl away. "Well, I'm stuffed."

I glance at his overflowing bowl and smile. "Me too," I say. "To the brim."

"Excellent." He stands up. "Then, let's go."

"Where to?"

"To check out your new gun," he says.

We set off to the Armory. But we don't go directly there, stopping off in Comms on the way. There, I call up Rufus Splinter and ask him to bring a supply of Devil's Dust to the Nest. He's not overly keen, which is hardly surprising when most of the howler army will soon be hammering on the Nest's door. But, when Nicolo tells him he'll be very well rewarded, the smuggler magically finds his courage and agrees to be here in two days.

Going on our way, I thank he boy.

"No problem," he says. "We'll give him a box of OxyPills. They'll not work for much longer anyway."

I follow Nicolo down yet another corridor. At the end of it, there's a door. It is a rusty-red colour, dented and badly chipped.

"This is it," says the boy, stepping up to the keypad and tapping in his number. The door opens with a click. But, when I go to enter, he stops me. "Best to knock," he says.

"Why?"

"Trigger, he's the Armorer, well, he can be a little – now, how to put this?" He thinks for a second, his fingers plucking at his chin. "Cranky," he says at last.

"Cranky." I nod slowly. "I see."

The boy knocks gently. "Trigger, it's me. Corporal Lupo. I'm coming in." He says this in such a way as to suggest coming in is a very foolhardy thing to do.

"Bugger off," is the curt reply. "I'm drunk and I'm holding a very big gun."

Nicolo sighs. "Oh no, he's been drinking." He turns to me. "I think I'd better go in first. He sort of knows me. Sort of."

"He's not going to shoot you, is he?" I ask.

"No, no." Then he frowns. "Well, possibly. But he's not a very good shot when he's drunk, so there's a 50% chance he'll miss."

"Oh. That's okay then."

As we creep into the Armory, I see it is very different to the rest of the Nest. To begin with, it's small, stuffed full of, well, stuff, and poorly lit. There's a lot of dust too. There's so much of it, I'm frightened if I sneeze, I'll never find my way out. As the stink of sulphur fills my nostrils, I look up. Hundreds of guns hang from the roof. They remind me of bats in a cave; so much so, I feel it best to walk softly and not risk waking them up.

Over in a shadowy corner, there's a workbench. It's littered with rusty springs, nuts, bolts and tiny screwdrivers. Sitting by the bench, holding a blowtorch, is a man. With a growl, he looks up from the pistol he's welding. "Didn't I just say – oh!" Resting the blowtorch on the bench, he gets up, sways a little. Then, thinking better of it, he sits back down. "Sorry," he says. "I didn't know it were you."

"This is Private Crockett," says Nicolo, "but everybody calls him Trigger."

The Armorer is incredibly thin. A scruffy fellow with grey whiskers and saggy pockets under his eyes. And he smells of alcohol. But cheerfully so, as though every drop went down smiling. He greets me with a nod and an owlish blink, befitting a man who spends his days hidden away in this dark, musty room.

"Good to meet you, Two Seven," he says, his words so low, so mumbled, I hardly catch them.

Suddenly, I get it. "You work with guns! That's why they call you Trigger."

"No," he says. The single word is cold, matter-of-fact.

"Oh," I say.

"I got it from this." He holds up his left hand and I see the tip of his trigger finger is missing. "A rat gnawed it off when I was a kid."

"Oh, em," before I can stop myself, I blurt out, "you must drop a lot of stuff then."

He eyes me coldly. Then, thankfully, a grin splits his craggy face. "I do," he says with a chuckle.

He pulls a grubby hipflask from his pocket, uncorks it and then, like a baby's dummy, he plugs it into his mouth. As I watch him suckling away, I wonder how old he is. He looks seventy; possibly even older. But, then, drunks often look old to me.

"Fancy a drop?" he asks, offering it to me.

"No thanks," I reply. "I don't drink."

"Very wise. This stuff will kill you."

"Then why drink it?"

"It's the best way of dying. Well, compared to being turned into a howler. Or suffocating."

I smile. A surprisingly logical answer from a man who's so drunk he finds it difficult to stand up. "But I am interested in a rifle that can shoot 5,327 feet."

Trigger grins. "I think I can help you there," he says, struggling to his feet. Then, wobbling a little as if the floor is the deck of a storm-tossed ship, he staggers over to a shelf, to where a box is sitting.

Pulling it down, he sways back over to us, setting the box on his bench. "This here is a Remington rifle," he tells us, opening the lid. "I did a bit of work on it for you. Extended the barrel. Put on a sling so you can carry it."

I'm not listening. I loved my old rifle. But this! I think, possibly, I'm drooling. It is, in every way, a monster of a gun. Shiny. Devilishly black. And, unlike my old rifle, not covered in dents. Gently, I pick it up. It's long and bulky, but surprisingly light.

"Under 6lbs," says Trigger, seemingly reading my thoughts. "The barrel's steel but the stock's polymer. It's a sort of plastic, synthetic with..."

"I know what polymer is," I interrupt him, remembering my lessons from sniper camp.

My eyes narrow, calculating. From butt to muzzle, it must be over 3½ feet long. I peer into the barrel, marveling at the size of it. You could shoot a rocket out of there, never mind a bullet. I think of Lily. Anybody shot by this monster will not be getting back up. Even her.

"Optics?"

"Here." He hands me a 10 x 40 scope with a laser sight and I slot it on. "Good up to 5,000 feet."

I look up.

"Don't worry. It'll stretch to 6,000 if needed."

"It'll be needed," I tell him, playing along. But not by me. But I must pretend it is. The rebels mustn't discover I'm only here to kill Crow. And find Level Seven. "Ammo?"

"Nine millimeter, hollow tipped." He throws me a box. "I call them Anvils. Invented them myself. If they hit it, they'll kill it."

"Good. Is there a silencer?"

"Yep, but I didn't think you'd want it. Not for this shot."

He's right. It'd just reduce the bullet's velocity. "So, Trigger, is there anywhere I can try this monster out?"

"You bet," he says with a grin.

We follow Trigger to the very back of the Armory, to a rickety-looking stepladder. Nimbly – for a man who stinks of alcohol – he climbs up it, elbowing open a trapdoor at the top. "Let's go," he calls down to us.

I pocket the box of shells and, using the sling, I hook the rifle over my shoulder. "See you up there," I say to Nicolo. I then follow Trigger up the ladder.

Getting to the top, I claw my way through the tightfitting hatch to find myself on the Nest's steel roof. The sun is so blindingly bright, it hurts my eyes and, within a second, my body is drenched, my uniform clamping to my skin. I feel my lungs constrict as they fight for oxygen. It's such a shock, I almost cry out. Thankfully, Trigger's there to hand me two OxyPills. I greedily swallow them, thanking him with a grunt. It's shocking. Two days in the Nest and I'd forgotten how horrid the world is.

As my pupils constrict, becoming accustomed to the bright light, I look around. To my left, there's a Chinook helicopter, lots of dented petrol drums and, just beyond them, glinting in the sun, a row of solar panels. To my right, there's a low wall topped with barbed wire. I walk over to it and peer over the top. I see I'm at the top of a steep cliff. Craning my neck, I spot there's a ditch at the bottom of it. It's full of digging rebels. So that's where they go every day. I feel sorry for them. Digging in the hot sun must be hell. Beyond the ditch, there's another wall. It's incredibly high and topped with broken glass. Beyond the wall, I see twenty Challenger tanks. I must admit, I'm impressed. Crow's not going to go down without a fight.

Looking beyond the tanks, I see desert. Dry creeks, rolling hills, all shimmering under the sulphur-yellow sun.

As the breeze stirs up the wispy sand, I can't help but wonder what I would be seeing if I'd stood here a century ago. Lush, green forests? A winding river filled with swaying reeds?

"Can you spot them?" Trigger interrupts my thoughts.

I frown. "Them?"

"I set up a bunch of target for you. Here." With a wink, he hands me his binoculars. "Check out the hill to the north west."

Using the binoculars, I soon spot them, a row of green petrol drums sitting innocently on an outcrop of rock. "How far away is that?" I ask.

"5,327 feet," he answers smugly. "I put them there myself."

"That's terrific!" Trigger is proving to be very helpful.

Handing him back his binoculars, I walk over to a gap in the wall. There, I unsling the rifle and drop down on my belly. Time to go to work...

With a sharp crack, I pull back the bolt and slip a shell into the firing chamber. I then push the bolt forward and down. Now, let's see if I can hit anything. I put my eye up to the lens and, by slowly turning a knob on the top, I focus in on the first of the drums.

"Wind speed?"

"Seven knots," responds Trigger, "gusting left to right."

"Humidity?"

"Zero."

I don't know why I bothered asking. It's always zero.

"Why's humidity important?" asks Nicolo.

I go to answer, but Trigger cuts me off. "If it's high, it'll slow the bullet down," he tells him. "Then it'll drop much sooner."

I'm impressed. The rebel knows his physics. Now let's see if I can impress him with my shooting skills.

The biggest problem with firing a bullet such a long way is, as Trigger put it, drop. It won't fly forever. And, when the bullet's velocity slows, gravity will pull it down. This bullet is going to be travelling over 5,000 feet, so it's going to drop A LOT! My work is to work out how much and then adjust for it. "So you see, Corporal Lupo," I say, "the job of a spotter is not simply to spot the enemy."

"So it seems," he says glumly.

"Don't worry," says Trigger, slapping him on the back, "I'll work with you. Old Crow's ordered me to help you in every way I can. Now, I don't normally listen to a word Crow says, him being such an annoying git, but I'll do my best for you."

Interesting. Although I try not show my interest, keeping my eye pressed firmly to the lens. So Trigger's no fan of Crow. Could he possibly be my first ally? I know he's a drinker but he's the person with the key to the Armory. Who better ally is there?

I flex my hand, shaking out any tremors. Then, I rest my finger on the trigger. It's important I relax. But how can I with Nicolo looking on? When I know, if I miss, he'll report it to Crow.

A fly hovers over me, buzzing annoyingly, And I'm gnawing so rattishly on my top lip, it's bleeding. Focus Amaryllis, I sternly tell myself. Focus.

I empty my lungs.

Hold it.

Hold it...

Very gently, I pull the trigger.

I know I bungled it. I knew it even before the bullet left the barrel. So I'm not surprised when Trigger, who's peering intently through his binoculars, calls a miss. Everything felt wrong. My old rifle was a part of me; another limb like my arms and legs. But I feel disconnected from this gun. It's as if it belongs to another sniper and I'm just borrowing it for the day.

"Where did it go?" I snap.

"Three feet left of target," he reports with a hiccup. He then delights us with a long, smelly burb before adding, "And seventy feet short."

Seventy feet! "Bugger," I mutter. If the petrol drum had been a barn door, I would still have missed it.

I'd better get my act together. I don't want Crow deciding I'm not up to the job. If that happens, he might send me away, and then I'll never get my hands on him – or find Level Seven.

I yank back on the bolt, ejecting the empty casing. Then I thrust in a second shell. But, when I press my eye up to the scope, I find the petrol drum is obscured. And, whatever's obscuring it, is moving! Could there be rebels over there? Annoyed, knowing I can't risk a second shot, I twist the lens, focusing in on...

Oh no!

My bowels churn horribly. Suddenly, I feel the need to vomit. It's not a rebel. It's Lily! And I think...yes, she is. She's holding a rifle. My rifle!

"Did you think I'd forgotten you, Amaryllis?" Her cold, scornful words fill my mind. "Remember, wherever you go, I'll find you."

Through my sight, I see a plumb of smoke erupt from the gun's muzzle. Did she...? Oh God, she did. She took the shot.

5,000 feet.

3½ seconds.

"Get down!" I yell. "Get down! GET DOWN!" Letting go of my gun, I grip hold of the closest foot – it's Nicolo's – and pull, flipping him over onto his back.

But I helped the wrong person...

The bullet hits Trigger between the eyes and he drops to the floor with a thud.

XX

The Skeleton Clock
1 month, 25 days, 23 hrs, 50 mins, 20 secs

I stand silently in Twig's room looking down at the sleeping boy. It's not difficult to see he's still suffering from a fever, his sunken cheeks - the skin so papery it's almost transparent - glow with it. He's as withered as the flower I drew in my burrow only a week ago.

Gently, not wanting to disturb him, I rest my old ragdoll on his pillow. Then, feeling horribly impotent, knowing there's nothing I can do until Splinter gets here with the Devil's Dust, I slump down on a stool. I look around. It's so tiny in here - and depressing. It's the sort of room mops and buckets should be kept in, not sick children. It stinks of disinfectant too. Tomorrow, when I visit, I'll try to remember to bring a few herbs with me from Level Six. I'll slip them under Twig's pillow; it'll smell much better in here then.

As I sit there, gently brushing my fingers through the boy's curls, my dark thoughts drift to where they always go...

To Lily.

It's not difficult to work out why she shot Trigger. She was sending me a message; her way of reminding me she can get to me whenever she wants. But how the hell did she do it? It's a 5,000 feet shot. It's not as if she's...

I scowl.

...a sniper.

Splinter told me this howler is different. What were his words now? "The slug allows the host of think. To remember stuff. They work together." According to the smuggler, Lily's host was a rebel sniper. So she'd know how to shoot. I slap my knee. That's how the Sheriff did it. The slug discovered a way of accessing the host's skills. Splinter was right, they do work together. It's a horrifying thought.

My mind travel back to yesterday. Within seconds of Trigger being hit, Nicolo crawled over to help him. The Corporal impressed me. Even if he is Crow's spy, there's no denying he's got guts. He did everything he could, pumping Trigger's chest - he even pulled off his socks and pressed them to the rebel's torn skull. But there was no saving him. Lily's bullet hit him between the eyes.

In the end, Nicolo called for help using his walkie talkie. Another medic turned up and, together, they stretchered him off to Medical. Crow showed up too with a reluctant-looking Doctor Atchoo in tow. When the doctor stepped in the pool of blood, he turned a sort of sickly-yellow. He looked so unwell, I thought he was going to throw up. Crow, on the other hand, didn't seem to be in the slightest upset by the turn of events. I suspect he's secretly delighted to be rid of Trigger. Now he can tidy up the gunroom so it's just as organised as the rest of the Nest.

And, through it all, I stayed silent. I had to. If I told Crow I'd seen the sniper, he would want to know everything: who she is, how I know her, and why I think she killed Trigger. He'd end up thinking I was in on it. I'm a mercenary. I'm not to be trusted.

Just then, Twig shifts on his bed, and his eyelids flutter open. I jump up, gently gripping hold of his hand. "How do you feel?" I ask.

"Cold," he mutters. Then he coughs so wildly, the bed shudders.

When he stops, I pull his blanket up to his chin. "It's the fever," I tell him.

He nods. "The doctor told me I need a drug."

"Yes. It's called Devil's Dust. The howlers put it in serf's food. Don't worry. In two days, a smuggler I know will bring it to the Nest. The doctor will inject you with it."

"Then I'll feel better?"

"Much better," I tell him. "And if the doctor injects you with a little less every day, soon you won't need it. You'll be cured." I'm just hoping the doctor knows what he's doing. From what I know of him so far, he seems to be an incompetent fool.

The boy rests silently for a second, his trembling fingers clutching his blanket. "When I'm better, will I be sent back to the howlers?"

"No, no, don't be silly," I chide him. "You can stay with me."

"Here?" he says, his eyes widening. "In the Nest?"

He thinks the Nest's steel walls will protect him from the howlers. That's a joke. But he's a serf and howlers don't tell serfs anything. So he can't know the Skeleton Clock's ticking down. He'll not even know what CO_2 is. And nobody's told him a howler army will soon be scaling the Nest's walls. Well, let him think he's safe. Why not? He's just a kid.

"Yes," I tell him. "For now." Where I'll be a month from now, who knows. "There's a rebel here called Nicolo. He's trying to get you into the school."

"School! And I can go there?"

"Yes, I think so."

"Cool. I know my letters. And I can spell lots of different words. My granny showed me how to do it. She..." The lights in his eyes dim. He's remembered. "Granny," he whispers.

I steel myself. I knew this was coming. "The thing is, Twig - " I stop. I know I must tell him the truth. But how?

"It's alright, Amaryllis. She'd be happy to know I'm here with you. It's what she'd want. For me to be safe."

I see he's getting tired, his eyelids drooping. But, before he sleeps, I need to find out a few things. He looks so much like my brother, Benji, it's uncanny. It can't be by chance. Nothing ever is. "Twig," I say, gently nudging him, "Why did the howlers pick you to work in the forest?"

"I don't know," he says. "I didn't often get picked. I'm not very strong. They mostly pick the older, bigger kids. But the new sheriff..."

"Lily?"

"Yes. When she spotted me, she told her knights to bring me along. Granny too. But I don't know why."

I nod slowly. I think I do. I'm betting Lily knew I had a brother. And she knew, if I saw a boy who looked just like him being whipped, I'd try to help him. Then, when I went running in, she'd spring her trap. And I fell for it. Thankfully, she'd not expected me to overpower three of her knights. I must admit, it's a clever plan. Although, for it

208

to work, she'd need to know what my brother looked like. She'd need to see my file. A file kept here, in the Nest.

I scowl. The plot thickens.

Just then. Doctor Atchoo walks in, interrupting my thoughts. "I think we'd better let the boy rest," he scolds me, peering at the monitor.

I nod. "I'll try to visit tomorrow," I tell the boy.

He nods sleepily.

I then turn to the doctor. "Yesterday, you told me to pop in for a checkup. As ordered, here I am."

"Oh! Oh, yes. I did, didn't I." He looks me up and down. "Been feeling tired?"

"No,"

"Dizzy?"

"No."

"Any memory loss?"

"I, er, don't remember." I grin. "A joke."

"Very funny." Then, with a roll of the eyes, he exits the room.

"See you," I say to the boy. And I hurry after him.

I catch up to him in the corridor. "Doctor!"

"Yes, what is it?" He keeps on walking, refusing to slow down.

"Nicolo told me he's going in the pod soon. Will it fix his leg and his injured face?"

"No. Just his..."

I grip hold of the doctor's collar and push him up to the wall. But I don't say anything. Why bother when my eyes can do the talking.

He swallows, his pale cheeks turning even paler. "Yes, yes. The leg and the cheek.

"The cut over his eye too."

"Yes, yes, the cut too. I'll see to it."

"Good. Now, moving on. Yesterday, you told me I was different."

"No, I didn't."

"Yes, you did."

"No, I…"

"Doctor, I don't wish to hit you but - ." I lift my fist.

"Alright! Alright! But if Crow discovers I told you, I'll be shot. So I didn't tell you. Understood?"

I nod.

"Your word on it."

"You have it," I growl. The doctor's a moron. I'm a mercenary who kills for a living. As if not keeping my word is going to keep me up at night.

He turns to look down the corridor.

"There's nobody here," I hiss. "Nobody's listening. There's just me and you. Now, spit it out or you'll be spitting teeth."

He sighs. "When you were in the pod," he begins, "it checked your blood to see if it was A, B…"

"Yes. Yes, I know," I butt in. "A, B, AB or O. I'm not stupid. Get on with it."

"It's not any of them."

I frown at him. "I'm not following."

"It's not A, B, AB or O. It's unknown."

Unknown! So that's what the U, N and K stood for on my monitor. "What are you trying to say, Doctor? That I'm dying?"

"No, not at all. What I'm saying is, you're not human."

XXI

The Skeleton Clock
1 months, 25 days, 11 hrs, 33 mins, 07 secs

The next morning, 0700hrs sharp, Nicolo and I return to Level Six to work with Akiyo. But, when we get there, she's nowhere to be seen. Annoyed – I could have slept in – I perch on Nicolo's upturned bucket whilst the boy wanders over to a pen of cows. As I sit there, my eyes idly hunt the craggy walls for a door. The door to Level Seven. This is Level Six so, logically, if a lower level exists, the way in must be here. But I see nothing of interest. I'm not surprised. If it's a secret level, there's not going to be a big, red door with the words 'This Way to Level Seven' flashing over the top of it. No, I need to look properly. And the only way to do that is to creep down here at night when everybody's sleeping.

"This is the howlers' crossbow." I jump and look up. On the pads of her feet, Akiyo walks over to me. She's like a cat on the hunt, her short legs swirling up her robe and the sword on her belt. I see she's carrying a crossbow and a fistful of arrows. "Do you know it?" she asks, holding it up for me to see.

I nod, absentmindedly rubbing my leg where I'd been injured. The pod erased the scar but not the memory. "I know it very well," I mutter.

She stops in front of me. "It's light but still very powerful," she says. "Whatever it hits, it'll kill." She shrugs. "If the target's within a hundred feet."

The Skeleton Clock

It didn't kill me, I think, standing up from the bucket, and I was only ten feet away. But, then, it wouldn't, would it. I'm not human.

I didn't sleep well – when do I ever? – the doctor's words swirling in my mind. Not human! It's impossible. I know I'm different. The speed I run. My strength. Still, I don't look different. I look human. Except for my eyes. But let's say the doctor's right. Then, what I want to know is, what am I? Was I born different or was I changed? And, if I was changed, how was I changed, why, and, most importantly, what to? The answers must be on Level Seven. Lily told me I'd find out 'everything there is to know' there. But I suspect discovering the way into it is going to be difficult, if not impossible.

"Hello! Anybody there?" Akiyo prods me with the butt of the arrow, interrupting my thoughts.

"Yes, yes." I can tell by her expectant frown she wants me to comment on the crossbow. "It's a handy toy," is all I can think of saying.

My tutor hooks her eyebrows. "This is not a toy," she scolds me.

"Sorry." I put up my hands in mock surrender. "It's just, this is the 22nd century. And that's from what? The tenth?"

"Sixth," she snaps. Swiftly, she fits an arrow to the crossbow's string, pulls it back and lets fly. The arrow hits a water barrel over a hundred feet away.

My chin drops to my chest.

"That shut you up," mutters Nicolo, who's returned from stroking the cows and is now standing by my elbow.

I nod. It sort of did.

"Do not be fooled by the crossbow's simplicity. Here," she hands it to me, dropping the rest of the arrows by my feet, "you try."

"Try not to shoot the cows," says Nicolo. "They like me."

"I'll do my best," I coldly reply.

I must say, he looks much better now he's been in the pod. I spotted on the way down he's stopped limping. And the burn on his cheek has been replaced by smooth, glowing skin. Even the cut's vanished. I'm happy for him. But that's not why I did it. He's now indebted to me; a debt I will soon insist he repay.

Clumsily, I try to fit the arrow to the string but, with a tut, Akiyo stops me. "Don't rush it," she tells me.

Annoyed with myself, I nod briskly. She's right. It's like chambering a bullet. Better to do it slowly and get it right than risk fumbling it.

"Remember to bend your left knee." She shows me and I mirror her. "Then, if needed, you can push off the back foot and run."

"Where to?" I ask.

"Away."

I frown. "Isn't that a bit..."

"Cowardly?" she interrupts me with a sneer. "Don't be so stupid. If you get killed today, you can't fight tomorrow."

I shrug. There's no denying her logic. Anyway, I'm a big fan of living.

Lifting the crossbow up to my eye, I target the barrel.

"Up a bit," mutters Nicolo.

I shush him with a grunt. I'm the sniper, not him. But, when I pull the trigger, the arrow hits the dirt ten feet short.

Crestfallen, I lower the bow.

"The crossbow's no different to the gun," Akiyo tells me. I'm just thankful Akiyo didn't tut – and Nicolo didn't say I told you so. "When a bullet travels, it slows down and drops, yes?"

"Yes."

"Why?" she asks.

"The momentum slows. Gravity pulls on it."

"Correct." She picks up a second arrow and hands it to me. "Gravity will pull on this too. You must try to correct for it."

I nod. Akiyo, it seems, knows her physics.

"For every 100 arrows you shoot, you will improve by 1%. Only 9,999 to go."

"Why am I doing this?" I ask. "I'm a sniper. I shoot bullets, not sticks."

"Can the enemy do it?"

"Yes."

"Then that is why. Now, I must report to Major Crow. He wants to be updated on how everything's – progressing." She bows. "Keep up the good work, Two Seven. I will return soon to check on you."

She turns and pads off, and I'm left under the watchful eye of Nicolo.

I spend the rest of the morning trying to skewer the barrel. It is surprisingly humid on Level Six – it must be all the sprinklers. Nevertheless, I keep on shooting and, by lunch, there's a nasty welt on my finger and the barrel's badly in need of a carpenter.

When I'm too tired – and bored – to go on, Nicolo, who's been fetching the arrows for me, asks for a go.

"Enjoy," I say, handing him the crossbow. I then sit by a patch of turnips to watch.

I must say, he's very good...at missing! I try to help him, but I can't seem to turn my thoughts into words. I just get muddled up - then he just gets annoyed with me. In the end, he only hits the barrel on his final attempt, the arrow ricocheting off and flying into the cow pen.

A long, grumpy, "Moo" erupts from it.

"Beef for lunch," he mutters.

I giggle – which is annoyingly girlish of me – so I stop.

When Akiyo returns from her meeting, she looks from my blistered finger to the splintered barrel and nods. "Bravo, Two Seven, I think you killed it." She then twists sharply on her heels and walks off. "Keep up," she calls.

With a shrug, I go after her, Nicolo following doggedly on my heels.

As we stroll along under the hot, red lights, I'm surprised to see the rebels don't just grow crops here. There are dozens of richly-tinted flower beds too - and hundreds of trees. In amongst the beds, I spy lots of tiny channels filled with flowing water. This must be what Nicolo referred to as hydroponics.

"Why not just grow food?" I ask, running to catch up with my tutor.

But it's Nicolo who answers. "When the war's won, Cinis must be replanted. Not just crops. Trees and flowers too. So we grow them all here."

"When the war's won, not if. The boy truly thinks Crow's plan will work. Well, I'm not going to burst his bubble. He'd not thank me for it. Messengers only ever get shot.

As I look out over the rows of flowers, my fingers itch to sketch them. "They look so innocent," I say wistfully.

"Innocent!" Akiyo stops and turns to me. "Did you know there must be over two hundred different plants that can kill. Two hundred! You might find the venom in the petals, the stems, the tubers, the roots, or even the bark. On this level, you will discover the sweet perfume of the hemlock, the deceptively pretty petals of the monkshood and, look, over there, the red berry of the cuckoo-pint. Very nasty customers and, trust me, not so innocent. But such plants can be effective tools in the hands of the rebels."

I suddenly remember the howler I darted in the forest. The tip had been dipped in a powerful toxin. A toxin sent to me by the rebels. Did it kill him then? I'd been told in sniper camp it just sent them to sleep.

"A coward's way to kill," I murmur.

"Don't be a fool," she snaps. "The rebels do what they must do to win. And, remember, we did not invent the clever ploy of murdering the enemy in his bed. The Thugs of Kali did in the 8th century followed by Hassan of Iraq and his fanatics in the 11th. You see, the assassin is part of our history, our world culture. Remember, a sniper's job is to hunt down the howlers and destroy them."

"With a bullet," I remind her. "Not with," I wrinkle up my nose, "this!"

She shrugs. "If you miss," she fingers the petals of the monkshood, "this might be the only way of doing it."

Nonsense, I think, my temper rising. I never miss. Not until recently anyway. But I keep my lips tightly shut.

We stroll by a plum tree, and I scoop a plum up off the dirt. It is shiny and plump but, when I chew on it, the yellow flesh is dry and surprisingly bitter.

"In Italy in the 16th century," Akiyo persists, "a lady, Madonna Teofania di Adamo, discovered the cure to the problem of annoying husbands. She actually sold her medicine in shops." She barks a laugh. "The result, six hundred fewer husbands and six hundred happy widows in the world."

We stop by a pond, and I look down at the muddy-looking water. It is crowded with fish. Twisting, fins flapping, they fight for room. I grunt. I know how they feel.

Suddenly, Akiyo sits down. "Gojo-Goyuko," she says.

A little perplexed, I sit down too.

"Well?"

Oh! She expects me to know what it is. "Em, is it a venom," I propose tentatively, "or a, em, way of fighting?"

"No, Two Seven," she sucks in her cheeks, "it is the Japanese word for the study of the flaws of the enemy."

"Oh, yes. I see." I nod wisely, trying to look as if this would have been my third guess.

Akiyo rubs her temple and ploughs on. "If the enemy is a coward, or too kind perhaps, or maybe just has a terribly short temper, a clever ninja can turn this on him." My tutor's eyes twinkle. She enjoys sermonising. "Using a bribe, flattery or a well-thought-out insult, the ninja can prod the enemy into doing whatever he or she wants them to do. You see, Two Seven, by understanding the enemy's flaws, they can be easily manipulated and controlled. That is Gojo-Goyuko."

I steeple my fingers under my chin and mull her words over. I know what my flaw is. I'm a selfish cow. Try manipulating that, I think to myself.

Akiyo sighs audibly and begins to suck on her teeth. I suspect my inability to instantly accept her wisdom annoys her immensely. "Allow me to offer an example," she mutters.

I nod. As if there's a possibility of stopping her.

"A powerful ninja is given the responsibility of murdering thirteen of his master's political opponents. Now, this assassin is a very intelligent chap. He looks down the list and sees Lord Nin Po is on there, third from the bottom. The ninja knows this lord to be a very kindly sort and very popular with his followers. He also knows if he is to succeed and kill all thirteen men on his list, he must murder Nin Po first."

My storyteller cocks her eyebrow and, still chewing on my disgusting plum, I nod my understanding so far.

"So, the ninja, confident in Nin Po's kindly ways, sits by the door to his castle and pretends to be a leper. The next day, on his way to temple, the lord spots the leper, walks over to him and drops a penny in his lap. The ninja jumps up and thanks him with the swipe of his sword. The assassin then allows himself to be captured and, under torture, he surrenders his twelve co-conspirators."

She looks to me with a quizzical eyebrow.

Reluctantly, I nod. "They were not his twelve co-conspirators; they were his other twelve targets." I see the logic in the ninja's plan but still there is no honour in trickery.

".Just so!" Akiyo claps her hands, no doubt misinterpreting my understanding for agreement. "The clever ninja knew how much the lord's followers adored him and he correctly judged they'd avenge his murder. They did the rest of the ninja's job for him."

"I admit it's a clever ploy," I murmur, "but it's still cowardly."

"No, Two Seven," Akiyo counters with a flaring of her nostrils, "not cowardly, smart."

"But..."

Annoyingly, she shows me the mollifying palms of his hands. "We can ponder the ins and outs of morality tomorrow. Now, however, we must return to work." She hops athletically to her feet and, crossly, I scramble up to follow her. It seems, according to Akiyo anyway, her word is law. There is no room for debate. I wonder if she is frightened I will find a gaping hole in her cold, hard logic.

".Jump it," Akiyo says.

Momentarily lost for words, I spit pulped plum on a bush. "What?" I finally muster.

"THE POND!" she trumpets, grinding her heel in the dirt. "Jump it," she tells me sternly.

I look to the muddy pool, my eyes narrowing. "You must be joking," I protest. "It's over twenty feet."

"Firstly, I never joke," she tells me stiffly, "and, secondly, you think too much. Whether it is possible or not is not important. Think only, I must jump this pond, I will jump this pond. Only then will you succeed."

I look over at Nicolo, but he just winks at me. "Watch out for the piranha," he says.

"Piranha!"

"Just kidding." He turns to Akiyo. "I'm kidding, right?"

Akiyo says nothing.

Ha bleeding ha! "Do you want to do it?" I hiss at him.

"I can't," he answers flatly. "I didn't bring my swimming trunks."

"Nor did I," I mutter.

I back up a little. Then, clenching my teeth, I sprint for the bank. I jump, pulling my knees up to my chin.

Six feet.

Seven feet...

I hit the pond with a gigantic splat, sending up a shower of mud and flapping fish. I'm just thankful it's not deep, the water only coming up to my knees.

"That was a big splash," says Nicolo. He's still up on the bank peering down at me.

I glower at him. Is he suggesting I'm fat? I sort of want to stamp my foot, but it's underwater so why bother. I see the boy's trying not to grin – but he's not doing a very good job of it. "Do you think this is funny?" I snarl.

"No, no." He steps swiftly back. I think he thinks I'm going to try to pull him in too; which was exactly what I was planning to do. "I'll, er, fetch a towel," he says, hurrying off.

My tutor twists on her sandaled heels and, whistling a cheery tune, she strolls off too. "Let's go, Two Seven. I think it's fish for lunch."

It seems, I ponder, a silver-scaled cod lazily circling my legs, Akiyo enjoys a good joke after all.

Standing there, dripping wet and wondering how long it'll take Nicolo to fetch a towel, I watch a man plod by the pond. He's old and wrinkly – like a prune – and looks way too doddery to be working on Level Six. He stops by a chestnut tree, his eyes darting here, there and everywhere, hunting for – what? Anybody who might be watching. But I don't think he sees me. How can he? I'm covered in mud and dangly bits of weed. Seemingly content there's nobody spying on him, he steps closer to the tree trunk and...

I blink.

Where did he go?

It was as if the tree – swallowed him up!

But I do know this. I think I just discovered the way into Level Seven.

XXII

The Skeleton Clock
1 months, 24 days, 10 hrs, 44 mins, 31 secs

After a disgusting lunch of cold, lumpy porridge – I'm considering shooting the cook – Nicolo and I plod up to the Armory to fetch my rifle. We discover a skinny, pimply-cheeked rebel girl in there who's been given the job of tidying up Trigger's mess. I feel sorry for her and wish her luck. Then, with pockets stuffed with bullets and the gun slung over my shoulder, we go up to the Nest's roof. There, I spend most of the afternoon trying to hit the petrol drums – and missing spectacularly! The problem is the wind. The bullet's flying for so long, even a tiny gust pulls it off target. But how do I adjust for it when the wind begins to blow a second after I pull the trigger? But I keep on trying. If Lily can do it, I can do it. I work a little on Nicolo's spotter skills too, showing him a trick I know for estimating wind speed. It's not a success. I know what I'm trying to say but I just get mixed up, and I end up confusing even myself. I think I must be the worst instructor in the world – or he's the worst student.

The next morning, I go with Nicolo to visit Twig in Medical. I remember to bring the herbs with me, thyme and a sprig of basil. When we get there, the boy's sleeping, so I slip them under his pillow. He still looks terribly sick. Sort of smaller too, as if he's slowly shriveling up like a punctured paper bag. I don't think the boy will last much longer. I kiss him on the cheek. Then, with Nicolo in tow, I return to Level Six to work with Akiyo.

When we get to the tiny patch of grass, Akiyo, as always, is nowhere to be seen. She must be a big sleeper! So I sit, legs crossed and try not to look at the tree. I don't want Nicolo to suspect anything. Tonight, I'm planning to creep down here to get a closer look at it; see if it truly is the doorway to Level Seven.

"Today, we will be working with the fist, the foot and the knee."

Startled, I look to my left to see Akiyo striding over to me. Oddly, she's carrying a wooden dummy. Arms. Legs. It's even got eyes. She plonks it down on the grass. "Hold this," she says to Nicolo.

The boy nods. Standing behind the dummy, he grips it by the hinged elbows.

"What do you want me to do with it?" I ask. "Dress it?"

"No," she answers with a smirk. "Hit it. Let's begin with the fist." She turns to the dummy and thumps it in the chest.

Goggle-eyed, I study what's left of the poor dummy's torso. Not much. The wood's splintered and there's a big dent in it.

"I think you killed him," I mutter.

"Now, Two Seven, let's see if you can throw a punch. The torso's a little, er..."

"Destroyed?" I suggest.

"Yes. So hit him on the chin. Hard."

Nicolo, who's still holding the dummy's elbows, protests. "She's going to mess up her hand," he says.

I'm surprised. I didn't expect him to try to stick up for me. I'm thankfully but irritated too. I stick up for myself.

Akiyo nods. "Yes, she is. Badly, I suspect."

"Then how will she shoot?"

"Don't worry, Corporal, she'll mend. If not, we'll stick her in the pod. It'll fix her up. Happy?"

I can tell by the throbbing artery in his neck and the way he's screwing up his lips he's not.

With a dismissive snort, Akiyo turns to me. "Is there a problem, Two Seven? If I remember correctly, you agreed to do everything I tell you to do."

"No, I say, smiling brightly at her, "there's no problem." I know she's testing me. Crow must be putting her up to it. He wants to know if I'll crack. "I keep my word," I say.

"Good." She nods to the dummy. "Then get on with it."

Gritting my teeth, I curl up my hand and thump it, almost shattering my knuckle. With lewd words spurting from my lips, I nurse my fingers in my armpit.

"No," she spits, her eyes flashing. "The punch begins in the legs." She slaps my knees. "Push off from here and don't forget to twist your hips. Got it?"

My eyes flash too but, dutifully, I follow her order.

Thud! Thud! Thud!

Akiyo grinds her teeth. "Pitiful," she growls. "This dummy is the enemy. He's trying to kill you. Not just you, your family too." Her eyes narrow. "Pretend he's the howler who murdered your little brother, Benji. Such a tragedy."

My top lip flips up into a snarl. She knows way too much. Way to much! And I very much want to rip the sneer off her face. But I still my temper, keep my wits and, with a blood-curdling growl, I turn my anger on the dummy.

THUD! THUD! THUD!

"Harder," Akiyo yells at me. "Unless you wish to stop."

"No," I cry.

THUD! THUD! THUD!

"Better, Two Seven. Not a lot, but still – better." She bows. "I will return soon to check on your progress." Without another word, she twirls on her heels and trots away.

Nicolo and I stand there watching her flapping heels. Then, when she's out of sight, the boy drops the dummy on the grass in disgust. "What a cow," he mutters. He steps over to me and asks to see my hand.

"No," I say, jumping back. I nod at the dummy. "Pick it up."

He frowns. "But..."

"Nicolo," I interrupt him, "if I don't win this contest, another sniper will. And when she's sent on the mission, she'll miss. That'll cost the rebels the war." I don't bring up the fact I presently can't hit a barn door. "If Akiyo thinks pulverising my hand is going to help me win, then that's what I'm going to do. Now, pick – it – up."

Of course, I'm lying. It's funny. I'm so good at it, even I'm convinced. But the truth is, if I don't follow Akiyo's orders, she'll rat me out to Crow. And, if that happens, he might find another sniper to represent Zulu Sector in the contest. A sniper who follows orders. He'll send me away and then I'll never find out what happened to my mother. Or discover what's on Level Seven.

With a resigned shrug, he picks up the dummy. "This is crazy," he says.

"No" I reply coldly. "This is my life."

Two agonisingly long hours later, Akiyo dutifully returns, but by then my fist is a blood-spattered pulp and my mood is volcanic.

She looks to the dummy and her eyes narrow. "Excellent," she murmurs. "Excellent! I see the chin is very slightly dented."

I pull a face. I don't think it is. The dummy's chin is rock hard and all I can see is my blood all over it.

"Look!" My tutor knocks on the wood with her knuckle. "I think you even splintered it."

"Yes, well, I pretended it was you," I say jokingly. Sort of jokingly.

Her eyes narrow to tiny slits, and I catch her hand shift a little closer to the sword on her belt. "Whatever works. Now, rest your fist," I nod thankfully, "and let's see how hard you can hit the dummy with your knee and foot."

I look to her in frank astonishment, my mouth opening and closing like a hungry fly trap. She must be crazy.

Akiyo claps me cheerfully on the shoulder. "Then, I think, it'll be time for you to jump the pond."

Thankfully, I'm saved from further destroying my body – and getting drenched – by the beep of Nicolo's walkie talkie. "Corporal Lupo, this is Command. Escort Two Seven to the hanger bay. There's a visitor for her."

My spirits lift. It must be Rufus Splinter with the Devil's Dust.

I snap off a bow. "Sorry. I'll, er, see you tomorrow, yes?"

With a sulky shrug, Akiyo returns my bow. "The dummy will still be here," she says stiffly.

"Excellent!" I smile sweetly. But not if I slip down here and burn it, I think to myself.

Nicolo and I plod up the steps to Medical. There, we pick up a box of OxyPills before sprinting the rest of the way up to the hanger on the top level. When we get there, I skid to a stop. I remember Nicolo telling me there's lots of tech in the Nest. Even so, I'm shocked to see seven helicopters in there. Seven! There's a mechanic too, up to her elbows in cogs, bolts and dirty rags. I didn't know mechanics still existed.

Scanning the hanger, I soon spot Splinter. He's standing by a Chinook, resting his elbow lazily on the helicopter's conical nose. He's being watched over by a stiff-backed sentry. To my surprise, Crow is there too.

"Where's my payment?" the smuggler calls to us as we walk over.

I grin. Although I thoroughly dislike the man, I do understand him. With Splinter, I know where I stand. He's not complicated. If I pay him, he'll do it – if it's not too risky. If I don't, he won't. End of story. In many ways, he's a lot like me.

"Here." I throw him the box. "The Devil's Dust?"

He pulls a crumpled bag from his pocket, drops it on the floor and kicks it over to me. I pick it up, blood from my injured hand dripping onto my boots. "There's not a lot in here," I say, peering in.

"Not a lot!" splutters the smuggler, puffing up his chest in a pathetic attempt at looking insulted. "It's potent stuff. Sniff it. Go on, sniff it. You'll be seeing unicorns for a week. Not a lot, my ass."

"Colourful, isn't he," mutters Nicolo.

"Okay, okay," I say to Splinter. "Keep your knickers on."

With his honour successfully defended, the smuggler stuffs the box of pills in his pocket. "I'll be buggering off then," he says. "Unless anybody's interested in a drop of pig penicillin." He winks at me. "Fifty percent off!"

"Fool," I mutter.

He turns to the sentry. "Interested?"

The sentry responds by stroking the trigger on his gun.

The smuggler shrugs and turns to go. Then he stops. "Where's the door?" he asks. "It's like a maze. I don't want to be lost in here when the howlers show up."

Crow, who up until now has stayed silent, steps up to him. "Did you see them?" he asks.

Splinter nods. "Ay. I spotted them on the way here. But they didn't spot me," he adds with a snigger. "I'm too tricky for them. Too sly."

"How many?" snaps Crow.

The smuggler looks the major up and down, his eyes calculating. I sigh. I know that look. "It'll cost you." he says.

"Tell me," says Crow, "or I'll fly this helicopter up to 1,000 feet and drop you out of it."

He says this so coldly, with so little grandeur, even Splinter seems to get he's not bluffing. "I were just joking," he says. "Always happy to help the rebels."

"Then tell me."

"Hundreds of them. Bleedin' hundreds."

Crow nods slowly. "I see. And when will they get here. Two weeks?"

"Two weeks! Where y' getting y' intel from? A blind man?"

"Then when!?" thunders Crows.

Startled, Splinter backs away, but he's stopped by the sentry's gun nozzle.

"Six days," he whimpers. "They'll be here in six days."

XXIII

The Skeleton Clock
1 months, 23 days, 22 hrs, 5 mins, 13 secs

When the bolt of electricity rips through my body, I jerk up in my bed. Pulse racing, chest thumping, I fumble with the S-TOX on my wrist. I didn't miss this, I think, jabbing wildly at the buttons. The shocks stop, and I peer drowsily at the glowing, red numbers. It's midnight. If I'm lucky, the Nest's inhabitants will all be asleep.

Slipping out from under my coarse blanket, I pull on my uniform. The scabs on my fingers rub the cloth and I wince. The rest of my body is a disaster too, my elbows, my knees, even the bottoms of my feet all cut to ribbons from hitting Akiyo's dummy. Thankfully, my body will recover in a day or two. I don't know how and I don't know why, but it will.

Softly, I pad over to the door. As I go to open it, I suddenly worry it will be locked. But, when I press the green button on the wall, the door slithers silently open. I smile. It seems the rebels trust me. How very stupid of them.

Stepping out into the corridor, I'm taken aback by how dark it is, the buzzing lights on the wall giving off a dull, sickly glow. Then I remember the Nest is powered by the sun, the energy collected and stored in a battery. The rebels must dim the lights at night to prevent it going flat. This is not altogether bad news. My night sight is good.

And now, if I bump into any patrols, they might not spot me.

I stand there giving my eyes a few seconds to adjust to the darkness. Am I doing the right thing, I wonder. If there is a Level Seven and I'm caught trying to get into it, who knows what the rebels will do. Torture me? Shoot me? But I know I can't stop now; I can't go back to my room and simply go to sleep. I need to find out if Level Seven exists. And, if it is there, what's on it. I'm not doing this for Lily. I'm doing it for me. I need to know what I am.

Steeling myself, I begin to walk down the corridor. I try to step softly, but the tapping off my heels on the steel mesh echoes off the walls. To keep my mind off the thought of being captured and interrogated, I think back to this morning. After the grumbling Splinter was escorted away by the sentry, Nicolo and I went directly to Medical to deliver the Devil's Dust to Doctor Achoo. He seemed delighted. He told me not to worry and insisted Twig would be up and about in a jiffy. A jiffy being two days. I'm not so confident; after all, the man's a clown.

My planning of what I'll do to the doctor if he kills Twig ends when I get to the first bend. I stop and listen. Nothing. No footsteps. No rebel chatter. Just the distant drumming of the water pumps. So I keep on going. Second bend. I stop. I listen. I keep on moving. When I get to the third bend, I press my back up to the wall and peer around the corner.

I can see the camera. It's perched high up on a wall halfway between me and the steps. I must try to get by it without being seen. Thankfully, I have a plan. Presently, it's pointing down the corridor towards the steps. When it begins to swivel, I duck back. Then I begin to count. 1, 2, 3 ... When I get to 15, I sprint around the corner, skidding to a stop directly under it. It can't see me here. I peer up at it watching for it to turn. Suddenly, the tiny motor hums to life and I'm off. 1, 2, 3, I get to 13 seconds when I hit the top of the steps and down I go.

Corkscrewing further and further down into the depths of the Nest, I feel my stomach tighten. The hand clutching the banister is trembling, the knuckle waxen and blotched, and my mouth feels as dry as a desert cave.

"I see you, Amaryllis." A sharp, acid-laced whisper stabs at my mind.

I freeze.

"Planning to shoot me, little girl?"

"No, I..."

"Planning to kill me?"

I say nothing. Like a lasso, the words drag at my feet, commanding me to turn and flee. But I'm rooted to the floor. It's as if my legs no longer work.

"Find Level Seven, little girl, or I'll kill you."

So it's her. Lily. She's the whisperer invading my mind, urging me to kill. To do her will. Well, no longer. I'm doing this for me, not her.

"Do I frighten you, Lily?" I hiss. a nervy jitter distorting my words. "Do I?"

The seconds tick ponderously by but there's no answer. Gritting my teeth, I command my legs to work and slowly, tiny step by tiny step, I go on my way.

When I'm almost to the bottom, I stop mid-step. Peering down into the gloom I can just make out a sentry. He's sitting by the door to Level Six, his chin nestled into his chest, his legs stuck out and crossed at the heels. He must be sleeping. But I can't creep by him; not when his feet are blocking the door.

I try to think. I could knock him out. But there's a good chance he'll wake up and sound the alarm. I suppose I could kill him. But I can't. I won't. I'm not Lily and he's not my enemy... My enemy! What is it Akiyo told me? I can prod my enemy into doing what I want him to do. I eye the sleeping man. I just need to discover his flaws; his Goyo-Goyuko. I shrug and proceed down the steps. How difficult can it be?

"Hello," I say stopping in front of his outstretched boots.

With a startled yelp, the sentry jumps to his feet, his stool tipping over and clattering to the floor. "Stop or I'll shoot," he croaks, his hand fumbling for the pistol holstered on his belt.

"I have stopped," I reply flatly, resisting the urge to disarm him.

"Oh," he says. "That's, er, good." He falters. I think I confused him.

Now I'm much closer to him, I see he's not much older than me. He's a scruffy fellow, his uniform shabby and frayed with bits of cotton dangling off it like untidy cobwebs. He looks dirty too and horribly underfed, his cheeks sunken, his skin a sickly-yellow. My eyes drift down to where his left hand should be, but all there is is a stump.

"Level Six is off limits at night," he growls, inspecting me with hard, flinty eyes.

"It is!" I do my very best to look innocent. "But why?"

"They don't want anybody nicking food."

I nod slowly. "But it's sort of understandable," I say grinning at him.

"Is it?"

"Well, the food's so nasty here, everybody must be starving."

He picks at his teeth with a stubby finger and says nothing.

Okay. So now I know his first flaw. He's not got a sense of humor. "Don't worry," I add, still smiling sweetly at him, "I'm not hungry."

"Then what you doing here?" he asks.

I see he's beginning to relax. His shoulders have dropped and the sternness in his jaw has softened. He no longer sees me as a threat.

I shrug. "I couldn't sleep," I say offhandedly, "so I thought I'd workout."

"Work out!?" He scowls, staring at me as if I just grew a third eye. "Work out what?"

"No, no, not work IT out. Work out." Okay, so he's thick too. "You know, get fit for the contest."

He nods, the penny dropping. "Oh, right. I get y'." He pulls a walkie talkie off his belt. "But I'd better check in with Command. Major Crow will want to know."

Blast! That's the last thing I want him to do. "Forget it," I say, turning to go. "He'll never let me." Now, let's see if Akiyo knows what she's talking about. I know the man's not very clever but is he greedy too? "I just know lots of rebels bet on me. They think I'm going to win, and I don't want to let them down."

"Hold up," says the sentry.

Smiling to myself, I turn back to him. It seems he is. "Did you bet on me too?" I ask innocently.

He nods. "Ten OxyPills," he says. "If I win, well, if you win, I'll get a hundred."

"A hundred!"

"If the howlers overrun the Nest, I'm going to need them. They'll keep me going for a month."

If he's lucky, I think. But he's right. If he gets away, he'll not last long without the oxygen enriched pills.

He looks at me, his eyes narrowed, trying to decide what to do. In the end, greed and the tiny chance of survival gets the better of him. He shrugs. "Go on then," he says gruffly. "But don't let me catch you nicking food."

"No, no, I won't." I beam brightly at him. Then, concerned I might be overdoing it a little, I thank him and hurry down the steps and over to the door.

There's not a lot of cover between here and the tree; just rows off turnips and the odd wheelbarrow leftover from a day's farming. And, unlike the rest of the Nest, this level is bathing in light. So I do the only thing I can do. I sprint for it. As I run, I keep my eyes peeled for another sentry. I see nobody. But for the sprinklers, everything is still. Hurrying by the cowshed, I dart along the path towards the pond. Then, when I get there, I slow my pace and creep over to the tree.

The Skeleton Clock

The Chestnut is, I think, the most magnificent of trees. And this is no different. It towers over me, and I must tilt back my head to see the top. I eye the broad trunk. If I was going to hide a secret door, this is where I would put it.

I begin by placing my hands on the rough bark, feeling for anything that might open a door. After a few seconds, I find a bump in the wood. I press it but nothing happens. I pull it. No, no good. I wonder if possibly there's a chink in the trunk; a gap where I can slip in my fingers and pull on a lever. But no matter how hard I look, I find nothing of interest. In the end, I try kicking it but all I do is stub my toe.

Hands on hips, I step back. I don't get it. When the old man vanished, he was standing right here. So where did he go? There's no lever to pull or button to press, and there's no trapdoor under my feet, just dirt. It's a mystery.

As I stand there trying to think of what to do next, I hear a sudden whirling sound. With a horrible sinking feeling, I glance up. There, hooked to a branch, is a camera. "Oh no," I mutter as the motor hums and the lens twirls. It's focusing in. It's focusing in on me.

"Good evening, Two Seven."

With a startled cry, I twist on my heels and find myself staring into the cold eyes of Akiyo. Very slowly, she pulls her sword. "The punishment for spying," she says, "is death."

XXIV

The Skeleton Clock
1 months, 22 days, 13 hrs, 44 mins, 60 secs

Gritting my teeth, I jam the tip of my foot into a cranny in the wall and pull myself up. There's still a long way to go to the top, but I'm determined to get there. It's my test for today and, if I'm to keep up my pretense of wanting to win this contest, it's important I put on a good show. Thankfully, the cavern wall is a hotchpotch of tiny nooks and knobbly, protruding rocks - it's covered in long stringy ivy too so it's excellent for climbing.

There's not only me clinging to the wall. Akiyo is too. I peer up, half-blinded by the glaring lights, to see she's almost to the cavern roof. I'm impressed; she climbs like a scalded monkey.

Two nights ago, when she discovered me by the tree, I thought she was going to attack me. But amazingly, when I told her I was having problems sleeping and I slipped down to Level Six to work out, she simply shrugged and then ordered me back to my room. Unlike the sentry I tricked, Akiyo is nobody's fool, and she must suspect I was up to no good. So why did she let me get away with it? Then there's Crow. Is he letting me get away with it too? Or did I just get lucky and nobody in Command happened to be watching the monitor when the lens zoomed in on me?

It's a big mystery.

The Skeleton Clock

There's a third person climbing the wall too; a rebel girl who kindly volunteered to help out. And who, according to Akiyo, is an expert climber. Saying that, she's presently ten feet below me and, if I keep up this rapid pace, she's not going to catch me up. It seems she's not such an expert climber after all.

For the first time ever, I'm in full ninja garb, or shinobi shozoku in Japanese. It is a sort of tight-fitting cloth and is surprisingly robust. I don't know where Akiyo got it from. Knowing her, she probably sewed it together herself. She's that sort of person; the sort who, if needed, could construct a bra out of string and coconut shells. Sadly, I'm not allowed a rope and grapple for this climb, only shuko, a row of metal studs on the palms of my hands and the typical ninja split toe boot to help me grip with my feet. But it's better than nothing.

As my eyes hunt the wall for my next hold, there's a sudden cry of, "Help me!"

I peer down to see the girl dangling by her fingertips from a narrow outcrop of rock. It's a fifty-foot drop to the cow shed below. If she falls, she'll be killed.

"Buddy!" I yell. Amazingly, that's the girl's name. It's what I'd call a dog. "Swing your foot up onto the ledge."

"I can't," she whimpers back. "My leg's cramped up."

I sigh. Buddy's a wuss. "Okay, hold on. I'm coming down."

Loosening my hold on the wall, I drop nimbly onto the outcrop of rock. But, when I turn to help the girl, I'm surprised to discover she's standing on the rock too.

"Oh," I say, "you got up by yourself. Good."

To be honest I'm a bit upset. I risked my life to try to help her and she didn't even need it. I sort of expect her to apologise. But no, she blinds me with a sunny smile. It's a warning, a flashing red light, but I miss it. I'm too slow.

Stepping up to me, she kicks me brutally in the kidneys and I reel back. My feet slip from the rock, and I plummet, the studs on my clawing fingers thankfully catching on the lip of the rocky outcrop. I hang there totally at her mercy.

I peer up at the girl. "I thought you were going to fall," I hiss at her. "I was trying to help you."

She sniggers, her eyes bold and pitiless. "I'm just a messenger," she says.

"A messenger! Sent by who?"

"The Sheriff."

Oh no, not Lily.

"She instructed me to tell you she's watching you. She wants you to get on with it or the next bullet will be for you."

I try to swing up my foot but, brutally, she kicks it away. "The Sheriff told me you can run like the wind. But what I want to know is, can you fly?"

"Don't do it, Buddy," I beg her "Don't..."

My fingers crunch under the heel of her foot and my hold is lost. Silently, I plummet to the cow shed below.

XXV

The Skeleton Clock
1 months, 20 days, 9 hrs, 11 mins, 36 secs

Two days later, I show Twig into my tiny room. He still looks unwell, his cheeks pallid - and, when I held his hand on the way down here, it was clammy, and I felt it trembling. Still, he's up on his feet and he's no longer got a burning fever. For all of my fretting, it seems the doctor's not totally incompetent after all.

"This is where you'll be sleeping," I tell him, steering him over to a low, steel-framed bed in the corner of the room. On it, there's a blanket, a puffed-up pillow and a fluffy toy rabbit that's a foot taller than the boy. And that's not all. There's a chocolate-drenched sponge cake sitting at the foot of the bed. "Will this be okay for you?" I ask.

With a squeal, the boy throws himself onto the rabbit and hugs it tightly. It seems it is. "Did you get this for me?" he asks, his eyes twinkling with joy.

I can't help grinning. It's good to see him happy. "No," I reply. "It's a gift from Nicolo."

"The boy in the helicopter?"

I nod. I'm surprised he remembers. "But I don't know where he got it from."

Nicolo has been a big help preparing my room for Twig's arrival. Yesterday, he delivered the bed, the blanket - a much softer blanket than the one he got me - and the pillow. Then, later in the day, he turned up carrying the toy rabbit. He wouldn't tell me where he got it from but, from the way he kept cuddling it and referring to it as Floppsy, I suspect it was his.

Suddenly, the boy spots the cake, and the rabbit is forgotten. "It's for you," I tell him. Dorothy baked it for him when I told her the boy was soon coming out of Medical. "He'll need fattening up," she told me, presenting me with a ribbon-wrapped box. I'd been so touched by her generosity, I decided there and then not to shoot her for being such a rotten cook. "Go on," I urge the drooling boy. "Try a slice."

Twig is looking at the cake in wonder; it's almost as if he's hypnotised. "I don't even know what it is," he says.

"Oh, yes. Sorry." I forgot; the howlers only ever feed serfs turnips. "It's called a cake," I tell him. "It's made from..." I stop; to be honest, I don't know what it's made from.

"A cake," he says slowly. He seems to enjoy saying the word. "And what's all the brown stuff?"

"Oh, that's chocolate," I say smiling. "Trust me, you'll love it." I press a spoon into his hand. "Go on."

"But, but - I can't," he stutters. "It's so pretty. I don't want to destroy it."

He's right, it is pretty, the frosted top sprinkled with all different sorts of nuts, and the word Twig spelt out using wafers. Who knows where Dorothy got it all from. "We don't want it to melt," I say sternly.

That did the trick. Looking at me in horror, he attacks the cake with gusto, scooping out a huge chunk. He puts it to his lips and holds it there, a blissful look on his face as the smell drifts up his nostrils. Then, with a sort of doggish whimper, he stuffs it in his mouth. "It's better than turnips," he says, spitting crumbs on the rabbit's belly.

I chuckle. I don't have a second spoon but I do have my fingers, scooping up a splodge of chocolatey mousse and putting it in my mouth. Wow! It is good. Soft and light and shudderingly sweet. It seems Dorothy is considerably better at desserts.

As we sit there, munching away, I can't help pretending that my life is normal. The world is not at war, nobody is trying to kill me and there's nobody I want to kill. And I didn't just spend the night in the MediPod with two broken legs and a dislocated shoulder. No, life is good. Just a little brother and his big sister, school tomorrow, mum's cooking dinner and dad's trying to help but just getting in the way. A family. But, in the end, my fantasy is interrupted by a knock on the door. "That'll be Nicolo," I tell the startled boy. "Sorry, I gotta go down to Level Six for a bit."

"Oh, okay," he says. "What's down there?"

"Nothing much," I reply. "It's where the rebels grow food. I just go there to work out." Jokingly, I flex my biceps. "It's important to keep fit." I don't tell him I'm soon going to be flying off to who knows where to battle it out with a bunch of snipers. It'll be too much for him. Better he thinks I'm staying here with him. For now anyway.

"So, er, what will I do?" he asks, looking frightened.

I tell him not to worry. "I'm going to drop you off at school first. It's up on Level Three. And I'll pick you up at the end of the day."

He nods jerkily, allowing me to brush the crumbs off his knees. "Do you think I'll like it there?"

I think back to my old school in the Netty. I was only six when I went there but I still remember there were thirteen other kids in the school, all of them hungry and frightened; and I was no different. I remember the bullying, the spiders in the desks, and how dirty everything was. It has to be better than that. "I think you'll love it," I say, ruffling the boy's curls. "There will be lots of other kids to play with. Nicolo went there and he told me it was the best fun ever."

"I'll do my best," he says.

"And that's all you can do," I softly tell him.

I stand up and stretch, the boy returning to the important job of demolishing the cake. "Will there be any left for me?" I ask him.

"Possibly not," he answers. He grins, showing off his chocolate-covered teeth.

Thinking I must find him a toothbrush, I grin too. "I didn't think so." Then, as Nicolo yells at me to, "Get a shift on", I hurry over to the door to let him in.

After dropping Twig at the school - a large, oblong room with a stripey red and yellow carpet, the walls plastered with children's artwork - Nicolo and I hurry down to Level Six. For the first time ever, Akiyo is there when we arrive. I wish her a good morning and she responds by instructing me to stand on a wobbly-looking, upturned barrel.

With a shrug, I do as she says.

"The ability to keep perfectly still is the most important of the ninja's skills," she tells me, sitting down on the grass and crossing her legs. Nicolo, looking a little bemused, sits down next to her. "You must be the tree on a windless day."

I stifle a yawn. According to Akiyo, every skill we work on is the most important.

"If you wish to successfully ambush your enemy," she says, "it's important he, or she, not see you. In battle, surprise is everything."

Not daring to nod, I blink my understanding. It seems my test for today is to keep perfectly still, and I'm determined to pass.

This is my seventh day of ninja school, and I'm so tired I can hardly keep my eyes open. When I'm not up on the Nest's roof trying to shoot petrol drums, I'm down here working with the sword, the crossbow, or simply pummelling the dummy until my fists bleed. Yesterday, I hit the dummy so hard in the ribs, it split in two, and now it's just a hill of splintered wood piled up by the shed.

"That'll do, Two Seven," says Akiyo, with a sharp clap of her hands. "You can jump off there now. I'm happy to tell you that you were the tree..."

My spirits lift.

"...on a very breezy day," she adds with a sneer.

Deflated by my tutor's endless criticism, I clamber down off the barrel. I feel horribly stiff and there's a nagging cramp in my left foot. I check my watch. "The meeting will begin soon," I say moodily. "We'd better go up."

Crow called the meeting for midday today. It's going to be held on the top level, in the Command Room. Nicolo told me the Skelton Clock is kept in there, and I'm interested to see it. I'm also interested to find out what Crow's going to say. With the howlers only a few days away, I'm hoping he's going to tell me when the contest is going to begin and where it's going to be held. I also want to know if Buddy's been captured and, if she has, whether she's been interrogated or not. She must know a lot; I wouldn't mind interrogating her myself I think, rubbing my still aching shoulder.

"Shortly," says Akiyo, hopping athletically to her feet, "but first..." She nods sharply at Nicolo who, with an apologetic shrug, plods over to the shed. He returns a few seconds later lugging a second wooden dummy.

"Sorry," he mutters, dropping it down in front of me.

"So, Two Seven," Akiyo rubs her hands briskly together, "what shall we begin with? The fist or the foot?"

A volcano seems to erupt in my belly, red mist blurring my eyes. A week of physical punishment and I snap. I storm up to the dummy and, in a ten second blaze of elbows, fists and feet, I smash it into splinters. With a growl, I turn to my tutor, my flashing, yellow eyes daring her to wheel out a third dummy.

Akiyo gawps at me, her eyelids twitching like a cow bothered by a fly. Nicolo, looking just as shocked, sits down on the upturned barrel.

"I'm off to the meeting," I hiss, flexing my battered fingers. "Coming?" Then, without another word, I storm off.

The Skeleton Clock

Having completed the long, agonising climb up the steps, I'm now sitting at a long, perfectly polished table in the Nest's Command Room. I'm trying to look indifferent to everything going on around me, legs extended, hands shoved in my pockets, eyes half-closed. I could almost be asleep. But I'm not; I'm taking everything in. The rows of computers, the screens filled with complex graphs and lists of flashing numbers. The tired-looking rebels sitting staring at them. I'm listening too, trying to catch the whispered reports of howler activity. I don't catch much, but what I do suggests the war's not going well.

On the wall across from me, there's the Skeleton Clock. I always thought it would look, well, like a skeleton - with a clock on it. But, of course, it's not. It's just a row of red, glowing numbers. My eyes drift to the last two digits, 27, 26, 25... Counting down to the moment humanity will be wiped off the planet.

Fixed to the wall under it, there's a much bigger screen. It's been divided up into grids, six grids in all each showing a different part of the Nest. I spot a Chinook helicopter in the hangar, a team of rebels working hard to attach rockets to the underbelly. They must be preparing it for the coming howler attack. The screen next to it shows Medical and Doctor Atchoo fiddling with his beloved MediPod. Seeing him reminds me I must bring Twig down there tonight for his shot of Devil's Dust. Three of the screens show corridors bustling with rebel troops and, although the screens are grainy, I can still see how frightened they look.

In the end, my gaze is drawn to the bottom, left-hand grid. It's been switched off, blackened-out as if the rebels don't want me to see what's going on there. I wonder what it normally shows. Level Seven possibly? Or the Chestnut tree?

The door to the room slithers open and Crow walks in in a crisp-looking, perfectly ironed uniform. Instantly, everybody stiffens, Akiyo, who's on my left, sitting up on her stool, Nicolo, who's on my right, putting down the pencil he's been fiddling with.

"Good afternoon," he barks, marching over to us. He thanks everybody for coming. Then he sits down, resting a thick wad of papers on the table; we all watch as he spends the next few seconds lining them all up. "I think it will be best," he eventually says, "if I begin by..."

"The howler spy, Buddy," I interrupt him. "Is there any news? Do you even know why she did it or where she went?"

Crow chews irritably on his lower lip. To him, it's probably important to discuss things in alphabetical order. Still, Buddy begins with a B, so what's the problem? Unless Apricots are on the agenda. "Buddy worked in engineering," he says. "Exemplary work record, or so I'm told, and recently promoted to Corporal. She'll be missed."

"Missed," I mutter with a roll of my eyes. "She's a howler spy, an assassin - AND she's annoyingly pretty. What's there to miss?"

Nicolo shuts me up with a sharp prod of his elbow.

"As to why she did it," says Crow, blatantly ignoring me, "I can only suspect the howlers offered her payment. Immortality possibly."

I can't keep silent any longer. "Rubbish," I cry. "Even if they stuffed a slug up her nostril, she'll not live forever. Howlers rot. They always do."

"Always?" says Crow, his eyebrows coming together to form a frown.

I go to answer, to fight my corner, but then I think of Lily - her perfect skin, how she smells of flowers - and I snap my mouth shut.

"Where is she now?" asks Akiyo, coming to my rescue.

"We don't know," admits Crow with a hint of a shrug. "After the attempt on Two Seven's life, she simply vanished. We searched the Nest thoroughly, every level, but..."

"Did you say every level?" I interrupt him. "All the way down to..."

"Yes," he interrupts me back. "All six. But we'll keep on looking until we find her."

I recall the cold, calculating look on the assassin's face. She was a girl with a plan. She'll be a long way from here by now. They'll not find her.

"Did she speak to you?" Crow abruptly asks me.

He's hoping I'll answer without thinking, but I'm not going to fall for his tricks. "No," I reply, the fib instantly forming on my lips. If this man asked me what day of the week it was, I'd still not tell him the truth.

"I see," he says, his eyes burning into me. I stare blankly back at him, giving nothing away.

The major sighs. "Moving on then. I wanted to begin by updating you on how the war is progressing." He turns to the rest of the room. "Bring up the satellite image of the Nest," he orders them.

One of the nondescript rebels sitting at a computer terminal clicks a button. Instantly, the six grids on the screen fizzle out, replaced by a shot of the Nest's roof.

"No, no," mutters Crow irritably. "Zoom out, zoom out. I need," he consults his papers, "grid reference 45-731 to 52-663."

"I didn't know we still had a satellite," I say, peering up at the gritty-looking image.

"We don't," says Crow. "It's old Chinese military. We only discovered it was still up there a few months ago. It took our engineers forever to patch into it."

"Did Buddy help?" I ask, remembering she was an engineer too.

"Yes," says Crow thoughtfully. "She did."

"No wonder it took so long," I murmur.

Although I hate to admit it, the major keeps on impressing me. A fleet of working helicopters, working computers, and now a working satellite. I thought most technology had been lost, but no! It's mindboggling!

"It's been orbiting the planet for over a century," Crow informs us, "so it can be little - temperamental. Still, it's better than nothing. It's how we intend sending the imagery from the contest back to the Nests."

Everybody in the room is silent as the camera slowly zooms out. Even the tapping of keys has stopped. At first, all I can see is golden desert. That, and the odd wiggly patch of dark brown which must be the remnants of old riverbeds. Then, in the bottom left-hand corner of the screen, I see a mass of tiny dots. Valley after valley of them. Mesmerised, I watch as they creep closer and closer to Rebel HQ; to where I'm sitting.

"How long until they get here?" asks Nicolo.

"In just under eleven hours," answers Crow evenly.

My eyes widen. They can't even be stopping to sleep.

"I fully expect the wall to hold for weeks. Still, I want you and Amaryllis out of here today."

"Today!" gasps Akiyo, sitting up even further on her stool. "I thought we had another three days. Two Seven's not ready. She can't even hold a sword."

I glare at her. Yes I bloody well can.

"Sorry," says the major with a shrug. "The howler army's moving considerably faster than we anticipated. When it gets here, we'll be surrounded. Cut off. There's been reports of the howlers using rockets, so even the Chinooks might have problems getting out. I don't want to risk Amaryllis getting trapped here and missing the contest. It's too important."

When did the howlers begin using rockets, I think. It's just as I suspected. The enemy's changing. Evolving.

"Why don't we just forget this stupid contest?" I say. "If I stay here, I can help you to defend the Nest. And let's face it," I wave my hand at the screen, "you need all the help you can get." I see a few of the rebels at the computer terminals nodding. Encouraged, I carry on. "Then, when the Nest's secured, I'll go shoot whoever it is you want me to shoot."

Of course, what I say is not what I'm thinking. What I'm thinking is, if I stay here, I still might find a way of accessing Level Seven; and there's still a good chance I can get Crow on his own and interrogate him. Then, with the rebels fully engaged fighting off the howlers, I can find a way of escaping the Nest and bringing Twig with me. Let Sniper Six Six try and shoot Crow's mysterious target. I'm not risking my neck on a crazy plan that'll never work.

Crow eyes me coldly. I can tell he's not impressed. "The other sector commanders will never go for it," he says. "They want this contest to happen, so it's going to happen. I need you to focus on winning. Don't worry, we'll hold off the howlers."

I shrug, sitting back on my stool. I don't get it. Why is it so important to keep the support of the other sectors? If I shoot the target and the rebels win the war, nobody is going to mind. They'll be too busy celebrating. I wonder what it is the major's not telling me.

Crow turns to Nicolo. "How's the shooting been going with the new gun?" he asks the boy.

"She's not missed yet," he says.

I stop myself from looking at him. I'm yet to hit a petrol drum and he knows it. So much for him being Crow's spy. I wonder if possibly I misjudged him; that he's on my side after all.

The major nods. "Excellent."

"Even if I do win," I say, "when the contest's over where do Nicolo and I go if the Zulu Nest's been overrun?"

"If Zulu falls, you'll be transported to Victor Sector. The commander there, Commander Rizzo, she knows who the target is. She'll direct you from there."

I sigh resignedly. "So where is this contest going to be held?" I ask.

"In the Kremlin."

"And where's that?" I ask.

He looks at me a long time before answering. "Moscow," he eventually says.

My eyes widen. "But that's in the Wilds! It's beyond the wall. Who knows what's out there."

"We do," he says evenly. "We've been sending helicopters there for weeks checking for enemy activity and setting everything up. Trust me, there's only desert and a few wild dogs. Anyway, it must be there. If we hold the contest in a sector controlled by the rebels, the sniper from that sector will have too big an advantage. And we can't risk holding it in a city controlled by the howlers. All that's left is the Wilds."

"Toxicity levels?" asks Akiyo.

He frowns. "Within, er, limits," he says. His hesitancy is not lost on me.

"What is the Kremlin?" I ask.

Crow snaps his fingers and, instantly, a black and white photograph pops up on the screen. I study it with interest. The most prominent thing on there has been labelled Palace; the architecture is stunning with hundreds of intricately decorated archways and tapered columns. But all I see are hundreds of shadowy corners snipers can hide in and take pot shots at me. Just to the north of the Palace, there's a cathedral. I see it's topped by a huge, conical-shaped belfry. That's where I want to be, I think to myself. From there, I will be able to see every foot of the killing zone. The Kremlin is encircled by a red-bricked wall; although it's not a circle, it's a wonky-looking square. Interspersed along the wall there are a number of towers. I count nineteen in all.

"A century ago, the Kremlin was the political capital of the USSR," the major informs the room. "It was bombed during the Third World War, by the Americans we think. So, as you can see, parts of it have been badly damaged. But the Palace is still standing, and most of the surrounding wall; the towers too."

Crow's right. Although the photograph is horribly grainy, I see much of the ground is pitted with craters, and the north end of the cathedral has caved in.

"Every sniper will be dropped by a different tower." Crow picks up a long stick and prods a tower on the south wall. "This here is the Borovitskaya Tower; it's where you and Nicolo will be dropped. You'll then have sixty seconds to get in there and find cover. The contest will begin 0700hrs on the dot. Understood?"

I nod, forcing myself to grin. I'm keen for Crow to think I'm up for it but all the time I'm thinking, my God, I'm going to have to go through with this madness.

Collecting his papers together, the major stands up. The rest of the room stands up too, and, reluctantly, I drag myself to my feet. "Be in the hangar at midnight," he tells Nicolo and I. "Full Kevlar. Helmets too. Low velocity shells only." He turns his gaze to Akiyo. "You know what to do," he says.

"Yes," she answers soberly.

Huddling his papers to his chest, he walks over to the door. I hurry after him. "Major!"

He turns back to me. "Yes, what is it?"

I hesitate, a little surprised by his abruptness. "The, em, secret," I say. "You were going to tell it to me when we first met in the Map Room, but you never did."

His eyes narrow.

"Don't you remember?"

Crow looks over my shoulder at the roomful of rebels and sighs. "Now is probably not the best time," he says with a hint of a smile. "Just try to focus on the contest. It's vital you win. Vital!"

I nod slowly. "Okay, " I say. This man is so full of secrets. There are so many things he's not telling me; things I need to know.

He steps closer to me, his dusty smell filling my nostrils. I remember when I first met him, I thought he smelled disgusting. But now, not so much. Now it's almost comforting like old slippers. "If you win this thing," he whispers, "when you return to the Nest, we'll sit down and I'll tell you everything I know."

I eye him skeptically. "Will you tell me what Project Liberty is?"

He scowls. "How did you - no, don't tell me. I don't want to know. And, yes," he adds after a short pause. "I will."

"And will it be just you and me?"

He nods. "Just you and me. My word on it." Suddenly, he lifts his hand to my cheek, his fingertips lightly brushing my skin. "You so remind me of her," he says.

"Of who?" I ask, a little shocked by his sudden intimacy. "My mother?"

"It's not important. Just remember, Amaryllis, the enemy is not always who you think it is."

Before I can think of how to respond to this, he turns on his heels and exits the room.

I stand there hypnotised by his final words. What was all that about, I wonder. But I do know this. If I want to get Crow on his own and find out what happened to my mother, I'm going to have to win this contest. I'm going to have to play the hero after all.

XXVI

The Skeleton Clock
1 months, 20 days, 3 hrs, 27 mins, 6 secs

That very afternoon, I'm back on Level Six, on my tiny patch of grass hemmed in by the corrugated steel cow shed and the rows of flowering herbs. But there's not just me here. Gathered around me is a crowd of rebels. Dusty-looking, most of them carrying shovels and picks, they have been pulled away from digging the ditch to witness the shinobi ceremony. Akiyo is standing next to me, and next to her a poker rests ominously in a bucket of glowing, red embers.

My tutor holds up her clenched fist and, instantly, the crowd is silent. "Today," she begins, "we welcome Amaryllis Storm to the rebel ranks. From this day on, she is no longer a mercenary or a stranger, but a part of this family. A sister." As I stand there inwardly cringing, she turns to me and, with a small bow, hands me a scroll. "As is customary, we will begin with the vow of loyalty."

Loyalty is not particularly my thing but, with a shrug, I take the parchment anyway. Unrolling it, I study the flowery-inked words. Wow, I think to myself, they honestly expect me to say this!? I glance over at Nicolo who's standing in the front row of the crowd. He rolls his eyes and mouths, "Get on with it."

I balloon my cheeks. Why not? If it'll keep them happy. "I vow to stand shoulder to shoulder with the rebels..." possibly, if it fits in with my plans, "to follow the orders of my commanding officers..." I don't think so, "and to do everything in my power to destroy the enemy." Okay, I'm happy to do that.

There is a muted cheer from the crowd, and everybody claps. Noticeably, they don't clap for very long. Looking out at them, I see hundreds of sceptical eyes. They don't trust me. I grunt. I don't blame them.

"Thank God that's over with," I say to Akiyo.

She grins manically. "Oh, it's not over yet," she says.

I watch as she pulls the poker from the embers. The blunted tip is glowing red and has been hammered into the crude shape of a six-pronged star. The rebels' emblem.

Bloody hell, I think. She's going to brand my wrist.

"Shouldn't there be one less prong?" I say, in a pathetic attempt at stalling her. "You know, now Golf Sector's been overrun."

She grins. "This might sting a little," she says in a scarily optimistic tone.

I suddenly find it difficult to swallow. The thought of the red-hot poker melting my skin is terrifying to me. I stumble back but my bottom hits the cowshed wall. "Can't you just draw it on?" I whimper. "In ink?"

"Draw it on!" Akiyo titters pitilessly. "Why would I want to do that? It would be no fun at all."

My eyes widen. No fun. No fun! The woman's a psychopath. "I don't think..."

She cuts off my protests my snatching my hand, twisting it, and stamping the poker's glowing tip to my tender skin. I yelp pathetically. Then my knees buckle and, with a cry, I drop to the trampled grass. There, I promptly throw up over Akiyo's sandaled feet.

My tutor peers down at me, a smirk playing at the corner of her lips. I expect her to be upset, angry, but she's not. Not in the slightest. But then, why would she be? She just discovered my Goyo-Goyuko. I'm frightened of fire.

"Welcome to the family, Two Seven," she says with a triumphant smile.

XXVII

The Skeleton Clock
1 month, 20 days, 2 hrs, 12 mins, 20 secs

"Is it hurting?" Akiyo asks.

I glare daggers at her. "Hurting!" I hiss. "You melted my skin! Yes, it's bloody hurting."

I'm standing on Level Six with my hand in a barrel of water in a futile attempt to stop the throbbing. There's just me and Akiyo here, the rest of the rebels having left to carry on preparing for the howler attack. Nicolo left too. He went up the gunroom to begin packing for the contest, although I suspect he's just as interested in chatting up the pretty girl who works there.

Akiyo sighs, mutters the word "Wimp" and then wanders over to a patch of herbs. When she returns, she's holding a purple flower. "It's lavender," she tells me, handing it to me. "Rub it on the burn. It'll help."

"I'd prefer to go in the MediPod," I tell her.

"No time," she says bluntly. "There's too much to do."

Reluctantly, I pull my hand out of the barrel and press the flower to my injured wrist. Amazingly, after only a few seconds, it begins to feel better.

"Sorry," she says.

My eyes widen in astonishment. I'm surprised she even knows the word.

"But it's important I did it. We had to show the rebels how - committed you were to the fight. I didn't enjoy doing it," she belatedly adds.

I say nothing, still remembering the glint in her eye when she stamped the red-hot poker to my flesh. She enjoyed it plenty.

"I need help," I tell her.

"Okay," she says, nodding slowly. "What with?"

"There's a little boy. He's a serf - well, he was. I rescued him. He's here with me in the Nest. He's staying in my room. If the Nest is overrun, can you get him out?"

I don't want to ask for her help, but there's nobody else. I can't ask Dorothy; the boy's still poorly and her cooking would probably kill him. The only other person I could turn to is Nicolo, but he's coming with me.

"Why is he so important to you?" she asks.

I shrug, attempting to lighten my answer. "He sort of reminds me of my brother," I say. "The howlers killed him."

"I see." She plays with the hem on her kimono. "I'll try," she says at last. "There's a secret tunnel running from this level to the foot of the hills. Tell the boy if the howlers get in to run down to Level Six and find me. I'll get him out through there."

Surprised, but awfully glad she's agreed to help me, I thank her. "He's a good kid," I tell her. "He'll do whatever you say."

"Then he must be very different to you," she responds with a grin.

I grin too and, for a second, it's almost as if we like each other. "So, any tips for the contest?"

"Simple. Stay away from Sniper Six Six."

"Is she that good?"

"Good! She's lethal. A predator." She sighs. "But she wasn't always that way. She grew up in a refugee camp. Her parents were killed by howlers so, being her grandmother, she was my responsibility. She was a good kid. Always happy. Kind too. Then, the day she turned seven, she vanished."

"Vanished! Where did she go?"

"I don't know. I still don't. But many years later, she turned up. By then, she was a sniper, the best in Victor Sector. I went to see her in her burrow on the enemy front, but she didn't know who I was. It was as if I'd been wiped from her memory."

I sit there, my mind whirling. I don't know what to say. Then, suddenly, I do. "When you visited her, did she get upset?"

"Very."

"And did her eyes glow yellow?"

"As yellow as yours did when you smashed up the dummy." She rubs her chin, her brow wrinkled up in a frown, contemplating me. "I see power in you, Amaryllis," I'm a little startled; she's never used my proper name before. Knowing this must be important, I listen intently. "I do not pretend to fully understand it but, if I may, I would like to offer you a little advice."

She eyes me warily and I nod for her to carry on.

"You must channel this - whatever it is, control it if you can or soon it will control you." She drops to a whisper. "But most importantly, you must not allow it to pick the targets for your bullets."

The Skeleton Clock

What is the 'it' she's referring to? The whisperer? Or possibly whatever it is that allows me to run, to jump, to shoot better than any other person I know. I smile blandly; my mind's a muddle but I cannot risk showing that to Akiyo. I know it seems she's trying to help me, but I do not trust her. I suspect she's simply probing for my second Goyo-Goyuko; a second way of hurting me. Deep down, I think she knows I'm truly her enemy and that soon, a week from now, a month from now, I'll be forced to kill her or she'll be forced to kill me.

For a second, I don't know how to respond. Then, from nowhere, I blurt out, "Why didn't you tell on me?"

Akiyo looks at me in puzzlement. "Sorry, I'm not following you."

My eyes shift momentarily to the Chestnut tree only a hundred feet away.

"Oh, yes." She shrugs. "It's not wrong to look for answers," she says.

"And will I find them there?" I press her. "Over by the tree?"

"Possibly." The corner of her lips twitch up; I think she's trying to smile. "But the answers you find will not change anything. You'll still be whatever it is you are."

"I still need to know," I persist.

She rubs her chin thoughtfully, gazing into nothingness. "A retina scan," she says at last. "It's the only way in."

So that's it! No wonder I couldn't find the door. Although now I'm presented with a new problem. Now I need to pluck out a rebel's eyeball.

Akiyo unfolds her limbs and hops to her feet. "It's time," she says. Her eyes flicker momentarily to the pond. "You never did jump it."

I spring up too. "No, I never did," I reply, squarely meeting her gaze.

With one last final bow to Akiyo, I set off up the steps to the top level. To the gunroom. There, I discover Nicolo chatting to the young, pimply-cheeked Armorer. Looking around, I see everything is now dust free and all the guns have been lined up in racks. She's even put them in alphabetical order! Crow, I think, must be delighted.

The Armorer hands me my rifle and, as I check it, she helps Nicolo to pack a rucksack. I'm surprised it's taking so long. The Corporal's been up here for hours; but he probably spent most of it chatting up the girl. They put in binoculars, a box of OxyPills and a high powered torch. A medical kit, scarily small, is fitted into the side pocket along with a compass and a handful of low velocity shells. When they slip off to the kitchen to get food, I do a little packing of my own, adding a box of high velocity shells – Anvils, Trigger called them – and a grenade.

Best to be prepared.

When they return - looking very pally I might add - Nicolo and I struggle into the Kevlar. It's a devil to get on - like putting socks on wet feet - but it's worth it, the cloth so tightly woven it'll stop a knife and most bullets. It's surprisingly comfortable too; even the helmets fit perfectly.

Nicolo thanks the Armorer for her help. She hugs him tightly, but all I get is a perfunctory nod. Not that I'm jealous, I tell myself. No, not at all. Then we set off to the hanger.

I'm surprised to find the corridor packed with rebel troops. As we walk by them, they cheer and slap us on the back. "Good luck," they shout. "We'll be watching."

Oh yes! I forgot. They'll be following our every move on a big screen Crow's put up in the canteen. I'm going to be a film star!

I find it all mind-boggling. The howlers are only a day's march from here and the only thing the rebels seem interested in is this stupid contest. Still, seeing so many shining eyes, I wonder if Crow might be right. Possibly if they see me battling it out with a bunch of snipers, they'll want to battle it out too. They'll want to keep fighting on. It suddenly occurs to me that, in a strange way, I'm responsible for these people. It is not a comfortable feeling so, with an angry shrug, I throw it off.

After successfully jostling our way through the crowded corridor, we enter the hangar. Over by one of the helicopters there's Atchoo. He's got Twig with him. Excellent. Yesterday, when I suspected we would soon be going, I called in on the doctor and asked him to bring the boy up to the hangar to say a proper goodbye. I'm surprised to see Crow's there too, his hand resting on the boy's shoulder.

"All set?" the major calls to us as we trudge over.

We stop in front of them. "I think so," is my curt reply.

"Excellent." His favorite word. "And do you have a plan?" he asks me.

"The belltower," I say.

"My thoughts exactly," he says waggling his annoyingly short index finger at me. "High up, excellent visibility. From up there, you'll pick them all off in no time." He rubs his chin thoughtfully. "Of course, the other snipers will soon work that out too. What if..."

"I'm going to get there first," I interrupt him.

He nods. "Then all there is for me to say is, the very best of luck. I'll be watching," he adds with a cold smile.

I say nothing. There's nothing to say.

With a click of his heels, he turns to Nicolo. "And the very best of luck to you too, Corporal. And, er, don't forget what I told you."

"No, Sir, I won't," the Corporal answers, snapping off a smart salute.

I scowl. What, I wonder, is the major up to now.

My distrustful thoughts are interrupted by Twig gripping hold of my hand. I drop to my knees and, playfully, pinch his cheek. He responds by hugging me as tightly as he can, burying his cheek into my neck. I'm surprised by how strong he now is; he must be getting better. "If the Nest is overrun," I whisper, "get down to Level Six. There's a tunnel there; a way out. Akiyo will show it to you."

"I'll find her," he says, whispering too. He knows Crow's listening and he must sense I don't trust him.

Letting the boy go, I stand back up and turn to the doctor. But before I can say anything, he holds up his hand. "Don't fret," he says, "I'll see he gets the Devil's Dust."

"A little less every day," I sternly remind him.

"Yes, yes," he rolls his eyes, "I won't forget."

I thank him with the ghost of a smile. Possibly, the doctor's not such a plank after all.

I shoulder my rifle and follow Nicolo over to the helicopter. The ramp at the back's been opened so we walk up it. But, halfway to the top, Crow calls my name. When I turn to him, I see he's now standing directly behind Twig, his hands resting on the boy's shoulders. "I'll keep my eye on him," he says, giving the boy a little shake.

To anybody listening, his words must seem innocent. Even kindly. But I know the truth. When he tells me he'll keep his eye on the boy, what he's really saying is, if you don't win, the boy will suffer.

"Message understood," I murmur.

The twin rotors begin to spin, so I hurry up the ramp and sit down, buckling myself in. The helicopter lifts off. Then, vibrating alarmingly, the nose dips and we fly out of the hangar door.

Settling back for the long flight, I look over at Nicolo. He's sitting opposite me, checking over the contents of the medical kit. "What was Crow referring to back in the hanger?" I shout.

"Major Crow," he corrects me for the umpteenth time.

I shoot him my 'whatever' look.

"I want to know," I tell him.

"Nothing much," he says offhandedly. He throws me two OxyPills and I pop them in my mouth. "He's been helping me that's all."

"Helping you?"

"Yes. he's a spotter - or, he was. He's been showing me how to do it. You know, how to work out wind speed, and how far it is to a target. That sort of stuff."

"Oh, I see." I remember my attempts at helping him were a total disaster. It seems I'm just not a very good teacher. "That's good," I say. And it is. I'm going to need all the help I can get.

"He even showed me how to work out bullet drop."

"Did he know." I think for a second. "A nine millimeter bullet traveling a hundred feet."

"It'll drop just over a foot," he instantly says.

I nod. "Correct." Then, rather childishly, I add, "The girl in the gunroom will be very impressed."

"Sorry?"

"Don't be," I say. I begin to fiddle with the trigger on my rifle.

"There's nothing going on between Cheryl and me."

"Oh, it's Cheryl, is it."

"Amaryllis..."

"It's got nothing to do with me," I say, lying down. "Now, I need to get a little shuteye. Tomorrow is going to be a very long day." I roll over, turning my back to him and silently congratulating myself for getting in the last word.

Although the burn on my hand is still stinging, within seconds the helicopter rocks me to sleep. It's almost as if my body knows it needs rest if it's to get through the next few days. Seven hours later, Nicolo wafts a cup of coffee under my nostrils and I sit up. I see he's covered me in a blanket. A little embarrassed, I thank him.

"No problem," he says. "You were shivering so..." He shrugs and, looking just as embarrassed as me, hands me the coffee.

There's a sudden blast of static from the tannoy, saving me from trying to think of what to say next. "This is the flight deck," the anonymous pilot says. "In a few seconds we'll be coming up on the wall. I thought you might be interested."

Interested! You bet I am. Trying not to spill my coffee, I I hurry over to the closest window. Peering out, I see it's almost dawn, the sun climbing up over the hills in a blaze of vibrant reds and egg-yolk yellows. Although we've been flying all night, the land here looks no different to the land in Zulu Sector. Desert. All I see is desert. And the odd wiry-looking bush. God, it's depressing.

"Over there," says Nicolo who's at the next window along. "To your ten o'clock."

I look to my left and there it is. The wall. The only thing separating Cinis from the Wilds. Even from up here it looks tall; magnificent. It towers over the deserts, the steel surface, although ravished by age, glinting in the morning sun.

"I never thought I'd see it," says Nicolo.

I nod. Nor did I.

"We'll be coming up on Moscow soon," the pilot informs us. "Be ready."

"Let's do it," I say.

I fetch my helmet from off the floor and slip it over my red curls, buckling it under my chin. I then pick up my rifle. Nicolo pulls seven low velocity shells from the rucksack and hands them to me. I slip the first of them into the gun's barrel, cocking it. The rest I put in my pocket.

I feel the helicopter suddenly lurch, coming to a stop. Briskly, I wipe the grubby window with my sleeve and peer out. The helicopter's hovering over a dry riverbed that runs parallel to the Kremlin's south wall. The Borovitskaya Tower is to my left. It's fatter, more dumpy-looking than the other towers, the red-bricked walls topped by a tall, green steeple. As soon as the helicopter lands, we must get in there. But I'm not planning on staying for long. My gaze shifts north, to the belltower and to the belfry strutting up into the sky. That's where I want to be; from there I'll see everything.

I see four other helicopters hovering over the crumbling city. The closest of them is only a hundred feet away. There's a girl crouched in the doorway of it; like me I see she's dressed in full Kevlar, a long-barreled rifle slung over her shoulder. She lifts her hand and, for a second, I think she's going to wave to me. But no, she pretends to shoot me with her index finger.

I wonder if this is Akiyo's granddaughter, Sniper Six Six. Well, whoever she is, I see she intends to win.

"Hold on!" the pilot calls over the tannoy. "I'm taking her down."

The Chinook plummets, my stomach rising up into my throat. Determined not throw up, I focus on the glowing, red digits on the helicopter's clock. Only sixty seconds to go until the contest begins.

Nicolo, who's hunkered down in the doorway next to me, is adjusting the buckle on his rucksack. I switch on the

S-TOX on my wrist. I'm returning to a world of toxic gas and slugs determined to invade my body. I'm going to need it.

I elbow the Corporal in the ribs. "Remember," I yell, "when we get out the door, we go for the tower. No sightseeing."

He eyes me quizzically, making a show of rubbing his side. "Why the rush?" he asks. "They won't shoot. Not until the contest begins."

"I'm a sniper," I reply coldly. "Snipers never stay out in the open. Ever."

He nods. "Got it."

Good. He's listening to me. The last thing I need is a spotter who won't do as he's told.

Crouching there, clutching my rifle, I feel my many problems crowding in on me. My inability to interrogate Crow, still not knowing what's on Level Seven, and the biggest problem of all, the ever-present Lily snapping at my heels. But, if I can win this contest, I'll be a step closer to solving a lot of them. I cock my gun, the thump of the bolt driving the problems from my mind.

Time to go to work.

The helicopter's wheels hit the deck with a terrific jolt and, instantly, we jump out of the door. I look for the tower but, annoyingly, it's lost in the swirling dust kicked up by the helicopter's rotors. Blast! I should have thought of that.

As I stand there trying to work out which way to go, a bullet zips by me, ricocheting off a rock by my boot.

"Who's shooting?" Nicolo yells. "It's not allowed," he huffs.

Wildly, I hunt the swirling dust for my enemy. I'm just as confused as the boy is. How did another sniper get eyes on us so fast? But there's no time to discuss it now. If I'm not mistaken, that bullet was high velocity; if it had hit us, it would have ripped through our Kevlar armor as if it was paper.

The helicopter's now climbing away and the dust is settling. That's good news - and bad. The good news is, we can now get to cover. The bad news is whoever's doing the shooting can now see us. The tower's fifty feet away at the end of a cobbled path. Thankfully, the path is strewn with craters; if we use them for cover we might make it.

"Go, go, go," I cry, pushing Nicolo brutally in the back.

Then, just when things can't get any worse, they do. A rocket shoots up into the sky, hitting the underbelly of our helicopter and destroying it in a flash of blinding light. A second later, the other four helicopters explode too.

Then it hits me. It hits me so hard I almost stop running. Almost. This isn't the work of another rebel sniper. This is a howler ambush!

Using the craters for cover, we zigzag over to the tower. When we get to the door, I don't bother with the lock, lifting up my foot and kicking it open. Then, as bullets ricochet off the tower walls, we tumble through the doorway.

In a spaghetti tangle of arms and legs, we lay there. "What the hell's going on?" pants Nicolo.

Untangling myself, I kick the door shut. "I wish I knew," I reply. But I do know this. This contest is no longer about winning...

The Skeleton Clock

...it's about staying alive.

Part III
Hidden Enemy

XXVIII

The Skeleton Clock
1 month, 18 days, 15 hrs, 44 mins, 50 secs

Rubbing my battered elbows, I slowly sit up. There's not much to see in the tower, just lots of dust and crumbling, red-bricked walls. The floor is tiled and richly decorated with flowers, but a lot of it is missing and the rest is riddled with cracks. Glancing up, I see there's not even a window, the only light coming in through a jagged hole in the roof. Nicolo, who's kneeling next to me, pulls the rucksack off his back and begins rummaging through it. He pulls out the torch.

"Don't," I whisper urgently. "Not yet."

Clambering to my feet, I creep over to the door we just fell through; the only door in the tower. It's too risky to open it, but I spy a tiny crack in the wood by the broken lock. Warily, I put my eye to it and peer out. There's not a lot to see, just a grey, swirling fog as if a blanket has been thrown over the door. I sniff, smelling smoke. It must be coming from the burning helicopters.

"Hello, Amaryllis," Lily whispers in my skull.

I almost jump out of my skin. So it's her who's doing all the shooting!

"Can't you see me?" she mocks me.

No, I think to myself, I can't. But if I can't see you, you can't see me. Thankfully, this seems to shut her up.

I turn back to see Nicolo has now moved and is huddled up in the corner of the room, his knees pulled up to his chin. Keeping low, I scamper over to him. "I have a plan," I tell him.

"So do I," he says with a misery-filled sniff. "Stay here and not get shot."

I chuckle. He's joking. Then, little by little, my grin morphs into a scowl. Or possibly not. "We must get to the belltower," I tell him sternly.

The Corporal's eyes widen in horror. "But, but - that's nuts! The howlers just took out the helicopters. There must be hundreds of them out there. Hundreds! No, we stay hidden. Everything that happens here is being transmitted to the Nests, so the rebels will know the helicopters were shot down. They'll send help."

I answer him with a scornful roll of my eyes. I remember thinking how gutsy he was when he went to help Trigger when Lily shot him. And now here he is cowering in a corner. What the hell happened? "I thought you wanted to inspire the rebels to fight on."

"I do," he spits angrily, my scorn not lost on him. "But everything's different now. We didn't plan for this. We didn't plan on being ambushed."

I drop to the floor, resting my gun on my knees. "War's unpredictable." I say this gently; I'm going to need him if I want to win this thing, and I don't think yelling is going to help. "To you, being attacked by howlers is a setback. But to me, it's an opportunity."

We lock eyes; a battle of wills. Then curiosity gets the better of him. "How?" he asks.

"If the rebels send a helicopter, how long until it gets here?"

He frowns, thinking it over. "Difficult to say. Yankee Sector is the closest, so they'll be coming from there. A Chinook can travel 300 kilometers per hour. Yankee's 2,000 kilometers from here. A 1/2 hour to prep the crew, then 6 1/2 hours flying time."

"So, if there's no problem with the helicopter, help should be here in seven hours?"

He nods.

"Perfect." Although I suspect it'll be much longer. A perfectly working Chinook might bomb along at 300 kph, but not the rust buckets the rebels fly. "The belltower is two kilometers from here. All we need to do is get there, set up, and shoot the other snipers when they run for the helicopter." I grin wickedly. "Pop! Pop! Pop! Contest won."

The Corporal's jaw drops open. "Two Seven! We can't."

"Why not?"

"Why not! Well, it's not very, you know..."

"No."

"It's not very sporting."

"Sporting!" I laugh. "Crow didn't send me here to be sporting. He sent me here to win. Anyway, it'll not kill them, it'll just - sting a little."

The Corporal nods slowly. "But the howlers?"

"Forget the howlers," I growl. "If they get in the way, I'll shoot them. Remember, they'll not be protected by Kevlar so even a low velocity bullet with a blunted tip will do the job." I know there's a box of Anvils in his rucksack, but I'm saving them for Lily.

Nicolo emits a long sigh and stuffs his hands deep into his pockets. "I don't know," he says. "It's so risky."

Risky! I stuff my hands in my pockets too. I'm not cold; it's to stop myself from strangling him. Did he honestly think traveling to the Wilds and fighting the best snipers in the rebel army was going to be risk free? "You must trust me, Corporal," I say as calmly as I can. "I know what I'm doing."

"Okay," he says at last. He looks up. "So, how do we get from this tower to the belltower and not get shot?"

I grin. Much better. Shuffling closer to him, I begin to draw a map on the dusty floor with my trigger finger. "To get there we must first get to the Palace. Agreed?"

"Agreed."

"This is us." I draw a wonky-looking cross to show him. "And this," I draw a second cross, "is the door we need to get to. Sadly, there's not much cover between them. Just a crater here," I draw a circle by the tower, "and a crater over here." I draw a second circle.

The Corporal frowns deeply, idly rubbing his now perfect cheek. I suddenly wonder if that's why he wants to stay hidden in the tower. He's frightened of getting another scar. "It must be a hundred feet," he says. "We'll be in the open for a long time. We'll be sitting ducks."

"It's closer to two hundred," I tell him evenly.

"Oh, well, that's much better," he says, throwing up his hands. "I enjoy a challenge."

277

"There's good news too. There's so much smoke coming from the crashed helicopters, visibility is almost zero. I don't think she'll see us."

"She?"

For a second, I say nothing, annoyed by my slip. Then I shrug. It's probably for the best; I can't keep it a secret forever. My eyes slowly travel the walls, looking for...

"There's no camera in here," Nicolo says.

Good. "The sniper's Lily, the sheriff of Zulu Sector."

The Corporal's eyebrows lift in astonishment. "How do you know?"

"I just do." I don't want him to know she's in my skull. "You must..."

"I get it, I get it. I must trust you."

"Yes."

Apart from a long, deep sigh, he says nothing. Taking his silence for agreement, I press on. "Speed is going to be everything. It's important to keep going no matter what happens. Don't stop for anything. ANYTHING!"

He nods.

"Say it," I insist.

"Don't stop for anything."

"And don't run directly to the door," I tell him. "Keep swerving and ducking, anything that'll keep her off balance. Remember, she's going to shoot where she expects you to be. The trick is not to be there."

"Got it."

I honestly hope so. If it is Lily and he's not 'got it', she'll shoot him between the eyes before he gets ten feet.

"How do you know it's just her?" he asks. "There could be two or three snipers out there."

"I can tell by the trajectory of the bullets. They were all coming in from the northwest at a 45 degree angle."

"So she's high up."

I nod. "And I'd say she's two kilometers away."

The Corporal frowns. I watch him, interested to see if he'll work it out. Suddenly, his eyes widen. He's got it. "She must be in the belltower," he says.

I nod.

"But if she's in there, how will we get in there?"

"I don't know," I say honestly. "But don't worry, I'll think of a way."

We check for worms – armpits, bellybuttons, feet – and pop two OxyPills. Then we walk over to the door. "Remember," I say, helping him on with his rucksack, "don't stop for anything. Even if I'm hit, keep going. If you try to help me, she'll simply shoot you too."

"And if I'm hit?"

"I'll try not to step on your corpse as I run by."

"Thanks."

I'm suddenly reminded of a joke Splinter told me a few months ago. Two rebels were walking along a street when suddenly a howler jumps out of them. The first rebel drops to a knee, lacing up his boots. 'Why bother?' says the second rebel. 'you'll never outrun a howler.' 'I don't need to,' the first rebel answers. 'I just need to outrun you.'

"On three then." I rest my hand on the doorknob. "One, two..."

"Was it Lily who shot Trigger?"

For a second, I don't answer, keeping my eyes locked on the door. The Corporal's no fool. "Yes," I finally say, "I think so."

"She's good then."

"Not good, no." I turn to look at him. "To shoot Trigger from there is, well, astonishing. It took 3 1/2 seconds for the bullet to get from her to him. 3 1/2 seconds! And he was moving. Moving!" I balloon my cheeks. "I don't even know how she did it."

"So she's better than you."

"I wouldn't say she's - ," I stop. Who am I kidding? "Yes, she's much better."

The boy nods. "Okay, Just so I know." He grins at me. I grin back. He seems to be over his shock which is good news. I'm going to need his help if I'm going to kill a sharpshooter as skilled as this howler.

I yank open the door and rush out into the swirling smoke. Twisting and turning, dropping low, I do everything I can think of to stop Lily getting me in her sights. Half way there and she's still not taken a shot. I wonder if it's the smoking helicopters preventing her or she's simply playing with me; holding off until I'm almost there. Then she'll pull the trigger.

After thirty seconds of running as fast as I can, I see the wall. Amazingly, I see the door too. But I don't stop, running into it and hitting it like a battering ram with my shoulder. But this door is big, the wood thick, and I ricochet off, landing with a jolt on my backside. Scrambling to my feet, I grapple for the doorknob and twist. No luck. It's rusted up.

Nicolo skids to a stop next to me. "What happened to not stopping?" he yells.

Smartass! "It's the door," I growl back. "I can't get it open."

A bullet thumps into the wood, showering us with splinters. I turn to see the smoke is much thinner now; the helicopters must be almost burnt out. I look up and, yes, just as I thought, I can now see the belltower. If I can see her, she can see me. And there's no cover – anywhere!

"Together," pants the Corporal.

I scowl, not getting it. "What?"

"You and I." He pulls me away from the door. "We'll ram it together."

"Oh, okay," I say, shrugging his hand off. I don't remember ever doing anything together with anybody. It's always just been me. But he's right. Together's the only way.

We run at the door, smacking into it with our shoulders. This time, the wood splinters, the lock ripping away, and we tumble into the Palace.

"Sort of getting sick of falling through doorways," the Corporal mutters, scrambling to his feet.

I scramble up too, slamming the door shut with the heel of my foot. I then toss the compass to Nicolo. "According to Crow..."

"Major Crow."

I roll my eyes. "What, even here!?"

He nods to the door. I turn to look and see, just over it, there's a lens peeping out of the wall. Oh yes, I forgot. I'm on TV.

"According to Major Crow, the Palace's a labyrinth of endless corridors and rooms. It's important we keep going north and don't get lost."

The Corporal begins fiddling with the compass. "And that's my job."

"Correct."

He slowly turns on the spot, stopping when the needle hovers over north. "And what will you be doing?" he asks.

"My job's to shoot any howlers or snipers who get in the way."

"Excellent plan," he says.

"Drop low if we go by a window," I tell him.

"Don't worry," he says fervently, "I will." He frowns. "How do you think she got here? Howlers don't fly helicopters. Or do they?"

I respond with a lopsided twist of my lips, shorthand for 'hell no'. I think back to when we were attacked by the crows. She turned up there too. How is she doing it, I wonder. She's not got wings. Although I don't know how she got here, I suspect I know why she's here. She's here for me. If the spy, Buddy, reported back to her, she'll know I didn't kill Crow and she'll know I still don't know what's hidden on Level Seven. She'll be spitting mad. But I don't tell the Corporal any of this. How can I when Crow's listening to my every word. "Help will be here in seven hours, right?"

He nods and checks his watch. "I got 0830."

"So they'll be here at 1530?"

He nods.

The Skeleton Clock

I step up to the lens. It twirls, trying to focus in on me. "Did you catch that, Major Crow?" I say testily. "I'm expecting the helicopter by 1530." To back up my words, I cock my gun. "Don't be late." I then turn back to the Corporal. "We'd better get a shift on. We've got seven hours to get to the belltower, shoot Lily, and get set up."

XXIX

The Skeleton Clock

1 month, 18 days, 14 hrs, 52 mins, 40 secs

With my rifle cradled in my hands and the compass cradled in Nicolo's, we set off through the dusty corridors of the Palace. Annoyingly, the mosaic-patterned floor is tiled, the click of our boots on the hard surface echoing off the tall, cracked walls. It's so awfully loud, I'm tempted to go barefoot - and order Nicolo to do the same. But with so many shards of glass on the floor from the broken windows, our feet would be cut to shreds.

As we creep by another of Crow's swirling cameras - they seem to be everywhere - I shiver. It's not because I'm being watched; although it is rather unsettling. And it's not because I'm cold; it must be over thirty degrees in here. No, I'm shivering because I don't like this place. The endless corridors smell musty, the dust kicked up by our boots tickling my nose. And, wherever I look, I see caved-in walls with yellowed skeletons, the skin tight like stretched parchment, peeking out of the rubble.

I nudge the boy. "What is this place?" I ask him.

"This is where the president of the USSR lived," he tells me. "But, as you can see, a lot of it was destroyed in World War Three."

Passing another window, we duck down, not wanting to give Lily - or any of the rebel snipers - anything to shoot at.

"Who was the fighting between?" I ask him. I don't know much about the war. But I do know it started before the comet struck.

"China and the USSR. Towards the end, NATO got involved too. Nobody knows why they were fighting and there's nobody left who remembers now. It's not important. The comet put a stop to it."

I'm reluctantly impressed. How is it he knows all this stuff? Then I remember he went to school in the Nest. I suspect it's much better than the school I went to in the Netty.

"So nobody won," I say.

"The comet won," he answers dryly. "When it hit South America in 2032 it killed almost everybody. The few survivors who were left were too hungry to fight on."

I sigh at the irony of it all. In many ways, the comet saved the planet.

Creeping down yet another seemingly endless corridor, we finally turn left, through an oval-topped door and into a room. It's huge and rather splendid-looking, the walls adorned with thick, velvet wallpaper, the colours still vibrant despite the years. The floor is no longer tiled but hidden under a plush, red carpet and, although it's worn and discoloured, it still feels soft under my boots. I look up to see much of the roof has collapsed, crows nesting in the exposed timbers.

"Look," says Nicolo. "Over there. There's a door."

I nod, ushering him over to it. I feel exposed in here. Vulnerable. There are too many windows and too many dark corners for enemy snipers to hide in.

"Oh," says the boy, stopping by a hill of cobwebby timbers and turning to me, "I forgot to tell you. Today's August 7th and it's your birthday."

I stop too, accepting the news with a deep frown. "I thought it was top secret," I say, wondering if he's just messing with me.

"It is." Then, with a shrug, he adds "Or, it was. Yesterday, Major Crow told me it was okay to tell you so I'm, er, telling you." He grins wildly. "Happy birthday!"

"I'm seventeen?"

"Yep. Hey!" He snaps his fingers almost dropping the compass. "Now you can legally drive."

"That would be difficult," I reply coldly. "No cars."

He scowls thoughtfully. "Tanks!" he suddenly says, his face brightening. "We have tanks."

"Fool," I say, suppressing a smile. Although driving a tank sounds like a lot of fun. "Where's my cake?" I ask him.

"Sorry," he says. "I didn't want it to get all smashed up in my rucksack. But don't worry, I asked Dorothy to bake you one. It'll be there when we get back to the Nest. We'll share it."

"Okay, it's a date," I say without thinking.

His eyes widen. "A date!"

"Oh, em, no," I bluster, my cheeks reddening, "not a..."

"A date it is!" He winks at me, checks the compass, turns, and sets off through the room.

"Why was it a secret in the first place?" I call after him.

"I don't know," he calls back. "Ask Major Crow. He'll know."

I intend to, I think to myself. I watch him as he clambers over the pile of broken timbers. He seems so dependable now, so - together. I want to trust him but I know I can't. He assured me there was no Level Seven. He told me he'd grown up in the Nest and knew every part of it. Yet, I discovered the entrance after being there only a week. He has to know. That or he's incredibly stupid. And I don't think he is. Still, a date's a date. And a girl can't be too picky, not in a world where pretty much everybody has been turned into a bloodthirsty monster.

I sigh, check the safety's off on my rifle, and set off after him.

It's only as we approach the door that I spot the torch resting on the carpet. It's turned on, standing upright, perfectly balanced, the light playing on the dusty crystals of a chandelier hanging over it.

I inhale sharply. Instantly I'm on high alert, the butt of my gun pressed into my shoulder, my finger curling around the trigger as I scan the room for my enemy.

"What's this doing here?" Nicolo asks me, walking over to the torch.

Is he crazy? "No," I hiss. "Don't!" But he's not listening and, with a shrug, he picks it up.

I watch in horror as a loop of rope tightens around his left ankle and he's hoisted up into the air. He dangles there, cursing loudly and crying out for help.

There's a sudden, almost inaudible 'Click'. To most people, it's an innocent sound and not frightening at all. But to me, a girl who's spent her life dodging bullets, it's the most frightening sound I know. It's the sound of a safety catch being flicked off.

Sick to my stomach, I twirl. But I know it's over. And there's nothing I can do about it. This is a trap; a trap so ridiculously simple, a child could have set it. And the legendary Sniper Two Seven, the hero of Zulu Sector, just fell for it. And, thanks to Crow's cameras, every rebel saw!

"Hold it!"

I stop, a little surprised to have not been shot.

"Twitch and I'll drop you. I'll not miss, Two Seven. Not from here."

For a second, I'm frightened it's Lily. It's not. The warning is followed out of the shadows by a tall, willowy-looking girl. She's strikingly pretty with large, puppy-dog eyes and cheeks so freckled the brown spots almost overlap. Similar to me, she's dressed in full combat Kevlar and she's carrying a rifle, the tip of the barrel level with my belly.

I grind my heels into the carpet, furious with myself for being so stupid. But there's nothing I can do; I'm totally at her mercy. "Okay, okay," I say, lowering my own rifle and pulling off my helmet. "For God's sake, don't shoot. At this distance, you'll kill me."

She scowls and, for a second, she looks confused. Then, she gets it. When Crow thought up this little game of his, he planned for the snipers to be shooting each other from hundreds of feet away. Not twenty! If she pulls the trigger now, the Kevlar won't stop the bullet. She'll kill me.

"Why should I care?" she snarls, her words husky and peppered with splinters. She steps closer to me. "You murdered Casper, my spotter. Don't deny it. And it wasn't a low velocity bullet you shot him with."

Lily, I think to myself with a curse. She's been busy. "I didn't kill Casper," I tell her, looking her directly in the eyes. "There's a howler in the belltower. It must have been her. She's been taking pot shots at us too."

The girl's scowl deepens. "How do you know it's a her?"

I mentally kick myself. Another blunder. It's becoming quite a habit. But I manage to cover my stupidity with a wry smile. "She's a very good shot," I tell her. "It must be a her."

"Sorry to interrupt," says Nicolo, who I see is still dangling by the rope, "But can you CUT ME DOWN! My leg's killing me."

"Shut up," spits the girl, not even bothering to look at him.

My eyes widen. Wow, she's almost as nasty as I am.

"Why should I trust you?" she says.

"Look, I'll prove it to you." I eject the shell from my rifle and hold it out for her to see. "Check it," I say. "You'll see it's low velocity." I'm just hoping she'll not want to check Nicolo's rucksack where I hid the box of Anvils. And the grenade!

She eyes me distrustfully. "Throw it here," she barks.

With a shrug, I toss it over to her. I watch as she inspects it. She seems to be in no hurry, turning it over and over in her hand. "It looks - okay," she finally admits, slowly lowering her weapon.

I snap my fingers. "The bullet. I want it back. An empty rifle is no good to me."

With a hint of a smile, she lobs it back over. I instantly rechamber it. I'm tempted to shoot her in the foot. Then I'd be another step closer to winning the contest and getting back to the Nest. But, annoyingly, there's a camera poking out of the wall, the tiny light over the lens blinking green. I don't think the rebels would be too impressed if I shot her now.

I'm a little disconcerted when she suddenly pulls a dagger from off her belt. It's long and evil-looking with a serrated blade. Holding it in her fist, she walks over to where Nicolo is still dangling.

"Hang on," I say, hurrying after her. But I need not worry. She simply cuts the rope holding him and he falls to the floor with a thump.

"Sniper Two Seven, yes?" she says, turning back to me. Her accent is oddly robotic, as if she's simply reciting the words and is not particularly interested in what she's saying.

"Yes," I reply. I see no advantage in lying.

She pulls a stray curl away from her eyes and, for a split second, I spy a long, jagged scar on her temple. It's identical to the scar on mine.

"I'm Sniper One Zero One from Kilo Sector. Do you know what is, er," she falters as if she's not been programmed with the right words, "happening?" she finally says.

"We were ambushed by howlers," I tell her. "But I don't know how many. And I don't know why."

"Howlers! But this is the Wilds. They don't go here."

"It seems they do now," I say. "What happened to your spotter?" I ask her.

She rubs her eyes with a balled-up fist. "When we ran from the tower he was killed." I see her eyes brim with pent-up fury. Possibly she's not as robotic as I first thought. "He only got a few feet. As you say, this howler is a very good shot."

I remember how Lily shot the Armorer from 5,327 feet away. Shooting the spotter would have been child's play for her.

"I'm, er, sorry," I say limply.

"Whoever did it will be sorry," the sniper growls, her eyes glowing yellow.

So it's not just me and (according to Akiyo) Sniper Six Six!

"The contest's over, yes?" She picks up the torch, turns it off, and stuffs it in a rucksack. "We must work together. Attack the belltower and kill the howler."

I nod slowly. "Okay," I say. She wants to work together! Now there's a novel thought.

"We must find Sniper Six Six," she says. "She's the best there is. No offense," she adds with an unapologetic smile.

"Just Sniper Six Six?" asks Nicolo who, up until now, has been moodily rubbing his injured ankle. "Why not Sniper Zero Seven and Three Six Nine? Can't they help too?"

I turn to him, rewarding his suggestion with an icy stare. My plan is to shoot the rest of the snipers when they run for the helicopter, not to become best pals with them. Next, he'll be suggesting we hold hands and sing songs around a campfire.

"They were killed," the girl says.

Stunned, I lock eyes with her. "But, but – HOW?" I stutter. "Were they shot too?"

"No." Her robotic tone is jaded now as if her battery is running low. "When the helicopters were hit, they crashed down on top of them. The spotters were killed too," she adds with a shudder. "I saw everything."

My stomach churns sickeningly. Two snipers, two spotters, and who knows how many pilots, all murdered. And for what? So Lily can show off her shooting skills. I think of the Anvil bullets hidden in Nicolo's rucksack. When I get this howler in my sights, I'm going to relish pulling the trigger. "So there's just you, me and Sniper Six Six left?" I ask her.

She nods.

In a sick sort of way, this is good news. I want to win this contest, get back to the Nest and check out Level Seven. And I'm now two steps closer to my goal. But, if I'm totally honest with myself, I want to know how good I am. I want to know if I'm the best sniper in the rebel army. And this is not the way to do it. Lily's doing all the work for me.

Staring at the girl, I try to decide what to do. I'm surprised to see she's trembling, and her cheeks look milky and cold. She must be in shock; that, or she's pretending to be. Is she hoping I'll feel sorry for her? That I'll forget how lethal she is and turn my back on her? Not bloody likely.

I glance over at Nicolo to see what he thinks. "We need all the help we can get," he says.

He's right. Annoyingly. Outwitting and outshooting Lily is going to be difficult, but with the help of another sniper, possibly two, it shouldn't be a problem. Although, from the way Nicolo's looking all starry-eyed at the girl, I suspect it's not her sniper skills that's won him over.

"Okay," I say, "we'll try to work together." I put a lot of emphasis on the word 'try'. "But only until we shoot the howler. After that, the contest's back on. Got it?"

She answers me with a lazy shrug. "Whatever," she says. "This contest's of no interest to me. It's all - politics." She spits the word. "My Nest commander insisted I enter, but I don't know why. I'm in this war for one reason. To kill howlers. They murdered my brother, Benji."

I stand there, my mouth hanging open, my mind doing cartwheels as I attempt to comprehend her words. The howlers murdered her brother too. And his name was Benji! But that's, that's – IMPOSSIBLE!

Seeming not to notice how shocked I am, she extends her hand and walks over to me. "Let's, em –," she frowns, "- now, how do you say it? Oh, yes. Let's shake on it, yes?"

For a spit second, I think I see a shift in her eyes, a kind of cold mocking that she blinks away as soon as I spot it. As she steps up to me, I look down at her offered hand. Only then do I see the glint of steel. It suddenly occurs to me, I don't remember seeing her put away the knife.

"Amaryllis!" calls out Nicolo in warning. He's seen it too.

She's only in front of the window for a split second. But, for Lily, a split second is all the time in the world. The bullet hits her in the back of the neck, driving her into my arms. Then, very slowly, she slithers down my body, coming to a rest in a pool of blood by my feet.

XXX

The Skeleton Clock
1 month, 18 days, 13 hrs, 43 mins, 11 secs

As I peer down in horror at Sniper One Zero One's inert body, I'm almost hypnotised by the flow of blood and I find myself wondering if, like mine, it's 'unknown' too. I feel hands gripping me. Nicolo's. But, for once, I don't shake them off, allowing him to drag me away from the distinct danger of a second bullet flying through the window. But, still, I keep looking back; I can't help it, my darting eyes zooming in on the steel object still clutched in her hand. It is the knife! Was she going to stab me then? Was her story of wanting to work together, of not being interested in who won the contest, was it all just an elaborate ruse to get closer to me so she could stick me with it? I remember Akiyo telling me back in the Nest how the only thing snipers know how to do is to kill. It seems she's right. And, if it wasn't for Lily, my sworn enemy, and her excellent marksmanship, it would be me lying on the floor; it would be my 'unknown' blood pumping out.

Standing there, trembling, icy cold in spite of the sun's scorching rays flooding the room, I recall Crow's words to me in the Control Room. "The enemy is not always who you think it is." Could he possibly have been referring to Lily? Did he know she'd be here? Was he trying to tell me she's not my enemy?

As my mind churns with endless whys, wheres and whens, a horrible feeling of loneliness engulfs me. I wanted to trust this girl, this sister sniper, so much, but it was foolish of me to even try. I should know better by now. I can't trust anybody. Then, like a speeding truck, it hits me. How much my life truly sucks. My knees unlock and, with a whimper, I drop to the floor. For the first time in my life, all I want to do is give up; all I want to do is sit here until the sand covers me over.

"Amaryllis!" It's Nicolo; he's gripping me by my elbow, trying to pull me up. "Amaryllis, let's go!"

"I - I can't," I snivel. And I'm not lying. Even sitting down, my legs feel like wobbly jelly. If I try to stand up, I'll just fall on my face.

Ignoring my pleas, he yanks me to my feet and literally drags me out of the room into a long, dark corridor. There, he lets me go. I drop to the floor like a sack of spuds. Resting my back on the wall, I pull my knees up to my chin and curl my arms around my hunched-up legs.

"Sorry," he says, nestling down by my elbow. "We were on camera in there so," he shrugs, "I didn't want the rebels to see you that way."

"It's okay," I reply. He's right. Collapsing to the floor in a shivering wreck is hardly inspiring.

The boy pulls off his rucksack and hunts through it, finding a canteen. He offers it to me. Gladly, I accept it, although, when I drink, my hand is shaking so much, most of it drips down my chin.

"Here, let me help." He covers my hands with his, steadying the canteen. Much better. Greedily, I gulp down the water.

"Did you see the knife?" he asks.

Handing the canteen back to him, I nod miserably. "Yes," I say. "She's still holding it."

"I don't get it," he says. "I thought she wanted to work with us."

"She was lying. She's a sniper, remember. A killer. Just like me. It's the only thing she – we, know how to do."

The boy's silent for a long time. I guess he's contemplating the fact that he's sitting in a dark corridor with a murderer. "I know it's difficult," he says at last, "but what you told me back in the tower, about this being an opportunity, you were right. Lily's doing the job for us, and now there's only you and Sniper Six Six left. We can win this thing."

"It's not important," I say. "Let Sniper Six Six win. Then she can go on Crow's mission, whatever the hell it is."

"But she'll miss the target."

"You don't get it, do you," I snap back. "Nobody can shoot a target 5,326 feet away. Nobody! It's impossible."

"You did."

"Nicolo..."

"Back in Sniper Camp. That's what Major Crow told us. Or was he lying?"

"No, but -," I sigh. "How many of Trigger's petrol drums have I hit? Go on! How many?"

"You got much closer yesterday."

I laugh jadedly. "Closer! It's not important how close I get. If I'm on target then I'm on target. If I'm not, I'm not. End of story. It's a miss. And don't forget, this is going to be a night shot and Crow thinks the target will be moving.

Trust me, it's impossible. Nobody can do it. At sniper camp, I just got lucky, that's all."

"Then you will have to get lucky for a second time," the boy says.

I roll my eyes. He's as obstinate as I am.

"I don't get you, Amaryllis. I never thought you were the giving up sort."

"I'm not," I growl, his words stinging.

"Then what is it? What's going on?" He rests his back on the wall too, uncomfortably close, our elbows touching. "Is it the howler in the belltower? Is she getting to you?"

I rest my chin on my knees, pressing my lips firmly together.

"Back in the tower, you told me to trust you," he says. "You must trust me too."

I snort mockingly. "Trusting people is difficult for me," I tell him. "And when I do try to, it never seems to work out. Anyway you'd not understand."

"Try me," he says.

Don't do it, I tell myself. Don't do it. He told me there's no Level Seven when I now know there is. He can't be trusted. Still, I can't help being drawn to this boy. I can tell he's broken. I can tell by the way his hands tremble and how he never looks anybody in the eyes. Even me. I sort of want to fix him. Which is odd as I'm not the fixing sort.

"Look," he says, "I lost my mom and dad to cancer when I was six years old, and I now sleep in a tiny, steel box. My life sucks. Whatever the problem is, I'll get it."

Up until now, we've been staring at the wall. But now he turns to me, his eyes finding mine. I think it's the first time he's ever looked at me - really looked at me - and, I must admit, it feels good. Why not, I think to myself. although the thought of confiding in anybody frightens me. The problem is I don't know how to do it. I'm stumped.

Nicolo seems to understand my difficulty. "Start at the beginning," he says.

Start the beginning. Right. "When Doctor Atchoo put me in the MediPod, it didn't recognize my blood type. It was unknown."

"So?"

"So, I'm -," I swallow, trying to push out the words, "- not human."

"You look human to me."

"Do I?" I say.

He nods, although I suspect he's just being kind.

"When I lose my temper or when I'm fighting for my life, my eyes glow yellow," I tell him. "And when I'm sick or injured I get better in almost no time at all. Do you remember me telling you I had five cancers? Five! But I still fought off three howlers in the forest and I didn't even get a scratch. I can run faster than you. I can jump higher than you. If I wanted to, I could punch a hole through a brick wall."

Nicolo is silent for a moment, his eyes hunting the corridor as if the answer is hidden under the piles of rubble.

"If I could just get down to Level Seven," I begin. "The answer's down there. I just know it is."

I feel the boy's body tensing up – a testimony to how close he's sitting to me. "There is no Level Seven," he barks.

"Yes, Nicolo, there is," I reply stubbornly. "And I think I discovered the way in."

"Think?"

"Know," I correct myself. "Akiyo confirmed it. Sort of."

The boy blows out his cheeks then, with a shrug, he says, "You think you'll find the answers there?"

"Yes, I do."

"Do you think it's got to do with Project Liberty?"

Surprised, I sit up. "How did..."

"On the helicopter when we first met," he interrupts me, "you asked me what it was."

"Oh, yes," I say, remembering. "You told me you didn't."

"I still don't. Why don't you enlighten me."

I shrug. "All I know is it's written in my file in Sniper Camp. I think it's got to do with my birthday and possibly my father."

The boy frowns. "There's no record of your father in your file at HQ. I'd know. As your controller, my job is to know every word of it. Do you remember him?"

"Sort of," I reply. "but it's all so," I sigh, "fuzzy. You know, out of focus. I can almost see him. Almost. But, then, the memory just slips away."

"Well, your birthday's no secret. It's today."

"But why's it been a secret for so long? And why tell me now?"

"I don't know," the boy says slowly. "But how's this for a plan? When this contest is over and we get back to the Nest, you and I will go hunt for this secret level together. We'll find the answers - together."

I eye him distrustfully. Why did he change his mind so suddenly, I wonder, and why is he offering to help me. What's in it for him? "Why are you helping me?" I ask him.

Why wouldn't I?"

I don't get it. "I don't get it," I say. "What's in it for you?"

He laughs. "Nothing," he says.

I feel my jaw harden. I don't like being laughed at.

"Okay, okay, Amaryllis, chill. Look, if I go down there with you and show you there's no Level Seven, I'm hoping you'll stop obsessing over it. Then you and I can focus on the mission - and saving the world," he adds with a grin. "Better?"

"Much better," I concede. "Just don't let me down." Which, even to me, sounds wrong. As if I think I'm doing him a favor by allowing him to go with me. So I quickly add, "Thank you." Followed by, "It gets sort of lonely doing everything on my own."

Very gently, almost if he's scared I'll hit him – which, with me, is always a distinct possibility – he puts his finger to my wet cheek, wiping away the wetness.

"Em, what are you doing?" I ask him.

It suddenly occurs to me how close he is. A very big part of me wants him to pull away. Another, even bigger part of me, wants him to get closer still.

"I was, em, thinking of kissing you," he says.

"Oh! Right! Um..."

"If you don't want me to..."

"No, no, I do." I back my words up with a fervent nod.

"Don't you want to know why I want to kiss you?" he says, resting his hand on my leg. "What's in it for me?"

"I don't need to," I reply. "I know what's in it for you."

With surprising gentleness, he puts his lips to mine. They feel hot, soft, taking tiny sips as if he's frightened of hurting me. God! Must a girl do everything. I yank him closer, pressing my mouth harder to his. I feel his teeth and taste the slightly salty flavor of his saliva. So this is kissing. Excellent!

"Wow!" he gasps when I finally allow him to pull away.

I can't help but grin. A 'Wow!' on my first kiss. Not bad. I must be a natural.

"Hungry?" he asks.

"Starving," I reply with vigor. I'm feeling much better. A good snog, it seems, is just what the doctor ordered.

I watch as he digs through his rucksack and pulls out a food parcel. To be honest, I'm a little disappointed. I've been referring to my lips being hungry, not my stomach. Still, I gladly accept a small bowl of beef strips and rice, and a bag of mixed nuts. Using plastic forks we tuck in; it's not too bad, although the beef's a little chewy.

When we finish, I watch, a little amused, as Nicolo packs everything up. There's rubble and shards of broken glass everywhere, and the boy's concerned about dropping litter.

He checks his compass. "All set?" he asks.

"I think so," I reply, scrambling to my feet. "Sorry I lost it back there. It's just..."

"Don't be," he interrupts me with a grin. It's a very 'toothy' sort of grin and, for the first time, I spot there's a chip in his front incisor. "Everybody needs a good cry now and then."

"I don't remember crying," I tell him stonily.

He digs into the front pocket of his rucksack and extracts a bottle of OxyPills. "Here," he says, unscrewing the cap and throwing me two of the orange-colored pills.

I thank him – although I'm still a little miffed by the crying remark – swallowing them down.

He checks his watch. "If the helicopter's on time, it'll be here in just under three hours."

I nod. It seems the boy's mind is back on the job, the kiss forgotten. "Then let's get going," I say.

Setting off down the corridor - and trying to ignore the crunch of the skeletons under my boots - I feel much, oh, I don't know, lighter I guess. As if, by sharing my problems with Nicolo – and a lot of saliva – it's helped to lift them a little way off my shoulders. But I didn't share everything with him; not by a long shot. I didn't tell him that, according to Lily, it's Janus who wants me to find the elusive Level Seven. And I didn't tell him Crow's responsible for my mother's death and, when I finish interrogating him, I plan to kill him. No, I didn't tell him any of that.

Turning a sharp corner, Nicolo elbows me. "You know, if Sniper One Zero One did intend to kill you, then the howler in the belltower saved your life."

Reluctantly, I nod. "Yes, she did," I reply. "But I don't think she spotted the knife, only the girl. Then she took the shot. Simple. If she saved my life, she did it by accident."

That must be what happened, I think to myself. It must be. Why would Lily save my life? It would make no sense. Anyway, there's no way she spotted the knife, not through a scope in under a second. But, as we clamber over another hill of rubble, Crow's words keep coming back to me. "The enemy is not always who you think it is."

For the next two hours, we work our way through the endless maze of corridors and rooms. Although Nicolo's compass keeps us going north, often as not we hit dead ends and are forced to backtrack. The clock's ticking and it's very frustrating. If we don't take out Lily before the helicopter gets here, she'll shoot it down. Every room we enter seems to get grander and grander but, after a while, I sort of get immune to the dusty chandeliers and the gilt-framed doors - just as I get immune to the skeletons crunching under my feet.

In one of the rooms we pass through, I see a small desk. On it, there's a silver-framed photo of a family. A mum, a dad and two children: a boy and a girl. Only a week ago, I would have grabbed it and added it to my 'pretend' family. But not now. Now, I don't I need to. Now, I have Nicolo and Twig. I know it's not much of a family - I hardly even know them - but it's better than nothing. Possibly it would be better if I do win this contest and go on the mission for Crow. Suddenly, I find myself caring. Suddenly I see a future for myself that's worth fighting for.

Finally, just as I begin to think Nicolo's got us totally lost, we turn a corner and there, in front of us, is a door. It's open, and beyond it I see the towering wall of the cathedral.

We did it!

But there's no time to celebrate. Just as I see the door, I see the silhouette of a girl standing not twenty feet away from it. Sniper Six Six! It must be.

This time, I'm not taking any chances. Dropping to my knee, I level my rifle at her chest and rest my finger on the trigger. But, just as I'm about to take the shot, the girl turns and looks at me.

"There's a howler in the belltower," she says. "and I know just how to get the cow."

XXXI

The Skeleton Clock
1 month, 18 days, 11 hrs, 11 mins, 37 secs

The room I'm now in is tiny, even smaller than my burrow, and is piled high with old, broken desks and saggy-looking sofas, rusty springs erupting up from the cushions. The room is egg-shaped which, in my mind, is a very odd shape for a storeroom as there are no corners to put anything in. There are three doors going off it, all of them shut, and there's a long, lightning-shaped crack running up one of the walls.

I plonk myself down on a badly-scuffed, wooden desk. Instantly, I wish I'd picked a different spot to park my bottom as it tips back and I almost tumble off. I shuffle forward – better – and rest my rifle on my legs, allowing my index finger to hover playfully over the trigger. Sniper Six Six, who I followed in here - I insisted she went first - sits down too, dropping onto the black, tiled floor and crossing her legs. I watch, amused, as she rests her rifle on her knees demonstrably directing the barrel at my midriff. There's a revolver hooked to her belt, a Browning nine millimeter by the look of the stumpy grip. It's holstered, but I see the catch is unclipped. Like me, this girl trusts nobody. Nicolo is nowhere to be seen. He wandered off to look for a loo, although why he can't simply pee in a corner is beyond me. Possibly, he suspected I wanted to talk to the girl alone.

He suspected correctly.

I pincer the bulletproof cloth covering my belly between two fingers and drag it away from my drenched skin. It's so hot in here, I'm beginning to worry I might melt. Unclicking the canteen from off my belt, I uncork it and suck greedily on the funnel. The water is tepid with a strong, metallic aftertaste, but it helps to soothe the dryness in my mouth and throat. Remembering my manners, I hold it out to the other sniper. She nods, so I toss it over to her, throwing it unnecessarily hard just to see if she can catch it. A silly test. She succeeds without spilling a drop.

"Thanks," she says, taking a long swig.

As she drinks, I can't help but look her over. I think she must be older than me, twenty possibly twenty-two, with tousled, chestnut-colored curls and a hard, granite-like jaw. I remember when I first saw her by the door thinking how surprisingly short she is; I'd say a foot shorter than me. She's incredibly slim too and her tiny, child-sized boots suggest tiny, child-sized feet. As I sit there, trying not to topple off the wobbly desk, I see there's a stillness to her, a thoughtfulness, as if she's never in a hurry but always knows exactly where she's going.

There's a long, long list of things I want to ask her, but when I open my mouth to begin, she cuts me off. "Have you run into any of the other snipers?" she asks.

I hesitate, then soberly I reply, "I think there's just us left. I know two of them were killed when the helicopters crashed down on top of them."

"Poor sods," she mutters with a sigh. "And the third?"

"She was killed by the sharpshooter in the belltower."

"You saw it happen?"

I nod, deciding not to show her the specks of One Zero One's blood still ingrained into my hands - and I don't tell her she was going to stab me and that the sharpshooter probably saved my life. I don't want her to think I'm in any way to blame for the girl's death.

With an angry growl, Six Six thrusts the cork into the neck of the canteen and lobs it back over to me. Like me, she throws it unnecessarily hard...

...but I can catch too!

"For the good of the many," I mutter. "Isn't that the rebels' motto?"

"It's bull is what it is," she barks back.

I nod, smiling. "Yes," I agree. "it is." Although I don't trust this girl, I can't help but be impressed by her. She's gutsy. I like gutsy.

She lowers her rifle, not all the way, but just enough to send me a message. I reply by uncurling my finger from off the trigger.

"So, Crow's plan isn't going very well," she says.

I frown, not following her.

"My Nest commander, Major Rizzo, she told me this contest is Crow's way of picking a sniper for a big mission."

"Yes, I think that's his plan," I say. "Well, it's what he told me."

"You don't trust him?"

There's no camera in here - which is why we picked it - so I can speak freely. "I'd sooner trust you," I reply coldly.

The girl grins.

Now I think about it, Six Six is right. Crow's plan is going terribly wrong. Soon there'll be no snipers left to go on this big mission of his. And then there's the second part of the plan. The contest was supposed to motivate the rebels to fight on. But, I suspect, watching us getting knocked off one by one by a single howler is not doing much for morale. As I sit there, I can't help but ponder if this was not the major's plan all along.

"When I'm angry, my eyes glow yellow," I suddenly blurt out, unable to hold it in any longer. "Do yours?"

For a few seconds, she says nothing, fiddling with the catch on her holster and refusing to look at me. "I think so," she says at last. "There's no mirror in my burrow so," she shrugs, "it's difficult to tell."

I nod my understanding, remembering what Lily told me. 'There's never a mirror in a sniper's burrow.' It seems, as always, she's right.

"But a few months ago, I was chopping wood for my log burner and I accidentally cut my finger. It was a stupid thing to do and I remember I was so angry with myself. When I went to clean it in a bucket, I was looking down into the water and I think, for just a second, I saw my eyes glow."

"How's the finger now?" I ask.

"It was a deep cut. I almost cut the bloody thing off. But it got better in just a few days." She holds up her left hand and inspects the top of her index finger. "Now there's not even a scar."

My pulse begins to race. Is it possible I'm not the only one? That I'm not alone in my abnormality? "Did you have a brother called Benji?" I ask her, jumping down off the desk. "Was he killed by the howlers?"

Her jaw drops open, her eyes widening in astonishment. "How did you know?"

"I had a brother called Benji too," I inform her. "But the howlers murdered him. I was only seven years old when it happened. I hid, cowered in a cellar, too frightened to..."

"Help him," she ends my sentence. "Yes, I know. I hid too. What the hell's going on, Two Seven?"

"I don't know," I reply honestly, "but I intend to find out."

"How?" she asks.

I sit down in front of her, crossing my legs like a bow. "I think there's a secret level in my Nest. A Level Seven. When this contest is over, I'm going to find a way of getting in there. I think, in there, I'll find the answers I'm looking for."

The girl scowls, her hands tightening on her gun. "Then I'm going with you," she informs me sternly. "I need answers too."

Before I can think of how to reply, there's a gentle knock on the door. It opens and Nicolo peeks in. "Am I interrupting?" he asks.

"No," says Six Six.

I grit my teeth. I was going to say yes. It's amazing! Only a day ago, I was facing the prospect of having to go into Level Seven alone. Now there's going to be three of us. It's almost a gang!

"Did you, er, find a loo?" I ask the boy.

"Sort of," he says, stepping into the room, "but there was a rat in there the size of a dog so I ended up peeing in a vase."

"Did the rebels get it on camera?" asks Six Six, winking at me.

Nicolo grins. "It will be good for morale," he says with a shrug, "By the way, I wanted to ask you, where's your spotter?"

The girl gets to her feet. I get up too. "Better if I just show you," she says. "Then we'll discuss my plan for killing the howler."

We follow her out of the room and back along the corridor to where we first saw her. I see the door is still open and, although the sun is blindingly bright, it's still easy to make out the cathedral wall rising up only a hundred feet away.

As we creep closer to the door, Six Six suddenly holds up her hand. "If we get any closer, she'll shoot us," she says, dropping to her belly.

I glance over at Nicolo who lifts his eyebrows. I shrug and, together, we drop down too.

Just beyond the door, there's a large, square courtyard. I see it's been badly bombed, the gravel pitted with craters.

"Look up," says Six Six.

Although I'm not a big fan of following orders, I do as I'm instructed. The wall must be fifty feet high and, perched on top of it, is the belltower. On top of that, there's the belfry. It's perfectly circular and ringed with six arched windows - although I can only see three of them from here.

"She's in there," says the girl. "But she's smart and keeps away from the windows. Even when she shoots."

"How do we kill her if we can't see her?" asks Nicolo, vocalising my own thoughts.

"That's the tricky bit," she says. "You asked me where my spotter is. Look over there, by the foot of the wall."

At first, I can't see anything of interest. So I lift my rifle and put my eye to the scope. Soon, I pick out the body of a boy lying on the gravel, the Kevlar where it covers his chest torn and bloody.

"I'm sorry," I say.

But the girl, it seems, is not interested in my sympathy. "Just there, it's a blind spot. The only way she could have seen him is if she peered out of the window."

I nod slowly, predicting her plan. "So, if one of us stands there, she'll have to show herself to shoot them."

"And that's when we take her out," she says. "Simple."

"Suicide," mutters Nicolo. He's not wrong there.

"Don't worry," she says with a cold smile. "I'm going to be the target. Your job, Two Seven, is to shoot her as soon as you see her. Don't let her get a shot off."

"Why you?" I challenge her. "Why not me?"

"Wouldn't it be better if I'm the target?" says Nicolo with a long sigh. "There's a much better chance you'll hit her if you both shoot."

"No," says the girl. "it has to be me. I'm the smallest."

I frown, not getting it.

The Skeleton Clock

"But for it to work," she says, "I'm going to need you two to get undressed."

XXXII

The Skeleton Clock
1 month, 18 days, 10 hrs, 33 mins, 41 secs

I'm a sniper, so lying on a hill of jagged rubble for hours on end is part of my job; it's what I do. But for Nicolo, who's nestled in by my elbow and who's used to the comforts of the Nest, it's a form of torture.

"For pity's sake, Nicolo," I hiss for the umpteenth time, "do try to keep still. If Lily sees you, she'll shoot you."

"Let her," he growls back. "She'll be putting me out of my misery."

I know I should send him away. He's putting everybody at risk, including me. But I don't. It feels good having him here. Comforting. And, anyway, the wind's picking up and I'm going to need his help judging it.

"Just try," I tell him with a long sigh.

It took a lot of hunting to find this spot, the spot being a dusty corner in the Palace's attic. The north wall's been badly bomb-damaged and a chunk of it's caved in, so now there's a gaping hole in it. Through it, with help from my high powered scope, I can see the belfry where Lily is reportedly hiding.

I shiver. It's not that I'm cold. Anything but. It's like an oven in here. But I do feel horribly exposed. For Six Six's plan to work, she needed all of my Kevlar – and Nicolo's too. After handing it over to her, the only thing I could find that even sort of fitted me was a flimsy, cotton dress. Cotton, sadly, is not very good at stopping bullets.

The Skeleton Clock

I removed the dress from off a skeleton. Before putting it on, I did a little surgery on it, pulling off the lacy cuffs and cutting away the hem at the bottom. Now, if I'm forced to run, there's less chance I'll trip up. Nicolo fared much better than me, discovering an old officer's uniform in a trunk. It's dusty and torn, the row of medals on the chest spotted with rust, but I still think he looks dashing in it.

It took Six Six forever to put on the two extra layers of Kevlar. But, after a lot of tugging and cursing, she finally struggled into it. Then she set off back down to the door. Now, all Nicolo and I can do is watch the belfry until she signals, the signal being three shots of her pistol. That's when she's going to run out of the door and over to where her spotter's body is lying. The plan's simple. When Lily attempts to shoot her, she'll be forced to show herself. My job is to shoot Lily first. The important word there is 'first'. Although Six Six has three layers of Kevlar on, who knows what sort of ammo the howler's using. For all we know, she might shoot a rocket at her! And no Kevlar is going to stop that.

Which reminds me. "Nicolo," I whisper, elbowing him in the ribs. "I hid a box in the front pocket of the rucksack. Can you get it for me?"

He nods.

"Oh, and Corporal, do it slowly," I add.

Grinning, he pulls the bag off his back, unzips the pocket and pulls out the box. "What's in it?" he asks, passing it to me.

"Do you remember the bullets I was using when I was trying to shoot the petrol drums?"

"Trigger's Anvils?"

I nod. "I thought it best to be prepared."

I'm expecting him to be angry with me. Crow did tell us to only bring low velocity shells. But, surprisingly, he's not, rewarding my refusal to follow orders with a toothy grin. "Good thinking," he says.

I grin back at him. It seems his loyalty to the Major is no match to a good snogging from Amaryllis Storm.

Ejecting the old shell, I replace it with one of Trigger's Anvils. I then lower my eye back down to the scope. I see the sun is almost on the belfry. Six Six is planning to go for it when the sun hits the window. Lily will be blinded so, even if the howler gets a shot off, it will be difficult for her to hit the target.

Not long now, I think. Not long now.

"Range?" I whisper. I know the answer, but it's always best to check. Anyway, I don't want Nicolo feeling left out.

"Two hundred and ten feet," the Corporal promptly answers.

Spot on.

"Wind speed?"

"It's blowing ten knots, left to right." Then he delivers the bad news. "But it's gusting up to fifteen."

I scowl, biting down on my lower lip. The wind's getting stronger by the second and, if I'm unlucky, it'll gust up just as I pull the trigger, dragging the bullet off target. But there's nothing I can do.

Then, to add to my problems, my alarm beeps. With a sinking feeling, I check it. 250 REMS. Blast! If we don't get out of here soon, it won't be Lily's bullets that kill us, it'll be the toxins.

"How bad is it?" asks Nicolo, pulling up his mask.

"Bad," I say, doing the same.

To keep my mind off the toxins filling my lungs, I mull over my latest plan. I know I must win this contest. So, after I shoot Lily, I'm going to shoot Six Six in the leg. It's the only way. Only then will I be welcomed back into the Nest and be allowed to meet with Crow, just him and me.

But the first thing I'm going to do when I get back there is find a way into Level Seven. I want answers. I want to know who I am. I want to know what I am. I'm hoping Nicolo will go with me. As for Six Six, I don't think she's going to be so keen; not after I put a bullet in her leg. I balloon my cheeks. And I don't think snogging her is going to help much.

I see the sun is now fully on the belfry window. But, oddly, there's still been no signal from Sniper Six Six. What's she playing at, I wonder. Has she bottled out? Or has it all been a big con? Her way of getting me to trust her. And, any second now, she's going to storm through the attic, guns blazing.

"Nicolo, do you think -," I begin, but then I stop, my eyes narrowing. "What's that?" I ask him.

"What's what?"

"That!"

"I can't – oh, hold on. I think – ."

But, before he can utter another word, it hits me. It's the drum of rotors. It's the helicopter!

Too soon, I think to myself. Too soon. If I don't kill Lily now – RIGHT NOW! - she'll shoot it out of the sky with a rocket.

"Where's Six Six?" I hiss. "Why's she not running?"

Only then do the three shots ring out. This is it! With my finger hovering over the trigger, I peer intently through the scope, willing Lily to show herself. The thump of the helicopter's twin rotors now fill the attic. It must be directly over us, the rubble under my body vibrating wildly, making it almost impossible to keep my rifle from shaking.

"Why can't we see her?" yells Nicolo over the din. "Where is she?"

I wish I knew. I suddenly wonder if she knows I'm here; if she knows it's all a trick. Or possibly it's the helicopter. She's not interested in Sniper Six Six now. She knows she must shoot down the Chinook first. Then, when all seems lost, my lens is filled with a bush of red curls. It's her! "Got you!" I hiss.

Suddenly, her cold tenor fills my skull. "Don't do it, Amaryllis."

Blast! She knows I'm here. She knows I have her in my sights.

"Listen to me," she growls.

"Go to hell," I growl back.

Next to me, Nicolo jumps. He must think I'm talking to him.

"If Crow's plan is to work, you need me," she says.

My eyes narrow. How can she possibly know...

"Shoot her!" Nicolo elbows me ruthlessly in the ribs. "Or she'll shoot Six Six."

The boy's right. The other sniper's relying on me and I can't let her down. Anyway, I suspect Lily's just playing with me, trying to get the upper hand. Just like she did back in my burrow. Gently, I pull back on the trigger. This time, she's not going to get her way.

"Have you forgotten what he told you?" she yells in my mind. "The enemy is not always who you think it is."

I freeze.

"Two Seven, wake up!" Nicolo snarls. "She's going to shoot Six Six. Stop her!"

But how can I when I'm in total and utter shock? Didn't Crow say the identical words to me only yesterday in the Nest? This is madness! Suddenly, for the first time in my life, I don't know who to shoot. For the first time in my life, I don't know who the enemy is.

Nicolo grips hold of the gun, trying to pull it away from me. "Hand it over," he growls. "If you won't shoot her, I will. Six Six is relying on us."

But, by then, it's too late, and I watch in horror as a bloom of smoke erupts from the barrel of Lily's gun.

"My God, you killed her," mutters the boy, and I know he's not referring to Lily. He's referring to me.

Angrily, I yank the gun away from him. All I can do now is stop the howler from taking a second shot. Zeroing in on her chest, I pull the trigger. But, in my rush, I don't so much pull it as jerk it back, the gun bucking wildly in my hands. Thankfully, I get lucky and hit her anyway. I watch, mesmerized, as she staggers back, blood gushing from her neck.

"Get up from that," I hiss.

I turn to Nicolo. "I'm sorry, but…" I stop, my words faltering on my lips, silenced by the look of contempt on the boy's face.

"You took too long," he says. "Why?"

I don't respond. How can I when I don't know the answer? Jumping to my feet, I slither down the hill of rubble. As I sprint through the attic, all I can think of is getting to Sniper Six Six…

… and seeing how badly she's hurt.

XXXIII

The Skeleton Clock
1 month, 18 days, 09 hrs, 16 mins, 21 secs

With Nicolo panting to keep up with me, I sprint through the long, dark corridors, and helter-skelter down endless flights of spiral steps until, finally, I'm back at the door. But, when I get there, a thought hits me and I skid to a stop.

"What is it?" barks the Corporal, almost sliding into the back of me. "Keep going."

I silence him with an angry scowl and a not so soft prod of my elbow. Before I take another step, I need to think this through. I'm suddenly wondering if this is a trap. A few weeks ago, when I shot Lily in the belly, she simply got up and brushed off the dust. Could she possibly be immortal? Didn't Crow suggest this to me in the meeting? And, if she is, did she get up now and, this very second, she's kneeling by the window with her finger on the trigger hunting for a target? Hunting for me.

"Amaryllis, we must get to her," protests Nicolo, pushing and shoving at me, trying to get by. "She could be badly injured. She could be dying."

With a growl, I whip around. "I know that!" I hiss. "Just shut up for a second and let me think."

He backs away, looking shocked as if I just slapped him in the face. But, then, he's never seen me angry before; he's never seen my eyes glow yellow.

"Listen to me, Nicolo," I say, taking a deep breath, "there's a strong possibility I didn't kill her."

"But you shot her." He eyes me distrustfully. "Didn't you?"

"Yes, I think so. But..."

"Did you or didn't you?"

"I did."

"Then there's no problem. Let's go."

"Nicolo..."

But he's not interested, slipping by me and running out of the door. I don't follow him. It's just too big of a risk. It's the sniper in me. Instinct. Or am I being too kind to myself and I should be calling it cowardice? I find myself counting down the seconds, ten down to zero. When I get to three, Lily's still not fired. She must be down. She must be. She's not immortal after all. It's as if a sack of cement has been lifted off my shoulders. I smile, jam another shell into my rifle, and go after him.

By the time I run over to where Six Six is lying in the dirt, Nicolo's kneeling down next to her, pressing his fingers to her neck and trying to find a pulse. I see Lily shot her in the stomach and, by the look of the spreading pool of blood, the three layers of Kevlar were no match for whatever bullets the howler is using.

"Is she - ," I stop, knowing I'm responsible, not wanting to say the word.

"She's still alive," he says. "Just."

I turn to look at the helicopter which is hovering a hundred feet to the north of us. The pitch of the twin motors tells me it's coming into land. But why is it landing all the way over there? Then I get it. If the pilot risks coming any closer, there's a chance the rotors will hit the towering belltower.

I balloon my cheeks. It seems, then, we must go to it.

I drop down beside the boy. I see he's upended his rucksack, the contents of the medical kit scattered in the dirt. He picks up a syringe and jabs the needle into the girl's thigh. It must be morphine. "Do you think you can carry her?" I ask him.

He looks up, peering over at the helicopter. "I can try," he says. "But how am I going to get by the howlers?"

Howlers!? With a horrible sinking feeling, I follow his gaze. Instantly, I spot three howlers standing between us and the Chinook, blocking our way. Then, to add to our problems, a further three howlers erupt from the belltower.

"They look properly pissed off," says the boy.

I agree. Armed with crossbows and swords, all six of them look big and strong and up for a fight. Although it's hardly surprising. I did kill their boss.

"Don't worry," I tell him. "Just get her to the helicopter. I'll cover you."

He shocks me by suddenly pulling me closer and planting a kiss on my cheek. I thought he was still upset with me. It seems not. "Try not to get killed," he says. Then he jumps to his feet, picks up the girl and lumbers off.

I stay sitting. Crossing my legs, I unhook the rifle from off my shoulder and rest it on my knees. I then hunt through the rucksack pocket for the box of high velocity shells. When I find it, I rip it open, lining the shells up by my feet. I have six bullets for six howlers. Perfect.

I see the three howlers from the belltower are now creeping up on me. Soon, they'll be on me. As always, my instinct is to protect myself. But I fight it, leveling the gun at the howlers blocking Nicolo from getting to the helicopter.

I hit the first of them in the chest. The second gets it in the shoulder, spinning him around before he drops to the dirt. The third is difficult; Nicolo's in the way and I'm frightened of hitting him. The boy seems to understand the problem and suddenly ducks down. I shoot, hitting the howler in between the eyes. He'll not be getting back up.

Suddenly, after weeks of doubting myself, I can shoot. It's as if a blindfold has been torn from my eyes. And I know why. Lily lost and I won. Finally, I'm free of her and I can do my job. I can rid this planet of howlers.

Now Nicolo's safe, I turn my rifle on the other three howlers. I bring the first two down in seconds. Bang! Bang! But the third is crafty, twisting and turning, making it difficult to target him. When he's twenty feet away, he lifts his crossbow and let's fly. I roll to my left, the arrow hitting the dirt just where I'd been sitting. Coming to my feet, I lift my rifle and pull the trigger. The monster keels over with a grunt.

I snatch up the rucksack. Then, hooking the rifle back over my shoulder, I sprint over to the helicopter. But, when I'm still fifty feet away, hundreds of howlers begin flowing out of the belltower door.

My only chance is to get to the helicopter before they get to me.

Thankfully, the gunner sees I'm in trouble and opens up with his M16. I help out by pulling the grenade from my rucksack, yanking out the pin, and lobbing it at a pack of howlers directly in my path. They scatter, the grenade exploding in a barrage of flying rocks. Now's my chance. With most of the enemy still cowering in the dirt, I sprint over to the helicopter and up the sloping ramp. "Go, go, go," I yell.

With a deep growl, the lumbering monster lifts off. The nose dips and we thunder away over the crumbling city.

"Going so soon?"

My eyes widen in shock. No, it can't be. It can't be. Slowly, I turn around. The pilot's still not pulled up the ramp and, through the gaping doorway, I see the Kremlin in the distance. There, sitting on top of the belltower, is a howler.

It's Lily.

"Be strong, Amaryllis," she whispers in my mind. "Remember, the only way we can win this war is if we work together. There's still much to do."

Work together! She must be crazy. How can we possibly work together when she keeps trying to kill me? When she's my sworn enemy? I thump my skull, trying to loosen her hold over me. But I can't. It's as if I'm hypnotised by her. As if she'll be with me forever.

"Tell Hubert he was right. Tell him I'm beginning to remember."

There is a sudden cranking of machinery and the ramp is winched up, locking into place with a thump. I stare at the metal door. The only Hubert I know is Hubert Crow. What the hell is going on?

As horribly confused as ever, I stagger over to where Nicolo is working on the girl. He's strapped her into a cot. There's a mask covering her nose and mouth and a dripfeed going into the back of her hand. There's blood everywhere.

"What can I do to help?" I ask him.

"Top drawer of the steel cabinet," he snaps back. "I need antiseptic. Lots of it."

Obediently, I open the drawer, fumbling in amongst scissors and packs of plasters until my hand finds a bottle. It's the only bottle in there. "Is this it?"

Glancing up, he nods sharply. "It'll do," he says, snatching it off me and emptying the contents over her stomach. Much of the blood is washed away revealing a large, jagged hole just under her rib cage. The skin around it is blackened and charred, the flesh red and raw-looking. I gulp down the bile rising up my throat.

The Corporal rips open a bag of surgical pads and, deftly, binds them to the wound. Then he wraps everything in a bandage. With a sigh, he steps back. "It's all I can do," he says.

"How long's she got?" I ask.

Wiping his bloody hands down his shirt, he shrugs. "I think the bullet ripped through her stomach, then clipped the lining of her right lung. It looks as if the lung's collapsed. The ventilator is helping but not much." He sighs. "She's lost a lot of blood too. She's going to need a miracle."

"Or a MediPod," I say.

His eyes narrow, calculating. "Possibly."

"Can you keep her alive until we get back to Zulu?"

"I'll do my best."

The monitor beeps loudly and he returns to the almost impossible task of trying to keep Six Six from dying. I, in turn, look over at the gunner, a surly-looking man, grizzly, with hollow eyes and liver spots on the backs of his big hands. He's dripping water from a canteen onto the glowing red barrel of his gun, trying to cool it down.

I thank him for saving me. Then, over the drum of the rotors, I yell, "Where's this rustbucket flying to?"

"Yankee Sector," he calls back.

Yankee Sector! That won't do at all. "We need to go to Zulu," I tell him sternly. "The Nest there has a MediPod. It's the only way of saving her."

The gunner looks up from the smoking gun. "Best discuss it with the pilot. Not that she'll listen to you. The Zulu Nest is under attack from howlers; hundreds of them. If we go there, there'll be nowhere to land. Then we'll all be killed."

Hundreds! My thoughts turn instantly to Twig. Where is he now, I wonder. Is he cowering under his bed cuddling my old rag doll, or did he listen to me and is on his way down to Akiyo on Level Six? But, even if he finds her, will she help him? Can she be trusted? I know the only way I can help him and the girl is to get this helicopter back to Zulu. With this in mind, a yank the pistol from off Six Six's belt. She's not going to be needing it anytime soon. "I'm going up to talk to the pilot," I calmly inform Nicolo.

As I turn to go, I feel his hand gripping my shoulder. "Don't do anything stupid," he says.

"Stupid! Me!" I cover his hand with my own. Then, gently, but determinedly, I unhook his fingers. "Never." Cocking the pistol, I storm up the helicopter towards the cockpit.

XXXIV

The Skeleton Clock
1 month, 18 days, 01 hrs, 25 mins, 57 secs

As the helicopter thunders through the night, I sit slouched by Six Six's juddering cot, a dripfeed snaking from the back of my hand to the back of hers. I don't mind giving her my blood although, according to Nicolo, this is not the best way of doing it. It seems an anticoagulant should be added to stop the blood from clotting; we don't even know if my unknown blood is a match for hers. But time's running out and, as the Corporal so aptly put it, "She's lost so much blood, if we don't try, she's a goner anyway."

The pilot's now agreed to fly us back to the Zulu Nest. When I first went up to the cockpit, she put up a bit of a fight. But when I told her how sick Six Six is - and jammed the butt of my pistol up to the nape of her neck - she changed her mind. Thankfully, the support crew back in Yankee Sector cleverly thought to fix an auxiliary fuel tank to the Chinook's underbelly, so we should make it - just.

The helicopter's been flying full pelt for just over seven hours, the rivets holding it together rattling under the stress. Like the rivets, Six Six is holding on too, helped by Nicolo (who's been doing wonders for her) and a few pints of my blood. The worry now is what to do if the Nest's been overrun by the enemy. If that's happened, there'll be nowhere to put this bird down.

The injured girl shifts in her cot, her eyelids fluttering, then blinking open. "Hi there," I say, sitting up.

She looks blankly back at me. I don't think she knows who I am. "I'm Amaryllis," I remind her gently. "I´m a sniper, like you. Don't you remember?"

The girl frowns, then nods. "Oh yes," she mutters. "My job is to shoot you."

I grin. She remembers. "So, I can't keep calling you Six Six."

"Rosolino." I'm surprised by how offhandedly she says it, as if it's of no interest to her; just another label.

She peers down at the lumpy dressing swaddling her belly. "The howler got me then. It looks – terminal."

"It is," I reply bluntly. Why bother lying; she's too smart for that. "But try not to worry. I, er, convinced the pilot to fly us back to the Zulu Nest. There's a MediPod there. It'll fix you up in no time."

She cocks her left eyebrow at me. "Convincing pilots not to follow orders can be difficult."

"It did prove a little tricky," I admit. "But I borrowed your pistol." I pull it off my belt to show her. "It helped a lot."

With a chuckle, she shuts her eyes. "I'm getting to like you," she says.

I stay sitting there, my gaze drifting between the resting girl and Nicolo, who's over with the gunner patching up a cut on his leg. When I was running for the helicopter and he was covering me with his M16, a howler shot him. But it looks as if the arrow just nicked his shin. He'll live.

"So nobody won," Rosolino suddenly says.

I scowl. "Sorry?"

"The contest. You didn't shoot me and I didn't shoot you. A draw. So, who's going to go on Crow's big mission now?"

I nod thoughtfully. She's right. Although I don't think she'll be up to going anywhere; not when there's a bullet lodged in her gut. But I play along anyway. "We could go together," I suggest.

"Excellent," she murmurs sleepily. "You can be my spotter."

"I don't think so," I reply with a grin.

Just then, Nicolo walks over, his hands overflowing with blood-drenched dressings. He dumps them into a bin. "How do you feel?" he asks the girl.

"Terrible," she says with a shrug. "But I'm hanging in there."

He checks her monitor. "Let's see now. Your blood pressure is 80 / 50. Well, that's much better. And your temperature's dropped to 37.1. Astonishing! It seems Amaryllis's blood is doing the trick."

The other sniper peers down at her hand and the curling tube protruding from it. "Thanks," she says, glancing up at me.

"You'd do it for me," I reply. Although, in all honesty, I don't think she would.

She drops her gaze, possibly thinking the identical thing. "Did you get her?" she suddenly asks. "Did you shoot the howler in the belltower?"

"Yes, I got her."

"Good." She sighs deeply, her eyelids fluttering shut. "It's just a pity she got a shot off first. How did she do it?"

I feel Nicolo's eyes drilling into my back. I suspect he's dying to know the answer to that too. But I don't reply, pulling up her blanket and telling her to try to rest.

I sit silently with her until I know she's asleep. Then I turn to the boy. "When can I get rid of this dripfeed?" I ask him. "It's hurting." What I don't tell him is I don't want to be tethered to an injured girl when we get to the Nest; not when there's every possibility it'll be overrun with howlers.

"Now," he says, gently pulling the needle from my hand. "She's had plenty, and I think she's on the mend."

Rubbing my tender skin, I clamber to my feet and shuffle over to the monitor. I stand there watching the green dot jump up and down, all the while listening to the beep of the girl's pulse. The Corporal's right; she is on the mend. If we can get her into the pod, I think she'll be okay.

"I know I let her down," I whisper, keeping my back firmly to the boy. "It's just," I chew rattishly on my bottom lip, trying to find the words, "Lily got to me."

"How?"

"In here." I thump the top of my skull to show him.

"How did she get in there?"

"It's a long story."

"It always is with you," he snaps. "The problem is you don't trust me. You don't trust anybody."

This totally gets my back up. Swinging around, I hiss, "You told me not to."

"So you keep reminding me."

"You did say it," I huff.

He sighs, scrubbing his fingers over his unshaven chin. "I know I did, but you must try to trust me." He steps closer. "You do know I have feelings for you."

"Feelings?"

"Yes, feelings."

"Anger's a feeling."

He laughs. "Yes, it is. But I was referring to a different feeling. I did kiss you, remember?"

"No," I retort, "I kissed you."

As I look into his eyes, I see an intensity there I missed up until now. I'm suddenly reminded of the boy's secret number to the doors in the Nest. 2727. I stupidly thought it had been randomly picked for him. It seems not.

"I'm sorry," I say. "I do trust you. Honestly. When we get back to the Nest, I'll tell you everything I know."

He eyes me sceptically. "Everything?"

"Everything."

He nods, and plants a kiss on my cheek. "It's a good start," he says.

The last three hours of the flight seem to go on forever. All I can do is sit there counting off the seconds until I can get Six Six into the pod. It's okay for Nicolo; he's got plenty to do, checking the girl's monitor, rewrapping her dressing, and keeping her topped up with drugs.

At last, when I don't think I can sit there for a second longer, there's a crackle from the helicopter's intercom. "This is the cockpit." It's the pilot. "ETA to the Nest 60 seconds. I'm going to fly low, under 200 feet, so this could get bumpy. Best buckle up!"

Buckle up! As if. Dashing over to the window, I peer out. It's morning now, the sun peeking over the tops of the hills. At first, all I see is golden sand. Then, finally, I see the Nest for the first time in three days. It's a horrifying sight. There seems to be howlers everywhere, hundreds of them, surrounding the Nest on every side and crawling over the burnt-out Challenger tanks like hungry ants. The only good news is the wall's still standing, the rebels nestled on top of it firing wildly down at the enemy mob. With the wall still up, there's no way for the howlers to get into the Nest, so it shouldn't be a problem to land in the hangar.

Suddenly, the helicopter banks wildly to port, and, like a ragdoll, I'm tossed to the steel floor, slicing open my finger on a protruding rivet. Cursing, I look up at the gunner. Like the rebels on the wall, he's firing too, a torrent of steel erupting from the M16's muzzle.

"This is it," the pilot informs us, panic lacing her words. "I'm going for the hanger. Hold on!"

This time, I do as I'm told, gripping hold of the leg of a bench, and pressing my feet up to the vibrating wall.

The Chinook plummets sickeningly. Determined not to throw up, I focus on Nicolo who's bravely flung himself over Six Six and is trying to stop her from tumbling out of her cot. Not wanting to, but knowing I'll hate myself if I don't, I clamber to my feet and lurch over the swaying steel floor to help him.

After 30 seconds - although it feels like forever - of stomach-churning dips and rolls, the wheels hit the deck with a jolt. Instantly, we unlatch the cot and, using it as a stretcher, we carry Rosolino over to the back of the helicopter. As we stumble by the smoking M16, I spot the gunner lying on the floor. He's been killed, shot between the eyes. My knees turn to jelly, my legs almost giving out from under me. Only Lily could pull off a shot like that. But she can't be here. She can't be!

Nicolo thumps the button and the ramp begins to drop. As soon as it's fully extended, we hurry down it, only to be met at the bottom by a panting Akiyo.

"Is she still alive?" she asks, gripping hold of Rosolino's limp hand.

I scowl, wondering how it is she even knows the girl's being shot. Then I remember the big screen Crow erected in the canteen. She'd have seen everything on there.

"Yes," says Nicolo. "But we must hurry. She's not got long."

I'm surprised to hear him say that. But when I look down at the girl, I see he's right. Her chest is hardly moving and her skin has a ghastly yellow sheen to it. I thought she'd been getting stronger, but it seems I was wrong.

Akiyo nods sharply, her face grim and determined. "Follow me," she says.

As she turns away, I almost call out to her. I want to ask her where Twig is and if he's okay. But I stop myself. I know I'm not the most sensitive person, but even I know this is not the best time.

Carrying the girl between us, Nicolo and I follow Akiyo through the bustling hangar and along the corridor to the spiral steps. As we struggle down them, the ends of the stretcher catching on the riveted wall, I can't help wondering who thought of putting Medical on the second floor!

When we finally get there, I'm shocked to see so many of the beds filled with badly injured rebels. The howlers can't have gotten into the Nest; not with the outer wall still standing. So how did they all get hurt?

I'm about to call to Akiyo to ask her what's going on when Doctor Achoo scampers over, looking highly upset. "Stop right there," he orders, puffing up his weedy chest. "She's not going in my pod. It's only for very important..."

A swift punch in the guts from Akiyo shuts him up, dropping him to the floor with a piggish snort. "Your job is to help the sick and injured," she scolds him. "All of them!" She turns to the room. "Everybody in here will be going in the pod. Everybody!"

Her words are met with a long, rowdy cheer.

"This is - this is mutiny," snivels the doctor, who's still cowering on his knees. "Major Crow ordered me to..."

"Screw his orders," Akiyo snarls. "Now, get up, assess who needs to go in the pod first, then wheel them in. Got it?"

"But..."

"Just do it," she barks, "or I'll have you arrested and thrown in the brig."

"Arrested!" The doctor gets shakily to his feet. "What for?"

"It's a long list, but mostly for being such a prat." Then, without another word, she turns on her heels and storms off.

Meekly, Nicolo and I sprint after her. I must admit to being impressed. It seems I misjudged the woman, and she's not Crow's puppet after all.

We hurry out of the ward and down a long, dimly-lit corridor. I remember the pod's in a room on the left, the second door from the end. When we get to it, Akiyo brashly kicks it open, and we storm in. Thankfully, the pod's still there, sitting in a corner looking shiny and new.

Nicolo and I watch as Akiyo picks her granddaughter up from the stretcher and rests her in the egg-shaped device. Instantly, the monitor beeps alarmingly, hundreds of tiny lights embedded in the glass flickering on.

I'm about to ask Nicolo how long it will take when, abruptly, the beeping stops, and the lights blink off. I frown. Is it over? Has the pod fixed her? But then why is she still just lying there? And why is her dressing still drenched in blood? Confused, I nudge the Corporal. "What's going on?"

But the monitor answers for him, a row of red text flashing up on the screen. It's cold, short, and horribly direct.

No life signs detected. Next...

With a hiss of escaping gas, the glass lid tilts up, the pod's way of announcing there's nothing it can do. Akiyo drops to her knees, gently brushing her fingertips over the girl's sunken cheeks. "I'm sorry I left you there," she says. "I let you down."

I'm so stunned, I'm having difficulty comprehending what's going on. "But she seemed so much stronger."

"I don't get it," says Nicolo. He begins pacing the room, scowling furiously. "Unless..."

"Yes?" I prompt him.

"The bullet nicked the spleen too. Then, when the helicopter landed, the jolt ruptured it. It's all I can think of."

"I thought the pod could fix anything."

"It can. but if the patient's already dead then -," he shrugs, "- it's not God."

Anger smoulders within me. Another of Lily's victims. But I vow she'll pay this time. Not today, not tomorrow, but she'll pay.

We watch Akiyo pick up the girl´s limp body and carry it over to a corner of the room. There, she rests it gently on the floor. I don´t know how to comfort this woman, but I try anyway, walking over to her and taking her hand.

She pulls sharply away, her face contorted with rage. "You did this!" she snarls. "You let the howler shoot her."

Shocked, I take a step back. I want to tell Akiyo what happened. Six Six was her granddaughter so she's got a right to know. But even now, when I know I should be feeling sorry for her, all I can think of is the gleeful look she had in her eyes when she thrust the red-hot poker to my skin. I don´t trust her. I never will.

In the end, it is Akiyo who turns away. "This isn't over," she says. Then she storms over to the door. "Doctor Atchoo," she hollers. "Get in here."

Within seconds, the doctor scampers in. He must have been hovering in the corridor, trying to keep watch over his beloved pod.

"Start wheeling them in," she orders him.

"I sent for Major Crow," he says slyly. "He's going to be livid when he..."

"I don't care!" Akiyo thunders. "Just do it."

Despite being much taller than her, the man cowers away. Then, with a whimper, he runs from the room.

"I'd better help him," says Nicolo with a long sigh. "I'm a medic after all."

"Then help him." I say. Pulling the pistol from off my belt, I eject the clip and count the shells. Only three left. But I'm not trudging back up to the Armory, so they'll have to do. "I´m going down to Level Seven, and nobody is going to stop me."

I feel the Corporal's eyes burrowing into me. Coldly, I return his gaze. "Coming?" I ask him.

He shrugs. "Why not? Atchoo's such a fool, I'd only end up punching him."

I do a terrible job of hiding my smile. I don't know what I'm going to discover on Level Seven, but I do know I feel much better now the boy's going with me.

We walk over to the door, but I'm forced to stop when Akiyo steps in front of me, blocking my way. I drop low, bring up my fists. I don't want to fight her, but if it's a fight she wants, it's a fight she'll get.

"Relax, Amaryllis," she says, putting her hands up in mock surrender, "I´m not going to hurt you."

Hurt me! As if. But I say nothing, uncurling my fists, watchful to see what she'll do next.

"You can't go down there," she says.

"Why not?"

"It's too risky."

"Risky!" I scoff her. "The only risk I can think off is slipping on the steps."

"There'll be howlers everywhere."

"Nonsense!" I hiss. "We just flew over the Nest. The wall's still up. There's no way for the howlers to get in here."

"Yes, there is."

My eyes narrow as I try to work out what she's up to.

"Do you remember I told you I'd get Twig out through a secret tunnel?"

I nod irritably; I'm in no mood for a Q & A.

"Well, I showed it to the boy."

"And?"

"He let them in. I'm sorry, Amaryllis, but Twig's a howler spy."

XXXV

The Skeleton Clock
1 month, 17 days, 21 hrs, 13 mins, 17 secs

In spite of Akiyo's dire warnings, we get down to Level Six with hardly a problem. When I say hardly, we did bump into a howler on the steps between Level Two and Three. Being in a hurry, I showed it no mercy, putting it down with a bullet between the eyes. Then we stepped over it and went on our way.

As we trudged down the steps, I couldn't stop thinking about Twig. According to Akiyo, when the howlers attacked, the boy turned up on Level Six and asked her to show him the tunnel. Using it, he left the Nest and, not long after, the howlers piled through it.

If Twig did let them in and he is a spy, a lot of stuff that didn't add up with the boy now do. How he sneezed in my cellar, giving us away. And how Lily's knight didn't seem interested in capturing him. But what I want to know is, why did the boy do it? Why is he helping the enemy?

When we finally get to the tree, we hunt the rough bark for the retinal scanner. Now I know what I'm looking for, I soon spot it; a tiny, red lens hidden in a gnarled knot halfway up the trunk. Now all I need is the eyeball of a rebel who has access to Level Seven.

Thankfully, things seem to be going my way, Nicolo spotting a body lying by the pond I attempted to jump over only a week ago. Hurrying over to it, we discover it's the body of a man, the chest torn open by a howler's claw.

Gently, we carry the body over to the tree and press the left eye up to the scanner. When I pull back the eyelid, there's a click and a hidden door in the trunk swings open.

Clever!

After resting the body on the grass, we peep through the door. There, we discover a set of steps spiralling downwards.

"Told you so," I can't help saying to Nicolo.

He looks at me, anger glinting in his eyes. For a second, I think he's angry at me. But no, he's angry at being kept in the dark. "I didn't know," he says. "Honestly."

I nod. I remember when we first met on the helicopter, he told me the Nest was full of secrets. He was right.

I go first, pistol up, my finger resting on the trigger. Every ten steps, a bulb's been screwed into the wall. There's a lot of dust on them so they only glow dimly. Still, better than nothing, particularly when I forgot to bring a torch.

Down and down we go

The steel steps are horribly rusty and, although we try to walk softly, they judder and wobble alarmingly the further down we go. The roof hovers just a foot over my skull, forcing me to bend my knees to keep the spider webs from getting entangled in my curls.

When we get to the bottom of the steps, we discover a laboratory. There's dust and cobwebs here too, as if nobody's worked here for months. Warily, we creep between the rows of desks; they look messy, cluttered, Bunsen burners sitting cold and idle amongst hills of top secret papers. I see many of the stools have toppled over, as if everybody left in a terrible hurry.

At the far end of the laboratory, there's a hefty-looking door. On it, in bold, red letters, there's a sign.

Keep Out

I see the door's bolted, the bolt secured with a padlock. Undeterred, I lift the pistol. "Get back," I warn Nicolo. I pull the trigger, the bullet striking the padlock and splitting it in two.

Pulling back the bolt, I kick open the door and storm through it.

I'm now in a tiny, oblong room. It's musty-smelling, cold, and totally empty but for a big computer screen on the wall.

"I don't get it," says Nicolo, walking into the room and standing by my elbow. "Why the locked door and the Keep Out sign if there's nothing in here to protect?"

I go to answer, but I stop when the screen blinks to life.

This is the Project Liberty Control Room.
How can I help?

My chin drops to my chest. Speechless, I look up at the screen in wonder. Is it possible? Can I finally find the answers I'm looking for? Here? In this dusty room?

"Let's see what it knows," whispers Nicolo. Then, addressing the screen, he says, "What is Project Liberty?"

Specify.

"Everything!" I thunder.

Project Liberty was set up to prevent the howlers from invading the last six rebel-controlled sectors.

"Go on," I say.

It involved kidnapping children from refugee camps and bringing them to the Zulu Nest. There, slug DNA was introduced to the subject at a cellular level by inserting it directly into the cerebral cortex.

My fingers find the scar on my temple. So now I know.

In the weeks following the procedure, the female subjects began displaying improved levels of strength, speed and intellect. The boys, however, responded differently, many of them dying. As a result, boys were dropped from the project.
The subject's memory was then wiped, and a new memory implanted. The memory was designed to instill hatred of howlers, including the brutal murder of a brother at the hands of the enemy, a murder the subject was too frightened to prevent.
The subjects were then sent to sniper camps. Then, when they were deemed Fully Skilled, they were deployed to the enemy fronts.

So now I know. I was kidnapped and taken here to be experimented on. I'm just a tool, a monster conjured up here, on Level Seven, and then used by the rebels to fight the howlers and stop them from invading. Not only that, they implanted a memory of me cowering in a cellar whilst my brother was killed by the enemy. A brother I now know never even existed.

I dig my fingers into my hands, trying to keep control, trying to do everything I can to stop myself from going crazy and shooting the screen. "Why were the, er, subjects' birthdays kept secret from them?" I want to know.

> The doctors suspected that, as a result of the slug DNA, the subject's aging would slow. In order to keep the subject's mind focused on killing howlers and not on this abnormality, birthdays were kept Top Secret, and mirrors were banned from sniper burrows.

I stare the the screen in wonder. They thought of everything.

"I'm so sorry," says Nicolo.

Gently, he rests his hand on my shoulder, but I shrug it away. I don't want sympathy. What I want is revenge.

"Is Project Liberty still active?" I growl at the computer.

Project Liberty was shut down by Major H Crow on 25th December 2131.

"I didn't know."

With a startled cry, I spin around to find Crow standing by the door. He's panting heavily, and there's a nasty gash on his cheek. "Only when I was promoted to Nest Commander was I informed of the project," he says. "It's barbaric. I instantly shut it down."

But oddly, now I know what I am, it no longer interests me. Now, I'm only interested in shooting the man responsible for my mother's death; the man standing right in front of me.

Slowly, determinedly, I lift the pistol. "Why did you do it?"

"But, but - I didn't," he says, stepping back. "I only discovered the project existed..."

"Not that," I growl. "Why did you kill my mother?"

His eyes widen in astonishment. "Kill your mother! I'd never do such a thing. It's, it's – crazy. I love her."

Now it's my turn to look astonished. I expected him to say a lot of different things, but never that.

"Why would I kill her?" he asks.

"Why!" I yell, my anger getting the better me. "I'll tell you why. In the Battle of London, when the howlers attacked, you peed your pants and ran away. You left her at the mercy of the enemy."

"That's not what happened," he says. "But the truth's – complicated."

I storm up to him and press the pistol to his chest. "Then uncomplicate it," I hiss.

For a moment, he just looks at me, a gentleness to his eyes I never expected to see. Then, in a few short words, he turns my life upside down. "She's my wife," he tells me.

I respond by almost dropping my gun. All I can do is stare back at him, feeling so numb, I wonder how I can possibly exist.

He lifts his hand then, just like he did in the Control Room a week ago, he puts it to my cheek, his fingertips brushing my skin. "Don't you understand, Amaryllis," he says. "I'm your father. And you met your mother. You met Lily."

XXXVI

The Skeleton Clock
1 month, 17 days, 19 hrs, 22 mins, 41 secs

Gently but firmly, he unhooks my rigid fingers from the pistol and hands it to Nicolo. "Sorry," he says to me, "I know this must all be a bit of a shock."

A bit of a shock, I think to myself. In the last hour, I've discovered the rebels infected me with howler DNA, my mother's a bloodthirsty monster, and my father's the man who I've been plotting to kill for the last two weeks. "Yes," I reply coldly. "It is a bit."

He grins, the mockery lacing my words not lost on him. "It's messy, I know, but possibly I can untangle it for you."

Standing there, I feel horribly vulnerable, and I find myself regretting I surrendered my pistol to him. But it's not only the possibility of being attacked by howlers making me feel this way. It's the thought of what this man might say to me and how much it might hurt. "Go on," I reluctantly tell him.

"When we lost the Battle of London and your mother was taken, I returned to the Netty to find you. But you'd vanished. Nobody knew what had happened to you. I hunted for weeks. Months. But nothing. I only discovered the truth when I was promoted to Zulu Commander. That the rebels were kidnapping children for Project Liberty."

"Why didn't you find me then?"

"I wanted to. I knew where you were; this computer told me. But it also told me the doctors had wiped your memory. I thought, if went to you and told you the truth, I'd only frighten you and push you further away. I was stupid."

"So you just left me there," I growl. "In a tiny burrow with the enemy on my doorstep"

He nods. "But I did keep my eye on you."

I frown, puzzling over his words. Then I get it, bits of the puzzle slotting into place. "The old Chinese satellite," I say slowly. "The bottom left corner of the screen in the Control Room is blank. Did it show..."

"Yes," he interrupts me. "I checked on you every morning and every night."

"And my mother," I say. "What happened to her?"

"Your mother had a plan, and I, reluctantly, went along with it. She thought, if she allowed herself to be infested by a slug, she could find a way of controlling it."

"But that's – crazy!"

"I know, I know, but," he shrugs, "it's very difficult to say no to your mother. She's very – stubborn. A lot like you."

Although I like the thought of being like my mother, I push it away. "Then what happened?"

"The plan was for her to infiltrate the Assembly at the highest level. Then, when we assassinated Janus, she'd step in and order the howlers to surrender."

"But it didn't work."

"To begin with, it did. But then the slug, Lily, proved too strong for her. It took over. I thought until recently, I'd lost her forever."

"But now she's fighting back?"

"Yes, I think so."

"She told me she's remembering," I blurt out. "She told me to tell you."

My father's eyes light up and he claps his hands together. "Six months ago, she contacted me with news of Janus's plan to drop a bomb in Esja volcano."

"So my mother's the spy in the howler camp."

The major nods, fiddling with the gold ring on his finger. "She has her good days and her bad. Days when she's Holly and she remembers who she is, and days when she's Lily and she's just a murdering howler. But I think, slowly, she's coming back to us. Back to her family."

"So the howler you want me to kill is Janus," I say.

"Yes. On the 25th September, he's going to address a crowd of howlers from a balcony overlooking the Cinis capital. That'll be your chance to take him out."

"And you think Lily..."

"Not Lily. Holly. That's your mother's name."

"Okay, Holly then. You think she's going to simply step up and tell the howlers she's the new boss and to surrender to the rebels. I don't think so."

"You must trust me, Amaryllis. And trust your mother. Remember, she's the host to a sheriff and most of the enemy see her as Janus's deputy. When he falls, when he's lying by her feet in a pool of blood, they'll listen to her."

I think back to when I was in the helicopter flying away from the Kremlin, and what she whispered to me. How we need to work together to win the war. Is there a possibility my father's right? If I kill Janus, will she step up and order the howlers to stop fighting? Will they listen to her?

"And if, in the end, Lily's too strong for her?" I ask.

"Then it's over," my father says soberly. "That's why it's so important it's you who kills Janus. Your mother will only find a way of overcoming Lily for good if she knows it's you she's helping."

Th major suddenly pulls me closer and hugs me tightly. I hug him back. I know I should be angry with him, but how can I be? I just got my father back.

"I think I'm going to vomit."

Up until now, Nicolo's been silent; so much so, I'd forgotten he's still in the room. Extracting myself from my father's arms, I turn to look at the boy. I see he's still holding the pistol and, unnervingly, it's levelled our way.

"My boss isn't going to be too happy if I let you shoot him," he says.

"Boss!" My father scowls, stepping up to him. "But I'm your boss."

"I don't think so," says the boy with a grin. "And you never were."

Then, just as I work out what's going to happen...

It happens...

Nicolo shoots my father in the chest.

XXXVII

The Skeleton Clock
1 month, 17 days, 20 hrs, 07 mins, 13 secs

I dash over to my father who is now lying on the floor, his hands clawing at his torn rib cage. Dropping to my knees, I rest my hands on top of his, pressing down as hard as I can. "Hold on," I say, ignoring the blood bubbling up between my fingers. "I'll get you into the pod."

"No you won't," says the boy.

With an animal-like growl I glare up at him. He's still holding the pistol, his finger curled around the trigger. It's the only thing stopping me from rushing him and ripping him to shreds. "Why?" I hiss. "I thought the rebels were your family."

He laughs bitterly. "The rebels murdered my family when they stopped my father from going into the pod. And I ended up an orphan, living off the pity of others. But I'm a talented actor and I played the role of," he frowns, "now what did you call me? Oh yes! A yes sir, no sir rebel grunt. I played that role perfectly. They thought I'd forgotten." His eyes harden. "But I never forgot."

Suddenly, I get it. It's as if a lightbulb flashed on in my skull. "It was you all along," I say. "You told the howlers my number, where to find me and how to get by my traps, and you told them I was going to the forest."

He rolls his eyes mockingly. "At last! Honestly, Amaryllis, I thought you'd never get it. Yes, I'm the howler spy."

"But how did you do it?"

"Think it through, Amaryllis. I work in Comms. How difficult do you think it is for me to contact the enemy and keep them informed?"

"Did you kill Six Six too?"

He shrugs lazily. He's not even got the decency to blush. "I didn't know you and her were," he smirks, "mongrels. And, by pumping her full of your blood, she'd recover so soon. So I overdosed her on morphine. It did the trick."

I sit there in shock. And I thought I was the cold-blooded murderer. Compared to the boy, I'm softer than melted butter! "But she was just a sniper," I protest. "Why?"

The boy steps closer to me and is now only six feet away. If he gets any closer, I'm going to rush him and try to grab for the gun.

"The howlers know Crow's devised a plan to win the war," he says, "and they know he needs a talented sniper for it to succeed. So they must all be killed. Then there's no risk of the plan working. Simple."

"I bet you thought up the contest too," I say bitterly.

"Let's just say I suggested it. By having all the rebel's best snipers together, the howlers knew they could pick them off one by one. That was Lily's job."

"If you wanted all five snipers killed, including me, why did you want us to stay in the tower?"

"Not us. Me. I didn't want to go out there. I thought, if I refused, you'd go off on your own. But you insisted I go with you. It was very annoying."

"Oh, I get it. Then, when the shooting was over, you'd swagger out of the tower and meet up with your pals."

"And get my reward, yes."

I frown. "I thought revenge was you reward."

"Oh, it is." He shrugs. "But I'm greedy. Janus promised, if I work for him, I could be a sheriff. But I think my reward is now going to be much bigger."

"Why's that?"

"Now, when I go to him, I can tell him what Crow's plan is. All of it. And I can tell him I killed the last of the snipers. You. Then there's Lily. Just think how he'll reward me when I tell him her host's remembering and trying to protect her daughter. He's going to be very happy with me."

He steps closer. Instantly, I jump up, grabbing for the pistol. But my hand is slippery with my father's blood, and the boy yanks it away. He shoots, the bullet digging into the rock by my feet.

"Now, now, Amaryllis," he says, 'you must try to stop playing the hero."

But I simply smile. When he pulled the trigger, everything changed. Now I can kill him whenever I want to. But, first, I need to know if he'll do it. If he's beyond saving.

"Let's get on with it," I tell him.

He nods slowly, looking surprised. "Turn around," he orders me.

I do as I'm told. A moment later, I feel the butt of the pistol pressing into the back of my skull.

"Did you ever have feelings for me?" I ask him.

The Skeleton Clock

His answer is simple, uncompromising. "I told you not to trust anybody."

Then he pulls the trigger.

Printed in Great Britain
by Amazon